MW00876826

A Corporate Coup

Adventures of a Jump Space Accountant

Book 4

Andrew Moriarty

THIS IS A WORK OF FICTION.

The character of Scott Russell is based, with permission, on my good friend Scott Russell, USMC. Semper Fi Buddy!

The character of Vincent Pletcher is based, with permission, on my good friend Vince Pletcher. If you have some money, need a spaceship, and don't ask too many questions, Vince is your guy.

Admiral Edmunds/Lieutenant Edmunds shares a name with Colonel Bryan Edmunds, USAF, retired. I will leave it up to his former squadron mates which rank from this book properly reflects his competence.

Special thanks to my dedicated team of beta readers – Bryan, Scott, Vince, and Alex.

CONTENTS

CHAPTER 1

"It's too dangerous. I'm not going to let you go alone, sir," Jose said.

"Oh? Are you going to assault me if I do?" Dashi asked. He strode toward the drop shuttles, Jose trailing along beside him. Dashi was small and neat. His mustache was trimmed, and his scalp was shaved. Jose was taller, younger, and could be called smooth, if not for his suit, which would be called flashy.

"It's quite an honor, sir, and about time."

"Nothing is permanent yet. I'm just going to a casino to meet some people."

"The chairman of TGI, the chairman of AFN, a Militia admiral, a Representative of the Free Traders' Guild, and a senior professor at the university are not 'some people,' sir."

"Carry on as necessary in my absence. It will only be for a day."

"I've heard rumors that you will be made the deputy chairman."

"Rumors abound. I place no trust in them." Dashi held

out his hand for his overnight bag.

Jose didn't give it to him. "Corporate regulations require that the deputy chairman have a bodyguard."

"I'm not the deputy chairman yet."

"I'd be a poor assistant if I didn't plan for any eventuality." Jose pointed to two men in TGI livery waiting at the lock. "You need guards. Watkins and Seth—"

"Excuse me. Coming through." A young couple in generic skin suits pushed by, each carrying a duffel and pulling an extra bag behind them. Jose and Dashi stepped back to allow them to pass.

"Watkins and Seth—" Jose began again.

"Sorry—sorry." Another man pushed by. "Apologies for my siblings. We're late. Have to catch the drop ship."

"You still have a few minutes, sir," Dashi said.

"Yes, but those two have probably misplaced their tickets, or the luggage is overweight, or something like that. I'll need the time to sort out our...well, their problems. Do you have brothers or sisters, sir?"

"One of each," Dashi said.

"You know how it is with the younger ones, then," the man said. "Always expect you to get them out of whatever fix it is, large or small, and no second thoughts, either."

"My siblings are singularly ungrateful as well," Dashi agreed. "The three of you are going on vacation?"

"Damn straight," the man said. He was tall, like his siblings, and dressed in a nondescript skin suit. "Saved up for six months. A nice break from corporate life. It's taken forever for the three of us to get the same three days off, given our jobs."

"Well, I hope your wagers are fruitful," Dashi said.

"Wagers? Oh, I'm not much for gambling, but I had to go along to keep an eye on those two. Alana would lose her whole wage chip in an hour, and then borrow more."

"Well, I'm sure you'll be able to ensure that will be unlikely."

"Alvin is just as bad. It's 'cause they're twins, you see. Not identical, of course. Fraternal."

"Twins often have similar interests and tastes. I'm sure you'll be able to handle them," Dashi said. He glanced at the time on his comm.

"Not that they pay any attention to their big brother, of course. I might as well be talking to a wall. Do your siblings listen to you?"

"No," Dashi said.

Raised voices rang out from the lock ahead—the twins arguing with the steward about whether their luggage was overweight.

"I see your assistance is required, after all," Dashi said.

"Emperor's hairy balls." The man strode off.

Dashi addressed Jose. "I am not taking your two thugs with me. I cannot arrive with an entourage. It would be impertinent of me."

"They are not thugs, sir. They are trained TGI security staff."

"Jose, I set up the training program for the security department. If they took that training, the only thing we can say with certainty is that they know which end of a gun should point away from them," Dashi said, "or that they frequently know this. Probably."

Jose shook his head. "I don't like it, sir. There have been rumors. The Free Traders are unhappy. They say that Dumarias, the rep, has sold them out."

"Minor rumors. Of no consequence."

"The Empire Rising faction has been throwing their weight around."

"A marginal group operating on the periphery of civilized society."

"There was a brazen hijacking at one of the smaller shared corporate stations. A group of calling themselves the Committee stormed the control room, confined the staff, and looted a warehouse before flying away."

"I have contacts with them. The Committee are not

our enemies. The Free Traders are not our enemies. Neither have ever operated against us."

"What about the Militia, sir, or the GG?" Jose said.

"They are constrained by tradition. The Militia are not our friends, but that does not make them our enemies."

"Still, the fact that the Free Traders and the others are not our enemies does not make them our friends either, sir," Jose said.

"*Et tu*, Jose?" Dashi said with a smile. "Nevertheless, I am pulling rank on you. Those two security men will not accompany me. It will send the wrong message to the emergency council."

"Very well, sir. You are the boss." Jose made eye contact with the two security men and jerked his head toward a corridor. They nodded and trotted off.

"Nor will I be accompanied by that operative pretending in vain to read the board back there," Dashi said, gesturing.

Jose turned around. Ten meters away, a chubby man in dirty coveralls was loitering in front of the drop ship status board.

"Sir?" Jose said.

"We collected him outside of my office, and he has been following us ever since."

"Could be a coincidence sir."

"The board hasn't changed the entire time we've been here, and he's still looking at it. He hasn't checked his comm or made any calls."

"Perhaps he is a slow reader, sir."

"There is a holster visible on the back of his belt, under his jacket, if you know where to look," Dashi said.

"Many people carry guns, sir," Jose said.

"His name is Alvagado. You've had him and one of his colleagues watching me for a week. I checked the receipts. There is a reason he's not expensive."

"Yes, sir." Jose sighed. "I should know better than to try to pull one over on you." He pulled out his comm and punched a number in. "Alvagado, don't look up. Make yourself scarce, and call me at the office later."

The man in front of the board cocked his head, listening, then sauntered off down a flight of stairs.

"As you wish, sir." Jose handed Dashi the overnight bag.

"Thank you for your concern, Jose, but these things have a rhythm of their own. It is not yet the time for overt confrontation."

"Well, you have told me you expect the possibility of...hostilities...breaking out soon, sir."

"Soon, but not today. I have to catch this drop ship, Jose."

"Sir." Jose didn't sound happy.

Dashi walked toward the lock. The twins' raised voices had been replaced by their brother's soothing mutters. The brother had his hand on the steward's arm, speaking in his ear. Something changed hands, and then the steward stepped back, and the group flowed into the drop ship's lock.

Dashi smiled. Graft was a tradition on drop ships.

"Ticket, sir?" the steward asked.

"Right here," Dashi said, handing over a chip.

"Yes, sir. A cabin just for you. Wait a moment while I close up, and I'll show you myself."

"I'm the last one?" Dashi checked his comm. He had spent a great deal of time with Jose. Their ship was dropping late.

The steward swung the hatch shut and locked the outer wheel. "The very last one, sir." He shuffled Dashi through the inner lock and spun the wheel behind him. Then he reached over to the wall, picked up a phone, and said, "He's here. We can drop."

Dashi walked up the corridor as the warning bongs sounded.

"Warning. Maneuvering in one minute. Low atmosphere in one minute. Zero gravity in one minute."

At the back of the shuttle, many couches were empty.

"I did not buy a first-class ticket. Why do I have my own cabin?" Dashi asked.

"Don't rightly know, sir. Corporate upgrade, maybe? Either way, that's where I'm supposed to put you, so, if you'll follow me." The steward beckoned. "You should get strapped in before we're underway."

Jose. Dashi shook his head and stepped into his cabin. It had a triple acceleration couch, a fresher, a porthole, and a locker with an emergency skin suit in it. Not big, but bigger than anything anyone on the deck would have. He looked across the hall.

"Howdy, neighbor," said the older brother from the corridor. "Finally got that shambles sorted out. A little grease in the right place covers everything, huh? Say, these cabins are something, huh? We figured if we were going to a luxury casino, why not a luxury ride?"

"Indeed. I wish you a pleasant journey." Dashi stepped into the cabin. He paused and stared at the door. The warning bongs had rung, but the ship hadn't started maneuvering. Almost like they were waiting for him to get settled.

☐

Jose sat at his desk watching the drop ship on his screen, with Alvagado across from him. Jose's office was not as luxurious as Dashi's. Instead of a wooden desk, Jose had a simple metal one. However, he did have a framed colored fabric swath on the wall, and a carved wooden statue on his sideboard.

"If anything happens to him...." Jose began.

"Stop worrying," Alvagado said. "The twins are deadly. She can hit a bullseye from twenty feet with her knives, and he can do the same at twice the distance with a crossbow."

"They carry crossbows? Do they have suits of armor too? Might as well join the Knights of the Round Table."

"Disassembled ones. They don't show up as weapons

on the scans. The bolts he uses are disguised as a belt he wears. He's got over a hundred rounds, and he can fire ten a minute."

"A crossbow, for the Emperor's sake."

The drop ship was just maneuvering away from the station. Jose pressed a comm button. "They've dropped. Keep in position," he said, staring out the window.

"What's a round table?" Alvagado asked.

"It's a thing knights did, on Earth."

"What's a knight?"

"There's a movie. I'll send it to you. He picked you up from the beginning, you realize."

"That was the plan. You said to be as obvious as possible."

"Well, you were good at that."

"The twins can handle any physical threat. Linc is a class-three med tech, and he has a full kit with him, as well as tools and commo gear—and unless I'm mistaken after watching that little charade, you have something going on with the steward on that ship."

"The pilots, too. All three of them get an all-expenses-paid vacation at the casino when they get there, and a bonus when they get back if they help keep an eye on Dashi. The pilots are former Militia. They can handle themselves in a fight."

"I didn't know that. You've got this guy ringed with security."

"Yes," Jose said, steepling his hands in an unconscious imitation of Dashi. "I do."

"Why are you telling me this? It's not like you to share sensitive information."

"Two things. First, I love that man. He's like a father to me. If anything happens to him...."

"And the second?"

"For once, I think he's wrong," Jose said. "We're entering a new era. There are more shortages. There is more low-level violence. People are starting to act different. Some people are scared, and scared people are unpredictable."

"He knows this."

"Yes, but he's not scared. He's never scared. Never even gets upset. I don't think he's taken into account what scared people will do."

"I hope you are wrong."

"Me too." Jose again stared at the screen, zooming in on the drop ship drifting slowly away from the station.

He had a perfect view as the shuttle exploded into pieces.

Chapter 2

"Can you get me a job?" Suzy Q asked.

"Doing what?" Nadine asked from the two-person metal table in the kitchen, having just finished her breakfast tray. It was tasteless, which made her happy. In the world of breakfast trays, the alternative to tasteless was disgusting, not delicious.

Suzy Q pulled the metal foil off her own breakfast tray and dug in. "Whatever you do. It sounds like a great job, sales consultant."

Nadine looked at her roommate for a moment, then dumped her tray in the mesh box. She wanted her deposit back. "What do you think I do?"

"Dress up and go to parties. Talk to people. Flirt. Drink. Have fun. Better than purchasing."

"That's not all I do. I have to promote products at these parties. Give out samples. Talk to people."

"Give things to men for free. Drink with them all night. I can talk while I do that."

"I have to travel a lot."

"Other than the farming settlement where I grew up, I've never been out of Landing. I've never been orbital at all."

"It's not a lot of fun," Nadine said. "It's like being inside a dreary office all the time."

"I'm inside dreary offices all the time now."

"Some of the stations aren't much fun. Dirty. Dank. Crowded."

"Different dirty, dank, and crowded, though," Suzy Q said.

"There are a lot of late nights," Nadine said.

"Yes, you woke me up coming in from middle-third shift last night," Natasha said, coming into the kitchen to grab a glass of water. Natasha occupied the apartment's

Andrew Moriarty

third bedroom. "Some of us have to work first shift, you know. Try to be quieter next time."

"Will do," Nadine said, smiling at Natasha. Suzy Q followed suit.

Natasha smiled back, then stepped through the front door and into the hall.

As soon as the door closed, Suzy Q dropped her smile. "Bitch."

"Why do you keep her around?" Nadine asked.

"She pays on time. She's annoying, but she's never missed a rent payment," Suzy Q said. She surveyed the apartment. "Finding roommates who pay on time is harder than you'd think, and I need both of you to afford this palatial homestead."

She waved her arms around. The room had a toilet, small sink, and shower at one end of the common area, and a microwave food tray slot and hinged table at the other. Three small rooms, two with single beds and a locker.

The third was larger than the other two combined, and had its own shower and toilet. That was Suzy Q's old room, now Nadine's. Officially, Nadine paid double what the other tenants paid, but Nadine suspected it was triple, if not more.

She didn't care. It was big enough for what she wanted, a short walk to both the shuttle port and the monorail station, and the area was busy, with plenty of bulk housing dating back to the Founding. Lots of university students lived there, so there was a large transient population she could blend into.

Best of all, her name wasn't on any paperwork—anywhere.

"Speaking of rent, where are we?" Nadine asked.

"You are two months ahead right now," Suzy Q said.

"Okay." Nadine ducked into her room. The closet-sized locker had a simple code-operated keypad. Easy for a professional to defeat. Once open, Nadine leaned down to open a much sturdier safe she'd had installed. It had a manual knob to spin, and was thus immune to electronic tampering.

She pulled out a handful of credit chips and closed the safe. An expert with the right tools could certainly break into the closet and, in time, the safe—but Nadine assumed that her roommates would notice if somebody were in her room working with a plasma torch for three hours. Besides, even if they didn't, the intruders would probably quit after they found the safe. Thieves wouldn't think to remove the outer wall panel to find what was behind there.

"Here's another three months," Nadine said.

"You don't have to," Suzy Q said.

"No problem. I owe you for the food too. Here." Nadine passed her another chip.

Suzy Q put the chip in her comm and glanced at it. "It's too much, Nadine. You don't eat that much."

"Put it on my account," Nadine said. "You know how I am. Come and go."

"Yes, you really are the perfect roommate. Pay your bills on time, and you're never here."

"It's the job. Come and go. Travel to events a lot."

"I wish you could get me work there."

"You wouldn't like it," Nadine said. "It doesn't pay well, for one thing."

Suzy Q looked at her and rattled the credit chips in her hands.

Nadine realized her mistake. "It doesn't, really," she tried to back up. "My salary from that job wouldn't pay even part of that."

Suzy Q raised her eyebrows and rattled the chips again. "Why work there, then?"

Nadine stared at her for a moment, then grinned sheepishly. "It's a good way to meet men. Rich men who want girlfriends." She shrugged. "Sometimes they give me presents."

Suzy Q stopped shaking the credit chips and thought

about that for a moment. She smiled. "Good for you. Did I tell you that Abdul made me pay for half of my birthday dinner?"

"Half? What a dirtbag. When he invited you out?" Nadine said.

Suzy Q nodded and began to catalog Abdul's failures. Nadine let out a sigh of relief.

She didn't really get presents, and she wasn't really in sales. Her regular job offered exceptional pay, and she didn't have to sleep with anybody. Unless she wanted to. She did sometimes have to shoot them, but usually she didn't have to. Unless she wanted to.

The rest of the conversation involved trashing current and former boyfriends. An hour later, after consigning the male half of the species to the deepest hells they justly deserved, Nadine went into her room, got dressed, and stepped out.

She twirled for Suzy Q, who indicated her approval. "Looks good."

"Thanks. I'm off to lunch."

"How long are you in town for this time?"

"Don't know. Up to my boss. He'll let me know."

"Is that who you are having lunch with?" Suzy Q asked. "Or one of your 'friends'?"

"He's just a boss, but I do have some friends in town."

"I hope your lunch is exciting."

"It's just a lunch." Nadine shrugged.

Chapter 3

"Bowling? You want to go bowling?" the brunette asked. "That is the most boring thing I've ever heard."

"It looks like fun," Jake said. "I'd like to try it. I've never been." He smiled at the brunette girl, Kyria. She was short and slim, with olive skin, black hair, and flashing black eyes.

"I've been bowling," Kyria's friend Zena said. "It's really boring."

They could have been sisters, with the same hair and eye color, but Zena had a slightly heavier build. She had a fairly substantial bosom, too, if you liked that sort of thing. Which the man sitting next to her—Zena's husband—clearly did.

Jake had just collected his lunch tray from the TGI main cafeteria and had been looking for somewhere to sit. He'd detoured away from a group of cargo handlers who smelled like eight hours of sweaty effort. Then he'd spied two pretty girls sitting with only one man. The math attracted him. *Can't win if you don't play, and they will surely smell better.*

As he'd gotten closer, Jake had recognized the man's face. The caf was crowded, so it seemed natural to ask if the seat was free. He and the husband, Ana, had chatted a bit and determined they had, in fact, seen each other around the station in some sort of work-related capacity, but neither of them remembered where or how. Ana was a big man, bulky, a wrestler's build, and he stood out in a crowd. Jake could not place him, but was sure he'd seen him.

"Why haven't you been bowling before?" Ana asked.

"I spend most of my time on smaller stations, not big ones like this."

"So you're the country boy come to big station, huh?"

Kyria said. "I thought I recognized a Belter accent there."

"I grew up in the Belt," Jake said, "but I've been traveling around for work."

"What are you doing here?"

"I'm just waiting for my next assignment."

"What kind of assignment?"

"Not sure," Jake said. "Maybe a cargo run."

In truth, Jake wasn't going to be doing any cargo runs at all. He was going to a far orbit. A very far orbit. He had a course chip that described how far out he was going.

At least, he thought it was a far orbit. It was mostly encrypted, but the parts that remained led Jake to believe that if he got far enough into the Outer Belt, he'd be near the orbit. Of course, just being near an orbit didn't mean that the thing you were looking for would be there when you got there. In addition to the shape of the orbit, Jake needed to know when the object would be passing by.

He didn't know exactly what it was—a tug, a cutter, a station, an asteroid, or whatever—but he wanted to get out there, and to get out there, he needed a fairly substantial ship and a great deal of time.

The course chip had belonged to his father. At least, as far as Jake knew. In a recent event, he'd almost gotten his legs shot off while hanging with his friend Nadine. While fixing him up, they'd found a course chip hidden in the heel of one of his boots. Boots that had belonged to his father before he'd died.

While Jake had been recovering, this course chip had been examined by his boss, Mr. Dashi. In simple terms, Jake's job could be described as "Do what Mr. D. says." For a few weeks, Mr. Dashi had had Jake working as a crewman on a cargo ship on a regular route. Jake had compiled lists of ships at different stations, with particular attention to the Militia ships and their maintenance status. He had dutifully counted and recounted, and managed to get a good look at a wide variety of Militia ships.

Then Mr. Dashi, via his assistant, Jose, had informed

Jake that he was on detached duty to follow up on this exact course chip. He'd also let Jake know that all the back pay Jake was owed was to be paid to him, plus some bonuses, and some money from the somewhat extralegal matters Jake had been involved in.

Jose had never said as much, but he had intimated that Jake's current expense account wouldn't be investigated too deeply if he went out and looked into that orbit, and there would be some extra money for "ship acquisition expenses," whatever that meant.

"Your collar flashes are TGI, but I've never seen that pattern before," Ana said. "What do you do for TGI again?"

"I'm in the insurance division. In accounting," Jake said.

Kyria laughed. "Accounting? That sounds boring. Did you actually go to school for that?"

"I did. Two years," Jake said.

"Two years?" Kyria said. "Two years learning about insurance and accounting. Holy Imperial sleepiness. How did you not shoot yourself?"

"Well, we didn't just do accounting all the time."

"What other things do you do?" Zena asked.

Jake thought about that. He'd gotten accused of a murder he didn't commit. Fled. Gotten shot. Hijacked and kidnapped and forced to shoot his best friend. Then coerced into the Militia, nearly killed by a boss who hated him, and had almost died of a deadly disease before being shot at by a madman with a ship big enough to have a rail gun. After, he'd inadvertently ended up running a sort of pirate base, shooting all his friends, and stealing a (sort of) shuttle and helping land it and a crew of escapees at TGI's new (sort of) secret shuttle base. Oh, and he'd almost drowned in the landing when the tide had come in.

"Well," Jake said, "we do a lot of auditing too."

"Auditing?" Kyria didn't look impressed.

"We go places and check the records and see if they are

correct. If things match up."

"Wow," Kyria said. "Accounting is way more exciting than I thought."

Jake was almost certain she was being sarcastic.

"Speaking of excitement," Zena said, "Ana, tell them what happened to you on your last ground assignment."

"Well, I was sent down to the surface."

Jake had to sit still for the next few minutes while Ana described the establishment of TGI's new alternate shuttle port and how he'd been involved in helping tow it to shore and get it fixed up for launch. Since Jake had actually been inside the craft the whole time, he just nodded and smiled. He had been warned to not talk about the whole event.

"So TGI has its own shuttle now?" Zena asked.

"It's not a shuttle, exactly. It's something else. It looks different, and it had a different name. It was called a...."

"A lifting body," Jake said.

"That's right. That's what it was called—a lifting body. It was like a shuttle, but not exactly." Ana gave Jake an odd look, but went on to describe the shuttle and the events surrounding its landing.

"Sounds cool, but I want more basic," Kyria said. "Anybody else?" She collected their various cups and went to the taps.

Zena looked at Jake. "She's not seeing anybody."

"What?" Jake said.

"She's single. If you're interested."

"Of course he's interested. He didn't sit down to talk to me," Ana said. "Did you?"

"I do know you from somewhere, but I can't remember where," Jake said.

"I've seen you somewhere too," Ana said, "but that's good enough for a nod, not sitting down. Anyway, when we're with Kyria, we're used to male attention."

"Just to warn you, she's into sport dating," Zena said.

"What's that?" Jake asked.

"She sees how much abuse you'll put up with. It's fun

for her," Zena said. "Lots of guys think she's worth it."

"Oh," Jake said. "Well, she is very pretty."

Kyria headed back to the table, a big man in a TGI security uniform in tow. "Look who I found at the taps," she said.

"Macon, how are you?" Ana said. He stood up and hugged the newcomer. "Great to see you. You're looking well."

"Isn't he, though?" Kyria said. She smiled up at Macon, then ran her hand along his arm. "Have you been working out?"

"Every day," Macon said, flexing a bicep. "Still pumped from the gym. "How's things in Finance?"

"Great. We've turned a huge profit this quarter," Kyria said, "and I'm looking forward to a big bonus."

"What are you going to do with your big bonus, little girl?" Macon asked.

"Dinner. A big expensive dinner, at that place off the mall. The one that has the buffalo steaks brought up from the surface—and orange juice."

"That sounds great. Why don't I go with you?"

"Now, Macon," Kyria said. "You know I don't buy dinner for men. Men buy dinner for me."

"What makes you think I can't afford it?" Macon asked.

"Because we know you," Kyria said. "You didn't join the security department for the money, that's for sure."

They all laughed.

Ana turned to Jake. "Macon and I grew up together. He isn't very...."

"Smart," Macon finished. "I'm not smart—but I'm big, and I like to fight. That's good for security."

"You aren't that dumb," Kyria said.

"Dumb enough. Certainly not smart enough to get a finance degree, not like a certain brainy girl," Macon said, winking at Kyria, then turned to Jake and smiled. "I don't know you. I'm Macon."

"Jake."

"Jake's in Accounting," Kyria said. "He likes bowling."

Jake shrugged. "I don't necessarily like it."

"Bowling? Sounds kind of boring to me," Macon said.

"Me too," Zena piped up.

"Boring as an Imperial rescript," Kyria said.

"Well, to each their own," Macon said. "Good for you, Jake."

"I've never actually done it," Jake said.

"Be proud of what you are. That's what I say," Macon said. "I'm dumb and proud of it, and, well, if you're boring, good for you. We need boring people."

"I was just interested," Jake said.

"Jake the bowler from Accounting," Macon said. "Your last name wouldn't be Stewart, would it?"

"It is. Why?" Jake asked.

"Security is looking for you. They have a package, I think. Let me ask." Macon produced his comm and typed something into it. "Yup, somebody is on the way. You should wait here."

Jake nodded. He was expecting a package.

Macon continued, "So, Ana, what's these rumors I hear about that new shuttle port?"

"It was pretty exciting. We were going to go down on the monorail, but there was some sort of problem. We had to wait till somebody senior from corporate came down and cleared it up, and we went down to the end of the line. Let me tell you, this place was small, and they'd had a riot or something. There were burned buildings all over the place."

Jake sat back and listened. He knew all this because he had been there, but he couldn't say it.

Two other TGI security persons approached the table. Neither was as big as Macon, but instead of Macon's shock stick, one was armed with a shotgun slung across his chest.

The other had his hands on his holstered revolver. "Hi, Macon. Which one is he?"

Macon gestured at Jake.

"You're Jake Stewart?" the first TGI guard asked.

"That's me," Jake said.

"I've got a package for you."

"Sure." Jake held out his hand.

"Sorry, need some ID and a DNA scan. Step over here, please."

Jake got up and followed the man to a table against the wall. The guard set up a DNA tester and took a pinprick from Jake's thumb, then waited a few minutes while it was analyzed.

In the meantime, Ana had finished his story.

"That sounds fun," Macon said. "Good job there, Ana. I'll bet you get a promotion for that."

"I might get a promotion, but I won't make as much money as Finance Girl over there does."

Kyria held up her glass in salute just as Jake returned with the guard.

"Nice meeting everybody," Jake said, "but my boss called. I have to go."

"Off to teach him bowling?" Zena asked.

"No, not exactly. He says I need to buy a ship, and today, so I need to get going."

The four at the table looked at him for a moment, then laughed.

"That's pretty impressive, Jake," Macon said in all seriousness. "Have fun buying your ship."

"Thanks," Jake said and hurried away.

As soon as he was gone, the girls laughed again.

"Macon, you are so gullible," Zena said. "He's not buying a ship."

"What do you mean?"

"He's not an executive ship buyer."

"Why would he lie?" Macon shrugged.

"Guys lie to impress girls, Macon."

"I don't. But that's 'cause I can't keep my lies straight. Will you take me to dinner with you, Kyria?"

"Not a chance."

"Stuck on that accountant guy, huh?" Macon said.

Kyria waved his comment away. "Hardly. He's boring. He's an accountant. Besides, he doesn't have any money. Look at that suit he's wearing. An old Belter semi. Can't he afford something new?"

Ana had been watching Jake's back as he strode away across the caf. "He was at the shuttle port."

"What?"

"That's where I saw him. He was in charge of the shuttle thing that came down."

"They put an accountant in charge of it after it landed?" Kyria asked.

"No, not like that. He came out of the shuttle. He rode it down when they brought it in the first time, and he was talking to the boss man—Jose or something like that. Seemed to know him well."

"You're saying he brought the shuttle down from orbit?" Kyria asked.

"There were two pilots, and a bunch of people in back, but he came out of the control room."

"He's a pilot? Or owner's representative, maybe?"

"Something like that."

The guard who had spoken to Jake returned to their table. "Thanks, Macon," he said.

"No problem, Nigel. These are my friends," Macon said, and introduced the others.

"Pleased to meet you all. I'm glad to get that knocked out so we can get back to the armory and drop these weapons. They're a pain in the ass on the station."

"Why carry them, then?" Zena asked.

"Policy. Whenever we're carrying a ton of cash, we have to be armed."

"Well, I could use some of that cash. Kyria is going to dinner at that expensive place in the commons."

"Oh, you are? Good for you. That Jake guy is paying, is he?"

"What? Why do you say that?"

The guard surveyed the table. "You think they sent an armed escort and a DNA tester to drop off lunch money? That guy just signed for a quarter million credits. Inter-company credits. Untraceable, too—once he has 'em, we can't get 'em back. He's mighty rich, that one."

The three turned just in time to see Jake retreat around the corner.

"You should have gone bowling with him, Kyria," Macon said.

Chapter 4

"So we should kill them all?" Don Pedro leaned forward and glared at Colonel Savard at the far end of the polished wooden table. "Is that what you want me to do?"

Colonel Savard frowned. "Not exactly. I don't want any unnecessary deaths."

"Why not?"

"Why not?" Colonel Savard looked at Commander Roi, who shrugged. "I don't understand."

"You said 'unnecessary deaths.' What makes some necessary and some unnecessary, and who gets to choose? What if I choose and I say just kill them all?" Don Pedro said.

Colonel Savard pulled himself up ramrod straight. He was the shortest person in the room, shorter even than his niece, Lieutenant Savard, who sat in silence next to Commander Roi. His uniform was unwrinkled and cut in a decidedly non-regulation way. The special cut was necessary to hide his growing weight issues. Commander Roi had the opposite problem. He was as skinny as a cancer survivor.

"We can't just have wholesale killings in the streets," Colonel Savard said. "This is not a coup. This is for the glory of the Emperor." As he pushed his chair back, the metal scraped into the wall behind it. He turned and looked at the scratch. "Sorry."

"That's carved hardwood," Don Pedro said.

"Sorry," Colonel Savard said again.

"Brought all the way up from the south continent."

"It was an accident."

"Perhaps if this table weren't so big," Commander Roi said.

"First you are telling me who to kill, and now you want to give me advice on interior decorating? In my own boardroom. Who do you think you are?" Don Pedro said.

"We'll buy you another table," Colonel Savard said, "but as for the matter at hand, as I said, we propose that we begin restricting shuttle access to only people on our joint approved list. That includes cargo. You'll do the same on the monorail. Shut down cargo transfers and passenger travel. If we control transportation, we control the economy. If we control the economy, we control Delta."

"You can't buy me another one. I had to organize a special expedition down there to get it. Twenty-five years ago. Had to have it cut and carved on the spot."

"Uh, right." Colonel Savard looked at the two Galactic Growing executives who sat on either side of Don Pedro, who stared back at him without so much as twitching. "Well, perhaps, afterward, we could move it into a bigger room, into one of the buildings in Landing."

"I don't want to go to Landing," Don Pedro said. "This is my favorite table in my favorite room. All my best decisions have been made here. My best acquisitions. Plans. Why, I even made the boy here, right on this table—twenty-five years ago, my wife and I, God rest her immortal soul."

Commander Roi and Colonel Savard looked down at the table, then at each other.

"Sir, I hope it's been cleaned since then," Commander Roi said in a low voice.

The young man at Don Pedro's side covered his face with his hand. "Please, Papa...."

"I hear bad things about Landing. It's dirty, wet, and you can't get a decent cider," Don Pedro said.

"We are not talking about cider," Don Pedro's son said.

"No, we're talking about killing a bunch of people on this list. This 'proscription' list they are talking about." Don Pedro looked closely at his son. "DJ, you are the spitting image of your mother, bless her. Did I ever tell you how we first met, her and I?"

"Many times, Papa. Many times." DJ took a deep breath. "Colonel, I think what my father means is that he is concerned about the number of people on this list of yours. You want us to detain all these people. TGI officials. Free Traders. Some university professors. Some other corps. There are even current and former Militia officers on this list."

"We strongly believe it is necessary to reform Imperial authority here on Delta," Colonel Savard said. "This so-called 'Delta Corporation' is just a commercial entity. It lacks any legitimacy. We will re-establish proper rule, in the name of the Empire. Until the Emperor returns."

"Until the Emperor returns," the other two officers echoed.

DJ looked blank for a moment, then turned to the GG official, a director of planning, at the end of the table and raised his eyebrows.

"We certainly wouldn't want to argue about the desirability of returning to Imperial authority," the director said. "After all, that's what the Delta Corporation was formed for, to govern in the Empire's absence. Certainly, we here at Galactic Growing feel that we should have more say in the Council's decisions than we currently have, but I do have some questions about the timing. This system is working. People get fed. The lights are on. Why change it now?"

Colonel Savard leaned back. "Explain it to them, Commander."

"Well, sir. Sirs. Don," Commander Roi said. "You're correct that people get fed and the lights stay on. For now—but nothing lasts forever. After the Abandonment, we were fortunate to have a large stock of materials on hand, especially in the Militia. Our capital goods have long amortization periods."

"'Amortization'? What?" DJ said.

"Spaceships last a long time," the director said. "They don't need much maintenance, and they don't break often."

"Yes, exactly." Commander Roi cleared his throat. "Well, we commissioned a study at the university. A secret study. It looked at the relative economic strengths of the different corporations, including how much of the economy each represents and what it produces. The first thing is—with the exception of food, of which we have a surplus—we have about twice the population we can support long-term."

DJ nodded. "We've found the same. We're short on energy, and the fusion plants decline a little every year. Not much, but enough. Over time, we'll have to start cutting off electricity somewhere. Either production plants or housing. Something. We're also starting to notice a shortage of critical materials for the printers. We can still make things—just not as many and not as fast—and the printers don't last forever either."

Commander Roi nodded. "Just so. At some point conflict will break out over resources. We want to make sure the reallocation of resources favors us while our relative economic positions are still intact, or at least not diminished."

DJ shook his head. "This is why I hated the university in Landing. What does that mean?"

"You're big dogs right now," Colonel Savard said. "You are bigger than any other corp right now. Are you bigger than TGI?"

"Sure," DJ said.

"How about a year from now?"

"Of course," DJ said.

"How about five years from now?"

DJ started to speak, but stopped.

"You see?" Colonel Savard said. "It's relative. You know that some things will stop working in five years. You'll have to close plants. Fire workers. Stop selling some things. Stop dealing with some people."

"So will TGI," DJ said. "We'll still be bigger, relatively."

"Will you? Maybe. Everybody is going to decline, but some are going to decline faster than others, and in different areas. You'll have to close some plants, and so will they. You're bigger, but they are more diversified. Ground and orbital. Food and manufacturing. They have services you don't."

"You're in the same boat as us," DJ said.

"Your Militia ships are starting to fail," the director said. "You're having problems with maintenance. You can't fix complex parts, and you have a limited ability to machine them. Ahhhh...." The director turned to DJ. "TGI has a...sort of a shipyard, really, at their main station. They've been quiet about it, but they haven't hidden it. They do repairs. They can swap engines from one ship to another. Anything that can be machined with local parts, they do. Rather than printing parts directly, they've made some metal forming items. Lathes, drill presses. They use them to make what they can."

The director turned back to the Militia colonel. "They can keep more ships flying longer than you can. You have an advantage now, but it will start to erode. At some point TGI will overtake you, and they'll keep that advantage, even as things fall apart."

Commander Roi nodded once. "By our reckoning, this moon and its system can support half the population we have now in a modern technological society. Half of us can have energy, food, medicine, clothing, entertainment, education, and a life. The other half will live in tents without clothes."

"Starve in the snow," the director said.

"No," Commander Roi said. "We'll always have a surplus of food, but not clothing or energy. They won't starve, but half of us will freeze in the snow."

"Well, I know which half I want to be in," Colonel

Savard said. "We can beat them right now, the two of us, and a few favored others. In the name of the Empire, we can—we must—take over the important parts of the economy and the Council. Run things our way. Properly. Stockpile. It's our patriotic duty. Until the Empire returns."

"Until the Empire returns," the other Militia officers repeated in chorus.

DJ looked at the other GG official and rolled his eyes, then turned back to Colonel Savard. "That's fine, Colonel, but what do we do with these people? We don't have a prison. We have a few jail cells on some of our settlements, but we can't hold this many people forever."

"Why not put them in barracks with the field workers?" Commander Roi asked.

"No locks," the second GG official said.

"And what if they resist?" DJ said. "We don't have an army, or even a police force. We have security. They keep order well enough, but they only have revolvers and perhaps a few shotguns. If we start collecting people from the streets, some of them will fight back, and that will lead to riots."

"Señor Pedro," Commander Roi said.

"Yes?" father and son both answered.

"Um, the younger, uh—you." Commander Roi pointed at DJ.

"Don Pedro is always my father," DJ said. "Pedro is the family name. Both of us are Señor Pedro, but only the head of our house is Don Pedro. My full name is Don Armando Julio Flores Pedro, but people call me Don Junior. DJ is an acceptable nickname. When my father passes, I will be Don Pedro. Until then, please use DJ."

"Señor DJ, are you saying you can't control the streets of your own settlements?"

"We already control the streets of our own settlements, but you want us to control monorail stations, other corporations' settlements, and send a sizable group to control the main monorail station in Landing," DJ said.

"You can't handle a group of soft executives and some accountants?" Colonel Savard asked.

"Many of these people are TGI, which has an exceptional corporate security department," DJ said. "Their senior people now travel with bodyguards. Armed bodyguards. Besides, the Militia people on this list have the same training as you. Do you call yourself soft?"

Colonel Savard frowned. "Be careful what you say, young man. We are soldiers of the Empire. Our honor is the Empire's honor."

DJ rolled his eyes again. "Colonel, most Free Trader ships have an arms locker. They usually have crews trained on their weapons. Some of those crews are former Militia. When you get away from the inner stations, things can be tense. They are used to confrontation."

"So overwhelm them," Colonel Savard said.

"In Landing? In Landing alone, there are three hundred people on this list. We have weapons for perhaps two hundred security troops."

"Brandy," Don Pedro said.

Everyone looked at him.

"Brandy."

"What about brandy, Papa?" DJ asked.

"They have good brandy in Landing, or so I've heard. Lousy cider, of course. We make the best cider here at East-27."

"Yes, we do, Papa, but we're talking about going into Landing. Bringing some of the security into Landing."

"Dangerous place, son. Bring a big group with you."

"I will."

"But you need to leave some here. We need to protect the cider."

"Of course, Papa. We will protect the cider."

"Good. You can take half of the security into town with you, but the rest stay here, and all the guns."

DJ frowned. "We'll need some of the guns, Papa."

"No. They stay here to protect the cider. You can take the men, but not the guns."

"Papa, you said Landing was dangerous. I'll need guns there."

"Yes. Yes, you will." Don Pedro frowned. "Ask these gentlemen. They have guns."

DJ turned back to the Militia officers. "My father is correct. You do have guns. You're asking a great deal of us here. We will need more weapons."

Colonel Savard turned to Commander Roi.

"Well, sir," Commander Roi said, "we could release some revolvers, perhaps twenty, and five shotguns."

Colonel Savard nodded and turned to the GG officers.

"No," Don Pedro said. "Five hundred revolvers. One hundred shotguns. Two hundred rounds for each, and half a dozen of those sub-machine gun things I keep hearing about."

"We can't do that," Commander Roi said.

"And twenty bottles of that brandy," Don Pedro said.

"Brandy?" Colonel Savard said.

"Yes. Apple brandy. They make it in Landing."

"That's a lot of weapons," Colonel Savard said.

"Yes." Don Pedro stood up and began to pace along his side of the table. "However, in return, we will capture all the people on your list that are in our area of operation." He began to tick things off on his fingers. "We will arm all our people and do it all at once. We will overwhelm them with a large force so they will be too cowed to fight. The monorail will be closed except to official traffic. Our official traffic. We'll collect all those people together, ship them to Landing, and turn them over to you. You can have control of them, and we'll leave their guards back in Landing to control the monorail station. My son will do this."

Colonel Savard looked at Commander Roi. "Give them one hundred revolvers, twenty shotguns, and one sub-machine gun."

"Don't forget the twenty bottles of brandy," Don Pedro said.

"You really want the brandy?"

"Of course. Why would we go into Landing otherwise?"

Colonel Savard raised an eyebrow at DJ.

"I am my father's man in all things." DJ shrugged. "If he wants weapons to do this, you had best give him weapons—and the brandy, as he said."

Colonel Savard rubbed his eyes and put his head in his hands. "Commander," he said, "how soon can we do this?"

"It'll take a while, sir, to divert some stores, ship things to the stations, and bring them down on the shuttles. I'll need to organize multiple shipments and confuse some inventories so that nobody knows what's missing, and to send somebody to buy brandy."

"Very well. Get started. Contact Don Pedro—" He looked up at the GG officials. "Actually, perhaps DJ will be handling this?"

"Comm me with the details about the weapons," DJ said.

"And I want to know when I get my brandy," Don Pedro said.

"Commander, contact Don Pedro and DJ as appropriate for their parts in this. Expedite this as much as possible, but make sure word doesn't get out."

"Yes, sir."

"I think that concludes our business for today." Colonel Savard stood up.

"Yes," DJ said. He stood as well and gestured to the other GG executive. "Raul will see you out."

Colonel Savard snapped a salute. "Till the Emperor returns."

"Till the Emperor returns," the other two officers said.

DJ and Raul looked at each other, and then Raul led the Militia officials out. DJ sat down and waited till the door shut, watching it in silence.

A minute later, Raul returned. "The Militia gentlemen have left the building."

DJ looked sideways at his father. His father's mouth was working, but no sound came out.

"Brandy? You want brandy?" DJ said.

Don Pedro burst out laughing. He sniggered. He chortled. He rolled around in his chair and spun it in a circle. Tears ran down his face.

"Why brandy?" DJ asked.

"Do you think they bought it?" Don Pedro asked.

"They think you are a crazy old coot—that's for sure, Papa. What made you think of brandy?"

"I've had some before."

"Is it good?"

"Horrible," Don Pedro said, "but that makes it hard to find."

"So some junior Militia officer will be running around Landing trying to buy brandy."

"Yes, and it makes me sound nuts—but it worked."

"One hundred revolvers, and the shotguns, too," DJ said.

"With what we have, that will give us enough to put a train full of troops into Landing."

"Won't they suspect?"

"We'll tell them a train with prisoners is coming into town," Don Pedro said.

"They only told us to arrest three hundred."

"We'll say they are friends, or family, or something, but we'll pack the train. We'll also be a day late."

"Why a day late?" DJ asked.

"There will be riots for sure. They'll spend their people trying to stop them, to occupy the other corporate HQs—all of that."

"But what will we do with all those troops in Landing, Papa?"

"What I've wanted to do for years," Don Pedro said.

"Occupy the Shuttle complex. Take over the city. Eliminate the Militia."

Chapter 5

"I'm angry with you," Admiral Edmunds said. He spoke quietly. Franz's on the plaza was expensive, discreet, and didn't put up with loud guests. Everything in the restaurant was quiet and soft. Soft cushions. Soft napkins. Soft lighting.

"Okay, and I should care why?" Nadine scanned the menu in front of her. "Buffalo ragout, or buffalo stew? What's pasta?"

"Why didn't you answer those last few messages?"

"I'll ask the waitress. She'll know." She raised her hand and gestured to a girl by the door.

"You can't just ignore me when I call you," the admiral said. "I count on you being able to give me detailed reports."

The waitress arrived. Nadine pointed at the menu item and gestured as if to say, *What is it?*

"It's a noodle, made from wheat," the waitress said.

"You can eat wheat?" Nadine asked. "I thought it was just something that rich people put in their greenhouses."

"You can. We pound it down, mix it with water, form it into strips, let it dry, and cook it with some oil. They did it in the Old Empire."

"It sounds horrible," Nadine said. "Who would eat oil? What's that taste like?"

"It's olive oil. I've had it twice. I really like it," the waitress. "It's got a unique taste. Mixed with the buffalo, it tastes fantastic."

"If it's so good, why have you only eaten it twice?" Nadine asked.

"Did you check the price?"

Nadine looked at the menu again. She whistled. The

only thing more expensive was the orange juice, and something called a lime.

"Please bring us a small plate of pasta, lightly oiled, as our appetizer, and then give us a few minutes," Admiral Edmunds said.

"He's quite generous, as long as I'm generous." Nadine winked at the waitress. "You know what I mean."

The waitress departed, and the admiral frowned. "Must you try to convince everybody that we're sleeping together?"

"I need to keep my acting skills up," Nadine said.

"You never answered my question. Why didn't you answer my messages before?"

"Because I'm not one of your employees. Because I do my own thing. I pick my own jobs. Because I don't owe you anything unless we agree to it ahead of time. What does this one pay, anyway?"

"You don't owe me anything?" Admiral Edmunds said. "Is that what you think?"

"I don't owe you a thing."

"I paid for all those schools. I got you all that training. I paid for all those ships. Set you up with all those people."

"Number one, those weren't favors," Nadine said. "You made me work those off. Number two, it wasn't charity. You needed something done, and I was the only one who could possibly do it, so you gave me the tools I needed to get what you wanted. That wasn't for me. Number three, this is all about guilt. Your guilt. You screwed up. You screwed up big time, and you think that by helping me out, you'll get some sort of cosmic forgiveness. Good luck with that, but it's not my problem."

Nadine raised her hand.

The waitress scurried over. "Ma'am?"

"Which is more expensive, orange juice or that lime juice thing?" Nadine asked.

"Well, the lime juice, but most people don't really

like—"

"Never mind that. Give me two big glasses of it."

"Two?" The waitress's eyes turned to the admiral. He scowled but nodded, so she sped away.

"Does it give you pleasure to spend my money like that?" Admiral Edmunds asked.

"I think of it as therapy for your guilt. I'm helping you deal with that. I'm a healing type of girl. You should be thankful."

The admiral glared at her for a moment, but then laughed. "You are just like your mother."

Nadine gritted her teeth. "Don't talk about my mother."

"Why not? You've already ordered the most expensive things on the menu. You can't cost me any more. Besides, it helps me deal with my guilt, as you say."

The appetizer and drinks arrived. The admiral snagged them, handed one to Nadine, and kept one for himself. "Free trades," he said.

"Free trades," Nadine said, clinking glasses.

They each took a big swig.

The admiral grimaced. "This is lousy."

"Blech," Nadine said, nearly spitting it out.

The admiral waved the waitress over. "There is something wrong with this lime drink."

"It's possible, sir, but I saw them squeeze the limes myself. That's how they are supposed to taste."

"Are you sure?" the admiral asked. "They taste horrible."

"Yes," she said, "you're not the first one to say that."

The admiral looked at Nadine, and they both started laughing.

"It'll be fine. Bring us two buffalo with pasta, please, and some orange juice."

The waitress hurried off, and Nadine continued to giggle. "People pay money for that?"

"Lots of money." He laughed. "Look, in return for

these dinners, I need you to stay in touch."

"I stay in touch when I'm on a job for you. Other than that, I'm busy."

"Busy with what?"

"You are not my only customer, and I do have a social life."

"You're gone three quarters of the time. You don't have time for a boyfriend."

"You would be surprised. But I came here for the food. Even with what you pay me, I can't afford to eat here. What do you want?"

The admiral picked at the pasta. "This is really quite good. You should try some."

Nadine had a bite. Her eyes widened. "This is wonderful. I've never tasted anything like it." She began to shovel the food into her mouth.

"I want you to get off-planet for a while. Far off-planet," Admiral Edmunds said.

"It tastes...delicate. You don't even notice the oil. What's that spice?"

"Far away. Outer stations, at least."

"It tastes fresh. What's it called?"

"Oregano. They grow it in the greenhouses."

"It's wonderful. It's not convenient to go off-planet right now."

"You were off-planet for a month with that Militia station thing."

"I wonder if there is any oregano in the buffalo."

"I need you to do it soon. I want you out of here right after this meal. Find somewhere far out and go there."

"Sounds like you want me to run away."

"I do."

"What ship will I take?"

"None. I need all my ships close by right now."

"You normally give me a ship."

"I normally don't have to worry about them being shot out of the sky."

Nadine put her fork down. "Shot out of the sky? What's going on?"

"Nothing has actually happened yet, but I need all my ships in close orbit right now, and I need them with full crews. Military crews, with gunners who can hit things."

"I can hit things."

"Not with ship weapons, you can't. You can drive things, but you have no gunnery skills."

"I have skills."

"Things are getting unstable."

"Besides, what do you mean, 'your ships'? You're not an admiral anymore."

"I'm not, but times are confusing. There are still some people who take my advice."

"So my leaving is part of some plan of yours?"

"Yes."

"Well, then you'll have to pay."

"I have to pay you to go somewhere safe?"

"Yup. I have a big clothes budget."

The admiral leaned forward. "You are infuriating. You drive me insane."

"Mission accomplished," Nadine said.

Admiral Edmunds started to speak, but stopped. He frowned, reached into his jacket, and pulled his comm out.

"It's rude to take a call when you're having dinner with a pretty girl," Nadine said.

"Which is why only a few, very important people have this code," the admiral said. He tapped the screen and then sat still, reading.

"Well, what exciting things are your important people telling you?"

"There's been an explosion. A drop ship was blown up."

"An accident?"

"That's the story. My people tell me otherwise."

"What do you mean?"

"There were a lot of important people on that ship."

The admiral looked up. "Are you armed?"

"Why?"

"I have to go. You have to go."

"I don't think—wait." Nadine gave him an odd look. "You look different."

"You have to go," the admiral repeated, scanning the tables around them.

"You're afraid. I've never seen you afraid before."

"Just go," Admiral Edmunds said. He sat up straight.

Nadine sat up straight up as well, looking around.

"Too late," he said.

Eight men and women in Militia uniform walked into the restaurant. Each carried a drawn weapon, either a revolver, a shotgun, or a shock stick.

"You need to get away—now. The Militia will be looking for you. Get away from close orbit. Go far, and go fast."

"I don't understand," Nadine said. "Why are they looking for you?"

"Good afternoon, Admiral. I need you to come with me," the leading man said, pointing his revolver at the floor.

"What for?" the admiral asked.

"I have a warrant for your arrest."

"No, you don't."

"So you must....What?"

"You've got nothing. Nothing official, anyway. This is a coup. That shuttle that blew up. You killed most of the TGI board, a bunch of the Free Traders, and some senior university people. This is a coup."

"I don't know anything about that," the man said. "I've got a warrant."

"You should check that."

"I'll do that later. For now, you have to come with me."

"Very well. Just let me take care of my young lady friend." The admiral turned to Nadine. "Sweetheart, I'm afraid lunch is over. You'll have to go." He smiled. "It's been fun, but things happen. Oh, I haven't paid you yet."

Admiral Edmunds looked up at the guard. "I always pay my bills. Do you mind?"

He didn't wait for an answer, but leaned forward and tucked a credit chip in Nadine's shirt pocket. Then he leaned closer and touched his lips to her cheek—close enough to whisper, "Get the guns. Bring them back to the loyal officers.'"

He leaned back and nodded at her. "Go now."

She pushed her chair back and got up slowly. "What's going on?"

"None of your concern, ma'am. Escort her out," the man ordered the others.

Two revolver-wielding Militia stepped behind her and gestured. She walked slowly toward the door.

"She looks familiar," one of the guards said. "I think I've seen her before."

"Run her though the system," she heard behind her.

Nadine didn't wait to hear more. "Excuse me, guys," she said.

"Yes?" The guard on her right turned.

She grabbed him and slung him into his partner, knocking them both down. Then she fled out the door and into the crowded street.

Shots rang out behind her.

Chapter 6

"She's out of your league," the man said.

"What?" Jake said, turning to the man next to him at the table.

"She's too much for you."

"What are you talking about?" Jake asked.

"I saw you looking across the bar. Over there." The man pointed. "You were watching her."

"I could have been looking at anything."

"But you weren't. You were looking at her, and you can't afford her."

"How do you know I want her?"

"I know that look. Especially from a young man. I wanted something like her when I was younger too. Great lines," the man said.

"She's very sleek," Jake said. "How expensive would she be?"

"Very, but that's not the problem."

"What's the problem?"

"It doesn't matter what you spend at the start. It's the maintenance."

"Maintenance?" Jake asked.

"You can't just spend some money and just leave her alone. You have to take her places. Buy her things. Food. And you....Well, look at yourself."

"What's wrong with myself?" Jake asked.

"You dress too plain. If you're going to be with her, you need new clothes. Flashy. Stylish. Expensive."

"I guess so."

"I know so. Sorry, kid. She's not for you."

"Couldn't I try her out for a while?"

"She'll break your heart, kid. She'll take all your money, and then you'll be high and dry."

"I guess you're right," Jake admitted, "but she'd be fun."

"She'd be lots of fun," the man agreed, "but she's not for you, kid."

"You are the world's worst salesman," Jake said. "Did you know that?"

"I'm a great salesman."

"Aren't you supposed to convince me to spend more money?"

"You'll spend everything you have and then some. I've seen the type before."

"What type of a salesman are you?"

"A very successful type. I'll get all your money, one way or another, but I don't think you have enough for what you want."

"I want speed, endurance, and a low price."

"You can pick one. After that, you start making compromises. Now, that girl you were looking at there...." He consulted his comm. "That's a Launch. Fast. Semi-streamlined. Thus, the curves. It's not streamlined enough to land on Delta, but it can land in a lighter atmosphere, or operate in the upper atmosphere of a larger planet."

"It's not streamlined enough to land on Delta? What's the use of having any streamlining, then?"

"It's an Old Empire design. It was designed to be carried on a much larger ship and zip people from a big freighter down to planets."

"How do you know it's an Old Empire design?" Jake said, eying the salesman. He stood tall, but he had white hair, and his face was heavily lined. "You weren't...."

The salesman laughed. "Kid, I'm old, but not that old. I wasn't alive during the Abandonment. My grandfather was, though. He worked on a long-haul freighter before he settled here, or jumped ship ahead of Imperial security. We're not sure."

"He crewed a big freighter? How come we don't have any big freighters here?"

"I asked him that. Nobody made them, he said. Big freighters were only for inter-system trade. Jump drives were expensive to operate and used a lot of fuel, so it made sense to only put them in the biggest ships. Intra-system traffic was always mass drivers. Load up what you wanted to sell into a container, fire it off to where the target planet would be in a few months, and let a cheap tug grab it."

"Oh. That's why we only have small freighters here. Cheap enough to operate in the Rings, where there are no mass drivers."

"You are a smart kid, aren't you?"

Jake turned from the viewport to look at the man. He might have been young, but he was experienced enough to know when he was being played. "But you said it can't land on Delta."

"There are more moons than Delta in the universe, kid. More planets, too. Some of them have partial atmospheres. Not enough to breathe, but enough to break things off if you try to land a big freighter."

"Oh," Jake said. "Good point. Regardless, I won't be landing on Delta."

"What type of ship are you looking at?"

Jake began to list statistics. Crew size. Consumables space. Power. Fuel size. Fuel loading systems. Flow rates. Cargo trusses. Major systems. Backup systems. Expandability. Maintenance spares. The salesman typed things into his comm.

"You've done your research, kid. That's for sure. What type of runs are we looking at?"

"I'm going to do general cargo to the Outer Rings. Tramp work. I'll be taking cargo on spec and transporting orders out. Bringing ore back in, probably."

"The Outer Rings?" The salesman stopped typing. "That's a good way to go broke, kid. It's way dangerous. You'll get thrown outside by pirates, or catch some strange disease, or get eaten by cannibals. Why not just find a mining station that needs a regular run?"

Jake grimaced. "I grew up in the Outer Rim. There are no pirates. We eat trays, like everybody else. We're not cannibals."

The salesman regarded him warily, like Jake might start gnawing on his arm at any second. "Says you. I got contacts out there. All sorts of strange things happen."

"It's perfectly safe."

"I hear there were some strange diseases out there. They had to change the medical protocols. Say, you've had all your shots, haven't you?"

"How much for a freighter?" Jake asked.

The man named a sum. It was high.

"How much for a small freighter?"

This sum was almost as high. Jake raised a brow in surprise.

"Look, kid, there's a certain base cost to these things. You need a control computer and some electronics—a radar and a telescope, at least. A couple radios. Those are all Old Empire, mostly, so they are expensive. The engine cost is pretty much fixed. You can have one, two, or four nozzles. Basic life support is the same for pretty much every ship. The only variable is how many container trusses you get, and those aren't that expensive. We fabricate them here."

"What does that mean to me?"

"It means that the difference in cost between a six-container freighter and a sixty-container freighter is only about 25 percent. It's the base stuff that costs."

"What about a loan?"

"We finance, but not for the Outer Rim."

"What's wrong with the Rim?"

"If you have a regular contract, a regular run, we take that as security. We contract directly with your customers. They pay us directly so that the mortgage gets covered, and we remit the rest to you. If there is any left."

"But what about trading outside of the main stations?"

"We're in business to make a profit, kid. The regular station runs make your nut, and we want it. Speculative trade isn't our thing." The salesman eyed Jake's clothes. "That a Belter suit?"

"I told you that I'm from the Outer Rim," Jake said.

"You talk like you know ships, but you're missing a few things."

"Like what?"

"I like you, kid."

"Thanks. What am I missing?"

The salesman sighed. "You did your research. You've thought about this. You have a plan. A plan with real numbers. I wish my grandson were like you."

"What am I missing, please?"

"I told his mother, but frankly, my daughter is just as useless as he is. You know what he's taking at the university?"

"No, I do not. What am I missing about the ship?"

"Imperial history. What's the use of that? He'll never get a job. I thought maybe he did it because the class would be all girls, you know? I figure, at least he's going to get laid—but no. Small class, 80 percent men. What's the point of that?" The salesman frowned and looked over Jake's head.

Jake grabbed the salesman arm. "Never mind your grandson. I'm right here, and I'm trying to buy a ship. What am I missing about the ship?"

The salesman looked at him. "Who's your patron?"

"My what?"

"Corporations have their own ships. They handle their own runs. The Free Traders and the Free Stations do their own thing, mostly, but if you touch at a corporate station, you need an in. Either you have a relative, a shareholder family member, or you have a patron."

"A patron?"

The salesman shook his head. "Maybe you aren't as smart as I thought. Even my grandson knows about something for the effort."

"What effort? What are you talking about?" Jake asked.

"Bribes, kid. Bribes. You have to cut a shareholder family or a corporate executive in. Those contracts only go to people on the inside. Part of the deal is that the person who wins the contract kicks some back to the people on the inside. You'll never get a contract at a corporate station without paying somebody off."

"What about the Free Traders? Are you saying they pay the corporations?"

"They do their own thing. They all own their own ships. Have for years. Most all of the Free Traders can trace their ownership of a ship back to a family member who was here at the Abandonment."

"Nobody ever becomes a Free Trader? There are no new ones?"

"Nope. They have a credit union of their own. If somebody needs a new ship, the credit union buys it outright, then mortgages it to the new owners. Plus, the new owners usually have family in the shipping business, or something like that."

"So there is no way to get a ship without paying off a corporation?"

"Not a big one. Not with a mortgage. Well, you could pay off the Militia, I think."

"No, not them."

"You don't like them?"

"What can I afford with what I have?"

They talked for a few more minutes, but the salesman shook his head. "I got nothing in that price range, and nobody else does, either. I'm sorry, kid."

"Any suggestions?"

"Go and get drunk."

Jake took that advice, sort of. The bar was dark, cheap, and served Belter beer. The décor was metal chairs, metal tables, and plastic cups, with a side of stale beer. He picked a corner and surveyed the crowd. For once, his choice of semi-hard suit and tool belt didn't stand out.

He fingered the course chip in his pocket. He had decrypted it enough to realize it was a course plot for a ship, but he couldn't get the details. He wanted to find this ship, or whatever was in that orbit. Problem was, he couldn't decode it completely. He needed another key. Even if he did decode it, he'd need a ship to get to that orbit.

The man next to him turned, interrupting his ruminations. "You're drinking Belter beer."

"So are you," Jake said.

"Yup. Rim-93, born and raised."

"Rim-37."

"I don't know where that is."

"That's okay. I don't know where Rim-93 is either."

The two exchanged desultory conversation for a while.

"Are you looking for work?" the man asked.

"Not really. Why would you think that?"

"No corporate flashes."

"I work for TGI. Well, I used to. Sort of. I'm kind of...between jobs for them."

The man laughed. "Sure, call it that if you want."

"What?"

"I understand. You jumped a contract. No shame in that. These corporate people are hard to work with. Don't pay what they promised. Extra charges. The labor contracts are a bitch, and if they catch you, they can ship you anywhere."

"I don't think—" Jake stopped. *He thinks I ran out on a labor contract.* "I don't think it matters."

"Nope. Just don't let them catch you, but if you want some advice, it's kind of dumb to sit around in a bar drinking while they look for you. You should get off-station, onto a ship or farther out to the Ring before you are seriously overdue."

"That's good advice," Jake said.

In reality, he was still on TGI's payroll. His boss, Mr. Dashi, had told him to take some time away from headquarters. Mr. Dashi had also strongly suggested that Jake investigate the course chip. Jake wasn't sure why Dashi would give one of his employees paid time off to pursue a private matter, but he was probably the smartest person Jake had ever met. Strategic, too. If Mr. Dashi wanted something done, there was a good reason.

Of course, the man next to him didn't know that. All he saw was a young kid who had taken a stupid labor contract and was now paying the price. This could work to his advantage.

"In fact," Jake said, "I could use more advice. This contract was a mistake. I'm getting out of here, but I'm tired of working for other people. I'm looking for a ship heading to the Outer Rings. One that needs crew—engineering crew. I can be an engineer. I, uh, I've also saved a bit of money. If there is somebody with a ship who needs a partner, or has one for sale? I might be able to work something out."

"You have enough money to buy a ship?" the man asked.

"Not on me. Don't get any stupid ideas. I put some money away. In the Free Traders Credit Union, where the corps can't get back at it."

"Smart," the man said.

"I have some family that comes here from time to time, too. They told me to keep my eyes open for a ship. One we could charter, or maybe buy."

"So go buy one, then."

"I don't have that much money, unless the ship was a great deal."

"This 'great deal' ship.... would it go straight out to the Ring, maybe, not come back here?"

"Probably," Jake said.

"Not come back here...ever?"

"That could be arranged," Jake said.

"Let me give you the name of a guy with a ship that needs to go away and not come back."

Chapter 7

"I'm sorry, miss, but you can't go in there," the guard at the side entrance said.

"What?" Nadine said.

"Only shuttle ticket holders, I'm afraid, miss." He stepped in front of the door to the shuttle station. "General public can't go in anymore. You have to go through the ticket kiosk."

Nadine glanced over at where he pointed. A line of people were waiting in front of the ticket window. "I'm just here on corporate business. I don't need to get on the shuttle."

"I'm sorry, miss. No ticket, no entry. You can ask at the window. They might let you in."

"Is this new? I don't remember waiting before."

"Militia Council put it in today, miss. There has been some pickpocketing, so they want better control of who is around the shuttles."

"Okay. Thanks." Nadine gave him a thousand-watt smile and walked back into the main street, looking back at the line. If she asked for a shuttle ticket, the Militia would sell her one, but they might make her get off halfway. She hadn't given them any reason to love her lately.

She still hadn't decided where to go. The admiral had said to run away, but why? What was going on? Besides, she had a firm rule that she didn't do anything unless she was paid.

Hearing a commotion, Nadine stood on tiptoe to see over the crowd.

A line of Militia officers with shock sticks was coming down the road, walking about five feet apart. They were letting the crowd pass, but looking at every face as they went by.

Uh-oh. Time to go back to the apartment. She turned the

other direction, but a second line was coming that way—and in the middle of it was one of the guards from the restaurant.

Nadine stepped back into the alley, turned to the guard, and gave him a once-over. He was old. His uniform didn't fit. Overweight. He'd called her "miss." She knew what to do.

She stepped just into his personal space. "Sir, I wasn't entirely truthful with you. I'm sorry, but, well, I'm supposed to be at work right now." She leaned forward even more and touched his upper arm, darting her eyes from side to side to convince him she was worried about who saw them. "I only have a few minutes till my boss notices I'm gone, but my boyfriend is in the Militia, and he's going up today. He's going on a long orbital patrol. He'll be gone six months. I just want to see him to say goodbye."

She stepped back and gave him a tremble-lipped grin. Just in case that wasn't enough, Nadine cocked her hip slightly and thrust her breasts forward. *Sympathy and sex appeal. That will get them every time.*

"Can you let me slip by, sir, just this one time? He'll be gone so long," she said. She made her lower lip tremble again, just a little bit. Older men were suckers for a trembling lip.

The guard looked around to see who was watching, then leaned toward her. "Miss, I'm sorry to hear that. Six months is a long time to be apart, isn't it?"

"Oh, yes," she said, "it is."

He put his hand on her shoulder and steered her to the side. "I feel bad for you. I have a son your age, you know."

Of course you do, Nadine thought, letting herself be led to the side.

"You remind me of his girlfriend. She's in the Militia as well."

"Really? Is that so?" she said. *I'll bet you wouldn't mind grabbing his girlfriend's shoulder either*, she thought, but she continued to smile.

His arm slid down from her shoulder to her lower back, just touching her belt. His hands caressed her belt area lightly.

Huh, she thought. *The old goat is still in the game.* She shouldn't have mentioned the boyfriend, but things seemed to be progressing well.

"Yes. She is. Wonderful girl. She's taught me a lot of things."

"Really? What type of things?" Nadine said. She switched her simpering smile for sexy smile number two. She always felt that sexy smile number one was too wanton, and sexy number three was a bit too subtle. She needed steamy but classy. That was smile number two. This was not developing as expected, but she could still handle it. Men were so predictable.

"Yes, she showed me all sorts of things," he said. "Things I didn't know before." He led her to the side and down a corridor, still propelling her along. "For example, she told me that the Militia never has six-month cruises. The longest is three weeks."

The man grasped her wrist with one hand and pushed Nadine into the wall. "And she showed me the holster for her ship weapon, which is what you are wearing. You're not here on corporate business, and you definitely aren't going to see a boyfriend."

He grasped her other wrist and drew them together. A pair of snap ties closed on them. "There's a reward out for you, Ms. Nadine, and since it's just me here, I get all of it. You are under arrest." He spun her around and stared her in the eye. "I'm taking you to Militia HQ. They'll deal with you."

Nadine flexed the cuffs behind her. "You're pretty sharp for an old guy."

"Thanks, Miss."

"Polite, too."

"Thanks again."

"I thought you were trying to grab my ass."

"It's exceptional, I'm sure. If I were thirty years younger and single, your scam might have worked, but by my age, you've seen everything."

"Not everything."

"No?"

"You haven't seen this, for example."

Nadine kicked him in the balls.

His mouth made a wide O, and air leaked out in a sort of moaning *ooooooohhh*. He hands dropped to cup his testicles, and he dropped to the ground and rolled on his side, continuing to moan.

"Sorry about that, old-timer, but I can't stick around." She crouched down, leaned forward on her knees, and pulled her hands under her legs to the front. She stood up, holding her hands in front of her.

"It's a good thing for you I do yoga," she said. "Otherwise I'd have had to kick you unconscious first while I worked these cuffs off. Now all I need is a knife to cut 'em. Where would I find that, old fart?"

He continued to moan.

Nadine heard a door lock open behind her. She turned to see another guard pushing through a door.

"Hey, Jim, did you want help with—hey—you! Stop!"

She bolted down the hall, shaking her still-bound hands in front of her. She hopped down the steps and across the street, dashing into an alley and ducking around a corner. She stopped and leaned against the wall for a second. Nobody was in view, so she stepped forward and bent at the waist. She pushed her elbows as wide apart as she could, then jerked her arms backward, aiming to hit her hipbones on each side. Her arms snapped into her hips, but the cuffs held.

"Emperor's testicles," Nadine said. "Empire-dammed cuffs. That always works in the vids." She caught her breath and tried again—and failed again. "Princess Patma's vagina, that hurt."

Motion at the end of the alley drew her eyes. "There she is!"

She sped away down the alley, turned left, then right, then left again into another alley.

The air carried the scent of cooking vegetables—there were food tray plants in this neighborhood. This alley was wider but dirtier, with giant, open bins full of vegetable waste lining each side. She darted down the alley, looking for an escape.

A dark door appeared on her right, and she jumped down the steps to it, but lost her balance and crashed through the door. It shattered as she hit it. She rolled onto her hands as she broke through it, pieces of cheap plastic splintering around her.

Nadine bounced back onto her feet and stood up. Dozens of men and women in Galactic Growing coveralls sat at tables and stood at a bar. It smelled of unwashed bodies, strong drink, and hard work. Everyone stopped talking, turning to stare at her.

She stood tall and strode to the bar. "*Hola*," she said to the bartender.

"*Hola, señorita*," he said.

"*Como esta usted?*"

"*Esta muy bien. Gracias.*"

"*Dos vodka grande, por favor.*"

The bartended glanced at her hands, still tied.

"*Dos vodka, por favor*," she said again. She held her hands up and beckoned with her fingers.

He shrugged, uncorked a bottle, and poured two shots.

Nadine stepped forward and grasped the first glass in her tied hands. She tried to bring it to her mouth, but it was too difficult. Instead, she put it back on the bar, wrapped her lips around it, flipped her head up, and drank it down. She spat the glass out. It shattered on the floor. Leaning forward and locking her lips around the second glass, she repeated the motion.

Standing straight, she straddled her legs wide, extended

her bound hands, and again slammed her forearms into her hips. "*Yaaaauuuuggggh!*"

The band snapped and flew off, landing on a beer-soaked table to her right. For a moment, the bar patrons stared at it, then started clapping.

"Thank you, thank you. I'm here all week." Nadine turned to the bartender. "What do I owe you?"

"Nothing," the bartender said. "It's on the house."

"Thanks." Nadine rubbed her hands and looked around. Everybody was staring, but nobody was reaching for a comm. She had a minute.

"How come your hands were tied?" the bartender asked.

"Maybe I'm into kinky stuff," Nadine said.

"These are Militia cuffs. Why were you wearing Militia cuffs?"

"'Cause the Militia put them on."

The bartender poured another shot and slid it across. "Good for you. We're not fond of the Militia here."

"Is this a GG only bar? And are you normally this full in the middle of the day."

"Not normally, but they laid off half their contract workers today."

"Laid off their contract workers?"

"Told us all to go home," a man at the beer table said. He picked up her broken cuffs and examined them. "They're bringing in some of the families from the outer stations. Corporate workers are fine. Part-timers are gone."

"Why were you fired?" Nadine asked.

"Not fired. Made redundant. Paid us off and sent us home. Why did the Militia put cuffs on you?"

"Maybe they like kinky stuff too," Nadine said.

There was shouting outside. One of the patrons stepped through the splintered door and peered down the street. He spoke rapidly in Spanish to the man at the beer table, too rapidly for Nadine to follow.

"Well, it's going to get kinkier," the beer-drinker said.

"There are four guards coming down the road. They have revolvers, and they're kicking in every door they see." He looked at the remains of the door. "Not much for them to do here."

"Well, thanks for the drinks. Emperor's blessing to you all. I'll just wait till they go into one, and be on my way."

The man at the door spoke rapid Spanish again.

"How come I can't understand him?" Nadine said.

"He has poor grammar. A thick accent."

"Really?"

"Yeah. Also, he's had nine beers."

"What did he say?"

"There are also two Militia officers with shotguns backing them up, and one with a funny-looking rifle thing. It has two metal bars sticking out, and something wrapped around them."

"Wrapped with a metal coil? Like a spring?"

There was a rapid exchange of Spanish.

"*Sí*," the beer-drinker said.

"Gauss rifle," Nadine said. "Hundreds of rounds per minute. They can go through plastic, wood, and sometimes metal." She turned to the bartender. "I need another shot, and a back door."

"No back door," the bartender said. "Still want that shot?"

"Nope," Nadine said. "What's up those stairs?"

"Storage. Food trays," the bartender said.

"Well, free trades, then," Nadine said. "Thanks again—gotta go."

She ran up the stairs, but the second floor held only a corridor. She opened each door in sequence. Nothing but piles of food trays.

There was a commotion downstairs. "Why's the door broken?" a voice said.

"The boys like to wrestle."

"Have you seen a tall blond girl around here?"

"In my dreams, every night."

A shotgun ratcheted. "Want to see those dreams sooner?"

Nadine slid over to the stairway and peered between two stacks of buffalo food trays. She leaned over the railing to see. The uniformed guards were facing away from her, confronting the bartender.

"She went that way," the bartender said, pointing out the front door.

The group turned toward the door. Nadine jerked back so she wouldn't be seen—and, of course, knocked the entire pile of trays down the stairs. They banged and clattered down the steps.

"That didn't last long," she said aloud. She raced up the next flight, footsteps pounding behind her.

"Up above—stop! We need to talk to you."

"Bite me," Nadine yelled back. She swung up several more flights, up and up.

"You can't get away. There are no exterior stairs," her pursuer called from below her.

"Still, bite me," Nadine yelled and ran up another two flights, spotting sunlight ahead. How tall was this factory? She ran out onto the roof, jogged to the edge, and looked down.

"Great view up here, huh?"

She turned around. A group of sweating guards were pointing their revolvers at her.

"It is a nice view," Nadine said. "I didn't realize the factories were so tall."

"Not all of them. This one is six stories. Only the corporate headquarters are bigger," the lead guard said.

"And Militia HQ, of course." A Militia officer clambered up the stairs.

Nadine hopped up to the parapet surrounding the roof. "Why did they make this one so tall, I wonder?"

"Prestige," the officer said. "GG wanted to impress all the other corps. They built big."

"Interesting," Nadine said. She skipped along the

parapet, looking over the side.

"There's no way down. We just want to talk. That's all," the officer said.

"I could jump." Nadine walked three more steps to the right. "A long way down. I wonder if I will survive the fall."

"Probably not, but anything is possible. Even if you lived, do you want to take the chance that you'd be crippled for life?"

"I'm a gambling sort of girl," Nadine said.

She jumped.

Chapter 8

Jake looked up at the sign over the counter. *Owl Ship Brokerage. We fly by night.*

"That's clever," Jake said.

"What's clever?" the gum-chewing girl behind the counter asked.

"That sign."

She stopped chewing and twisted to look, then turned back to Jake. "What's clever about it?"

"The reference."

"Huh?"

Jake looked her over. Her skin suit was new, stylish, and perhaps a bit too tight. Her hair was long, and not in a ponytail. He figured she spent a lot of time taming that hair in low gravity.

"The Old Empire reference. Owls. Flying by night."

She snapped her gum. "Old Empire?

"Yeah, they use that phrase in Old Empire books," Jake said.

"Books?" she said. "I don't read. I watch videos."

"You don't read?"

"Nope. How can I help you?"

Jake looked at her. "I was told to ask for Vince."

"Mr. Pletcher is busy this morning. I'm his assistant. What is this in regard to?"

"I was told he had a ship for sale that I might be interested in. I'm looking for a smaller freighter with a very specific fuel capacity and a number of other options." Jake began to list everything he needed—dimensions, power requirements, heating systems.

The girl listened for moment, then put her hands up. "Easy, tiger. Too much information," she said. "Wait a minute." She picked up a hard phone and spoke into it. Jake could hear a voice from the other end.

"Okay," she said, hanging up and pointing to a door.

"If you would wait in that room over there."

Jake stepped through and sat down on a metal chair, facing a wall with another door.

After a few minutes, a tall man appeared in the doorway, dressed in a business suit over a stylish skin suit.

"Vincent Pletcher," he said, extending his hand. "How may I help you?"

Jake shook the proffered hand. "Jake Stewart. Mr. Pletcher, I'm looking for a ship."

"Call me Vince, please. Ships we have," Vince said, glancing at Jake's outfit. His gaze lingered on his boots, tool belt, and chest plate. "Are you a Belter?"

"Yes," Jake said. *Pretty slick. He had me pegged right away.*

"So not for corporate runs. You are going to be trading in the Belt."

"Yes, and only in the Belt. Nothing in-system."

Vince nodded once and gestured to the door. "Come into my office."

Vince's office was extremely neat. The metal desk was cleared off, as was the credenza, but one wall held a dozen pictures of a young girl at various ages, from about three to seventeen. One look could tell you she was Vince's daughter.

"What type of ship are you looking for?" Vince asked.

"I gave all the details to your assistant," Jake said.

"You'll have to tell me again. Sorry."

"But I gave her all the specs."

"I don't really employ her for her ship-selling skills."

Jake furrowed his brow. "What do you employ her for, then?"

Vince smiled and pressed a button on his comm. "Ashley, come in here, please."

The receptionist appeared a moment later. "Yeah?"

"Could you unplug that heater and take it out front to the desk, please? Somebody will be by for it shortly." Vince pointed at a heating unit plugged into a wall conduit.

Ashley stepped to the corner of the office and bent

over to fiddle with the cord. Her skin suit was even tighter than Jake had imagined. The view from behind was spectacular. She grunted and fiddled, finally having to get down on one knee to pick it up.

"Thanks, Ashley," Vince said.

"No probs." She sauntered out, heating unit in hand.

Vince waited till she was gone. "Any other questions?"

Jake shook his head and began to explain what he needed, providing Vince the same specifications he'd given the other salesman. Vince took notes, waiting for Jake to finish before asking questions.

"Are you sold on two nozzles? They and the associated support systems will add 50 percent to any price I quote."

"I could do one nozzle, I suppose, if it's that big a difference."

"If I found you a two-nozzle system with one of the nozzles removed, you could use that extra interior space to meet much of your fuel tankage requirements. Since it's next to the existing fuel storage, you wouldn't need the extra pumps and piping that an external system would take, and you wouldn't have to buy an entire extra fuel truss. You could just cut holes in the existing H and O_2 tanks and double their size for minimal cost. Would you be up for that?"

"That's a great idea," Jake said.

"You mentioned extra consumables. Is this for long journeys?"

"Yes, we'd have some long runs. I'll need more trays and spare part storage."

"Belters work outside a lot. Would you be okay with external storage? Willing to go out and drag some stuff inside once or twice a trip?"

"Why does that matter?"

"Internally, you can only get the amount of storage you want with a second habitat module. That's pretty expensive, and you don't need the extra lounge, freshers, or cabins. They would be wasted on you. Plus I'd have to upgrade your life support power requirements. If your storage is external, it doesn't need life support. It doesn't have to be rated for blowouts, and we don't need sensors."

"What about freezing?"

"Heaters are cheap. You could just convert a container to handle what you need, but you'd lose the cargo capacity, and then you'd have to wrangle a container around out in deep space. I think I can find you a storage boom. It's basically a truss extension with lockers on the end. You weld it to the truss behind the control room or behind the container modules. It sticks way out, but you'd have a bunch of lockers on it. They can't take much in mass, but they have lots of volume. Food is light. Filters are light. Parts are light."

"That sounds great. How much does it cost?"

"Almost nothing in the grand scheme of things. It's just a bunch of metal."

"How long would it take to have that installed?" Jake asked.

"I have one with that installed already. Special deal for a long-range prospector. He worked for a few years, but it didn't pay off. I was going to remove it before sale, but in your case, you can keep it. Plus, you could put a radar on it. You'd get good coverage. Of course, the radar doesn't meet corporate standards for close maneuvering near their stations."

Vince stopped for a moment, obviously thinking his last statement was significant.

Jake was supposed to respond somehow. "Well, that's a good point. What are the implications of not having the correct radar?"

"Corporate stations expect three or sometimes four different radars to get full coverage, plus a standard telemetry module to handshake with the station systems. This wouldn't be part of that."

"In the Belt, we usually don't have telemetry repeaters, or they aren't working, anyway."

Vince nodded.

"In fact, in the Belt, we don't use much in the way of sensors, other than basic radar. We just find the stations and eyeball it from there," Jake said.

"So you don't need a full sensor package?"

"Nope, just radar and maybe a telescope—and a radio."

"One or two?"

"One is enough."

"Refurbished?"

"Sure."

"You understand you'll have problems at corporate stations with that type of setup? They'll want you to have a tug at every station. That could get expensive."

"I can deal with that," Jake said.

Vince nodded. "Got it. So what we're looking for is a standard single-nozzle, with extra interior tankage, a single habitat module, couple of cargo trusses, and no sensor package included. Add a storage boom, mount a refurbished radar on that, and put a single radio in the control room, also refurbished."

Jake nodded. Vince had done this before. With only a few questions, he'd narrowed Jake's search down, cut the number of ships they had to look at by 90 percent, and probably cut the asking price by two-thirds or three-quarters.

Vince ran a few numbers on his comm and named a price. It was much, much better than the price that Jake had heard before, but still too much. Vince waited for Jake to speak. They stared at each other. They both knew that in a negotiation, the first one to speak loses. But Vince had more experience with this, and seemed perfectly comfortable sitting in silence.

Jake broke first. "That's still higher than I wanted."

"It's a fair price."

Jake tried to wait him out again—and, again, failed. "I was told sometimes you have special ships for sale."

"All of my ships are special."

"Extra-special ships, then."

"Oh?"

"Ships that...might best be gotten out of here fast. And never come back."

"Why fast?" Vince's expression revealed nothing.

"Maybe somebody is looking for them," Jake said.

"You mean stolen?"

"Yes."

"I don't deal in stolen ships," Vince said. "You've been misinformed. Sorry. All my ships are legitimate."

Jake looked at him. Vince had just denied everything, but he didn't seem upset. He needed something else. Jake racked his brain.

"Restricted covenants," Jake said.

"Yes?" Vince said. "Go on."

"Do you have any ships that are restricted in where they can operate? Former corporate ships that used to do a run but that are being replaced?"

"What do you mean?"

"I studied this in school. Sometimes a ship owner will sell an old ship with the understanding that the ship can't be used to compete on the same runs, so they'll make a condition of the sale that a ship can't be used in certain areas or on certain runs."

"I've heard of that," Vince said.

"Do you have any ships like that?"

"Sort of. I have one that I'm brokering. The owner has insisted that the ship not be used on any of the inner or middle stations at all. Only on far stations."

"Or the Belt?"

"The Belt wasn't mentioned, but I'm sure it would be acceptable."

"I'd expect a large discount for such a restriction," Jake said. "It shouldn't cost more than half what you mentioned before."

"Would you buy the ship you specified before for half

the price if we impose those conditions?"

"Sure."

"Let's go see a man about a ship, then." Vince got up.

Jake followed him out the door, checking his watch. This man had just sold him the single most expensive item he'd ever buy in eleven minutes.

Chapter 9

"I think you're in the wrong place," the hostess said.

"No, I'm not," Nadine said. "I have reservations for lunch."

The hostess looked Nadine over. "What did you do to your hair?"

"It's the latest style," Nadine said. She'd had some issues with decaying fruit gumming up her hair, and had had to cut it off rather than comb it out.

"Shaving half your head?"

"It's only a third. It balances out the eyebrows."

"You look weird with only one eyebrow."

"Thanks for the fashion tip. I'll remember that if I ever end up working in a restaurant. As a hostess. Part time."

The hostess glared at her. "I don't see you on the list. Sorry, but you can't come in."

"You haven't looked at the list."

"I don't need to. You're not on it."

"Are you looking for trouble? Because I've had a heck of a day, and I'd love to give somebody a good beating."

The hostess stepped backward, and Nadine marched toward her. There was a sucking noise. Nadine stopped. They both looked down at Nadine's feet.

"Are you...squelching?" the hostess asked.

Nadine clenched her fists and narrowed her eyes.

"How can I be of service?" a voice behind her asked.

Nadine turned around. A maître d' and three staff members were confronting her. Two of them were big men. She could take those if she had to.

Who she couldn't take was the small woman—the one holding the stun stick. Nadine looked more closely. A stun stick with the power turned up to max.

"I'm meeting somebody," Nadine said.

"Of course you are," the maître d' said. "What is their

name, please?"

"He doesn't like me to use a name in public."

"We are very discrete here," the maître d' said. "We will not tell."

"Perhaps I can just go and look." Nadine started toward the door.

"We don't encourage that." The maître d' tilted his head, and the two big men stepped to his sides. Nadine stopped and glared at them. They didn't move. The girl with the shock stick slid to one side.

"Are you stopping me from going in?" Nadine asked.

"Our guests value quiet. We don't like to disturb them."

"What happens if I cause a disturbance?"

The maître d' smiled broadly. "If you turn around and walk out of here, we'll just let it go. If we have to move you out, you get shocked, and the Militia gets called."

"You'd call the Militia?"

He smiled even more broadly. "We'd rather not. If you fight and make a scene, you still get shocked, but we don't call the Militia. The boys will give you a beating to remember. Don't cause a scene."

"I won't cause a scene," Nadine promised. "I'll be good."

"Good," the maître d' said.

"However, I do have one question before I go."

"Yes?"

"BRAD, ARE YOU HERE? I'M BACK," Nadine yelled at the top of her lungs.

The men stepped forward and grabbed her. She didn't resist. There was silence from the room behind the maître d', then the scrape of a chair. "Nadine?"

"The buffalo here is excellent. I've had it before. They have orange juice, too," Nadine said, flipping through a menu.

"I can't afford orange juice. How about apple?" Brad

suggested.

"How about we never date again?"

"Your scale position doesn't justify orange juice." Brad was a tall, muscular man, and he wore a Militia shuttle pilot's uniform. Nadine had described him to her roommate as "scrumptious."

"My 'scale position'? What does that mean?"

"Why are your feet squelching?"

"I jumped off a roof into a bin full of rotting vegetables. There was a lot of juice. What scale?"

"Why did you do that, and why did you shave your head?"

"Gumming your hair up with rotting vegetables and then cutting it off is all the rage now. All the cool people are doing it. What scale?" Nadine asked.

"And your eyebrows."

A waiter arrived. "Drinks?"

"I'll take an apple juice vodka," Brad said.

The waiter tapped his pad.

"Me too," Nadine said. The waiter didn't move. Nadine looked at him, and he looked at Brad.

"The hot-crazy scale," Brad said.

"What's that?" Nadine asked. Brad didn't say anything. Nadine turned to the waiter. "What's this hot crazy thing? Have you heard of it?"

"The ratio of a girl's hotness to her craziness," the waiter said.

"What?"

"It's a guy thing," Brad said.

Nadine looked at the waiter, who nodded. She looked back at Brad. "Tell me?"

Brad and the waiter glanced at each other.

The waiter gave in. "It's okay for a girl to be really crazy, as long as she's also really hot. The crazier she is, the hotter she has to be to get away with it."

"Are you saying I'm not hot enough for you?"

Brad glared at the waiter.

"I'll bring you those two drinks," the waiter said.

"You're plenty hot," Brad said.

"But?"

"The craziness has gone up a notch since the last time I saw you."

"What's crazy? I'm just here for lunch."

"You have only one eyebrow. Half of your scalp is shaved. Your boots are overflowing with rotten vegetable juice."

"It's my new look."

"Also, your arms are scratched. One of them is bleeding on the tablecloth."

Nadine pulled her elbows off the table and dropped them into her lap.

"How did you not notice that?" Brad asked.

"I have a high pain threshold."

"You have a high craziness threshold. Your craziness has gone up a notch. Two notches."

"Can you smuggle me in the hold on the next shuttle trip?" Nadine asked.

"Three notches."

"I'll owe you. A lot."

"Nope. That's too much."

"Brad, you know I love you."

"No, you don't."

"Okay, I lust after you a lot. A big lot." Nadine tried smile number one.

"I'm not buying it. I'll buy you lunch. It will probably be the last lunch we'll have."

"You don't want to see me anymore?"

"I'd be happy to see you again. I just don't think the restaurant will be."

"They'll be happy if you spend enough money. You can spend some of the money I'm going to give you."

"Dirty, vegetable-smelling money?"

"Money has no smell, they say," Nadine said.

"Who are 'they'?"

"Some Old Empire founding race. The Romans or something like that. Not important. My friend Jake would know. I need to get in that shuttle. I'll pay double."

"It's not about the money. It's not for me. I only use it to pay off the others. I am happy to see you."

"But you won't help me now?"

"No, I won't."

"Because I'm off this stupid scale of yours?"

"Yes," Brad said. "Your craziness has gone up several notches, but that's just an excuse."

"I'm not hot enough? My looks haven't changed."

"It's not just looks. It's a combination thing. Getting on a shuttle right now is too dangerous."

"A combination?"

"A composite."

"What type of composite?"

"Well, things. Looks. Fun. Activities."

"Oh." Nadine looked around, then leaned over the table and whispered softly to him.

Brad nodded once, then again. She reached over and grabbed his hand, still whispering. Brad nodded again, then sat very still. After a minute, his head came up, and he gestured for the waiter.

"Drinks up in a second, sir," the waiter said.

"Change the order. Two screwdrivers."

"Screwdrivers? You mean vodka and orange juice?"

"Yes, orange juice."

"Do you want to see the menu, sir? To check the price?"

"I know what they cost. Two screwdrivers."

"Right away, sir." The waiter scurried off.

"Quickly, please. We have a shuttle to catch."

"Come down out of there slowly, and we won't shoot you," the guard said.

Nadine finished climbing down the ladder from the hold. "Thanks," she said to the cargo crewman who had put the ladder up. "Worst trip yet. What's wrong with this pilot?"

"What are you doing in the hold?" the guard asked.

"Coming to this station, of course." Nadine said swung her backpack off and put it on the floor.

"Show me your ticket."

"I don't have a ticket." She stretched her arms over her head and cracked her shoulders. "We were banged around all over the place. It took this guy five tries to dock. What is this, amateur week?"

"If you don't have a ticket, you are an unauthorized passenger."

"So?"

"Unauthorized passengers are to be arrested. Militia orders."

"Brad said it would be fine."

"I don't know a Brad."

"Are you sure? Because Brad said to give you this." Nadine bent over and reached for the backpack. The guard drew his revolver and pointed it at Nadine.

"Easy here. I'm just going to get a chip. I'll be slow." Nadine reached into a side pocket.

"What's that?"

"This is a credit chip," Nadine said. "With credit on it, obviously. Brad told me to give it to his friend. His friend who had my ticket." She spun the chip in her fingers. "Of course, if you don't know Brad, then I guess it's not for you."

"Why would Brad have you give us money?" the guard asked.

"To pay for my ticket, of course. His friend is a sort of travel agent. Arranges tickets. That sort of thing," Nadine said.

The crewman behind the guard coughed and raised his hand. "I know Brad. I was expecting a friend of his. I can take care of this."

The guard swung around. "You know this Brad?"

"I do. Good guy. He sends up special people from time to time."

"Why don't I know about this?" the guard asked.

"You can't issue tickets, Dev," the crewman said.

"You can't either," the guard said.

"Yes, but the major can."

"The major is going to give her a ticket?"

"Well, Sarge does the paperwork, but the major signs. It's all legit."

The guard holstered his revolver. "I don't get it. I should have been told."

"Dev, let it go. Let this lady go. We'll sort it out later."

"I'll just give you this and be on my way, then," Nadine said, proffering the chip.

The guard looked at it. "Maybe I should contact the major."

"Now, Dev," the crewman said, stepping forward. "That's hardly a bright idea. Remember what Sarge said when you did that last time?"

"Last time?"

"When you called the major about the sarge's niece? Remember that?"

"Oh, right." The guard frowned. "Sarge was pretty unhappy with me."

"Yes, and we don't want that, do we?" The crewman stuck out his hand, and Nadine handed him the chip. He put it in his comm, typed a bit, and then looked at the screen and smiled. "I'll take care of the ticket paperwork, ma'am. You can go."

"Thanks, boys," Nadine said, shouldering her pack. "Free trades."

As she walked away down the corridor, she could still hear the men's conversation.

"Don't bring this up with the sarge," the crewman said.

"No?" the guard asked.

"You know he doesn't like paperwork. I'll just do the paperwork and give him the chip. Later."

"Thanks, Sindar. You're a pal," the guard said.

Nadine strode down the docking ring corridor. The admiral had told her to get out of the system. She had checked with several contacts who said that the Militia and GG were looking for her. They hadn't said why, but she had done a lot of things in the past that might have made either or both of them unhappy. It seemed best to get off-planet for a while, until things sorted themselves out. It would be even better if she could get away from the inner stations. She needed to find a nice, long cruise out to the Rings.

As a matter of course, she also kept track of a number of contacts that could be useful for her. Some of them didn't know they could be useful to her, but she didn't mind. She had heard that one in particular, her old friend Jake Stewart, was on this station, and that Jake was looking for a ship. Jake was boring, a bit of a bookworm, a bit too intellectual, and not what you would normally call a man of action.

On the other hand, he seemed to have the spirits of dead emperors watching over him—he could fix anything, and he came out on top in a lot of situations that should have left him dead. Every time Nadine interacted with him, she seemed to leave with more money than she came with, and Jake seemed to end up with even more.

Not to mention he was kind of cute.

She knew where all the ship brokers' offices were, and she found him on the fifth try, standing outside a nondescript office, chatting with a man.

"Hello, Jakey. I'm here," Nadine said. "Have you found our ship yet?" Turning to the salesman, she said, "Hi. I'm Nadine. I'm Jakey's pilot—and partner."

"I'm Vince. You're his partner?"

"My partner?" Jake said.

"Yes. Jakey handles engineering, purchasing, operations, ordering, administration, computers, sensors, pricing, buying, selling, cargo, trading—all that stuff," Nadine said.

"I see," Vince said, giving her a once-over, "and what are your responsibilities here?"

"Mostly I just look pretty."

"You do that well," Vince said.

"Thanks." Nadine gave Vince an obvious once-over herself and then smiled at him. He smiled back.

"Jake and I were just talking about pricing, as well as some of the options," Vince said. "Would you like to hear about the requirements we've discussed?"

"Oh, I leave all that stuff to Jake. He's much better at it. What's the price?"

Vince named a figure. Nadine was impressed, but didn't say anything positive about it. This wasn't her first negotiation either.

"I leave those sorts of things to him," she said again.

"About that...." Jake said, grabbing her arm. "My partner and I need a few minutes, Vince. Do you mind waiting?"

"Not at all."

Vince stepped back, and Jake guided Nadine away.

"Hi, partner," she said.

"Nadine, what are you up to? Why are you here?"

"Aren't you glad to see me, Jake?"

"Yes, I am," Jake said. He blinked. "Did I say that out loud?"

"You did. Life too boring without me around?"

"It's never boring when you're around. What do you want?"

"I want—" Nadine stopped as her comm pinged her. A special ping.

She flipped it open and looked at it. It was from Brad. *Militia have traced you to station. Station security and on-board Militia are looking for you right now. Shoot on sight. What did you do? 1,000-credit reward posted for information leading to your location or arrest. Shuttle crew will turn you in for sure. Nothing I can do about it. Get out soon. Good luck, kiddo. It's been fun.*

Nadine stared at the comm. "I need to get off this station right away," she said, "and I want you to help me."

Chapter 10

"It's a rust bucket. You'll be lucky to get out of here alive," Lakowski said.

"It doesn't look so bad to me," Jake said. "It's got everything I need."

"Everything you need to do what? Die a slow and painful death?" Lakowski said.

"What do you mean? How would that happen?" Nadine asked.

Nadine, Jake, and Lakowski, the ship surveyor, were standing in the engineering spaces. Jake wore his semi-hard suit, and Nadine was in a skin suit and ready to get underway.

"Well, miss, let me give you the results of my survey." Lakowski was short and stout. Not fat—just a big man who worked out a lot. He wore a greasy skin suit and a stained ball cap. The ball cap had a chin strap to keep it on in zero-G.

Jake coughed. "I believe I commissioned this, Mr. Lakowski."

Lakowski turned to Jake. "Right you are, Mr. Stewart. Let me start." He pulled out his comm. "We here at Lakowski and Associates—that's me—" He tapped the company name emblazoned on his name tag.

"Who're the associates?" Nadine asked.

Lakowski ignored her. "—Marine Surveyors, duly licensed for ship inspections by the Free Traders' Coalition—"

"Free Traders? Why not a corporate firm?" Nadine asked.

"Too expensive," Jake said. "Continue, please."

"—Are licensed by the Free Traders' Coalition to inspect such ship systems as necessary for safety and normal operation. In accordance with generally accepted industry standards, a reasonable operator—"

"Skip that part," Nadine said. "Tell us how we're going to die."

Lakowski looked at Jake.

"I'm acquainted with the waiver," Jake said. "Perhaps you could let me approve that, and we can move on."

"Of course, sir. Let me read it out. In return for certain valuable consideration, I, Jake Stewart, agree to save and hold harmless—"

"That's fine," Jake said. "Just page forward thirteen pages to the signature block, and I'll thumb it."

"Thirteen pages?" Lakowski asked.

"Yes. I read your standard contracts online this morning. I'm happy with them. Thirteen pages, and then I'll thumb it." Jake extended his hand.

Lakowski frowned, and began paging through. "Eleven...twelve...thirteen. Huh, there it is. Here you go, sir." He handed it to Jake, who thumbed it and handed it back.

"Okay. After extensive work with our suite of testing equipment"—Lakowski hefted a meter from his tool belt—"we have discovered several discrepancies, and several hazards to life and limb, that do not allow us to certify this ship safe for flight. You can't leave the station."

"What? What do you mean?" Nadine asked.

"Nadine." Jake touched her arm. "Give me a minute here. Mr. Lakowski, how many issues are there?"

"There are three main ones."

"They are...?" Jake asked.

"Well, first of all, you only have one radio."

"We only need one radio," Nadine said. "Who uses more than one?"

"If your radio gets damaged, you can't call for help. If you have problems, you'll be stuck out there until you die."

Nadine shook her head. "Radios don't break. I've never heard of one breaking."

"It could happen. The regulations are clear," Lakowski said. "No second radio, no certification."

"The Free Trader regulations say there must be two long-range radios onboard the ship, correct?" Jake asked.

"Sure," Lakowski said.

"They don't specify where they are installed. Correct?"

"They don't. You can put them wherever you want, as long as you have them onboard."

"Good. I'm from the Belt. I have a long-range radio installed on my suit. It counts."

"A suit radio? That's not ship equipment."

"I believe, if you check, the regs just say, 'equipment that is regularly carried on a ship.' The regs further specify that there must be one suit per passenger and crew carried, so since I'm going to be on the ship, my suit must be on the ship. Therefore, the radio is regularly carried on the ship. It counts."

"Huh." Lakowski looked at his comm. "Still, how do I know it's long-range?"

Jake turned slightly and popped a panel on his chest with numbers written on it. "Radio part number here. I believe it's on page two of your list—the third one down."

Lakowski's mouth worked as he read the part number. He tapped his comm and read, then looked back at Jake. "Well, you learn something new every day. Okay, you've got all your radios. You'll be able to call for help before you die."

"Before we die of what?" Nadine asked.

"Of thirst, or starvation, or system failure," Lakowski said.

Nadine frowned. "Why would we die of thirst or starvation? We can count. We know how much food to take."

"But you don't know how much fuel you have. You have no functioning backup gauges on any of your tanks."

Nadine looked around. "Gauges? You mean, like, mechanical things? Who uses those? We use the sensors."

"The sensors need a backup. It's in the regs."

"When do sensors fail? They're solid-state electronics."

"It happens."

"Never happened to me. This is all a scam by the corps to force you to buy more stuff," Nadine said.

"Look, miss—" Lakowski began.

Jake coughed again. "Did you take note of the fuel levels when you did your survey?"

"Sure. I wrote 'em down when I checked the sensors."

"All the document says is that the crew must have an alternative mechanical measuring method."

"Yes."

"I also believe it says that the test for this method is approved if the crew can demonstrate that it gives the same reading as the sensors, within 5 percent. Correct?"

Lakowski looked at Jake, again read his comm. "Exactly what it says here."

Jake leaned forward, pulled a wrench out of Lakowski's belt, and hefted it in his hand. Lakowski stepped back.

"Jake, don't you think it's a little early in the day to give somebody a beating?" Nadine said. "I mean, he's an officious twit, but still."

"I'm just doing my job, missy," Lakowski said.

"Don't call me 'missy.'"

Jake looked at Nadine, then back at Lakowski. He raised his eyebrows, then turned and tapped the H tank on the top with the wrench. It rang hollow. He began to tap the side of the tank, moving down a few inches at time, listening to the sound. Then he changed his tapping to move even slower. After a few tries, he focused on a precise spot.

"Okay, it's a four-cubic-meter tank, mostly, but that part is a cylinder. The level right now is at about twenty-five centimeters. Figure the diameter of the circle...." Jake closed his eyes for a few seconds, lips moving as he thought. "22 percent."

"What?" Lakowski said.

"We have 22 percent fuel remaining. What did your numbers say?"

Lakowski looked at his screen. "22.3 percent." He looked back at Jake. "Okay, you win this one. One final thing, though. Come with me." He turned and headed up to the truss connecting the engineering spaces to the control room.

Nadine leaned close. "Jake, that was amazing! I didn't know you could measure fuel like that."

"I'll bet he didn't either."

"How do you tell the differences between the sounds?"

"You can't," Jake said in a low voice. "I faked it. I wrote down the numbers while he was searching earlier."

They trooped up to the habitation module behind the bridge. Lakowski pulled open a vented panel on the wall. "You are missing some of your standard sensor package. There should be a backup carbon monoxide sensor here, and one in the other backup station."

"It's not there?" Jake asked.

"See for yourself," Lakowski said.

Nadine pushed her way in front of the two men and looked inside. "It's too dark. I can't see a thing."

Jake produced a flashlight from his belt and illuminated the far side of the alcove. "Do you see a blue box with narrow red stripes on it?"

"I see a blue box with black stripes, and a green box."

"Green is O2. The one with black stripes is the CO detector."

"What's the red-striped box?"

"All CO2 detectors are blue with red stripes."

"There isn't one here." Nadine stepped back.

"There certainly isn't," Lakowski said. "Let's go to the second life-support station." He continued down the corridor.

Jake stopped for a moment and shone his light in. "Huh. Somebody cut it out."

"How can you tell?"

"Look in there, where it's supposed to be." Jake pointed his light into the alcove. "You can see the burn marks where they cut the lines."

Nadine looked past Jake, then turned to him. "Where?"

"Right there, between the smoke detection system and the ozone sensor."

Nadine gave him a blank look. "How can you tell which is which?"

"You don't know the color codes for the sensors, do you?" Jake asked.

"Nope."

"What about the color codes for low voltage, high voltage, commo lines, and such?"

"There are color codes?"

"You've never looked inside a life-support unit, have you?"

"No."

"Why aren't you dead? These things can break."

"I've never had any problems. I never even knew this stuff was here. Is this a Belt thing?"

"No, it's not. Maybe." Jake thought about it for a moment. "You've never had to fix a sensor, or fix the life support?"

"I know how to change filters and monitor the O2 level, but everybody knows that."

"But none of this other stuff. Never had to swap it out?"

"Never."

"I had to do it all the time at Rim-37. Help friends or family swap sensors around, or move them from old ships."

"Oh, 'cause you were poor," Nadine said.

"No."

"No, you weren't poor, or no, you didn't have to change things out a lot?"

"We were poor, and I did have to fix a lot of stuff."

"So it is because you were poor."

"Nadine," Jake said, "I know you were a pilot and all, but I've seen you with other people's ships. What did you do when they needed maintenance, or you get an alarm or something?"

"Before we flew it, we ran the standard diagnostic, and if anything wasn't green, we called somebody, and they replaced anything that was doubtful or close to the end of its service life," Nadine said. "Why? What did you do?"

"We had to fix this stuff ourselves. We bought used parts off the Free Traders and waited till something broke, then put a new one in—if we had a spare that worked. Sometimes the spare was bust as well."

"My spares always work, and when we use them up, we buy new. Besides, how often do sensors break? I've never had one go."

"That's 'cause you're rich," Jake said, "or your family was rich."

"I guess so. How would I know that? I seemed the same as the other kids around me when I was growing up. Didn't you?"

Jake looked at her. Customized skin suit. Expensive station slippers. Her hairband and wrist ruffs weren't cheap, either.

He looked at himself. He dressed better now. He had a customized suit, but he was wearing his Belter suit with a tool belt, extra pockets, and a carrying harness. He had more and better tools than before. But he didn't look rich.

"We had to check everything out. None of our ships were new. Stuff broke all the time, and people stole parts. Stripped the ships. That's what happened here. Somebody took those sensors."

"Well, what would they do with them?"

"Sell them to somebody. Probably us." Jake turned and followed Lakowski.

"Us?" Nadine said. "What do you mean sell them to us?"

Lakowski stopped, pointed into the secondary life-support cupboard, and began to talk. Jake didn't interrupt him, just kept nodding.

"So, that's it, Lakowski said. "You are missing two CO2 sensors, a spare CO sensor, and a spare ozone sensor. I can't certify you to fly until you replace them."

"That's good news," Jake said. "Thanks."

"I understand you would be upset—wait, what?"

"Sensors are an important matter. Thanks for pointing that out," Jake said. "I'm glad you didn't certify us."

"You are?"

"Indeed. Wouldn't expect a man of your standing to let that pass," Jake said. "You have a reputation to keep up. Much better to find these things out here than out in deep space. Don't you agree, Nadine?"

"Agree?" Nadine asked.

Jake elbowed her.

"Oh, yes. What Jake said."

The three stood and stared at each other in silence. Lakowski coughed, but Jake only tilted his head.

"So, that's the survey, then," Lakowski said.

"Yes," Jake said.

"I can't certify you, so the ship has to stay."

"Of course you can't," Jake said.

"Yeah."

"It's just the sensors that are keeping us here," Jake said. "We've met your other two objections, so if we got new sensors, you would clear us."

"Well, of course," Lakowski said. "I'll sign off on everything else. Just the sensors."

"Indeed," Jake said.

"If you buy new sensors and install them, I could certify you right away."

"Big station here," Jake said. "Could take us a while to find them."

"I suppose."

"I'm not from here, so I don't really know the local vendors."

"No, I suppose you wouldn't." Lakowski stared at Jake, and Jake stared back. The silence stretched. "I could recommend somebody, I suppose."

"Please," Jake said.

"You could call A&G services. They have a good selection."

Jake popped his comm open, did a quick search, and pressed a button. He held his comm out so everybody could hear him.

"A&G services," a voice said.

"Hello. My name is Jake Stewart. I'm here with a Mr. Lakowski. He says you are dealers in sensor suites. Can you help us out with some?"

"We are. We can. A couple of CO sensors, ozone, and an O2," the voice said, then named some part numbers and an exorbitant price.

"That's exactly it. Could you have them brought to me right away?"

"Sure. We can have them there in ten minutes."

"We'll wait for you, then," Jake said, hanging up. He turned to Lakowski. "Since my new sensors are on the way, perhaps we can go over the paperwork we will need once they are here."

They pulled out tablets and compared documents. Each began to thumb items on the other's tablet.

Nadine pulled him away during a break in the discussions. "Jake, I don't like this."

"Why?"

"How come they have those exact pieces in stock?"

Jake smiled at her. "One time you showed me a neat trick you could do with your knives. You did this flip thing with your arm, and it ended with knives in both your hands."

"I did. So what?"

"Can you still do it? If I asked you, could you do it right now?"

"Sure, just say the word. But why?"

"You are asking the wrong questions."

"So what's the right question, Jakey?"

"The right question is not why they had those parts in stock. Lots of places have parts in stock. The right question is why I didn't have to tell them which docking bay to bring them to."

Five minutes later, a young man rounded the corner, carrying a small satchel. "You Jake Stewart?" he asked.

"Yes?"

"I've got some sensors here for you. 8,200 credits."

"I want to see them first," Jake said.

The boy opened his satchel and showed Jake four blocky items. They were solid black or green, with narrow, colored stripes on them. Jake extended his hand, but the boy held the items back. "I'm supposed to get the money first."

"We need to test them," Jake said.

"We'll replace them if they don't work."

"Of course, but then Mr. Lakowski would have to wait till they were installed."

"I can't wait for that," Lakowski said.

"Well," Jake said, "then I guess we won't be buying these after all. If we have to wait to test them and get our certification, we'll have time to search over the station. Look for other suppliers. Do a price comparison."

Nadine grabbed Jake and pulled him said. "Jake, I don't have time to wait. We need to get out of here soon."

"Not now, Nadine. Don't worry. There's a rhythm of sorts to this," Jake told her. "We're in good shape."

Jake stepped back to the boy. "Anything else?"

"Um, you don't want them?"

"Not if we can't test them, we don't. We're running on a time frame here. These are only worth it to us if we can guarantee that they will get us our certification. Since we can't, we won't. Thanks for your time."

The boy looked worried. He looked at Lakowski and then back at Jake. "I can't go back without the money."

"You're not getting the money from me. I don't want

them anymore."

"Mister, I'll get into trouble."

"What's your name?"

"Jason."

"Jason, you're in trouble already. It's a question of how much more you will get into. Take 'em back."

Lakowski scowled. "Mr. Stewart, A&G services is a reputable firm. I'm sure that their equipment works, and you look like somebody who's handy with a set of tools. I bet you would have no problems installing these items."

"Well, if I install them myself, I would expect a discount," Jake said.

"I would be willing," Lakowski said, "to certify your ship right now, on receipt of the parts. You could install them later."

Jake smiled. "That's great. We do need the certification, after all. Let me just confirm our cash flow with my partner." He stretched and leaned toward Nadine. "Slide over until you are behind that kid, and be ready for my word."

Then Jake looked at Jason. "Jason, how much is the discount for self-installation?"

"Discount?"

Jake nodded and began to describe how discounts were calculated. He talked about time and materials, standard labor rates, cost of goods sold, differing taxes, prevailing wage rates—it was all quite detailed. Detailed enough that Nadine was able to slide behind Jason.

"So," Jake said, "taking that all into account, I believe a fair price is 800 credits." He nodded at Nadine.

"No way," Jason said. "My parents told me that I was to get the full price, and not to come back unless—"

Nadine flipped her knives out of her wrist ruffs and pointed them at Jason's eyes.

"Leave him alone," Lakowski said, producing a revolver and pointing it at Nadine. "Let him go."

"Jake, he has a gun," Nadine said.

Jake didn't move, staring closely at the gun. Then he smiled. "Everything will be fine, Nadine. Let me test a theory. Jason, nod your head very carefully if you are listening to me."

Jason's eyes tracked to the two knives, then back to Jake. He gave Jake a tiny nod.

"Good. Now, in a moment, Nadine will pull those knives away a little bit, and you are going to very slowly hand that package to your"—Jake stopped and looked at the two strangers—"your uncle, I think. You will hand the package to your uncle. You are his uncle, aren't you, Mr. Lakowski?"

Lakowski kept his gun on Nadine but glanced at Jake. "Great-uncle."

"Good of you to help out the family by steering business their way. However, we are on a bit of schedule, and it be tiresome to have to argue this point back and forth for hours. So I think it best if young Mr. Jason just hands those parts over to you, then runs back to your office. You'll have a good story to tell everybody about those crazy Belties. Nadine?" Jake motioned at her.

"Jake, what are you doing?"

"Everything is fine, Nadine."

"I don't like bringing a knife to a gunfight." She frowned. "Why are you so calm?"

"Everything is okay, Nadine. Trust me."

Nadine shrugged and stepped back. Jason nearly threw the box at his uncle, then scampered down the hall.

Lakowski looked at Jake. "I ought to shoot you for threatening my family," he said. He could hardly keep the revolver pointed at Nadine with the boxes cradled in his other arm.

"You are the one who brought them here. We just wanted to do some business," Jake said.

"I should call the Militia. Charge you with theft."

"First of all, you're the one with the gun in your hand. Second, you're holding a box of stolen ship parts that even a cursory investigation would show were removed from our ship. Third, you've got an obviously falsified set of ship certifications on your tablet, and I'm standing here holding an anonymous credit chip for a thousand credits. All very suspicious," Jake said. "So, you can call the Militia and see how it plays out. Of course, then there's Nadine here."

"Yes, you forgot about me," Nadine said.

"She's kind of crazy. I bet she'd stab you just for fun."

"I am kind of crazy. Too crazy, apparently. Jake, have you heard of something called the 'hot-crazy scale'?"

"Of course. All guys know this."

"This is a stupid conversation," Lakowski said. "Shut up and put those knives down, or I'll...I'll...."

"You'll what?" Jake asked. "Shoot us? Call the Militia? Run away? What?"

Lakowski hesitated.

Jake smiled. "All I want to do is give you money. I know you stole those parts from the ship. If you sign the certification and give us the parts, I'll give you six hundred credits, and we can all part as friends."

Lakowski pointed his gun at Jake, swiveled it to point at Nadine, then back.

"Emperor's balls," Lakowski said. "You two are hard cases."

"We didn't start it," Nadine said. "Where am I on the scale, Jake?"

"Six hundred credits," Jake said, not looking at her.

"You said there are a thousand credits on that chip?"

Jake nodded.

"Give it to me," Lakowski said.

Jake extended the chip. Lakowski leaned forward, then realized that he had a gun in one hand and a box of parts in the other.

"Give me the parts." Jake put out his other hand.

"Give me the credits," Lakowski said.

"Put up your gun," Nadine said.

"Sign the certification first," Jake said.

"Put your knives away," Lakowski said.

There was silence for a moment.

"I'm putting the credit chip on the ground," Jake said. "Drop the parts, Lakowski. Nadine, put those down. Lakowski, you do the same."

Nadine and Lakowski glared at each other, but managed to lower their weapons at more or less the same time. Lakowski crouched down and put the parts down. Jake kept a foot on the credit chip until the parts were on the ground.

"Well?" Lakowski said.

"If you'd just press the 'certify' button on your comm unit," Jake said.

Lakowski looked at Nadine. She slowly pushed her knives back into her arm sheathes. He holstered his revolver and played with his tablet. It bonged, and he held it up for Jake to see. Jake's comm binged.

Jake didn't look at it, but slid the credit chip over. Lakowski pocketed it, then slid the parts over for Jake to pick up.

"Pleasure doing business with you," Jake said.

"You crazy kid, you could have gotten us all killed," Lakowski said. "This is no way to do business."

"I wasn't worried. I knew you weren't serious about shooting us," Jake said.

"How in the Emperor's name would you know that?" Lakowski said.

"I watched you draw your gun. I've been watching videos about these things. You couldn't have shot me."

Lakowski tilted his head. "I couldn't have shot you? If you had taken a slice at my great-nephew, I would have shot you."

"You couldn't."

"I couldn't? Why not?"

"Yes, Jakey, why not? Why couldn't he have shot you, or me, or both of us?"

"I watched your hands. You drew the revolver, but you didn't disengage the safety."

"The safety?" Lakowski asked.

"Yes, I've been watching Old Empire movies. They were talking about the safety. I watched you. You didn't disengage the safety."

"The Empress's royal vagina," Nadine said. "Jakey, you got this from a movie?"

"Yep. Clever, huh?" Jake said.

Lakowski laughed. "In this movie, did you look closely what kind of weapon they had?"

"Well, it was a pistol," Jake said.

"Did it look like this?"

"I'm not sure. Why?" Jake asked.

"Jakey, those movies had pistols. These are revolvers."

"So?" Jake asked.

"Well, Mr. Stewart. Pistols have safety catches. Revolvers don't."

"What do you mean?" Jake asked.

"What he means, Jakey, is that he could have shot you any time. He didn't need to fiddle with any catch or anything. He could have just pulled the trigger and fired."

Chapter 11

"Jakey, we need to get out of here. Now," Nadine said.

They were in the control room of the ship that would soon be Jake's, the *Castle Arcturus*. It had room for four consoles, but only two were installed. Nadine had claimed the traditional pilot's spot, but her board was locked. Jake sat at the auxiliary station, tapping away.

Jake didn't respond.

"Jakey, I said we need to get out of here." Nadine leaned forward, put her hand on Jake's arm, and gave him her thousand-watt smile.

"The inspector missed a whole bunch of stuff," Jake said. "None of the exterior lights seem to be working. The cargo sensors don't work either. We'll have to manually check them all."

"When are we leaving, Jake? We've got no time for all this."

"At least the hatch sensors are working. Why do 'we' not have time for this? I've got plenty of time, Nadine. I haven't even decided if I'm going to buy this yet." He looked up at her and smiled back, then took her hand off his arm and dropped it in her lap.

"But I...but we...." Nadine stopped and looked at her arm.

"Yes?" Jake said.

She regarded him for a moment. "Nothing. How long till you finish your inspection?"

"A full day, probably. I was planning on doing this alone. You just invited yourself."

"Jake, we've worked together before, and things worked out well for you."

"You mean you were foisted on me by my boss. I don't want you here."

"Who exactly is your boss, anyway?"

"You shot me," Jake said.

"You shot me too, and had me locked up in jail. We're even."

"You stole all that metal from me."

"Last time we had this argument, you said it wasn't yours," Nadine said. "You cheated me out of all that potassium."

"You decided not to take it. You took silver instead. Not my fault if you don't know the market rate of bulk goods."

"You seem to have made out well, Jakey. You even have enough money to consider buying a ship."

"You are a complication I don't need," Jake said.

"Suspiciously well, now that I think about it. Jakey, would your finances handle scrutiny? Any ill-gotten gains that might stand out?"

"I've got receipts for everything, Nadine."

"Of course you do. Jakey, I'm a better pilot than you. I'm used to ships, used to voyages. Taking me along would make your life easier."

Jake stood up and stretched. "You haven't asked me where we're going or for how long."

Nadine leaned over and again put a hand on Jake's arm. "You know you can trust me."

Jake looked at her hand, but he didn't remove it this time. "I can absolutely not trust you. You steal things. You shoot people. You locked me up. You are the definition of untrustworthy."

"Exactly—and sometimes you need that. You steal things with paperwork. I use knives or guns. Good thing I had my knives with me. Your little inspection scam wouldn't have worked without me, would it?"

Jake ignored her, scrutinizing a checklist on his pad. "I need to check fuel and consumables."

"You know you need somebody like me, Jake. I'm a hammer, and sometimes you need a hammer."

"I don't trust their list on food trays. I'll have to check it. I wonder if they loaded that truss thing. I'll have to suit up and go outside."

"How long will that take?" Nadine asked.

"A couple hours."

"I've got nowhere to be. I'll just wait here."

"Fine with me," Jake said, "but don't think that just because you invited yourself here, you are coming with me."

"We can talk about it when you come back."

"Prepare to be disappointed." Jake slid out of the cabin and walked to the main airlock.

Nadine waited until he was gone, and began to type a sequence into her board. There was a quiet bong, and a message appeared. She typed the sequence again slowly, but the message reappeared. "Emperor's rosy anus!" she said.

She stomped down to the lock and glared at Jake, hands on hips. It made her look curvy. Jake would like that.

"Why do you always lock your board?" she asked.

"It's a good habit to get into. You never know who will come into the control room and play with switches. I learned that in Space Scouts."

"Play with switches?"

"That, or try to do an emergency undocking."

"Screw you and your Space Scouts. I'm going to get a drink." She turned around and tromped to the station-side lock.

"Nadine, you know you can't get back in?" Jake strolled down the corridor behind her.

"What?"

"We're not supposed to be here. The inspector had a one-time code that he used to get us in for the inspection. I just kept the lock open. If we shut it, we can't get back inside."

"Fine. I'll leave it open. You do your inspection thing, and I'll be back after a drink or two." She turned and walked out the lock, leaving the exterior door open. She hadn't gotten more than two meters when she spied a group of Militia guards heading down the corridor toward her lock. A well-armed group. She saw shock sticks, revolvers, and at least one shotgun.

She rushed back into the ship lock, slammed the outer door shut, and spun the locking lever.

"Didn't we just have this conversation?" Jake said.

"Jake, will this ship fly? Like, right now."

"Nadine, I told you."

"Jake. I'm in trouble. There are people looking for me. There's a group coming down the corridor, trying all the ship locks."

"Nadine, given what you do, there are always people looking for you."

"They have guns, Jake. Lots of guns."

"Well, you would fall into the category of 'armed and dangerous.'"

Nadine stopped and took a deep breath. "Jake, I can't get ahold of my boss. He hasn't answered his comm. He normally has an automated message for me. It changed."

"So?"

"Jake, it's not his 'just wait' automated message. It's his 'something is badly screwed up and you have to run away' message."

"Oh."

"I think the Militia got him."

"What do you mean, 'got him'?"

"Jake, I think that the Militia killed him. I got a warning to get out of town for a while. Then I got another warning that the Militia are looking for me. They want to shoot me. If they are willing to shoot me, that means they aren't afraid of what my boss will do afterward—which means they don't think he can do anything."

"Oh."

"You say that a lot."

"You're not the first one to notice," Jake said. "What do you want me to do?"

"Drop. Get me out of here. I just need to get away from them, get my feet under me."

"Nadine, this isn't our ship. I mean, it isn't my ship yet. I have to finish the paperwork."

"Damn you and your paperwork, Jake!" she said. A banging sound came from the closed airlock behind her. Nadine gritted her teeth. "I need your help. Please help me."

Jake blinked. "That's new. Never asked for help before."

"I thought you were getting better at this, Jake, but look at you—still an accountant."

"Being an accountant got me where I am now. Besides, that tactic doesn't work on me anymore."

"Which one?"

"The shaming. Nor does the flirting, nor the fake seduction."

"You've changed," Nadine said.

"Yes."

"I think I liked the old Jake better. I would have sweet-talked him into doing this."

"Probably. I'm different now."

"Yeah, but will it get you where you need to go next?

"I think so."

"Never mind. Once an accountant, always an accountant. I'll be in the control room. I'm going to monitor the comms and see if I can figure out what's going on." She turned and ran down the corridor to the bridge.

"Emperor's scrotum," Nadine said. "Why in the name of the Imperial succession is the Militia always trying to get me when Jake Stewart is around?" She looked at her screen at the Militia guards on the exterior camera. They'd given up banging on the door and called station ops for an override code.

They wouldn't even need that. A warning blinked on

her console. *Lock B, outer door open*, it said.

Jake had betrayed her.

She keyed her intercom. "Jake? Jake, what are you doing?"

He didn't answer.

"Unlock the board and let's get out of here, Jake." Still no answer. "Jake, if you let them in, I'm not going to go without a fight."

No response. Nadine hustled across the habitation module and into her cabin. She pulled a utility belt on, then unclipped a harmless-looking battery from the belt, reached down, and pressed on the heel of her boot.

A shallow compartment popped open, and she removed a metal coil with a plug on the end. Next she popped open a container in the other heel and produced a rectangular metal housing. The battery, coil, and handle clipped together, and a light flashed green on the gauss pistol.

"Eat samarium-cobalt, dirtbags," she said, concealing the pistol by her side and striding back down the hallway.

Jake came around the corner, and Nadine raised the pistol. "Sold me out, did you?"

"Hey, Nadine. 1713. Why are you pointing your gauss pistol at me?"

"I saw the airlock door open."

"I know."

"You know?"

"I tested the airlock alerts first thing. You were there when I did it with that inspector guy, so I know you saw it. 1713."

"I hadn't noticed. Where are the Militia?"

"What about the Militia?" Jake said.

"What's 1713?" Nadine asked.

"That's the year the treaty of Utrecht was signed."

"The treaty of who?"

"It's an Old Earth treaty. Some of the empires that were precursors to the Old Empire....They had a war, and they signed a treaty over some land. In Europe."

"I'm up?"

"Europe."

Nadine closed her eyes for a moment, then glared at Jake. "Jake Stewart, you are the most infuriating man. The Militia is hunting me on this ship, possibly trying to kill me, and after all that we've been through together, all the times we've helped each other and shot each other, you're letting them onboard...and now you're babbling on about some history lesson that nobody cares about and won't help us at all."

"The treaty of Utrecht was a major milestone in early Earth history. Paved the way for the empires that formed the first Terran empire. Everybody cares about the treaty of Utrecht."

Nadine kept staring at him. Jake looked disappointed. She looked down the corridor behind him. There was still nobody there.

"Except, whenever you babble this weird information, it usually has some real-world use," she said.

Jake nodded.

She lowered her gun. "And I don't see the Militia behind you, either." She thought for a minute, then turned and ran to the control room.

Jake's code, 1713, unlocked her board. She began a quick pre-flight and flipped the screen display. It was black—no signal.

"You undocked us?" she said.

"Yes. I disengaged the docking clamps and pulled the station power and comm connections. Only the magnets are holding us now."

"Great," Nadine said, punching the magnets. "Floating free. Do the thrusters work?"

"Yes. You can take us out."

"Fine." Nadine adjusted the thrusters, and the ship rocked slightly. They edged away from the station, and Nadine spun a wheel, then tapped a pad. The ship pivoted and began to drift away.

"Call station ops for clearance," Nadine said, "and turn on the radar so we can see what's out there."

"I'll turn the radar on, but, remember, we bought the discount package, so we don't get 360-degree coverage."

"Whatever. You're sensors. I'm pilot. Call the station and get clearance."

Jake manipulated the second board. "Station. *Castle Arcturus*, requesting drop."

"*Castle Arcturus*, you appear to have already dropped. Clearance seems redundant."

"Yeah, sorry about that. The pilot was...hasty. Reporting departure."

"Departure logged. Free trades."

"Free trades to you too, station." Jake manipulated the sensors. "It looks clear in front of us."

"So we're good to drop, then," Nadine said.

"Well, we only have a small sensor cone, and only facing forward, but it's clear."

The comm beeped. Jake pressed the button.

"Station to *Castle Arcturus*. Will you accept a call on a secure channel?"

"Roger. Change to 223," Jake said.

"Putting call through on 223," the station said.

Jake tapped the comm channel. "*Castle Arcturus* on 223. Jake Stewart here." He put the call on speaker.

"Ah, the absconding criminal, Mr. Stewart. Good morning," said a familiar voice.

"Mr. Pletcher, how are you?" Jake said.

"Vinnie, sweet cheeks, how are you doing, big guy?" Nadine yelled from her station.

"The luscious Ms. Nadine. How nice to hear your voice."

"Yours too, Vinnie. Sorry we had to go. We could have had some fun together."

"I think so, yes. It would have been fun. However, there is the small matter of my ship, which you have stolen."

"How come she gets 'luscious,' and I get 'criminal'?" Jake said.

"We didn't steal it. We bought it," Nadine said.

"Actually, Mr. Stewart insisted on a double escrow account. You still have all your money, and you have my ship."

"That's a great deal. Good for Jake," Nadine said. "What's a double escrow account? Is that twice as good as a single escrow account?"

"Of course, I'll have to list it as stolen, and you two as absconded."

"We haven't absconded," Nadine said.

"Do you even know what 'absconded' means?" Jake asked her.

She ignored him. "Tough beans there, Mr. Vince, but we'll take good care of it."

An alarm flickered on the screen. *Remote engine shutdown*, it said. Even more alarm lights began to flash.

"About that....I have taken some measures to protect my property," Vince said.

Nadine hammered her board and pushed a pedal on the floor. "Jake, I don't have any control. What's going on?"

"Remote lockdown of the board. There will be a remote control buried in the system. I can bypass it— given time." Jake began to page through the screens.

The lights went out. The hum of the fans stopped.

"Life support just shut down," Nadine said.

"I have a great respect for Mr. Stewart's mechanical ability," Vince said. "I can't really allow him to practice it unmolested, so I've shut down all the systems while we work this out."

"Jake?" Nadine looked at him.

"I can bypass all of this, but it takes time, and we'll have to be in suits for all of it. Besides, we did plan on actually buying the ship."

"There is the matter of the double escrow," Vince said.

"Look, I have most of the money. 80 percent of what you want."

"And the other 20 percent?" Vince asked.

"Perhaps a vendor take-back mortgage?"

"What type of terms?" Vince asked.

They began a lengthy conversation regarding interest rates, amortization, document fees, and processing times. They argued back and forth for about ten minutes before Nadine got involved.

"Boring," she said. "When will this end?"

"We're almost done," Jake said. "We've decided to set up a joint firm to split the profits, and a second, separate company to hold the mortgage, run by Mr. Pletcher and some of his investors. However, we're arguing about the corporate structure."

"Please, call me Vince," Vince said. "I have some investors who want to park some cash in investments, but they are fairly prominent dirt-side, and want to limit their corporate exposure."

"You realize we're drifting, don't you? We might hit something. Could we speed this up?" Nadine asked.

"We also have to discuss the amortization period. Vince insists on a 360-day interest calculation period, rather than the industry-standard 365-day year."

"What are you talking about?" Nadine said. "Our year is, what 123 days?"

"That's Delta's year. This is a financial year."

"A financial year? You mean like an Imperial Standard year?"

"A financial year is used in loan calculations. The shorter the year, the higher the effective interest rate. If I charge you 8 percent a day, that's a lot more than 8 percent every one hundred days. I'm holding out for the longer period to decrease our interest expenses."

"But as I've told you, Mr. Stewart, this is the standard in our documentation," Vince said. "We need to follow standard procedures."

"Vince, if you give Jake what he wants, I'll have dinner with you when we get back."

"Just dinner? How about dinner and dancing?"

"Dinner's all I will promise. The rest is up to you."

"Huh. Okay, why not? Mr. Stewart, send us the paperwork, I'll certify it, and then you are on your own. At least, until the first payment is due."

"Done," Jake said. "Let me send some messages." Jake busied himself on the board. The lights came back on, and the life-support fans could be heard again.

Nadine regained control of the ship and pointed them away from the station. "I need a course, Jake."

"Well, Nadine, our course depends on who you are running away from," Jake said.

"How about them?" Nadine said, pointing.

A ship showed on the radar. She had focused the telescope on it, and it showed up clearly on the screen. A Militia tug was heading right for them.

Chapter 12

"This is no fun," the copilot said. "We're just burning fuel, the chances of catching this ship is minimal, and even if we catch up to it, we can't do anything." He punched a button on the intercom in front of him. "You hear that back there? This is a waste of time."

The intercom crackled. "We're freezing. Turn up the heat."

"We're a tug. There is no heat except what you brought."

"Why can't we get in the cab?"

"Because there is only room for two people in the cab—the pilot and me. We might be able to jam a third in, but there are three of you."

"Looked like lots of room to me. We could float on that panel in front of you."

"Until we fired the thrusters. Then you'd bounce around the cabin."

"We can take it. We don't mind some bouncing."

"Really?" The copilot looked at the pilot and raised an eyebrow.

She only shrugged. "Bouncing, coming up."

The copilot keyed the intercom again. "Okay. Just as a test, we're going to drift for a second, then keep chasing them. We'll even give you a countdown. You ready?"

"Of course we are. Fire away."

"Poor choice of words," the pilot said. "Freefall in three...two...one....Now." She tapped a control. She and the copilot gently pressed against their restraint belts, then settled back.

The pilot listened to the intercom. There was a muffled curse, a thump, another curse, and another thump.

"Emperor's balls," the voice said. "Don't be so rough."

"Accel in three...two...one....Now," the pilot said.

The main engines engaged.

"The Empress's hairy armpits," the intercom voice said. "We're bouncing around like a roller derby team back here. I thought you said this was going to be gentle."

"I love roller derby," the copilot said. "I made a bundle betting on the last match. The Belt Bashers were awesome."

"I can't really get into it," the pilot said, "but I do like some of the outfits. They really go all out coloring their helmets."

"Are you trying to kill us up there? I think Suza broke her wrist."

"Are you strapped into the cargo nets back there?"

"Cargo nets?"

"The nets," the pilot said. "You're supposed to drape them from side to side and climb in the middle of them. That way, no matter what direction we accel, you just float around in the middle."

"Oh, so that's what they're for?"

"Haven't you ever been in a ship?" the copilot asked.

"A shuttle, not a crap ship like this."

"Don't talk about my tug like that. Penelope is the best tug ever. Aren't you, girl?" The pilot patted the console.

"Penelope? You named this crap-box Penelope?"

"It's an ex-girlfriend of hers," the copilot said, "but it doesn't matter what she calls it. What matters is that that was only gentle maneuvering. If we have to do anything radical to close in on that ship, you'll end up squashed like a bug. Can you strap in?"

"We can try."

"Try harder. We're gaining on them, and we'll have to maneuver soon."

☐

"Jake, they're gaining," Nadine said.

"I know. They're a tug. Three nozzles to our one. They can out-accel us."

"So what do we do?"

"We need to stay ahead till they run out of fuel," Jake said. "Lots of acceleration, but no fuel capacity at all. At this rate, they'll burn all their fuel off in less than an hour and reverse course. At least, if they want to get back."

"Empress's vagina," Nadine said. "We just have to avoid them for an hour?"

"That's a personnel container on the back. There will be a boarding crew there."

"A straight stern chase? I hate those. They're so boring." Nadine put her legs up on the console and stretched.

"Let's make it more interesting, then. Spin and give me a side vector, then one in reverse. Change our orbit completely. Do some random stuff and see what type of tug pilot that is."

"I'm comfortable here," Nadine said.

"Tugs are short-range, and they normally just bang containers around. A mid-space rendezvous is trickier. Let's see if their pilot is as good as you."

"Jakey, are you saying I'm a good pilot?"

"I've always admired your piloting skills. It's your other personal idiosyncrasies that bother me."

Nadine began to punch buttons on her screen. "Strap in and hold on, then, Jake. You're in for the ride of your life." Nadine stared at her screen for a few moments, then sighed. "Jake?"

"Yes, Nadine?"

"What does 'idiosyncrasies' mean?"

Nadine spent the next half-hour making random course corrections, reversals, jinks, and jumps. Jake had directed her out to a higher orbit, so she made sure that the general trend was where Jake wanted them to go.

"They haven't boarded us yet," Nadine said.

"That's kind of self-evident," Jake said. "I think I would have noticed several armed Militia clanking up the corridors.

"They should have, though. You're right that they're faster, Jakey. They have been pulling closer, but not fast. They're holding back."

"How are they holding back?"

"Their reactions are slow. Watch." Nadine pushed a pedal and swung the ship 90 degrees left, then another ninety up.

The rapid maneuver flung Jake against his straps, back against his seat, and then against the straps once more, but he kept his eyes centered on the display.

"They're following," Jake said.

"Watch closely, Jakey. There's a delay while they wait for us to commit, then they do a much smoother version. They have more accel on the smoother curves than we do, but it's like they can't do anything quickly."

"We're burning fuel I'd rather not use right now. If there's a way to stop that, I want to use it. Try a couple more of those rapid changes," Jake said.

The two watched in silence for a minute.

"For some reason they can't adapt quickly, or won't," Nadine said.

"That gives me an idea," Jake said. "Let's try something."

"They cut their engines," the pilot said.

The copilot looked up from her fuel calculations. "What?"

"Look, Mom, no engines. Huh, there go the thrusters."

"That's a big roll."

"It sure is. Several G's, at least. He-haw, now a yaw."

"Plus a bit of a pitch. They're all over the place."

"Easy to catch up to them now."

"Yes. Like they want us to."

The copilot pressed the intercom. "We'll be up to the target in about twenty-two minutes."

"About time," the intercom voice said. "Let us know when we're docked."

The two pilots looked at each other. "Docked?" the copilot said into the intercom.

"Yeah, when you have us at the airlock. We're supposed to capture that Nadine girl. I'm ticked at these jokers. Once we're locked in, me and the girls are going to go in, guns blazing."

The pilot shook her head, and the copilot punched the intercom button. "You know we don't have an airlock, right?"

"Oh. Right. Yeah, just get us next to their lock, and we'll force our way in. We've got tool chest back here."

"Riiiighhht. Things might not work out the way you expect."

"We don't tell you how to do your job. You don't tell us how to do ours."

"Actually, you've spent the last hour doing nothing but telling us how to do our job, but I don't care. We'll get you within ten meters of that ship. Think you can handle the rest?"

"Of course. Unlike you, we know how to get things done," the voice said.

"Okay. Hang on. We're going to cut thrust and do some maneuvering, but we'll be gentle." The copilot nodded at the pilot, who dropped the main engine and gave a gentle tap on the thrusters.

The tug took a full minute to spin around. Then the pilot tapped the thrusters again and pulsed the main engines. She rolled the ship and positioned it so that the *Castle Arcturus* began to fill the forward viewports. It took longer than expected, but they did catch up.

"We're in position," the copilot said over the intercom. "Suit up, meet up on channel 452, and come on up."

The three female Militia crew double-checked each other's suits, then attached their shotguns to bulky leg holsters that held them along their thighs. One of them hefted up a giant tool rack with mallets, crowbars, and wrenches.

The leader nodded and popped the rear doors. The air exited in a plume of vapor as the water froze out. They hand-crawled along the container, pulled around the outer edge, and grasped a grab bar, then pulled themselves up until they were able to climb up onto the cabin.

"Emperor's scrotum. How do we get onto that?" one asked.

The *Castle Arcturus* was farther away than the promised ten meters—more like fifty—but that was because it was spinning, rolling, and pivoting all at the same time. It was a tumbling mass that moved on all three planes. The containers locked on the hull flexed against their chains as centrifugal force tried to pull them off. The airlock flashed by about every eight seconds, moving fast. A jump toward the ship was possible.

It would be easy to hit—the tug was at rest relative to it—but locking onto it would be impossible. Even if you weren't crushed as the revolving hull slammed into you, the spin would throw you off into deep space, magnetic boots or not.

"There's your airlock," the pilot said. "Off you go."

"Can't you get us closer?" asked the Militia leader.

"And that will help, how?"

"It will make it easier to jump."

"No, it won't. It will just make it more dangerous. We're plenty close now."

"Can you fire a grapnel or something?"

"Sure can, but we're not going to."

"Why not?"

"Because we're a tug. We do container collection, not boarding, and we normally shoot at something that isn't moving. That way we won't break our grapnel."

"That is, if it even sets," the copilot said, "and doesn't just get banged off, come whipping back, and cut you three in half. Don't worry, though. If that happens, your boots should still stay magnetized, so your legs will stick.

We'll be able to get a good DNA sample for the death certificate."

"Hilarious," the Militia leader said, then switched to a private channel. "Either of you two have any ideas what we're supposed to do here?"

"We're supposed to pick the aspect that is moving the least and maneuver around to that side, fire our grapnel, and then jump on from there, stopping just short and trying to latch on," said the shorter of the two women.

"It's spinning in all directions. There isn't an easy way to do this," the leader said, "but we'll give it a try. Jelleaux, take the magnetic grapnel from the tool rack and jet out there. When it comes around again, fire a shot into the side of the engineering module and hold on."

"Uh, Boss, I don't really want to do that."

"It's not a request. It's an order. Do it. Jump on that ship."

"I'm going to puke," Jake said.

"If you puke, Jakey boy, I'll kill you," Nadine said.

"That's fine. I feel like I'm dying anyway, and I'm not dying fast enough."

"You want to die faster? I can help with your problem. Besides, this was your idea."

"It was," Jake admitted. He stared out the viewport. It didn't help, but it didn't make things any worse, either. He'd had Nadine cut the main engines and use the thrusters to spin the ship violently, and randomly, in all directions. Now he alternatively was thrown into the side of his seat, a bit up, and completely forward. Every few seconds he could see the pursuing tug spin across the viewports.

"Can you still reach the controls?" Jake asked.

"Yes. We're spinning, but not so fast that I can't stop it if need be."

"The tug looks like it stopped."

"It looks like it to me too. I see a group of people

scrambling on top of the cab."

"They can scramble all they want," Jake said. "They won't be able to board unless they have heavy equipment. Extra strong lines. Reinforced winches."

"They are playing with something now. Looks like a big shotgun, but with a plate on the front."

"Like a food tray?"

"About that size."

CLANK.

"What was that?" Nadine asked.

"Grapple gun," Jake said. "Magnetic plate backed up by a coiled line. They fired it at us. I wonder if they had the gunner chained in or not."

"Can they pull us in?"

THUMP. Something hit the viewport, then flew away.

"What in an Imperial dinner basket was that?" Nadine said.

"They kept the shooter chained."

"Chained?"

"There's a chain on the gun. If you attach your tether to it, you don't lose the gun when it fires."

THUMP. Another shadow passed over the viewport.

"Again? What's going on?" Nadine asked.

"The person who fired was chained to the gun. The magnet hit us and locked on. Since we're spinning so fast, it just pulled the shooter off the tug, and it's going to—"

THUMP. Another shadow.

"It's going to keep doing that," Jake said. "The shooter will get pulled around and around and keep banging against the ship until they get tired—"

THRUM. The sound was quieter this time, and the shadow barely noticeable.

"Get tired of banging against the ship," Jake said, "and release their tether and go flying off into space. Are they maneuvering?"

"Let me check," Nadine said. She played with her board, but with some difficulty. Controlling the ship under these conditions wasn't quite as easy as she had told Jake. "Their main engine is firing."

"They're going to pick up the lost crewman, the one spinning out into the void."

"That's a horrible way to die. Speeding off into the dark, all alone."

"Stop worrying. They won't be going that fast. The tug can catch them easily. I think. Anyway, put us back on course for the Outer Belt, and let's get out of here."

"Can we stop this spinning?"

"For now," Jake said. "Get us out of here and on our way. Try not to burn too much fuel."

"When do I burn too much fuel?"

"All the time. You are profligate with fuel. 'Profligate' means—"

"I know what it means, Jake. You've told me before. I'll be anti-profligate."

"I'm not sure that's a word."

"It is now." Nadine deftly manipulated the ship to near-stillness, pointed it in a different direction, and fired the main engines again. "So we're home free?"

"Not quite. I figure they'll have another chance once they get that crewman back. They can still burn to catch up to us, but they will have to get close again, and they'll still have a problem with getting a magnet on us. Let's watch and see."

They headed out on course for about twenty minutes. Jake continued to run tests and check his screens while Nadine kept track of the pursuing ship. With their limited sensor cone, she had to spin the ship around to point the radar and telescope back where they had come from.

"Jake, they seem to have grabbed their girl back, and they're gaining on us again."

"You sure?"

"Yes. Radar has shown them closer in each of the last two sweeps."

"Okay. Let me think about this."

There was silence for a few minutes, then Nadine again stopped the main engines and spun the ship to bring the radar around so it faced the pursuing ship. "They're still gaining. I'm going to push the engines harder."

"No need for that," Jake said. "They will be a little gun shy. Besides, they don't know much about rendezvous in deep space, or they wouldn't have bothered to try hitting us with the magnetic grapnel."

"What does that have to do with the engines?"

"Just keep us on our course as efficiently as you can, but give us a gentle roll. That way we stay on course, but they'll have to maneuver to match us. I'll bet they are going to be too scared to try to board again."

They waited and watched for a few minutes.

"Okay, spin us back to face them, Nadine," Jake said.

"Face them? You mean slow down? Retro fire?"

"Nope. Just spin so we face them, so we are nose to nose."

"They'll be able to catch up."

"They'll also match our velocity and spin. If we're lucky."

"How will that be lucky, Jakey?" Nadine asked.

"They've already tried to board us once manually. Now I bet they'll try the tug's equipment."

"They've cut thrust. They're drifting up to us."

"Are they rolling?"

"Starting to."

"Good. I need to get some special tools, and then go out the airlock."

"What for?"

"To teach them the difference between tensile strength and shear strength."

Ten minutes later Jake was on the hull. He'd had Nadine pitch the ship slightly so he wasn't visible to the pursuing tug. He slid around a corner and moved in behind the truss holding the storage box, where he fiddled with some electrical and control wires.

"I need you to turn on light number sixteen," he said.

"Why not just turn on the master?" Nadine asked.

"No, I need the shadows. Just turn on sixteen."

There was a pause. "It's on," Nadine said. "Why do you need shadows?"

"I don't want them to know I'm out here. Are you sure the light is on?"

"Yes."

"Toggle the switch."

"I did. On now?"

"No, it's not. Wait one...." Jake pulled out a meter and plugged the control and power cables in. The meter glowed green. He thought for a second, then leaned forward and looked inside the housing. There was no lamp. "Emperor's testicles."

"What?"

"I thought it was the control runs. It's not. The light is missing. I'll have to get another one."

"Jake, what's going on?"

"No time to explain." Jake slid behind the truss and began climbing.

The climb was easy. The truss was an open lattice of metal with lots of hand- and footholds. He climbed up to where a light fixture was bolted to the hull. He climbed around the front and began to loosen the two bolts that held the lamp assembly.

"Jake, they are slowing to a stop. Less than fifty meters away."

"There should be a contraption just under their cab, behind the capture block. It will be a sort of a winch thing, with one of those magnetic plates next to it. Can you see it?"

"Sort of. The shadows make it hard."

"Can you see vapor leaking off it?"

"Water vapor? Yes, sort of. Why?"

"It's a hydraulic launcher. You load it with steam, the

pressure trips the release, and it fires the magnetic grapnel out."

"You use steam on a spaceship? Not electromagnets?"

"It's a tug," Jake said. "Superconducting magnets are Old Empire tech. That's expensive. Hydraulics are cheap and easy to fix. I need to get this light working. Watch them closely. When you see a bunch of steam start to leak out, they're building up to fire. When you see that, move us out of the way."

"How?"

"I don't care. You're the pilot. Do some pilot thing. Just give me some sort of warning."

"I won't be able to give you much," Nadine said.

"I'm used to it." Jake clamped his magnetic boots to the truss and spun the wrench. The first bolt released. He pocketed it and began to work on the next one.

"Steam," Nadine said. "Ready....Ready....Now."

The ship seemed to lurch sideways. It was an odd motion. Jake had never felt one quite like it before.

The line with the magnetic grapnel flew by off to one side and hung there. After a moment, it started to retract.

"Missed us, suckers," Nadine said.

Jake removed the second bolt, pocketed it, and pulled the light fixture. The fixture was small, so he slid it into the net bag attached to his arm and pulled the drawstring, then began to climb down the truss.

"How long does it take to recharge?" Nadine said.

"About thirty seconds, but they can't start recharging until they've pulled the whole line back and the plate locks back into the steam launcher."

Jake reached the bottom and began to bolt the light fixture into the front of the truss. "Can they see me?"

"Nope," Nadine said. "I'm keeping the control room nose-up. You're hidden."

"Don't let them get below us."

"Sure. Steam—stand by."

Jake double-checked his boot magnets, then continued

bolting the light in.

"More steam," Nadine said. "Now."

The ship did that strange leaping thing again. Jake had no idea what she was doing, but it seemed to be working. The grapnel flew by.

"Missed again," Nadine said. "This is a fun game, but it will get boring after a while. What's your plan, Jakey?"

The light came on in Jake's hands as the bolt tightened enough that the fixture made contact with the recessed plug. He gave it two more turns to make sure it would stay in, then stepped back behind the truss.

"Let them catch us," he said.

"What?"

"Let them catch us. Pivot so that they can see the top of the control room and behind. Make sure they can see that storage truss and the area in front of it."

"And then?" Nadine asked.

"Then they will see a nice, flat towing plate attached there, as it is on every freighter ever built. Bolted directly to the frame, strong enough to take the full weight of a thousand-ton ship, and with two towing bollards and chain attachments if they needed to pull us. As soon as they see that, they'll shoot their next mag grapnel right there and catch us."

"Catch us? Then use that as a boarding line and come across?"

"I won't let that happen. I have a plan."

There was silence on the radio.

"Okay," Nadine said, sounding subdued. "You usually do. I'll trust you. What should I do?"

The pursuing tug took longer than expected. Nadine had changed the ship's angle so they could see the towing platform abaft the control room, but the tug didn't take the bait right away. It took another few minutes of maneuvering before the tug fired its grapnel straight at the middle of the towing plate.

"At least they finally have decent aim. Jake, there's a crew coming out of the container on the back."

"Let 'em. Are they crawling down to the line?"

"Yes. It's hard to see, but the first person has clipped on. Jake? Problems—they've got guns."

"What type?"

"Two revolvers and a shotgun, I think. Hard to see with the shadows. Two shotguns."

"Good."

"Good? They'll shoot you."

"They can't see me."

"How can they not see you? You're right there on the hull."

"Behind a truss, and behind a bright light pointing right at them. They can't see me."

"They can see you on infrared sensors."

"Please, Nadine. This is a tug, not a Militia cutter. Sensors cost money. They don't have any. Are you keeping tension?"

"Yes. I'm just barely spinning, keeping that line nice and tight. Why are we making it easy for them?"

"We're making sure they won't think too much. Let me know when they are halfway over."

"They're just starting along. Jake, we're locked on. I don't think I can break free."

"I'm going to cut the line."

"You're going to cut the line. The line they are using to hold the hundreds of tons of ship. That line?"

"Yep. Starting right now." Jake stepped out from behind the truss and slid his magnetic boots across the hull. The grapple was locked to the towing plate in front of him.

"Will you cut the power line?" Nadine asked.

"Not unless I want to be electrocuted." Jake unlocked his boots and flipped over to the cable, grasping it in his hand. The cable was a braided metal line with a shielded power line wrapped loosely around it.

Letting his boots float free behind him, he grasped the grapnel housing with one hand and produced a small set of pliers with a sharpened point. He carefully inserted the point of the pliers between two of the metal cable strands and snipped one. He clipped another strand, and another.

"Jake, they're halfway."

"Have they seen me yet?" He snipped another.

"I don't think so."

"Keep the tension up." He snipped again.

"Jake, they're still coming."

He snipped another strand, then two more.

"This is taking too long," Nadine said. "Speed it up."

He put his pliers around two strands at once and pushed hard. That worked. He began to cut two at a time.

"I thought you were going to cut the cable," Nadine said."

"I am. One strand at a time."

"How many strands are there?"

"Lots. Where are they?"

"Three-quarters over, and one of them has seen you. They've stopped. She's aiming her pistol at you."

Jake continued snipping, now over halfway through. He tried to snip three strands at once, and the line started to strain under the tension. He tried four strands. Too many—he couldn't cut them. He went back to three.

Sparks flashed from the corner of his eyes—a bullet hitting the hull. He looked up.

The group was much closer than he'd expected. The woman in front had a shotgun over her back and was climbing hand over hand along the line, her tether attached and trailing along behind. The second and third woman were all tangled up. The second must have fired and bounced back into the third.

He kept cutting.

"Jake, the lead one has gone past me. I can't see her anymore."

The lead women had almost reached the ship. Rather

than detaching her tether and clamping onto the *Castle Arcturus*, she was reaching behind her to pull the shotgun out. It had gotten stuck while she was climbing across. She was having trouble pulling it free.

"Keep the tension on the line, Nadine," Jake said, snipping three more strands.

"Jake, the other two are coming now too."

Jake ignored her and cut another three strands. There were barely ten left. He snipped again.

The woman had given up trying to pull the shotgun over her shoulder and was now unbuckling the whole harness. Jake snipped again. Only a few to go.

He felt a pressure against his shoulder and looked up. It was the shotgun.

Jake couldn't see the woman's face, but he slowly opened his hands and raised them. The wire cutters floated free. He reset his feet carefully, punched his chin button, and set his boots to maximum.

"Nadine," Jake said. "Full-power roll, spinward with the tension. Right now."

Nadine must have had her hands on the controls because the ship rolled immediately. With a jerk, the cable snapped.

Jake's world rocked, the pressure against his boots increasing. He staggered, but stayed attached.

The woman with the shotgun rocked as well, but stayed on the hull. *Emperor's anus. She's locked on too.*

But as the cable whipped off into the distance, the woman's tether, still attached, ran free to the end stop, where it stuck.

The magnets weren't stronger than the tether. She was yanked off the hull.

"Empress's royal lunch. What did you do, Jake? They're all collapsed in a ball at the end of that line."

"I told you—tensile strength versus shear strength. Now cut this roll before I get sick, and get us out of here."

Chapter 13

"So they're all dead?" Colonel Savard asked, revolver in hand. He pointed it at the wall and pulled the trigger, but the trigger didn't budge. He tried to spin the cylinder on the revolver. "Stuck."

"We think so, sir," Commander Roi said.

"What do you mean, 'you think so'? Can't you tell whether a man is dead or not? It's not a complicated test." Outside the window of Colonel Savard's office, the city of Landing stretched out between him and the mountain. There was a lot of smoke, and at least one visible fire.

"No, sir, it's not, but some of them we can't find."

"How do you lose dead people?" Colonel Savard pulled a lever, and the cylinder swung out. He popped all the bullets out and put them on his desk, then tried to spin the cylinder again, but it remained stuck.

"The bomb went off fine in the shuttle. We blew the main passenger compartment and got most of the delegates. Both of the university professors, and the Free Traders. Most of the passengers as well, truthfully."

"I don't care about the passengers, Commander. Keep your head in the game. What about Dashi?"

"He wasn't in the main compartment. The problem is he'd booked a first-class room."

"So he traveled first class. Why is that a problem?" Colonel Savard grasped the cylinder and managed to click it to the next setting. "Needs oil."

"He never does that. We've been watching him. He always travels economy. 'Wise stewardship of the corporation's money,' he would say. So we expected him to be in the back. The cabins are somewhat protected. The blast wasn't powerful enough to completely destroy the ship. It wrecked the passenger compartment, but the forward part of the ship was largely intact."

Colonel Savard began to rummage in his desk. "So he's alive?"

"Well, it decompressed. We can't find anybody back of the control room. They'd all disappeared."

"Killed?"

"Sucked out, we think...but without any bodies...."

"If they survived, they would be on the vids, so they must be gone. Aha!" Colonel Savard pulled a bottle of oil out of his desk and began applying it to the cog behind the cylinder.

"As you say, sir."

"But...?"

"But I'd like to find at least one body from up front."

Colonel Savard frowned. "Why do you need a body?" He clicked the cylinder one pawl at a time, adding oil.

"The front decompressed, but slowly. By the time the rescue tugs got there, it was empty except for the pilots. If the rest died of decompression, shouldn't we have found at least one of them there?"

"Could they have gotten into suits and survived, or gotten into emergency bubbles?"

"Yes, sir, they could have, but where did they go? The tugs didn't find anybody alive except the pilots, and the pilots said they had no communications after the hatch was shut. They couldn't exactly go back and look."

"Were there any indications of what happened?"

"Just reports of blood in some of the cabins."

"Have it tested," Colonel Savard said. He tried to spin the cylinder, but it stuck after three clicks. He applied more oil.

"Sir, we'll have to send somebody to the scrapyard to get a sample, and it may have degraded or boiled off."

"I didn't think I stuttered. Send them. Today."

"Sir."

Colonel Savard got up and paced. "Find out. I want to make sure TGI is out of the picture. What about the current chairman?" He picked up the revolver, finally able to spin the cylinder, though not fast.

"She's seventy-eight, sir. Hardly a threat."

"Dashi is a threat, though, and it won't go well for you if I have to report to the Officers' Council that you didn't remove that threat." Colonel Savard pointed the revolver at him. "Will it, Commander?" He shifted the revolver to the side and pulled the trigger.

The cylinder swung, and the hammer fell with an audible click.

"No, sir," the commander said, eyes tracking the barrel.

Colonel Savard examined the weapon. "We need to go shooting sometime, Commander. Just you and me. A little revolver action."

"I'd love that, sir."

"Of course you would. What about weapons and the Growers?"

"Things are looking better on that front, sir. We delivered them some weapons. Not as many as we promised, and not as much ammunition, but some."

"What about the machine gun?" Colonel Savard swung the cylinder out and lined up the bullets to load the revolver.

"We gave them one. They would have noticed if it were missing."

"True. They're getting ready to come into town?"

"Loading up a train right now, sir."

"Good. Your surprise is ready?"

"Already set, sir. We've seized all the weapons in town and armed extra troops. We'll be waiting when they get off the train."

"Excellent. Any issues?"

"One small one, sir."

Colonel Savard's eyes narrowed. He loaded the second bullet. "How small?"

"We can't find the admiral's weapons cache."

Colonel Savard pointed the revolver at Commander Roi's head. "He's not an admiral anymore."

Commander Roi's eyes widened as he stared down the barrel. "No, sir."

"He's a traitor."

"Yes, sir." Commander Roi was sweating now.

"Not a true servant of the Empire."

"No, sir."

"So don't call him an admiral." Colonel Savard began to wave his gun around. "He's traitorous scum. A disgrace to the Militia. Guilty of treason." He paused, and his voice dropped. "His weapons cache?"

"He held responsibility for the reserve unit's weapons and for the repair shops."

"There is only one reserve unit. How many weapons could it have?"

"Well, sir, he changed the regulations while he was in charge. Originally, every Militia person surrendered their weapons to the reserve command when they retired."

"Every retired Militia person? Well, that's not a huge number." Colonel Savard spun the cylinder again.

"He changed the rule, sir. It was every retired person, but it's now every discharged person. He did this about five years ago."

"Every person who leaves the Militia has to surrender their weapons....Are you saying all he got every one of those guns in the last five years?" Colonel Savard again pointed the revolver at Commander Roi.

Commander Roi squirmed, trying to see if there was a shell in the next breech that would come under the hammer. "1,205 revolvers, yes, and seventy-two shotguns."

"He has 1,205 revolvers?"

"No, sir."

"Oh, good. You had me worried for a moment." Colonel Savard sat down and holstered his revolver, then turned and stared out the window.

Commander Roi took a deep breath to calm himself before speaking. "He has 1,537."

"He has more?"

"Anything that went to the repair shop. After it was repaired, it went back to him."

"Where are these guns?"

"He put them in two containers and shipped them off-planet."

"Where?"

"Not sure. However, we do have a manifest and some routing details. Encrypted, of course."

Colonel Savard took a deep breath and raised his eyes to the ceiling. "Emperor's testicles. There are 200,000 containers in this system. Which one is it in?"

"We're working on the encryption right now."

"He must have had the encryption key with him, or sent it to somebody," Colonel Savard said.

"We figured out that it's a double key. He sent half of it off-planet and kept the other half."

"So somebody needs both sets. Who did he send half of it to?"

"One of his operatives. Her name was Nadine."

"Well, it's no good to her unless she has the other half, and she doesn't have it."

Commander Roi said nothing.

Colonel Savard looked at him. "I said, it's no good to her unless she has the other half, and she doesn't have it, does she? Does she, Commander?"

"Well, sir...."

"Yes?" Colonel Savard stood up again, revolver in hand.

"Well, sir, when we captured the admiral—I mean, the traitor—he had a girl with him. We thought she was just a floozy of sorts, but after we reviewed the video, we were able to identify her as this 'Nadine' operative." Commander Roi thought he glimpsed a round in the next breech. Sweat beaded on his brow, but he didn't dare wipe it away.

"With half of the key?"

"Half of the key sent to her electronically, yes."

Colonel Savard closed his eyes and shook his head. "Out with it, Commander."

"Sir, the ad—the traitor gave her a credit chip as payment when she left. We checked all the personal keys we found on the ad...I mean, the traitor, and he didn't have the other half."

"You think he gave her the second half of the key with the credit chip."

"Yes, Colonel."

"So she has both keys. Where is she now?" Colonel Savard pointed the gun directly between Commander Roi's eyes. "Where is she, Commander? Tell me now, or I'll blow your head off."

"Sir, she just left High-42 with a known TGI associate. They have acquired a ship. We put out a warrant for her, just as a matter of course, but it wasn't particularly advertised. We didn't know that she had all this."

"You idiot." Colonel Savard put his finger on the trigger.

Commander Roi's eyes focused on the round ready to rotate under the hammer. Time slowed down. He saw the colonel's finger clench and the trigger pull. The hammer came down in slow motion.

Why can't I move? Commander Roi stood frozen in place.

The revolver clicked. Colonel Savard looked at it closely. "Misfire." He lowered the weapon. "Catch her. Find those guns. Do it now."

"Yes, sir. We'll do that." Commander Roi turned and marched away.

Colonel Savard again looked out the window. The smoke was thicker. "Commander?"

The retreating man stopped and turned around. "Yes, sir?"

"The guns have to be somewhere already. A station."

"Yes, sir."

"We need the guns. Send a transport ship with a

company. We need those guns," Colonel Savard said again, "even if we have to kill everybody with them."

Chapter 14

"So the Militia are chasing me, and there's a price on my head. We need to go somewhere there are no Militia, and nobody who will take money to turn me over to them." Nadine looked over her board. "Right now our course could be described as 'thataway,' which I don't think is a good long-term solution."

The two were sitting in the control room at the two consoles. Jake had warmed up two trays and brought them back to the control room. Nadine was looking at a navigation screen, and Jake had some sort of complex schematic up on his screen.

"Where's the tug?" Jake asked.

"I can't see them on radar anymore. Last I saw, they were heading back to their station."

"Okay. Let us drift for a bit while I bring up a course."

"Do you have another set of cutlery?" Nadine asked.

"No." Jake continued eating and working on his board.

"No?" Nadine asked.

"No," Jake said. He looked at Nadine, sighed, licked his spoon clean, and handed it to her. "Don't lose it. It's super valuable."

"Ick, I'm going to get cooties. It's light, though. What is it?"

"You won't catch anything. I've had more shots than you. At least, I think I have. Have you had all your shots?"

"It's titanium, I think," Nadine said, still examining the utensil. "This is super expensive. Why have titanium spoons?"

"Because in the Belt, you carry a ton of stuff. Spoons. Screwdrivers. Wrenches. All that mass adds up. I try to keep things light. Have you had your vaccinations?"

"We have tools on the ship. Why not use those?"

"Seriously, I need to know about the shots. It will

control where we go next. And I like my own tools."

"Tools. Boys and their toys. Why did you help me?"

"If I take us to a station, I need to make sure we won't infect them with anything. I'm paranoid after that last incident. You've at least had a regular course of shots recently, right?"

"You could have just left me there, or turned me in. There was a reward."

"You would have shot me."

"Well, yes, I would have." Nadine shoveled the last of the tray food into her mouth, then handed the spoon to Jake without cleaning it. "I've shot you before, though, and that seemed to work out for you, so you shouldn't have been worried about that."

Jake held up the dirty spoon and waved it at Nadine. She took it from him and held it in front of her mouth. She began to slowly lick it with her tongue, sliding it in and out of her mouth.

Jake tried to ignore her licking, but couldn't tear his eyes away. "I wish you would stop doing that."

Nadine pulled the spoon out of her mouth. "Why? Does it bother you?"

"Not 'bother,' exactly," Jake said.

"What does it do, then?"

"Nadine, you know what it does. That's why you are doing it."

Nadine laughed. "True, Jake. It's one of my skills."

"Indeed," Jake said. "You have quite a skill set, really."

"I do," Nadine agreed, studying Jake, "and I have to admit, you've learned a lot in the last few years. You have some skills yourself."

"Oh? Like what?"

"Well, when I steal a ship, it's with a gun. When you do, it's with a varmint fake montage."

"Vendor take-back mortgage."

"See? You know all the right words. You do well with anything to do with ships."

"I've had lots of practice."

Nadine unstrapped and stretched, noticing from the corner of her eye that Jake was watching. Good. She stepped behind him. "In fact, that was pretty impressive, what you did outside with that boarding crew." She gave his shoulders a hard rub.

"Mmmmh, that feels good," Jake said.

"Very manly, Jake," Nadine said. She rubbed harder.

"Umh."

"I'm glad I got away. You know there's a big reward out for me, Jake."

"I don't care about that."

"You don't? You wouldn't turn me in, would you, Jake?"

"No. We're pals."

"We're pals? 'Pals'? What does that mean? Like friends?"

Jake squirmed in discomfort. "Kind of. We're not just acquaintances. We help each other out. You've gotten me out of some situations in the past. I won't turn you over to the Militia."

"Not even for a reward?"

"Yes, not even for a reward. You'd do the same for me."

"Don't count on it, Jakey. Enough cash, and I'd sell you out."

"Even to GG and the Militia? After all they've done to you?"

"Jake Stewart, you are one of the most naive men I've ever met. Everybody has their price. Everybody. Offer me enough money, and I'd turn you over to them in a heartbeat."

Nadine stopped rubbing his back and collapsed into her seat. She looked down at the spoon in her pocket, wiped it on her leg, and handed it to Jake, then turned back to the screen.

Jake slid the spoon into his pocket. "So you'd turn me

in for a reward."

"Yes." Nadine was silent for a moment, then smiled. "You're right, though, Jake. You have helped me out. It would have to be one big reward."

"How big?" Jake asked.

"Stupendously big," Nadine said. "Enormously big."

"See? I knew it," Jake said. "I'm safe with you."

"Safe enough. Until there is a lot of money on the table." Nadine leaned over to look at him. "What are you looking at there? It looks familiar."

"After my little...incident...with the revolver back there, I've decided to learn about guns. I'm looking at schematics of how to construct a revolver so I can be more dangerous with them."

Nadine looked at Jake and laughed. "Jake, you are many things, and you could be many things, but 'dangerous' isn't one of them."

"You just finished telling me I'm useful."

"At some things. Are you serious when you say you wouldn't turn me in?"

"I wouldn't turn you in." Jake paused. "Nadine?"

"What?"

"You don't have to stop that back rub. It felt kind of nice."

Nadine stood up and stretched again, then stepped behind him, settled her feet into the straps, and continued rubbing.

"That feels good," Jake said again.

"So what are we doing now?"

"We just drift for a while, until we're totally out of that station's radar range. Then we do some course corrections. That will be quite a few hours, though."

"A few hours with nothing to do." Nadine leaned forward, unclipped Jake's belt, and pulled him out of the seat.

"What are you doing?" Jake asked.

She towed him out of the control room. "Just payback

for helping me out."

"Nadine, not yet," Jake said.

Nadine stopped. "Not yet?"

"You don't have to do this."

"You helped me get away, Jake. You deserve some sort of reward."

"Nadine, I didn't help you so you would sleep with me. I helped you because you asked for help."

"So you don't want to sleep with me?"

"No."

"You realize that makes you different from 99 percent of the men I know, and I don't believe those odds."

"Well, eventually, but not this way. I'd like something on a more permanent basis."

"Permanent."

"Less transactional."

"What does that mean?"

"Maybe we could be more than friends. Do things together."

"'Things'? Like go on dates?" Nadine grinned. "Jakey, you are not my type. You are cute and sweet, but I like excitement. Action. Gunfights. Shooting. Adventure. Danger."

"Adventure like stealing a spaceship?"

"Well...yes."

"Like I just did?"

"Well, yes."

"Excitement like evading a tug? Danger like fighting off the Militia with guns? Like I just did?"

"You did do that." Nadine nodded.

"Since you came running up for help, I've managed to find you a ship, steal it from the station, avoid station security, swindle the lender out of half their mortgage, and fight off one Militia boarding party by flinging them off into space. Then I single-handedly did it again with only a pair of wire cutters, and took us out to the Rim to a secret base that the Militia will never find...and you say I'm not exciting."

"But....You....Well, you seemed so calm about it. Organized. Plus, we never got shot or captured."

"You only like incompetent adventurers, then?" Jake said. "Ones who can't get things done? Who gets shot?"

"I'm not sure," Nadine said. She glared at him. "Jake Stewart, you are way too confusing. I'm going to my bunk. Alone." She stomped off.

Jake watched her go. "Does this mean no more back rub?"

"Jake, are we out of range of that radar yet?" Nadine asked. She'd come back to the control room, but hadn't spoken much.

"Not for a few hours yet."

"Where can we go when we're past it?"

"Well, anywhere, really."

"I see. Jake, how did you pay for this ship? You put down a lot of money."

"My boss gave it to me. He told me to buy a ship. He needed somebody to look into some things for him."

"So you bought him a ship?"

"No, I bought me a ship. It's in my name."

Nadine rolled over. "Wait, you own this ship? Like, really own it? Not just using it while a corporation owns it?"

"My name's on all the paperwork and on the mortgage. They didn't want any corporate ownership on it."

"Then it's totally yours? But who's going to believe it?"

"It was a good deal, and a lot of the money is mine. I could have put a down payment on a ship and run it, but I would have had to mortgage the rest of it. This way I didn't."

"Then you could just take this ship and run, and nobody could do anything about it? Not even that Vince guy?"

"He got more than he expected off this. The rest is

extra. Our pulling out didn't bother him that much. I'll make a few payments, then approach him with one big payment for, say, one-third of what I still owe, and he'll take it."

"Really? Won't he send somebody after you?"

"He'll send some lawyers after me, and after a negotiation, we'll settle up. He's a smart businessman. Shooting people and such doesn't go down well with the corps, but cease and desist orders they're fine with."

"Why not just head out and not come back? Maybe be the Belter Free Trader? Do your own thing. Get away from your corporate overlords."

"I can't."

"Why not?"

"It wouldn't be proper."

"'Proper'? I just saw you cut a tow cable and send a three-man boarding crew flying out into space. Twice."

"It isn't their ship. They had no right to do that. Besides, only an idiot tries to board a spinning ship."

"But you knocked that person out into the dark."

"I'm not responsible for other people's stupidity, Nadine. I have enough of my own."

"Wasn't it kind of stupid for them to give you all that money, knowing what you are?"

"I'm not like that, Nadine. Now, giving you all that money? That would have been stupid. You would have taken it and headed for the Outer Rim in a heartbeat."

"Half a heartbeat, Jake. Half a heartbeat."

They kept drifting for a while until they were sure they were out of range of any radar from the tug's station. Jake had the orbital track in the computer, and after it passed behind Delta, he gave Nadine a series of course corrections.

"Where are we going? Some out-of-the-way craphole to hide in?"

"Yes," Jake said. "A Rim station I know."

"One where they won't ask too many questions," Nadine said.

"Oh, they'll ask a lot of questions. They just won't share the answers with anybody."

"How do you know that?"

"I was born there."

Nadine laughed. "Jake, are you taking me home to see Mom?"

Chapter 15

"We should have taken things over long ago," the Militia recruit said. He twirled his stick and stared around the monorail station.

"We are in position, Lieutenant," Sergeant Russell said into his comm. "No, ma'am. Very quiet. Just backing up the station staff." He turned to the recruit. "What are you yapping about, recruit?"

"Look at all these lazybones, Sergeant. Just sitting here. Hanging out in the restaurants."

Sergeant Russell peered around. He and his half-squad of three recruits were walking around the main concourse. Each recruit wore an ill-fitting dress uniform, creases still showing, and a holstered revolver. Sergeant Russell had a well-worn but neat uniform, without a single crease. His holster was spotless, but looked well used.

The concourse was crowded with passengers recently arrived on the eastbound line, and those lining up to board for its return journey. The restaurants lining the concourse and the square outside were full.

"What do you expect people to be doing, McLusky?" Sergeant Russell said.

"They should be out working. Paying taxes. Not lazing away on their daily stipend."

"What time is it, McLusky?"

"Sergeant?"

"Check your comm. What time is it?"

The recruit flipped his comm over. "Almost mid first shift, Sergeant."

"Also known as...?"

"As what, Sergeant?"

"Also known as lunchtime. It's lunchtime. Where do you expect people to be at lunchtime? They're on their break, McLusky. Stop your infernal yapping. Emperor's anus." Sergeant Russell touched his ear. "Who? An inspection? We look good, sir. Send 'em down." He turned around. "Listen up. Senior officers of some sort are coming by for an inspection. Look smart. Stand up straight."

A crowd of farm workers surged into the departures area. Most were carrying shopping bags from stores in town. They slowed and looked at the Militia squad as they passed.

"Look at them. Just eat, sleep, and screw. Spend their stipends on ridiculous stuff. Look at that guy." McLusky pointed at a man wearing a shiny new suit. "They just come in here and waste their money."

"You are just jealous 'cause he looks sharp in that suit. You wouldn't look nearly as good as him in that," the shortest trooper said from behind him.

"That's my tax dollars at work, Shorty." McLusky said.

"You get paid by tax dollars, Tex," Shorty said. "You're a drain on the economy now, not a productive worker."

"I mean before. Before, when I worked for GG, all the taxes I paid went toward that guy's suit."

"You loaded potatoes on the night shift," Shorty said. "Casual labor. All the taxes you paid on that might buy him an old pair of socks. This Militia gig is the best job you ever had."

"That's not the point. I worked hard."

"Yeah, one day a week."

"I work hard. I'm twice the man any of you guys are. Twice the man."

"That's what your mom said," the other trooper said.

McLusky turned toward the crowd, pulling his gun partway out of his holster. "Just look at them, the lazy good-for-nothings. Things will be different now." He pulled the gun all the way out, but didn't point it at anyone. "I'm glad it's finally coming to a head. Things will be different now."

"McLusky," Sergeant Russell said.

"Sergeant?"

"I see your revolver is in your hand. Your revolver should be in your holster, not your hand."

"Yes, Sergeant. Sorry, Sergeant," McLusky said, putting the revolver back.

"If I find it in your hand again without my permission, I will take it and put it somewhere else. You will not like where I will put it."

"That's what his mom said," said Shorty.

"Enough of that," Sergeant Russell said. "Everybody relax and smile. We are just securing the station against potential issues. No gunplay."

"Sergeant, why are we here?" Shorty asked.

"I don't need to know, and if I don't need to know, you certainly don't."

"Yes, Sergeant. My cousin says there is rioting in some of the neighborhoods. Fires and such."

"I don't know anything about that. We're just here to secure the station."

"Heads up, Sergeant," Shorty said. "Seniors approaching."

Two men in Militia uniforms strode over to the squad.

Sergeant Russell called the recruits to attention. "Commander. Schloss. A surprise to see you here." He saluted.

Commander Roi's bodyguard, Schloss, nodded at Sergeant Russell but kept his hands on his shotgun, clasped to his chest. "Sergeant Schloss," he corrected Sergeant Russell.

Sergeant Russell glared at Schloss for a moment, then nodded. "Sergeant Schloss."

"It's nice to get out of the office from time to time. How are things?" Commander Roi asked.

"Completely quiet, sir. No change at all. It's like nothing is happening."

"Well, nothing is happening, really. We've secured most of the city without incident. We're in charge now."

"'Most' of the city, sir?"

"There have been a few areas with some noise. Nothing to concern yourself with."

"Of course, sir," Sergeant Russell said. "Is there something special I can help you with?"

"No. I'm just waiting for the eastern express to come in. GG is sending some of their security forces to help us out."

"GG is sending troops, sir?"

"Corporate security, Sergeant. They are coming in to help us out."

"We don't need any help from anybody's corporate security, Commander. Especially not GG's," Sergeant Russell said.

"The Officers' Council says otherwise, Sergeant. I have the orders right here." Commander Roi tapped his comm. "We wait for them, greet them, and they will be assigned to security duties in several areas. The station will be one of them."

"As you say, sir."

They all stood and watched the crowd surge around them. People were giving them looks. There was a sudden, muffled boom, and the ground shook. The crowds halted, and people stared around.

Another boom. The crowd started to speed up.

Sergeant Russell unbuckled his holster flap. "Is that something that we should concern ourselves with, Commander?"

"I'll see what's going on," Commander Roi muttered, pulling out his comm.

The crowd edged around them. Some pointed at the Militia crew and got on their comms, and others moved outside. Still another group rushed into the station, some wiping dust from their clothes. Something smelled burnt.

"Main comms aren't working," Commander Roi announced. "I'm switching to backup."

Sergeant Russell checked his own comm unit and

nodded. "Shorty, go out front and report where that smoke is coming from."

"Terrorists," McLusky said.

"Shut up, McLusky," Sergeant Russell said. "Shorty, don't run, but go quick."

Shorty nodded and trotted toward the doors. He had to push his way out through the crowds.

"Orders, Commander?" Sergeant Russell asked.

"I need to talk to the Officers' Council," Commander Roi said, playing with his comm. "Stand by."

Sergeant Russell gave him a look, then turned to watch the door. Shorty reappeared with a different Militia recruit in tow.

"Shorty?" Sergeant Russell said.

"Smoke from over by the shuttle dock, Sergeant. Could be coming from the H tanks."

"Who are you?" Sergeant Russell asked the second trooper.

"Owens, sir. Comms are down. The Lieutenant Shutt sent me. She says to collect your squad and reinforce her over by the bank."

"Commander?"

"I'm busy, Sergeant," Commander Roi said.

"Lieutenant says to collect the squad and head over to the bank," Sergeant Russell said.

"Not now, Sergeant. Stay here."

"Yes, sir." Sergeant Russell waited. "....And?"

"What, Sergeant?"

"Any other orders, sir?"

"Keep the station secure while I sort this out."

Sergeant Russell was about to say something, but then clamped his mouth shut and turned to Owens.

"You go back to the Lieutenant Shutt and tell her we're not coming. Commander's orders," he told the recruit. "Shorty, find the rest of the squad. They should be outside the side entrance. Bring them all here. If you see any friendlies, bring them as well."

"Friendlies, sir?"

"People dressed like you, Shorty. People dressed like you."

"Yes, Sergeant." Shorty sped off.

The crowd surged back and forth. A large group appeared to be pushing out of the station away from the platform, starting to brush against the squad.

"Shock sticks out," Sergeant Russell ordered. "Clear a space for Commander Roi." He stepped up next to him. "Sir, we should move out of the foyer. We're just in the way."

"We need to be visible, Sergeant."

"Lots of ways to be visible, sir."

The shock sticks held the nearer crowd away, but the burning smell had intensified, and even more people were pushing their way into the station. The recruits were caught in the middle. Near the door, shouting started up.

Another Militia squad was pushing their way through the crowd, swinging their shock sticks, but without the power on. That made them just clubs, but they were effective enough.

Lieutenant Shutt arrived. "Bad time to not follow orders, Sergeant," she said.

Sergeant Russell jerked his head toward Commander Roi.

"Oh, didn't see you there, sir." She saluted. "Till the Emperor returns."

"The Emperor," Commander Roi agreed.

"My comms are out, sir. What's going on?"

"I'm waiting to hear from the Officers' Council."

"Yes, sir," Lieutenant Shutt said. "Should we perhaps move somewhere else? Somewhere more secure?"

"I have to greet the arriving GG security."

"Of course, sir," Lieutenant Shutt said. A screen flashed above their heads, letting them know the eastern express was arriving. "Here they come now, sir."

Both Lieutenant Shutt's and Commander Roi's tablets

emitted a loud bong.

"The low-bandwidth secure comms are working now," Commander Roi said. "Orders from the Officers' Council. Highest encryption. That will take a few minutes to chew through. Let's go meet our new friends."

Sergeant Russell began to issue orders. The troopers used their sticks to push through the crowd. Midway, they met Shorty returning with the rest of the squad and a few others they had picked up along the way.

Altogether, almost two dozen Militia surged onto the platform. They shooed the waiting crowds away, clearing the platform until only Militia stood there. Sergeant Russell lined them up about down the length of the platform, and Lieutenant Shutt stepped up behind Commander Roi.

"Can you share your orders from the Officers' Council, Lieutenant?" Sergeant Russell asked.

"Not yet, Sergeant. The encryption is pretty strong. Takes a while to work out."

They stood waiting. The monorail coasted to a stop, and the doors opened. Nobody got out for a moment, but then a single figure walked off the train. Commander Roi stepped forward to greet him.

Lieutenant Shutt's comm bonged. "Done," she said. "Let's see what's going on." She pulled up the message. Sergeant Russell glanced at her as Commander Roi greeted the stranger.

"Welcome to Landing. I am Commander Roi."

"Thank you. I am Don Mendoza. You've brought a lot of troops to greet us."

"Yes, well, we were told to give you a warm welcome."

"I see."

"I understand you are to take over security for the station. How many security guards have you brought?" Commander Roi asked.

"A number adequate to guard a station, I think," Don Mendoza said.

Commander Roi looked down the length of the train.

Nobody had yet exited.

"Of course," Commander Roi said. "You have weapons, should the need arise?"

"I think we have enough, yes."

"Are your troops going to disembark?"

"Shortly. We just wanted to make sure you were ready to receive us. We wanted no misunderstandings."

Commander Roi peered down the length of the train. The doors were open, and he could see inside most of the compartments. There appeared to be security in every one. "There seem to be a lot of you. How many did you bring?"

Lieutenant Shutt gripped Sergeant Russell's shoulder and shoved the comm unit in front of him. He looked at her face, then down. It was a standard electronic order. The icon for a secured communication flashed, as did the authentication code.

The message was short.

GG planning counter coup. Treat all GG security forces as hostile. Over one hundred on eastern express. Use force to keep them out of town.

"Enough for the job," Don Mendoza said, reaching for his holster.

"Militia, draw weapons." Sergeant Russell pulled his gun and pointed it at Don Mendoza. "They're here to fight. Disarm them. Shoot them if they resist."

"Sergeant, what are you doing?" Commander Roi said.

"New orders from the Officers' Council, sir," Sergeant Russell said.

Don Mendoza didn't look bothered. "There are several hundred of us, and perhaps twenty of you. We are the ones who will be doing the disarming. Throw down your weapons. You have no chance." He turned to the train. "Send them out now, Manuel."

The troops began to jump out.

McLusky fired first.

Then gunfire surrounded them.

Chapter 16

"Get out of my way," the Free Trader said as he shoved Jose aside.

Jose stumbled and put a hand on the wall.

"Watch yourself," the security man next to Jose warned the Free Trader. "Push us again, and I'll push back."

The merchant stopped, turned around, and held his fist up. "You want some of this?"

"Sure." The security man flipped the shock stick out of his belt and held it up. "Let's go."

The Free Trader glared, made a rude gesture, then turned around and kept moving.

"Imperial turd," the security man said under his breath. "You okay, Jose?"

"I'm well, thank you, sir." Jose was polite—the security man was a vice president.

"You shouldn't let people push you around like that. Dashi wouldn't have."

"Thank you, Mr. Rajput," Jose said, "but it's not important right now. We need to finish our business here and get to the meeting."

"What business do we have here?" Rajput asked.

"I need some messages hand-carried to various places," Jose said.

Another Free Trader approached them. "I'm Winn, master of the Danube. You have some chips for me?"

Jose nodded and handed them to him. "One message, one credit chip. Any change in your itinerary?"

"None. My cousin will be here in five minutes."

"Master of the Rio Plata?" Jose asked.

"The same. Free trades." The trader strode off.

Another group of Free Traders rattled past them. They were moving fast and heavily laden with boxes and bags.

"What's going on?" Rajput asked. "Why are the Free Traders spooked?"

Jose pulled out his comm and played with it. "Lots of activity on the Free Trader bands, and lots of requests for Free Traders to drop. I wonder how they found out so fast."

"Found what out?"

"Let's get to the meeting." Jose started walking.

"Found what out?" Rajput repeated.

A board meeting was in progress when Jose and Rajput arrived. Four members of the TGI board were questioning a VP of maintenance.

"How many people could get killed?" the acting chairman asked.

"From the bombardment, the explosions, or the decompression?" the VP asked.

"Do we get to choose?" the chairman said.

"Everybody on the station. The Militia could send fifty ships."

"That will kill everybody on the station."

"It could happen," the VP said. He began to lay out a series of scenarios involving lasers targeting the power plant, rail guns firing shots into the station, and teams of Militia boarding parties rampaging down the corridors.

The assembled group of TGI executives looked horrified. Scared.

Jose let them talk for a while. *What would Dashi do at a time like this?* he thought. He pondered that while the debate raged back and forth. *Wait, listen, learn, think, then speak. That's what Dashi would do.*

Eventually the room fell silent, and he saw his chance.

"No," Jose said. Everyone turned to him. "None of this is going to happen."

"You are Dashi's assistant, aren't you?" the vice president said.

"Yes, sir, I am," Jose said.

"Sorry about that. He was a good man."

"He's only missing, sir, not confirmed dead."

"Yes, but after that explosion, and the bodies they found...."

Jose just gave them his best Dashi smile and turned to the head of the table. "Mr. Chairman, may I have the floor?"

"Why?" the chairman asked.

"I have a few points to make."

"I think those were rather convincing statements by Mr. Rustigo. Do you disagree?"

"I do." Jose said.

The silence stretched.

"With which statement do you disagree?"

"The entirety of them. I think they are somewhat fantastical, and of unlikely probability," Jose said.

"Well, you sound like Dashi, anyway," muttered a member of the board.

"Explain," the acting chairman said.

"Let me take them in order. First, they won't send fifty ships. They don't have fifty ships available."

"How many do they have?" the security man asked.

"They have a hundred, or close to it."

There was a murmur from the crowd. They fell silent as the chairman glared at them.

"So they will send more?" the chairman asked.

"No. Only two-thirds of their ships have working drives. The rest are parked. Only two-thirds of those ships have working weapons, so they can't bombard anything. Only two-thirds of those have working fusion reactors that can power weapons, engines, and life support at the same time. They also only have enough crew to man two-thirds of the remaining ships."

"So, that's two-thirds of a hundred."

"No. They are not all the same ships. It's more like two-thirds times two-thirds, times-two thirds again, times two-thirds. "

Jose sat and waited while the board of directors tried to do the math.

"Sixteen eighty-firsts—less than two-ninths," one of the sharper vice presidents said.

"Yes. Then there is an issue with the crew. There aren't that many career Militia out there. Most do a one- to four-year stint and then call it good. Many on the crews will be from a station, or have family and friends on a station. Not all of the career people are behind this Empire Rising group. Enough don't care for this so-called Officers' Council that they will restrict the group's flexibility. Plus the training issue—they are perennially understaffed."

"How many?" the chairman said.

"They can crew about eight armed ships with loyalists. Perhaps a hundred armed crew, if they stuff them full. They have to keep some ships back to protect the shuttles and their air gates. They can keep some of their second-line ships near the smaller stations. The threat will keep them in line."

"What about the bombardment, explosions, and decompression?" the security man asked.

"There won't be any bombardment. This station is too valuable for them. Several members of their Officers' Council have argued during Council meetings that excessive damage to the station would amount to destruction of Imperial equipment, and that would be against their oath to the Empire. So no bombardment, and no explosions."

"How do you know this? What they say in their Council meetings," one of the board asked.

Jose simply gave his best Dashi smile.

"You have someone on the Council," the chairman said. "Dashi put one of his people in there." He peered closer at Jose's smile. "At least one."

"I have it on good authority that there will be no bombardment. If one of the ships goes rogue and fires on the station, at least one other ship will fire on them."

The board of directors looked at each other.

The chairman spoke again. "No bombardment and no

explosions, but you didn't mention decompression."

Jose grimaced. "The plan is to put armed teams in suits onboard. They are willing to selectively decompress sections of the station to gain access to the control rooms and fusion engineering stations."

"How can we stop them?" the vice chairman asked.

"We can't," Jose said. "We have no external defenses. They will inevitably gain access to the station because we can't stop them outside. Once inside, we can fight them with small arms if we wish, but we will be outnumbered, and we'll have only revolvers and some shotguns."

"At least they don't have any heavy weapons," the security man said. "There is only one printer on Delta that can print weapons, and it's never done mortars, or any sort of crew-served weapons."

Jose coughed.

"Yes, Mr. Jose?" said the security man. "You have something to add?"

"Sir, there have been some incidents in Landing. It appears that the Militia has seized control of the monorail station, fusion power station, and several corporate headquarters."

"Is this a coup?" the chairman asked.

"I think it's more of a putsch, technically," Jose said.

"How can it be a coup if they aren't taking over the shuttle?" a member of the board asked.

"The already run the shuttle, idiot," the chairman said.

"Well, yes, but, at least there is no fighting there."

Jose coughed again.

"Yes?" the chairman said.

"There is further information. There appears to be fighting going on near the shuttle port and the monorail station as well."

"Who's fighting?"

"It appears that GG is launching a counter coup," Jose said. "They have shipped troops into town. Fighting between the two has occurred."

"So they will be too busy fighting each other to fight us?" the chairman asked.

"No, sir. I have reports that there are Militia naval units on the way to us right now."

"They are on the way already?"

"Yes," Jose said.

"Can we stop them?"

"No, sir. We don't have any weapons that will stop them boarding us."

The members of the board looked at each other.

"Right. We have to evacuate," the chairman said.

"We lack the facilities to evacuate all of our staff and their families," Rajput, vice president of security, said.

"You aren't going anywhere. You signed up for station defense, so defend the station. I'm getting on a ship and getting out of here," the chairman said. He stood up.

"Sir," Jose said, "I understand Mr. Rajput will be in charge of the security forces, but as Mr. Dashi's deputy, I have some other operatives, and since I have a better feel for the political situation, I believe that while he remains in tactical control, I should have strategic oversight. I also have some other ideas—"

"Rajput. Defend the station. Resist," the chairman said.

"Resist who?" Rajput said.

"Anybody. Everybody. Jose will tell you who. He's in charge till the shooting starts. Then it's you."

Rajput looked at Jose. "Great."

Jose bent to his tablet and began to type quickly. "Sir, I will need some codes, and some additional authority. If you could check your mail right now...."

The chairman glanced at his tablet. "What do you want control of the operations and maintenance budget for? Authority to override HR and change job titles...? Fine." He tapped several screens and pressed his thumb against another. "Done. Good luck, you two."

The chairman strode from the room. The other board members had already gone.

Rajput looked at Jose. "Do you have a plan?"

"Always," Jose said. "I have to get some people moving and send a few messages. Then I have to ship a container of medical supplies to the Outer Rim, and we need to buy some things."

"A force of peeved and possibly insane Militia troops are collecting to attack us, and you want to go shopping?"

Jose looked up and nodded. "Yes. Shopping can be very therapeutic."

Chapter 17

"Well, that was an Empire-dammed fiasco," Sergeant Russell said. Broken glass crunched underfoot as they walked down the alley, away from the train station.

"Could have been worse, Sergeant," the corporal said.

"How, exactly?" Sergeant Russell stopped at a group of people bending over a wounded Militia man. "McLusky, how badly are you hurt?"

"Bad, Sergeant. They got me. I might not make it," McLusky said. He was lying on the ground, half his face covered in blood.

Sergeant Russell looked at the medic applying a sticky bandage. "Well? How bad is it?"

"Superficial. Lots of blood, but a big scratch, really. Give this bandage about ten minutes and he can go back to work," the medic said, "but he does whine a lot."

Sergeant Russell glared at McLusky, who gave him a weak smile. "It hurts, Sergeant."

Sergeant Russell leaned over, grabbed McLusky by the collar, and hauled him high enough that his legs dangled in the air. "I'm sure, but what I'll do will hurt even more. Go back to the barricade."

Sergeant Russell dropped him. After some crawling around, McLusky stood up and trotted to the end of the alley, where group of Militia with drawn revolvers stood behind a makeshift barricade.

"McLusky?" Sergeant Russell yelled after him.

"Yes, Sergeant?"

"How many reloads do you have left?"

McLusky reached into a pouch on his belt and counted. "Seven, Sergeant."

"Give 'em here," Sergeant Russell said, holding out his hand.

McLusky trotted back and poured the loose bullets into Sergeant Russell's hand, then headed for the barricade again.

"We only issue them in multiples of six. How did he manage to end up with seven?" Sergeant Russell wondered aloud.

"He dropped five reloading," the corporal said.

"At least five," Sergeant Russell said. "Shorty, how are you doing?"

The recruit had his arm in a cast and was sitting on the ground. "Shotgun slug broke my arm, Sergeant. They put on one of those quick foam things and gave me something, so I don't feel it. I can work."

"At least it's your left arm. You can still shoot."

Shorty frowned.

"Don't tell me you're left-handed?"

Shorty nodded. He awkwardly pulled his revolver from his holster and offered it to Sergeant Russell.

The sergeant waved it off. "Keep it. Give me your reloads."

Shorty counted twelve bullets into Sergeant Russell's hand, and they moved off. Sergeant Russell stopped twice more to collect bullets from seated troops.

The corporal cleared his throat. "When can we expect ammunition resupply, Sergeant?"

"I'm going to HQ to find out." Sergeant Russell walked down to a crossroads and stopped at another barricade. "Well?" he said to the two Militia men guarding it.

"They are a long way down the road. Couple hundred meters. We stick out heads out every so often. At first they fired a few shots, but nothing came close. They hit the other side of the street once. If you dash across, you'll be fine."

Sergeant Russell turned to the corporal. "You're in charge. The Empire will return."

"The Empire," the three said, saluting.

The dash across the road was uneventful, and it was only a fifteen-minute walk to Militia HQ. Sergeant Russell's uniform gained him entrance into the foyer. The shotgun-wielding guards didn't even challenge him.

He greeted Lieutenant Shutt behind the counter. "Good to see you mobile, ma'am. That was a nasty shot."

"Not exactly mobile, Sergeant," she said, pointing to her legs. One was in a cast, and a cane was leaning next to her chair.

"Huh. Sorry about that. How long?"

"Weeks, the docs say. Lots of bruising."

"That's too bad. Ma'am, when can I expect ammunition resupply?"

"Never."

Sergeant Russell said nothing.

"Will there be anything else, Sergeant?" she asked.

The sergeant looked left and right, scanning the room. "I don't see the Council members, ma'am."

"Meeting," she said, her expression unchanging.

Sergeant Russell turned around and checked behind him, but didn't see anybody watching them. He leaned over the counter and lowered his voice. "Clarisse. Emperor's anus. We need more ammo. I've got them bottled up at the monorail station, mostly, and we've got six of the seven roads blocked or watched, but I've only got about twenty rounds per gun, and that's only counting the thirty right on the barricades. I've got maybe a hundred others who have fully loaded revolvers, but no reloads. We need more ammo."

"We don't have any," she told him, "at least not regular ammunition."

"How can we not have any?"

"Nobody counted. They figured this would be quick. We intimidate everybody, fire a few rounds into a few ceilings, and we're done. So we didn't do an inventory."

"I thought we had a bunch at the armory."

"There was supposed to be, but they weren't there. I think Edmunds swiped them and hid them somewhere. Besides, three-quarters were frangible, for the ships. That's what got me." She tapped her leg. "The Growers have the same problem, we think. A lot of our casualties are like this—bones, or just major bruising. The rest of the supply has been depleted over time. Every recruit would shoot twenty-four or so. That adds up."

"So how much do we have?"

"Less than ten thousand."

"So give it to me."

"A hundred people, a hundred rounds each. Do the math. We can't give your folks all of it. We'll need some in reserve. Most of them can't even shoot."

"Can't argue with that," Sergeant Russell said, "but can't we make more? What about the printers?"

"We've got exactly one printer that will handle bullet-making, and it's slow. Actually, from what I've heard, we can make a revolver faster than we can make ten bullets."

"I don't need any more revolvers."

"Are they pushing you? The Growers, I mean?"

"No. We've blocked them off at the station. They're staying put. No change for the last few hours."

"Good. I've got another job for you," Lieutenant Shutt said.

"Do I get bullets?"

"Nope."

Sergeant Russell closed his eyes and rubbed his forehead. "What, then?"

"Crowd control. There are groups wandering around the city, taking advantage of things—beating up citizens, looting, starting fires. Go stop them."

"With what?"

"Take about thirty of those people who can't shoot. Give 'em shock sticks, or just batons, and tell them what Imperial losers they are. Then send 'em out to break heads."

"I want to leave now. We'll take what you want, and where you want, but it will be expensive to wait," the Free Trader captain said.

"How expensive?" Jose asked.

"What are we carrying?"

"One self-contained container with full life support, two containers of mixed goods, one container of medical supplies, and five crew."

"Five crew?"

"Three doctors, and two nurses. The doctors are a specialist surgeon, an anesthesiologist, and a neuro specialist. The nurses are nurse practitioners. They can apply drugs, act as midwifes—all sorts of things. There are various scanners in both containers, but I'm not sure what. Whatever the medics wanted. They are authorized to fix you up with anything medical you need on the trip."

"Where to?"

"Here." Jose produced a course chip.

The Free Trader examined it. "All the way out there?"

"It is."

"So...I just take them out there? That's all?"

"They need access to both medical containers full-time during the trip, and you have to supply power to both containers full-time."

"That's hard."

"Yes. That's why I'm paying so much."

"How much?" the captain asked.

Jose named a sum.

The captain was impressed. He might make that much in a full year. If he was lucky. "I just drop them off?"

"There is a contact protocol on the chip. Just dock, and you'll be approached."

The Free Trader captain thought for only a second. "Done. Half now, half on delivery. When can you get them here? As soon as the money reaches my accounts, I'll drop." He paused. "I can't get everything together right away. The medical stuff first—that will take you several hours to set up, at least. The two mixed containers will take longer, probably a shift and a half."

Jose reached into his pocket and handed a chip over.

"Here's the money. The crew will be here in fifteen minutes. The containers are attached on the break-bulk deck. You'll have to collect them next."

The Free Trader looked at Jose. "You don't look like much of a tough guy. What's to stop me just going now, without them, or not waiting for the containers, just taking the money and going? What are you going to do if I do that?"

"Nothing." Jose smiled. "It's a lot of money, isn't it?"

"It is," the captain admitted.

"I have a large budget. If you let me down on this, I'll just put double that amount out. As a reward. For your head—and your crew's heads. I won't even care whether they are still attached to your bodies. You're right. I'm not tough. I'm not rich, either—but I'm employed by rich people, and I can pay tough people. Lots of them."

The captain nodded once, then picked up his comm. "Jersey?"

"Yeah, Cap?" a voice said.

"Get Salvo to clean up five staterooms and put some food in them. Then prepare for two containers. Full power hookups. We'll be in a hurry, so I'll drive. You and everybody else will be outside. Hook them in as fast as possible."

"Even young Bobber? He's pretty useless, Cap."

"He can haul a chain. We can't afford to mess this up," the captain said.

Jose nodded once and strode away.

Jose's outer office was packed. There were probably twenty people there, and a bunch of strange equipment.

"Listen up," Jose said. "I'm Mr. Jose, your new employer. Anyone who is answering the welding ad, wait out in the corridor with your gear. Anybody who is an electrician, hang out here for a few minutes. I'll be right with you."

"I'm a master welder, but I don't have any welding

equipment," one man said. He wore a full hard suit with distinctive yellow and blue striped collar tabs. "It's down on the surface."

"I pay double for people with equipment," Jose said. "Um, it doesn't have to be your own equipment, just as long as you are authorized to have it. You got a brother, or a coworker who's on vacation? Maybe you can borrow their gear and bring it here."

"I got my own gear, but there's three sets back at my office and nobody to use them," a woman said. "I'll rent them to anybody who needs a set."

Jose looked at the woman. "If you still have any left after you've rented them out, bring the extra gear. I'll pay a 50 percent bonus for every extra set of welding gear you bring in, even if there is nobody with it."

"I hear the Militia are coming," the woman said.

"That's true."

"They are going to take the station over from TGI."

"That's possibly true. We will resist, of course," Jose said.

"I ain't resisting. I don't work for TGI. I'm not going to get shot by some Militia fanatic for you."

"It won't come to that. In fact, I'm going to broadcast a station-wide announcement shortly that people should stay in their rooms, with adequate supplies of food and water, for at least thirty days."

"Thirty days?"

"Yes. We have plenty of food, and I'm authorized to give it away for free. If everyone stays hooked up in their rooms, there won't be any casualties."

"If I bring that welding gear in, who's going to use it?" she asked.

"That's my worry, ma'am, not yours—but if you like money, I've got some, and I need some welding done."

The woman nodded and huddled up with several other welders.

Jose looked around the group again. "Now, which one

of you is the liquid nitrogen salesman?"

When Jose finished with the nitrogen salesman and closed the door to his inner office, it was even more crowded. There was Rajput, the security man, and his deputy, Sundarampli, plus the detective Alvagado and his assistant, a woman named, of all things, Smith.

"'Smith'? Couldn't you have found a better fake name?" Jose asked.

"It's my real name," she said.

"Nobody is going to believe that," Jose said.

"Who cares what they believe? I'm Janet Smith from Landing, seventh-generation dirtsider."

"They'll spend all this time hunting for your real family."

"My parents are dead, and I have no other family. It's just me."

"All of your opposition will knock themselves out trying to find out the truth behind that," Jose said.

"I know. It's wonderful, isn't it?"

Jose shook his head. "Right. To business."

Rajput and Sundarampli looked at each other, and Rajput cleared his throat. "How are we going to defend this station from the Militia, the rebels? Keep them off?"

"I don't think we can," Jose said.

"Explain," Rajput said.

Jose did. In detail. The security forces were small. They were not well armed, mostly just shock sticks. There were so many vulnerable areas. The fusion reactor. The operations center. Life support, but at least there were multiple backups of those. Fighting could harm civilians.

"So why are we here, then?" Rajput asked.

"I'm going to be taking some defensive measures that will give the Militia pause without endangering anybody. I'm also arranging the removal of some critical supplies to secure areas."

"You are running with the gold reserves?" Smith asked.

"Nope. I will be here, at my desk, until the very end. However, I'll need your staff to help coordinate the defense operation."

"Coordinate what?" Rajput asked.

"Stand behind some people and make them do their jobs."

"And shoot them if they don't?"

"No. A blast with a shock stick should do it. Truthfully, I think most of them will find it funny. I foresee almost no problems."

"And you'll be here at your desk?"

"I'll be sitting here in my office until the Militia comes through that door."

"What do we need to do?" Rajput asked.

Several hours later, Jose sat down at his desk with a cup of basic. He was exhausted, having been speaking to large groups for a long time. Still, there was so much left to do.

He checked the station's orbit. They were just coming within voice range of Landing and would remain so for several hours as they passed overhead. For a time there would be a delay in speech response of up to a few hundred milliseconds, but it was manageable.

He made several calls, each to different commercial entities on the surface. After the initial greetings, they switched to either code phrases or further encryption. There was no way to hide who he was talking to, but he did want some confusion as to the contents of his conversations.

Most of the conversations were companies allied to TGI, who wanted reassurance that TGI would be able to protect them, more money for goods ordered, or, in several cases, to express polite refusal to live up to previous contracts.

"I'm really sorry to say no, Jose," the manager of a glass factory said. "We've done business for a long time, but I'm family-run, and I don't want to get any of my people killed in some dispute between the intergalactic order of boardroom weasels."

"You're saying I'm a weasel?"

"That remains to be seen. You have treated me well so far, but the situation down here is bad. These guys are definitely weasels."

"How bad is it, really? Have many been killed?"

"There was a lot of activity at the monorail station. Shooting. I've heard of deaths and a lot of injuries."

"Whose deaths and injuries? Militia? GG?"

"Both. They shot it out when a trainload of GG goons came into town to help the Militia goons."

"Who won?"

"Neither, I think. The train station is blocked off. You can't get near it. There are Militia-manned roadblocks all around it."

"So the Militia has the station, then?"

"Nope. I've got commo with a few people down that way. GG is defending the station and a few buildings around it, and the Militia has retreated out of weapons' range. The two are kind of leaving things alone. Not bothering each other."

"So who is fighting who?"

"It's a stalemate down there, but there's a lot of unrest. Lots of kids—the ones without jobs—they took advantage of the noise to, well, act out. Smashed windows. Set fires. Stole stuff. Settled old scores, I guess. There were rampaging mobs last night. The Militia has been involved in taking care of that. They shocked some people and arrested others. Everybody is staying home from work, just waiting it out."

A non-ferrous metals broker was even more specific. "I got a cousin in the Militia. They had some sort of split with GG—GG would get half the town or something, and the Militia the other half. They were initially told that GG was sending troops into town as their friends, then they got a priority call that GG was coming in to take over."

"Take over?" Jose asked.

"Counter-coup. GG was double-crossing them, going to take everything for themselves. He got a comm right as the train was arriving. Told him to hustle down to the train station and shoot it out. GG brought in way more guns than the Militia expected, and it was touch and go, so they pulled all the Militia gunmen from the rest of town to hold the line. There was a lot of shooting."

"What about the fires and such?"

"That started small. Right at the beginning there were only one or two, but then they had to pull all their people down to fight off GG. That left the rest of the city uncovered, and the mobs just ran wild the whole night. Today, though, they pulled a lot of guys off their barricades and gave them shock sticks, and they went down and broke heads. The mobs won't stand up to discipline. Funny thing, though."

"What?"

"Only shock sticks. No handguns or shotguns or any type of weapons," he said. "Just shock stuff."

"Maybe they don't want to hurt the crowds."

"Maybe, but they did let my cousin keep his gun, and made him give up any ammo he had. Oh, and another problem."

"What?"

"The Militia has pulled about three or four ship crews out of the line. They're on their way up to the shuttle. Going to crew some ships."

Jose took a break from his calls to eat a tray and drink some more basic. He checked his orbit, then called a clothing wholesaler, switching to an encrypted channel to discuss delivery.

"We're encrypted now?" Jose asked.

"Yes. Should I put him through?" the clothing merchant asked.

"Yes. It's probably best for you if you don't hear this conversation."

"Don't worry. I want nothing to do with this. Stand by." The line went silent for a moment, and then a new voice came on.

"Yes?" This voice was higher-pitched than Jose had expected, and sounded lazy. It was a young man's voice.

"Don Pedro?" Jose asked.

"Julio. Hello, Jose."

"Hello, sir."

"How is my favorite cousin?" DJ asked.

"I am well, sir—and only a second cousin, once removed."

"Still family. Say, I see Morena from time to time. You remember Morena, don't you?"

Jose gritted his teeth. "How is she, sir?"

"Oh, she's well. I keep her well. You know what I mean."

Jose gritted his teeth harder and closed his eyes. "How goes the plan, sir?"

"We are...proceeding...here."

"You are in possession of the city of Landing, then?" Jose asked.

DJ laughed. "Mr. Jose, I know all about your spy ring. Don't pretend you don't know we're just around the monorail station."

"You said your surprise attack would defeat the Militia."

"It would have, if we'd had time to move out and position ourselves. Instead, they were waiting for us at the train station."

"They fired as you came in?" Jose asked.

"No, they didn't. They let us get most of our people off. It's a good thing, too, or they could have killed all of us. As it is, we managed to push out into the city, but they pushed back," DJ said.

"So what's happening now?" Jose asked.

"Not much. We tried pushing out. We'd have some success, then they would push us back. Ammunition is the limiting factor right now."

"How so?"

"We underestimated how much we would use. We gave most of our men fifty rounds. They went through that in about ten minutes. Now we're being stingy with reloads."

"We had an agreement," Jose said. "Once you captured the city of Landing, we would declare for you."

"I remember our agreement, but we've had difficulties. I do notice that you have taken advantage of our inattention to seize the western monorail line."

"We told you we would proceed as far east as we could. We're blocked at that pass. There is a train parked there, and we can't get around it."

"I know. We'll worry about our train agreements later."

"Unless you keep up the pressure, the Militia will be able to withdraw some of their people and begin seizing the orbital stations. We don't have any defenses against that."

"We'll do what we can. We're collecting more weapons and ammunition right now."

"Where from?" Jose asked.

"We're negotiating with a third party," DJ told him, "or a fourth party, I guess, who claims to have several containers of revolvers and sufficient ammunition."

"I see. You should take special care to see that those negotiations are closely held."

"Why do you say that?"

"Well, when you arrived in Landing...." Jose trailed off.

"Yes?"

"The Militia were waiting for you, weren't they?"

"Yes," DJ said. "So?"

"How did they know what you were going to do?"

DJ did not answer.

"You understand what I'm saying, DJ," Jose continued. "Somebody told them. One of your people sold you out."

"That possibility has occurred to us. We're looking into it right now."

"Don't take too long."

"Oh, don't worry," DJ said. "Our methods produce results—and soon."

After DJ hung up, Jose returned to his desk and worked for several hours, sending and receiving a large number of encoded messages. All his corporate partners got at least one, and quite a few agents got specific instructions.

Jake Stewart, for one, got a lengthy message, sent to his home of record, Rim-37. He would get there eventually.

Mid third shift, Jose heard a special bong on his comm. It was Rajput. "We're just loading the last container now. Once it's loaded, that Free Trader guy will hook it up, and we'll go."

"Good. He stayed behind, then? Didn't ask to leave early?"

"After I put three of my guys on board—on the bridge, engineering, and the galley—the topic never came back up."

"Good. Take as many of those workers with you as want to go."

"About half, I think. Are you sure you don't want to come?"

"My place is here. We have the best commo and banking connections here, and that's how my war goes."

"Let me know if you change your mind," Rajput said.

"Even if I do, there's no second guessing now," Jose said. "I'm staying. You know what the man said."

"What?"

"Let the dice fly high," Jose said.

Chapter 18

"Colonel Savard wishes to address the troops," Commander Roi said as he and Lieutenant Lanny walked down the corridor toward the shuttle launching bay.

"He wants to...what?" the lieutenant said, stopping.

The commander was in the full-dress uniform of the Planetary Militia, all creases and shined boots. Lanny wore the shapeless coverall of the orbital forces, with station slippers and toolbelt. His uniform ran more to oil stains than creases.

"Speak to the troops. Explain our motivations. Inspire them with tales of our glorious future under the reborn Empire."

Lieutenant Lanny stared at him open-mouthed, then nodded. "Inspiration. Empire reborn. Got it." He turned and continued walking.

"You don't agree?" Commander Roi asked.

"Outstanding idea. I'm all in favor of motivation. Lieutenant Motivation, they call me. Looking forward to watching Colonel Savard motivate the crap out of them."

"Colonel Savard is of two minds. Should he appeal foremost to their patriotism as soldiers of the reborn Empire, or should he discuss the perfidiousness of the former corporate government?"

"I wouldn't use the word 'perfidiousness.'"

"Too harsh, do you think?"

"Too many syllables. Especially for the maintenance crews."

"I see. What have you found is the best way to motivate the troops?"

"Smack a couple on the head and threaten to throw them out an airlock without a suit."

"That will motivate them?"

Lieutenant Lanny looked at him again and shook his head. "Probably not."

"What do you suggest, then?" Commander Roi asked.

"Skip the threat part. Just start with the 'out the airlock' part. We're in here." He gestured down a connecting hallway.

Commander Roi examined Lieutenant Lanny's collar flashes. Time-in-service markers lined a full second row. "I see you have a long and storied career in the Militia."

"You could say that."

"I have never met anyone with your level experience, with this combination of awards, and a rank of...." Commander Roi faltered.

"You mean somebody this old who is only a lieutenant? I started as a recruit."

"How long have you been in?"

"Thirty years, next month."

"You must be looking forward to a glorious retirement."

"Glorious indeed," Lieutenant Lanny said. "I have big plans."

"Outstanding. What will you do with your time?"

"Haven't decided, exactly. I'm thinking the last weekend I'm still in, I'll go home, buy a bottle of good whiskey, sit alone in my cube in the dark, clean my service revolver, and contemplate life under the glorious new Imperial regime."

Lieutenant Lanny paused at a door marked *Auditorium*. "Right, let's meet the Militia's finest. Say...." He turned to Commander Roi. "Your boss....He's a ground forces guy."

"Yes."

"Has he had much to do with the orbital forces? Spoken to them before?" Lieutenant Lanny asked.

"He has not had the honor," Commander Roi said.

"Well, watch and learn. Watch and learn."

"We will cleanse this infection from our glorious land. Your ships shall be like the surgeon's scalpel, exorcising the sickness from the corporate tyranny that affects us.

The Empire will be reborn in glory!" Colonel Savard said, finishing his speech. He waved his hands and looked around the packed auditorium.

Nothing happened.

He waved his hands again. "Glory!" he repeated.

Nobody moved. A sergeant in the first row began to clap. He was the only one. He stood up, turned around, and glowered at the room. The crowd immediately began clapping. It went on for perhaps three seconds before fading away.

The sergeant turned around again. The clapping picked back up and continued until the sergeant turned and sat down.

The room fell silent, and Lieutenant Lanny stood up. "Great speech, sir. Thank you for coming to see us."

"It is my pleasure and my honor, Lieutenant," Colonel Savard said. "I will now take questions about our operations and what must be done to remove this cancerous growth that masquerades as a government."

"Sounds like a personal problem to me," a recruit in the first row said, nearly inaudible.

"What was that, Shamus?" Lieutenant Lanny said. "I couldn't hear you."

Shamus coughed and stood up. "Sir, personally, I have no problems at all with this, personally, but I was wondering about the communications plan. How much bandwidth will be available? Will we have extra channels for inter-ship communications between departments, in addition to the command channels, so that we can properly liaise for the duration of these operations?"

Commander Roi leaned over to Lieutenant Lanny. "That is a young man to be watched," he said. "He is thinking ahead."

"He sure is," Lieutenant Lanny said as Colonel Savard began to answer the question. "I forgot the netball quarterfinals are that week, and he runs a book on them. He'll need a lot of bandwidth to take all those bets."

"He takes bets on the secured channels, and the officers know of this and do nothing?"

"No, no. I take it quite seriously."

"Good."

"Yes. I get a full extra point on the odds."

Another recruit stood on the floor. "Sir, I have a question about the command orders."

"Yes?" Colonel Savard said, looking confused.

"You used the word 'affect,' sir. That implies that we are receiving. I would think that is a little disempowering as we're telling our own story, not having it appropriated by others."

Colonel Savard blinked, but didn't answer.

Lieutenant Lanny stood up. "Sit down, Hans. Any other useful questions for Colonel Savard?"

A hand went up in the back.

"Yes, Tobias?" Lieutenant Lanny said.

"Sir, would you say this counts as a class one emergency operation?" Tobias asked.

"As much as anything is an emergency, Tobias," Lieutenant Lanny said.

"But what does Colonel Savard say, sir?"

"Well, of course it is an emergency," Colonel Savard said.

"But are you saying that it is a *class one* emergency operation, Colonel, sir?"

The question was met with creaking and rustling as everybody in the auditorium sat up straighter to focus on Colonel Savard's reply.

Colonel Savard looked sideways at Commander Roi, who only shrugged, confused. "Yes. Yes, that's what I'm saying," Colonel Savard said.

Smiles appeared in the auditorium, and a happy murmur ran through the crowd.

"Could you tell us how long this emergency will last, sir?" Tobias asked.

"Well, until we occupy the major stations, of course. A

few days."

"A few days, sir. Till the end of the month, perhaps?"

"Yesss." Colonel Savard looked sideways.

Lieutenant Lanny had flipped his comm open and was checking something. He looked up and smiled at Commander Roi.

"It will be in effect till we are done," Colonel Savard said. "Until we occupy the stations."

"Perhaps, for the sake of argument, sir, that might take a day or two longer. Would you say this state of emergency be in effect till, say, the second day of next month?"

"At least that long. Perhaps a day or two longer," Colonel Savard said.

The crowd went wild, and everybody stood up to cheer and clap. A chant started up. "Long live the Emperor! Long live the Emperor!"

Commander Roi had to stick his head to Lieutenant Lanny's ear to be heard. "Why are they so happy now? What just happened?"

Lieutenant Lanny spoke into Commander Roi's ear. "We get a monthly bonus if we're on duty for a class one emergency. A small one for a day, a bigger one for four, and a really big one if it lasts longer than seven days. And it's per month of proclamation. It's the total length that matters, not the length in each month, so even a day at the beginning of the month counts for full payment."

"What?"

"Your boss just tripled everyone's pay for the next two months."

Chapter 19

"Empress's hairy anus, what a dump," Nadine said, looking out the viewport at Rim-37, slowly growing as they approached.

"I was born here," Jake said.

"How does that make it less of a dump?"

Jake shrugged. "It doesn't, I guess."

"It looks like it's made up of busted pieces from three or four stations," Nadine said.

"It is, kind of," Jake said. "The main ring on the top—the A ring—that was the original station, back in the Founding. The second ring, the B-ring, was never finished. It's partially filled in with quarters, you see, but the rest is just truss work."

"What's that at the top? That big ship-like thing."

"It was a ship. Now it's just a second fusion plant. The main plant was running down, and now it can't handle the load, so about twenty years ago the station council scavenged that ship. It had a fusion plant but no nozzles, so they converted it to a power source. It's not operating at peak efficiency either."

"Where do we dock?"

"At the bottom."

"Those things that look like random pieces of metal and boxes welded together?"

"That's it. There are three docks, but I've never seen more than two in use at any time. They're empty right now. See the big letter A? Head for that."

Nadine maneuvered the ship down a bit and pointed at the dock. *Give Jake his due*, she thought. His course work up to now had been spot on, and they were gaining on his station ever so slightly. They would almost not need the thrusters to dock.

Jake Stewart had a lot of skills, when he had time to exercise them.

"You call the station and ask for permission," Nadine said.

Jake looked at her blankly. "What?"

"Call station ops and ask for permission."

Jake laughed. "It's the middle of the night. Station ops won't be manned."

Nadine looked at him. "Jake, we're in space. Things go on 24/7."

"Not here, they don't. We don't even power most of the station during third shift. Some critical areas stay up, but all the common areas and work areas are shut at night. Completely during third shift, and they power down a lot of stuff during second shift."

"'Power down'? Get real, Jake. People would freeze."

"The residual heat keeps anything from really freezing, and people generate a lot of heat. It does get cold at night, though. When I had to work second shift at the mill, it was really cold getting back."

"Where's the mill?"

"Over there." Jake pointed at a series of structures attached to an asteroid floating close by. "No gravity to speak of there, but it's good for crushing and doing some basic concentration. See those piles? They do different elements once a week. First they run aluminum through the evaporator for a few days, then once it's full, they run iron, and so on."

"What about the expensive stuff? Gold, platinum, that sort of thing?"

"There are some small, privately owned evaporators. You can pay them. We're almost there."

Nadine returned her attention to the board. She'd docked ships with no help from stations before, or without communications, but never with neither. She spun the ship sideways and docked the dorsal lock with the station, so at least the station's spin would give her a down. The grapples clicked into place, and they had a hard lock.

She got up and popped their airlock. They came up in

the floor of the station lock. Jake slouched over to the lock and pulled the door open. He seemed somehow...diminished.

They stepped through their lock into a dirty holding area and began to walk down the corridor. It was cold, cold enough to see your breath. Nadine shivered. Jake walked up to an office and pulled the door open.

A short, slight man with black hair sat there. He looked up. "Young Mr. Stewart," he said.

"Glen," Jake replied.

"What are you doing gallivanting around this time of night? Shouldn't you be in bed? Why'd you come up here and bother me?"

"I've just docked my ship, Glenn," Jake said.

Glen laughed. "Of course you have." He paused. "Come to think of it, I hear you've been away."

"I have," Jake said.

"Coreward, wasn't it?"

"Yes."

"A few months, I heard," Glenn said.

"Just over four years, actually."

"Is that so?" Glen said. "Seems like a long time to be away. Shouldn't take long to see what you need to see."

Glen turned back to his screen. Jake stood there, nonplussed. A smile began to tug at Nadine's lips.

"I saw your mother the other day," Glen said, not taking his eyes from the screen.

"Is she well?" Jake said.

"Well?" Glen looked at him. "How should I know? I'm not a doctor. She had some tomatoes she'd grown."

"Tomatoes?"

"Aye. Looked good, too. I thought about buying them, but she wanted too much for them. Always the proud one, your mother. Thinking she could grow proper tomatoes."

Nadine's smile became a full-fledged grin.

"I'll ask her about them when I see her," Jake said.

"You do that. Three years in the Core, huh?"

"Yes, Glen. Three years. Have you ever been to the Core?"

"Never saw the need," Glen said.

"You might try it."

"Did they have Rim beer?"

"Rim-brand beer?" Jake asked.

"Yes."

"No," Jake said. "We couldn't get Rim-brand beer there."

"Oh. I wouldn't like the Core, then. Well, off with you, young Mr. Stewart. I have work to do."

Nadine laughed.

Glen looked up. "Who's this, then?"

"Glen, this is Nadine. She's with me."

"On your ship?"

"Yes," Jake said.

Glen looked Nadine over. "She's a skinny one, isn't she? Not much meat on her bones."

Nadine giggled. "You think I'm skinny?"

"Aye," Glen said, "I do. Well, off with the two of you. Jake, do you really have a ship docked there?"

"How else would we have gotten here, Glen?" Jake asked.

"Don't know and don't care."

"It's at Dock Three. How long can I leave it there? It's a big ship."

"Of course it is. Nothing scheduled for another month. You can leave it there that long."

"Thanks," Jake said. "Does Jacqueline still have that company that does those tank repairs? The special fuel tanks?"

"Not anymore. Not enough work. She had to let the others go. She still does repairs, though."

"Too bad. I'm going to comm her anyway."

"Good enough. I'll make a note. Give me your crew list, and I'll count you off."

"Count us off? It's me, Glen. This is a station ship.

You don't have to count us off."

"Well, I guess not, but you've been away a long time. Don't get in any trouble. Having lived here before won't help you."

Jake got them both rooms at some sort of transient hostel near the yard. He apparently wasn't in a hurry to see his family. Nadine got a good night's sleep before meeting him in the morning.

"We'll be safe here for a while," Jake told Nadine. They were in Rim-37's cafe, standing in line for a late breakfast, as Nadine liked to sleep in. "This is a quiet place to rest and refit for a bit."

"You mean it's a dump at the end of the road that is so boring that nobody will ever think of looking for us here. What is that smell?"

"Vinegar. We use it to clean things, and put it on food."

"That's disgusting."

"It's cheap and easy to make," Jake said.

They reached the front of the line.

"What have you got for breakfast?" Nadine asked.

"Red-green-blue tray," the lady behind the counter said, sliding a tray across the counter.

"What else?" Nadine asked.

"'What else' what?"

"What else to eat?"

"That's it. Why would we have something else?"

Jake intervened. "Two trays, please. How much for basic?"

"Three credits. That comes with as many basic refills as you want, till you leave."

Jake collected his tray and went in search of a table. Nadine looked down at hers.

"I hope lunch is better," Nadine said to herself.

"Lunch is the same," the woman said. "Dinner is the same. Every day. We go till the trays run out."

Nadine blinked at her, then went to sit with Jake. "She said that all they have is red-green-blue trays. "

"It's a small mining station. Not a lot goes on here. Anyway, I did my part and got you out of the Inner Rings. What are you going to do now?"

"But there's more than one type of tray. Why not vary it?"

"They serve whatever they were able to buy for cheap." Jake pushed his cup at her. "Here, have some basic." He pulled his cutlery out from his pocket and began to eat his food.

"What do we do now?"

"Well, I imagine this message will help." Jake slid a chip across to her.

"What's this? Where did you get it?"

"I stopped by the comm shack while you were sleeping. It's a message chip, hand-carried here by a freighter. There was one for me, too."

"Who from?"

"My new boss."

"What did it say?" Nadine asked.

"It said to help you do what you have to do, and afterward I can take a vacation out here. "

Nadine frowned. "Jakey, you are a terrible liar. What did it really say?"

"More specifically, there's been a coup on Delta, and a group of Militia officers, those Empire Rising people, in conjunction with Galactic Growing, have seized control of the government and started an insurrection. There's fighting across the system. It said you're working for some Militia admiral who has access to a bunch of weapons. He told you to go get the guns he had hidden and bring them to a group of loyal officers who would help put down the rebellion. I'm supposed to help you with that." Jake took a big slurp of his basic. "Then I get my vacation."

Nadine stared at Jake, open-mouthed. "It told you all that?"

"Yep. It said your contacts for the guns would approach us here."

A skinny man with bad facial acne approached. He eyed their food, then sat down at their table. "Jake, how is ya doin'?"

"Good, Pickles. I haven't seen you in a while. How are you?"

"Oh, good. You know. Great. Lots going on. Got a line on a job on the cargo bay."

"You don't say," Jake said, and continued eating.

"Yep, casual work, ya know, but they pay. I'm pretty much good for the job. The foreman said I can start any day."

"That's good, Pickles," Jake said.

"Course, I got a bit of a problem, Jake."

"Oh?"

"Yeah. I need to get some gear. A line, new skin suit. Just need some money to get started. A friend of mine will sell me a used skin suit, cheap. Fifty credits."

"That's a good deal for a skin suit."

"That's an insane deal for a skin suit," Nadine said. "I've never heard of one that cheap."

"That's right, that's right," Pickles said. "The thing is, Jake, I need a loan. To pick up that skin suit, get started."

Jake simply continued eating.

"I could get you back from my first pay, ya know."

"Sorry, Pickles. I don't have any money to spare right now. Times are tight. You know how it is."

Pickles eyed the food again and licked his lips. "Say, you got any smokes?"

"You know I don't smoke," Jake said.

"That's right, that's right. Your mom does, though."

"She did, yes. Have you seen her lately?"

"Sometimes. She sells tomatoes to my cousin, you know. Are you going to eat that red there?"

"I'm going to eat the whole tray, Pickles."

"Oh. Oh, okay. Can I have some of your basic?

Haven't had anything in two days."

"You know I don't share, Pickles."

"Jake," Nadine said, "he's hungry."

Jake just shrugged and continued eating.

Pickles turned to Nadine. "Hey, I'm Pickles."

"Nadine," she said.

"You don't smoke, do ya?"

"No," Nadine said.

"I could really use some food, ya know. Haven't eaten in three days. Maybe give me some of your tray."

Nadine looked at Jake, who was ignoring the conversation. She frowned at Jake, and then pushed her tray over to Pickles. He produced a metal spoon from his pocket and began to shovel the food into his mouth. Jake looked at Nadine, then Pickles, and shook his head. Pickles grabbed Nadine's cup of basic and slurped it down.

"Hey—no sharing," the clerk yelled from the serving hatch. "You have to pay extra for another person."

"He's having mine," Nadine said.

"Basic comes with the meal. If you want basic for more than one person, you gotta pay more," the clerk said.

"How much can basic cost?" Nadine asked.

"Pickles, you going to pay for that basic?" the clerk asked.

"Nope. Up yours," Pickles says. He shoveled another spoonful of food into his mouth, drank the basic down, and then jumped up. He dumped the tray onto the floor, spilling the remains of the food everywhere, then flipped the cup at the clerk, splashing the dregs on the wall. Making a rude gesture at the clerk, he skipped out. "See ya around, Jake."

Nadine looked at the mess on the floor, then the wall. The clerk came out from the serving hatch.

"You owe me—" she said.

"One credit for basic," Jake said, proffering a chip. "Here it is."

"Who's going to clean this up?" she said.

"You are," Jake said. "Cleaning up is part of the job. You know that."

"Your girlfriend here should do it."

"I'm not his girlfriend," Nadine said. "He was just hungry. Why don't you feed him?"

Jake actually laughed.

The clerk looked at Nadine. "You're a stupid one, aren't you? Must be the blond hair. Better be careful, or they'll take you for everything you got."

"What?" Nadine said, but Jake only smiled and finished his food. "I missed something," she said.

"You missed a lot, actually," Jake said.

"Yeah, poor Pickles," the clerk said. "Did he tell you he hasn't had anything to eat for two days?"

"Yes," Nadine said, "or was it three?"

"Did he try to borrow money?"

Nadine nodded. "He tried to borrow money for some gear for a job he was going to get. He was going to buy a new skin suit. He had a great price."

Jake and the clerk smiled at each other.

"He eats every day," Jake said. "The station has him on rations. He picks them up at the station office. There is no job. There is no suit. He doesn't work. He just begs off people. Strangers like you are the best."

"He said he was hungry."

"Not anymore. He just ate your breakfast, and I'll bet he's off right now to get his daily tray. He'll sell it."

"Sell it?" Nadine said.

"Yup. Some chandler will give him a quarter credit for it or something, or one credit for ten. The miners buy them for long hauls. He'll spend the money on beer."

"Oh," Nadine said. "I guess I should buy another breakfast."

"Yup," Jake said, "and you need to buy some other things."

"What?" Nadine said.

"The courier that delivered those messages. He left

this as well." Jake produced another chip. "Instructions on where to meet the contacts for the guns. You should be able to decode it, but first we need to go to the chandlery."

"Why?" Nadine asked.

"He stole your cutlery when he got up," Jake said.

Chapter 20

"Final approach," came over the speaker.

"Right. Everybody strap in. This will be a combat landing," Commander Roi said. "Seal your suits. Clear your weapons. Keep unnecessary chatter off the radio. We're going in hard. Heavy weapons squad to the front. Nobody move until my signal. We will storm the station and clear out this nest of traitors. Who is ready to die for the glory of the Empire?"

He turned and faced the troops sitting in the shuttle. Nobody spoke.

Commander Roi frowned. "I said....Who is ready to die for the glory of the Empire? Who is?"

Still no answer.

Sergeant Russell cleared his throat. "Permission to ask a question, sir?"

"Of course, Sergeant."

"Just about that comm traffic statement, sir. Is a question permissible comm traffic?"

"Well, I suppose," Commander Roi said.

"Thank you, sir. Just wanted to get that out of the way, you understand."

"Er, yes."

"With the discussion about keeping off the radio and all. Didn't want to break any rules."

"Yes. Fine, Sergeant. Yes."

"Ah, good, sir, because I have another question," Sergeant Russell said.

"Yes?"

"This 'storming' thing, sir. Aren't we supposed to be occupying this station as an asset we need in the future?"

"Well, of course, Sergeant, but we need to destroy the traitors."

"Of course, sir, but are we sure that all the people there

are traitors? Most of them will just be workers."

"What are you saying, Sergeant?" Commander Roi said.

"Well, perhaps a more measured approach would work, sir. Going in quietly and just introducing ourselves, taking over easy-like."

Commander Roi just glared at the sergeant. "Traitors to the Emperor will be dealt with harshly, Sergeant. As will those who assist them."

"Of course, sir." Sergeant Russell regarded Commander Roi without emotion. "Well, sir, about strapping in...."

"Yes?"

"Well, we're already strapped in, sir. Shuttles only have the small harness. So I'm not clear on what you mean about 'strapping in' because we're already strapped in."

"Well, that's fine, Sergeant."

"So, we can ignore the order about strapping in then, sir?"

"Yes, Sergeant, you can. Yes."

"Also, sir, are you sure you want us to seal our suits?"

"Of course, Sergeant. We're going in hard. Want to be safe."

"Safety's my middle name, sir. Sergeant Safety Russell. But we only seal our suits going into an airless environment. This station is fully aired up. Also..." He regarded Commander Roi.

Commander Roi sighed. "Is there more, Sergeant?"

"Well, sir, this 'coming in hard' thing...."

"Yes?"

"Well, we're not an assault shuttle like you see on the vids. We're just an older-model orbital passenger shuttle."

"I see."

"More like a...well, a bus full of people, really."

"Is there a point to this, Sergeant?"

"Well, the pilots don't dare do a hard landing, sir. We'd just crumple."

"I see."

"Like a wadded-up piece of paper, sir."

"Thank you, Sergeant."

"Just like a piece of paper crushed underfoot, really. We'd all be tossed out and slammed into the station, or off into space. Wouldn't end well."

"Thank you, Sergeant."

There was a quiet *bong* and a gentle tap, then another announcement. "We're docked. Hard seal. Disembark when ready."

Commander Roi glared at Sergeant Russell, who looked back blandly.

"I think we're here, sir," Sergeant Russell said. "Keep strapped in?"

"No, Sergeant, you can unstrap."

"Seal the suits up now, sir?"

"No, Sergeant. Not necessary."

"Very good, sir." Sergeant Russell stood up. "Listen up. McLusky, Samar, Park, and Sundarampli—front and center. The rest of you, unstrap, unseal, and wait."

Four Militia at the rear of the cabin hopped up and ran forward to the airlock.

"Here you go, sir," Sergeant Russell said to Commander Roi, who looked the four over.

"Sergeant."

"Sir?"

"These men have no weapons," Commander Roi said.

"Yes, sir."

"No weapons at all."

"Yes, sir. No personal weapons at all."

"Why are you presenting me with four unarmed troopers?"

"To storm the station," Sergeant Russell said, "as the commander requested."

"I requested four unarmed troopers to storm the station?"

"Not precisely, sir, but you did request these four troopers."

182

"When, in the name of the Emperor's hairy anus, did I ask for four unarmed troopers, Sergeant?" Commander Roi screamed.

Sergeant Russell stared at him for a moment before answering. "The commander requested the heavy weapons platoon to the front. This is the heavy weapons platoon."

Commander Roi looked at the three men and the woman. "Where are their weapons?"

"In the cargo hold, sir."

"Why—" Commander Roi drew in a breath. He seemed to be having some difficulty controlling his voice. "Why, Sergeant, are their weapons in the cargo hold?"

"Well, sir, they are too big to load into the passenger cabin."

"Too big?"

"Yes, sir, and too heavy."

"Too heavy?"

"Yes, sir. That's why they are called heavy weapons."

Commander Roi hung his head and knocked it against the wall.

"Are you okay, sir?"

"I'm fine, Sergeant. Alright, you win. We'll do it your way."

Commander Roi led Sergeant Russell and team of eight—armed, this time—through the lock and into the cargo dock. He sniffed. The station exuded some sort of pine scent rather than the burnt oil he was accustomed to. The lights were brighter than on Militia stations, and there were more of them.

Commander Roi strode toward the cargo desk, where a woman sat behind a glass window with a speaker in the middle. He drew his revolver and pointed it at the women. "Are you a true servant of the Empire?" he demanded.

The cargo lady was blond, thin, pale, and quite unimpressed. She tapped the window and pointed down. "Speaker," she said.

"I said, are you a true servant of the Empire?" Commander Roi repeated.

She only pointed down again. "Use the speaker, jerkwad."

Commander Roi looked at Sergeant Russell.

"Push the button next to the speaker, sir, and lean forward so she can hear you."

Commander Roi tapped the speaker and yelled. "Are you a true servant of the Empire?"

"What? Can't hear you."

"A servant of the Empire. Are you a servant of the Empire?"

"A savant of piles? What are you talking about? Get your mouth closer to the speaker."

Commander Roi bent at the waist and put his mouth next to the speaker. "Are you a true servant of the Empire?"

"Servant of the Empire? Listen, mister, I'm just the door clerk. What do you want?"

Commander Roi lost his temper. "Let us in." He stepped back and pointed his revolver at the woman's head. "Let us in. We are the true servants of the Empire, and we will clear out this nest of traitors. Let us in, or die."

The woman regarded him levelly, then pushed the button for her speaker.

"That's a .38 revolver."

Commander Roi blinked. "What?" Then, remembering, he hammered the speaker button. "What?"

"I think that's a .38," the woman said. "Not very powerful. This is armored glass. Vacuum-safe. We're supposed to be able to monitor the deck even when it's in vacuum. Turn it sideways so I can see."

Commander Roi glanced at Sergeant Russell, who nodded, and turned the revolver sideways.

"Move your fingers so I can see the ID number. Yup, that's a .38. That's not going to break this glass. You'll need something heavier."

"If you don't....Emperor's testicles." Commander Roi pushed the speaker button again. "If you don't let us in, I'll call for heavy weapons and blast our way in."

The blond woman regarded him for a moment, then pushed her button. "Okay, you're in. Anything else?"

"What?"

"You're in."

"You need to unlock these doors," Commander Roi said.

The blond lady shrugged, then pushed the microphone again. "They're not locked. We leave 'em open. Unless you have cargo to declare, you can go where you want."

Commander Roi stared at her for a moment. Pushing the button, he said, "Thank you."

She just shrugged and waved him off and went back to her desk. Commander Roi looked around. Sergeant Russell's face was blank. There was a stifled sound behind him, almost like a smothered laugh. Commander Roi looked around, but didn't catch who did it.

"Forward," he said. "For the Empire. Death or glory."

"As you say, sir," Sergeant Russell said.

The squad rounded the first corner. Farther down, the corridor was blocked with a series of thin metal bars that had been welded to the walls. Each bar had a bottle welded to it. A man in a formal skin suit holding two metal bottles stood in front of them.

"Surrender or die," Commander Roi said.

"I choose surrender, please," the man said. "Are you in charge?"

"I lead this party of liberation, yes," Commander Roi said.

"Oh, good. Alphos Burasian. Here you go—these are for you." The man handed Commander Roi his two bottles. "Thanks for coming. Good luck with your liberation. Have a great day."

He started to walk down the corridor.

"Seize him," Commander Roi said.

The troopers looked sideways at Sergeant Russell. He rolled his eyes, but nodded. One of the troopers put out a hand to stop the man, then pointed at Commander Roi.

"What?" Burasian said, turning. "I surrender. You win. I don't have any weapons, and I'm not resisting. You are in charge. Let me know what happens."

"This was a TGI-run station," Commander Roi said. "Who is the ranking TGI officer?"

"It was a TGI station. It's a Militia one now, right? You are Militia, aren't you?"

"I have that glorious privilege."

"Good," Burasian said. "Well, as I said, congratulations."

"But who is the ranking TGI officer, and where are they?"

"You mean former TGI officer."

"Well, yes."

"In his office, of course." Burasian again started to walk away.

Sergeant Russell rolled his eyes and nodded at his troops. They stuck their hands out again, stopping the man.

"Where, and how do we get there?" Sergeant Russell asked.

Burasian started to speak, but looked at the sergeant and apparently changed his mind. He pointed. "Straight down this corridor to the inner ring, anti-spinward 40 degrees. He's in his office there."

"Can we just comm him?" Sergeant Russell asked. "Ask him to surrender?"

"He said he'll surrender the entire station, as soon as you get to his office."

"How do we comm him?"

"You can't. He destroyed his comm system. However, he told me to tell you his office is right next to the central control system, so if you work your way down to the central system, he'll be there to surrender to you."

"Glorious!" Commander Roi said. "Onward to victory." He strode around the corner.

"Don't forget your bottles. They're important," Burasian said, holding them up. Commander Roi didn't turn around, so he handed them to Sergeant Russell.

The sergeant weighed them in his hands. "What are these?"

Commander Roi's voice echoed down the hall. "Corporal, use your laser to cut these bars out of the way."

"Not a good idea," Burasian said.

"What do you do again?" Sergeant Russell said.

"I sell liquid nitrogen," Burasian said, "in bottles like these."

"Why do we care?" the sergeant said.

"Well, I sold him—the TGI guy, Jose—a thousand full bottles and five empty bottles. Oh, and one hundred liters of liquid oxygen."

Sergeant Russell thought for a moment. "Where did the liquid oxygen go?"

"Into the five empty bottles."

"Then where are the five empty bottles, labeled as liquid nitrogen but actually containing liquid oxygen?" Sergeant Russell asked.

There was a flash and a boom from around the corner, followed by screaming. Smoke and dust pulsed around them. Sergeant Russell started coughing, tasting the acrid stench of burning metal and plastic.

"Oh, they're around here somewhere," Burasian said.

Chapter 21

"This is the most disgusting bar I've even been in," Nadine said.

"What do your contacts look like?" Jake asked, shutting off the comm he had been talking on.

"No idea. They said they would send somebody to meet us at Mega-Thrusters," Nadine said, looking around. The bar was three stories high, with balconies ranging up to the ceiling, creating a theater-like effect.

"This is Mega-Thrusters," Jake said.

"This is a big bar for a small station," Nadine said.

"Not much else in the way of entertainment here, so people drink a lot. Plus, there aren't a lot of large public spaces here, either. They have the quarterly election debates here, and lots of other public events. They do a sort of net ball thing sometimes, too."

"Who owns it?"

"Station council, really. They get a cut of the profits. Honest Bob operates it."

"Honest Bob?"

Jake gestured at a fat man behind the bar. "That's what everybody calls him."

They were sitting drinking Belter beer at a stand-up table on the bottom floor. The chairs and tables were all metal, as were the glasses. Jake had acquired a spare set of glasses and cutlery for Nadine to add to his set, so they didn't stand out as much as before. Jake did all the ordering. That was good because it cut the price of a round by 50 percent, but it was bad because he ordered the local Belter beer.

"This beer tastes like the Emperor's anus," Nadine said. "Who were you talking to on the comm?"

"Yes, it does," Jake replied. "Cheap to make."

"It's freezing cold in here. Are you getting more heaters

installed on the ship?"

"Saves money on heat. No, just got Jacqueline to fix up our fuel tank."

"Why am I breathing so hard?"

"Lower O2 levels. Saves money on life support."

"I could never be a Belter," Nadine said.

"Well, I don't think you will ever be offered the opportunity," Jake said.

"Lousy beer, lousy food. No entertainment, horrible working conditions. Boring, boring, boring," she said.

"Thanks for pointing all those things out about my home station, Nadine," Jake said. "Glad you could come to visit."

"Just saying the truth, as I see it. Can you argue with it, when you look at...look at this?" Nadine swept her arm around the bar.

It was over half full, and for the first time Nadine saw more hard suits and semi-hards than regular suits. Most people didn't bother to wear anything in the way of coveralls, and those that did only had dirty and worn ones.

"Do we have to wait?" Nadine asked.

"You said your contacts would meet us here."

"Jake, there's an old man asleep in a pool of beer over there. At least, I hope it's beer," she said.

"He's not bothering anybody," Jake said.

"That girl over there has no shoes on. That's wretched."

"Nadine…"

"This bar is a dump. This station is a dump," Nadine said. "Jake, I'll tell you what. We'll find the people with the guns, shoot them, and take the guns."

"That's your method?"

"That's my method, Jake."

"Sometimes it pays to plan and wait, Nadine," Jake said, "and trust the people you work with."

"It does not. I don't trust anybody. Direct action is the only way to go. If you want something done, do it yourself, and don't trust anybody else to help you out."

"And yet," Jake said, tipping his glass and drinking up, "and yet you are the one who had to flee Delta ahead of the Militia, jumping off a roof into a pool of rotten vegetable juice and sneaking into the cargo hold of a shuttle—"

"The pilot owed me a favor."

"—and then we had to flee the station in a stolen ship because a Militia squad was chasing you—"

"You said it wasn't stolen. You said it was a vendor take-back mortgage, or something like that."

"—and then there was that armed entry team that chased us in the tug...."

"Except that they didn't catch us because of my awesome piloting skills."

"Which brought us here, to this station, which I suggested. That you hate so much, and that is the one place we seem to be safe from all the people chasing you."

Nadine glared at him. "What are you saying, Jake?"

"Planning. Trust. Patience. You should try them."

"I don't do any of those."

"So you don't want to wait?" Jake asked.

"Fine, but you could have let me wear a better outfit."

"Ruffles and neck bands make you look like a tourist," Jake said.

"Do you get a lot of tourists out here?"

"No ruffles."

"Spoilsport," she said. "I'm in hell. Look at all these people. I need another drink." She waved at a waitress carrying a tray of beers.

The waitress came over. "Two credits each."

"Done," Nadine said. The waitress didn't move. Nadine watched her for a moment. "I said two beers."

"I heard ya," the waitress stuck out her hand. "Pay first."

"Pay now?"

"Yep.

"Can we run a tab?"

"Nope."

"Are you saying we don't look trustworthy?"

"Nothing to do with trust. Everybody pays first."

"What if we want more?"

"I'll sell you more. When you pay more."

Nadine shook her head and handed a chip over. The waitress put it in the machine, extracted the cash, and handed it back, then walked to the next table.

"That's weird," Nadine said. "Why did she do that?"

"She's sort of an independent contractor. She buys a tray from the bartender at a discount, carries it around and sells the beers, and takes the profit."

"That's pretty awkward."

Jake shrugged. The two watched the group around them while having another beer, but nobody approached. The level of their beers sank steadily.

"I'm going to get another. Want one?" Jake asked.

"No. Yes. Fine. Bring me another of those crappy beers," Nadine said.

Jake walked toward the bar, and Nadine glared around her. Two young women had sat down at the next table and were flirting with the waiter. They were slightly better dressed than most of the women around. Something about the cut of the clothes. Hippy-ish, or perhaps Francois. Both were short and slight. One had a long, brunette ponytail, and the other had darker, almost black hair, worn in a French braid.

The women finished talking to the waiter. Nadine flashed him a brilliant smile, and he smiled back. One of the girls scowled at her, and Nadine returned the look.

Nadine continued sulking until the waiter returned to the next table with the girls' drinks. They tried to flirt with him some more, but Nadine smiled her thousand-watt smile and waved him over. He came running, as she expected. A quick sob story about her boyfriend being late coming back with her drink, and he hurried off to get her a round of decent beer. In bottles.

After he left, she turned and grinned at the two girls. One made eye contact and didn't break it. The other gave Nadine a quick look, then turned to the bar. The first girl got up, strode over to Nadine's table, and sat in Jake's seat.

"Who you talking to there, girl?" the woman asked. Her accent was strange.

"Whoever I want to," Nadine said.

Jake chose this moment to arrive back at the table. "Excuse me," he said, tapping the woman on the shoulder. "I think you might be in my—aaraugh!"Jake yelled as the women he'd tapped on the shoulder pulled his hand forward. She pivoted and pulled his arm forward, then bent it backwards at the elbow joint.

"That hurts!" Jake yelled at her.

"That is the point, you pervert. Do not touch me."

"I was just trying to talk to you."

The woman yanked Jake's hand around harder.

"Ow, ow—okay, no talking," he said.

She kept bending his arm around, and Jake twisted until he finally collapsed on the ground, rolling around in pain. The two women looked down at him as he flopped on the ground.

"I think you lost that fight, *mon ami*," Brunette Ponytail said.

"I didn't know I was in a fight," Jake said.

"That's why you lost so fast," French Braid said. She stood up as Nadine came around the table. "You want some of this, blondie?"

"Maybe I do," Nadine said. She looked down. "You get beat up by a girl again, Jakey?"

"Ow," Jake said.

"That's a yes." Nadine turned to the girls. "You want to explain why you did that?"

"Just for fun," French Braid said. "We like a little excitement."

"Me too. I like a friendly fight from time to time,"

Nadine said.

A few of the other tables began to clap as she stepped away from the table and into the cleared area. A chant started up. "Fight, fight!"

Nadine grinned. "Ready when you are."

French Braid's hand slashed out at her face. Nadine ducked to the side as nails scored along her face. She tasted blood, but reached up, grabbed the hand, and rotated, trying to pull the woman's arm over her shoulder for a throw.

It didn't work. French Braid flipped over Nadine's shoulder alright, but rather than Nadine's throw slamming her into the ground, she pivoted midair and broke the hold. French Braid used her momentum to lift Nadine off the ground.

"Empress's vagina," Nadine yelled. She hit the ground, rolled, stumbled, and kept rolling.

Normally she was better than this. She lurched back onto her feet to face her opponent.

French Braid immediately kicked out, but Nadine grabbed her leg and twisted right, hard. Instead of falling to the ground, French Braid spun in a circle and came down on her feet.

Nadine felt herself counter-rotate, then dove to the side and rolled. She couldn't brace herself at all. "What in the royal testicles is going on?"

"Never fought in low gravity, have you, blondie?" French Braid taunted.

Nadine rushed her.

There was a flurry of blows. Nadine managed to connect with her hands and feet several times, but each time, she bounced off.

French Braid danced around. Nadine rushed her again, and Braid danced backwards and flipped over a table. Nadine chased her.

"Stand and fight," Nadine yelled.

"Come and get me." Braid dove past Nadine and rolled

over the ground. Nadine pivoted and chased her. Braid came up facing the wall and jumped—high. She pulled herself up to the second story and flipped up onto the railing.

Nadine stopped and stared. "Wow. That was actually impressive."

Braid made a rude gesture.

Just then, Nadine noticed her heart pounding—much too hard. Why was it racing?

Low oxygen, she thought. *This is a setup*. She tried to catch her breath and looked up. Braid stuck her tongue out and made another rude gesture.

That was a long way. She was breathing hard already. If she climbed up there, she would just be even more out of breath.

"I'm not playing this game," Nadine said. She put her hands down, stepped back, and waited.

Braid made a few more gestures and raced around the bar. The crowd clapped and cheered. Nadine didn't follow, but made a few rude gestures of her own. The crowd cheered for that as well.

"Nadine, what are you doing?" Jake climbed to his feet.

"Saving your butt. Stay loose."

Jake began to massage his arm. "I believe she wrenched my arm out of its socket. Can't get more loose than that."

Nadine kept an eye on Braid. "What's the short brunette doing?"

"Just standing there by the wall," Jake said.

"Something isn't right," Nadine said. "I need to get my hands on Braid."

When Braid got tired of dancing around, she came in swinging at Nadine. Nadine didn't even try to get out of the way. She took the hits with her arms and shoulders, stepped into Braid, and grappled at her. Nadine didn't try to throw or hit her—just leaned in and grabbed.

Braid didn't expect that. She tried strikes and kicks, but Nadine was having none of it. She was too close. She leaned in and forced Braid to the ground. Pushing her arms apart, she began to beat at Braid with both hands, then paused.

"That was a neat trick," Nadine said, "but I'm just as tricky as you are."

"Not as tricky as us," a voice behind her said. She tried to turn around, but didn't manage it before the shock stick touched the back of her head. She shook and shook, then shook some more.

Things were woozy for a while, but Nadine came to as she was laid on the ground. She sat up and looked around. She was in a makeshift cell, a storage area of some sort. Benches leaned against the back wall, and some sort of mechanical parts lined one side, with boxes of food trays along the other. Metal fencing spanned from floor to ceiling along the front, with a fenced door in the middle.

Jake came over and helped her sit up.

"Wow, that was fun. What happened?" Nadine said.

"Shock stick," Jake said.

Nadine looked around. Braid was slumped on the bench in the corner, and Brunette was helping clean her up.

"What are they doing here?" Nadine asked.

"We don't mind a bit of fighting from time to time," a voice behind her said. Everyone turned. Standing behind the mesh was Honest Bob and one of his bartenders. "We don't like things getting out of hand inside the bar, though."

"Because you are worried about your elegant decor being damaged?" Nadine said.

"Because I have rent to pay, and fights get in the way of me selling drinks," Bob said. "What you do on your private time is up to you. This is sort of your private time. Here's the rules. We leave you here for a full shift to sober up."

"We're not drunk," Jake said.

Bob looked closer at him. "That's Jake Stewart, isn't it? Welcome back to the Rim. You went coreward to get an education, didn't you?"

"Merchant's academy. Two years."

"Good for you, Jake. You always worked hard. I have to say, I'm surprised to see you in here. Never happened before."

"I was helping out a friend," Jake said, giving Nadine a hand up.

Bob gave Nadine a once-over. "Also surprised to see you with a friend who looks like that. Must have learned something coreward." He shrugged. "Any-who. You four stay here a shift, till we think you won't cause any more trouble. All four of you walk out, or none of you walk out. If anybody has to go to medical, all of you go up in front of the station council. A fine and expulsion will be the least of your worries. Jake's a local, so we'll just let him out, but the tacit agreement is that that somebody's buddies will put a whaling on him, and nobody will say a word."

"What if the person being beaten up doesn't have any local buddies?" Nadine asked, gesturing at the two Francois girls.

"In that case, buddies will be provided. We have rules here. So, you can continue to settle your differences if you want, provided you are smart about it, or you can all keep your hands to yourself and walk away. Any questions?" Bob looked at each of them in turn. "Good. Camera's up there." He pointed to the roof. "Nobody watching, but if anything happens, we can go back and see who started it. See you at shift change."

Bob and the bartender marched out.

Nadine sat back on the bench and glared at the girls. Surprisingly, they smiled at her.

"I'm Yvette," Braid said, "and this is Odette. You hit hard."

"Not hard enough, apparently. You're still talking."

"No reason to be like that. You need to talk to us, and this gives us an excuse to be seen together."

"Why do I need to talk to you?" Nadine asked.

Jake looked hard at the girls. "I know you," he told Yvette.

"You do?" Yvette asked. "Where could we possibly have met?"

"Nadine knows you too," Jake said.

"I remember all the guys I've beaten up. I don't think I've beaten you up before," Yvette said.

"I've never seen them before, Jake," Nadine said.

"You were too busy stealing a case full of money to pay attention," Jake said. He turned to the girls. "No, you didn't beat me up. You were hauling a couple containers of stolen weapons onto your ship. You and a girl named Marianne."

"You know Marianne?" Yvette asked.

"Not well, but I shot out an airlock so she could get away."

Yvette leaned forward and looked more closely.

"*D'accord*," Yvette said. "I know you now. You are the accounting man. Marianne said you were dangerous—you think. I know why you are here now."

"Well, I don't know why you are here," Nadine said. "What's going on?"

"Nadine, meet Yvette and Odette. They are here to sell you some guns," Jake said.

Chapter 22

"Okay, Jakey, let's set this up," Nadine said as they exited the makeshift jail and headed down a corridor. "Here's my plan. Take your ship out, hide behind a rock, and drop a few credits. We'll meet this ship, pay some money, do a swap, and then we have a container of guns. Whatcha say?"

"No."

"What?"

"No, that's not how it's done. If you do that, we'll all go to jail."

"Then you've done this before? Transferred stolen goods, moved hijacked weapons, paid a ransom, and fled the law?"

"Well, sort of. Not myself, but I know how it's done."

"They teach you in school? Was there a class called 'How To Be a Reprobate 101'?"

"Of course, but it was more of an apprenticeship thing," Jake said. "Everybody has a cousin or a friend or knows somebody. Follow me."

While they were locked up, Jake and Nadine had finished a long talk with Yvette and Odette. They had guns. Nadine had access to money. Things could be worked out, but there were complications. It wasn't just a straight container swap. Some assembly was required.

Jake proceeded to a spoke set of stairs. Nadine had to jump over a missing step.

"Where are we going, Jakey?"

"To see a criminal mastermind. Say, where did you learn a word like 'reprobate'?"

Nadine stuck her tongue out at him. "Who says he's a mastermind?"

"Ask anybody. Ask him." Jake led the way down the corridor. They hurried up to another spoke and began to climb down.

A short man with stringy blond hair was coming up the stairs. "Jake," he said.

"Fowler. How are you?"

"Good, good. What are you doing here? I heard you went coreward for school. Are you back here, then?"

"What's Ari wearing these days? Suit?"

"Leather jacket."

"Emperor's testicles."

"Went back to his roots."

"Not really convenient."

The man turned to Nadine. "Who's your friend?"

"Nadine, this is Fowler. Fowler, Nadine."

Fowler shook hands. "Pleased to meet you. I see Jake hangs with a better class of person these days."

"Was he kind of a lowlife before?"

Fowler laughed. "No, that would be me. Jake was helpful. He's good with numbers." Fowler turned to Jake. "I owe you a beer or two. Let me know if you need it."

"Will do. Thanks," Jake said.

Fowler gave a wave and headed up the stairs.

"Who's he?" Nadine asked.

"Fowler? He's a drug dealer."

Nadine stopped and looked at him. "A drug dealer?"

"Yeah. C, whatever you want."

"He said you helped him. What did he mean by that? Were you a drug dealer?"

"No, no. Never did that, but you cut the drugs—mix the pure drugs with stuff."

"I know that."

"So, he was interested in how much he could cut the drugs. I did some math for him. If you keep two-thirds strength, most people can't tell the difference. Go much below that, and they notice."

"How did you figure that out?"

"Questionnaires."

"You gave drug addicts questionnaires?"

"I set up a survey. The break points are two-thirds and

50 percent. Anything above two-thirds most people consider 'pure.' Above fifty, it's 'good stuff.' Below fifty, they think it's crap. It might as well be 10 percent."

"He kept things at two-thirds, then?"

Jake shook his head. "No, of course not. After I showed him the optimization graphs, he set everything at 10 percent, but charged half as much. Maximized profits."

"Of course. I misunderstood." Nadine looked at him. "Jake, I didn't think you approved of drugs."

"I don't," Jake said.

"Why don't you turn him in, then?"

"I went to high school with him. He was on my net ball team," Jake said.

"You played net ball?" Nadine asked.

"They were short a guy."

"Right. What was that about the jacket?"

"Ari's jacket?" Jake asked. "Ari thinks he's a big man. He's got an exaggerated opinion of himself, and that manifests itself in his clothes. When things are going well, he swanks around. Suit, nice clothes."

"This is a fashion thing?"

"He's not that smart. He screws up a lot, botches deals. The smarter crooks have to teach him a lesson from time to time. They beat him up. Ruins his suit. Then he's back to a jacket till he makes enough to buy new clothes."

"We don't need this guy," Nadine said. "We can do this ourselves."

"Sometimes it's best to help other people out. Make it a win-win for everybody you're working with."

"I'm interested in it being a win-win for me."

"And me, of course," Jake said. "Besides, he's got success clothes."

"You choose your partners based on a fashion statement?"

Jake stopped and thought for a moment. "I never really thought about it, but yeah, that's how things are done here. People worry about clothes."

"You kept me from wearing my new clothes at the bar."

"Wrong type. You had actual nice clothes. Stylish."

"They were stylish."

"Right, but not for here. In the Core, everybody would know you were rich by those clothes. Out here, they're just weird. If you buy expensive clothes coreward and wear them out here, nobody knows what they are. They don't know how to react to you. They think you're just strange, rather than rich or important. The reverse is true too. People here dress up like they think they're important. Then they go a little coreward, and you Core people still think they're hicks."

Nadine stopped and thought about that. "That's true. I always made fun of your semi-hard suit."

"Here it's respectable. Not expensive, but respectable."

"Wrong social signals," Nadine said.

"Exactly," Jake said. "Social signals are important. Don't turn in your local drug dealer. Beat up the local thug if he gets out of line. Don't overpay for bribes. That destabilizes the system."

"I don't care about social signals, Jake. I care about winning. Pay some appropriate bribes."

"Nope. See Ari, and pay a man to go on vacation."

Ari met them in the caf at a table. He was on the short side, chubby, and had close-cut brown hair and a small mustache.

"Jake. Are you back in town?"

"Just for a few days to see some family. How are you, Ari?"

"I'm great. Things are going really well. Business is booming."

"Good to hear," Jake said.

"Selling things. Buying things. Best year ever."

"Glad to hear it."

"Got some deals going on right now. Big stuff. All

sorts of big stuff."

"That's great, Ari."

"So, what can I do for you, my friend? Need something? Brother Ari can help you out."

"Do you still know that guy with the dock? The one who goes prospecting a lot?"

"I do, I do. Got a good dock. Great dock. You need to use it? I can work that out for you. Wouldn't cost much."

"I'd like more of an introduction, really. Can you set that up?"

"I can. Tell me what you need and when, and I'll do it."

"I think it's best if you just give me an introduction, and we work it out directly with him from there."

"No can do, Jake," Ari said. "He's pretty shy. Very shy. Extremely shy. I should organize things."

"I don't think I want that, Ari. I just want an introduction."

"You tell me what you need, Jake, and I'll tell him what to do. Shyness and all."

"I don't think so," Jake said.

Things went back and forth for a while longer. Ari wanted to be the broker, and Jake kept saying no. They argued about pricing, policy, timing. Jake was adamant that they just wanted the introduction. After about fifteen minutes, they parted amiably.

"You can always bring it up with him, Ari. See what he thinks. I'll pay for the introduction."

"Sorry, Jake. That's not the way I do things. All in, or all out."

"Let me know if you change your mind. Free trades."

"Free trades, Jake."

Jake and Nadine walked down the corridor. "What now?" Nadine asked. "Ari just said he won't introduce you to this guy."

"He needs the money. Wait a day or two, and he'll approach us in the bar."

"He said he'd never break trust with his 'friend.'"

"That's a lie. He'd do it for a used food tray. Just wait till he runs out of money. Besides, we have a few things to do."

"What do we have to do?"

"Go meet my family and old neighbors."

Jakes family—what there was of them on-station—was very welcoming. His mother was there, along with some of her friends who'd known Jake as a child. They had arranged a party of sorts mid second shift. Nadine was introduced as his "business partner," and they seemed to accept that. His mother was kind, if somewhat spacey. He had a sister who was married, but she wasn't on-station. Nadine talked a lot with different neighbors.

"Will you visit his sister?" his mother's friend Sue asked.

"I don't think so. We don't have a lot of time. We took almost a week getting here."

"Shame to come all the way out here and not go the extra day or so out to see her."

"Wouldn't it be easier for her to come here? If it's only a day, as you say."

"Long way for her to come in, though. Difficult."

"How can it be difficult for her to come here, and easy for us to go there?" Nadine asked.

Sue just looked at her and shook her head. "You people from away. Don't understand travel."

"I guess not," Nadine said. She chatted with Sue for a while, and then another neighbor stopped to talk to her.

"Pretty expensive in the Core stations," a man called Radwa said.

"It is," Nadine replied.

"I hear that beer is ten credits a dozen."

"Sometimes," Nadine said.

"That's too much. Who can afford that?"

"Well, it's not Belter beer, so it's more expensive. I think it tastes better."

"Not to my liking."

"Well, regardless, wages are higher in the Core."

"High enough to pay for that? I don't think so."

After four or five similar encounters, Nadine had had enough. She went over to see Jake, who was talking to a woman called Clair.

"So, my Tanya—you remember Tanya, Jake?" Clair said. Clair's eyes flicked to Nadine, but the woman didn't greet her.

"Yes. She was a year ahead of me in school. Works at the cargo dock, right?" Jake said.

"Yes, couple years. She got a promotion. She's head checker now."

"Good for her."

Clair nodded. "Yes. They say four or five years and she could be the assistant dock officer."

"That would be great," Jake said.

"You studied accounting, didn't you?"

"Among other things, yes."

"She could put in a good word for you, you know. Get you a job there."

Nadine turned to Jake, but didn't join the conversation. Jake shook his head. "Thanks. That's great, but I have a job right now."

"Good money as a checker," Clair said.

"I'm sure," Jake said.

Nadine was tired of being ignored. "How much does a checker make here?" she asked.

Clair named a sum. It was not impressive.

"That's not much," Nadine said. "She'd do better as a waitress in a Core station."

"Waitress and make that much? Coreward? That's funny." Clair continued talking to Jake.

Nadine waited as long as she could, then grabbed Jake. "Jake, we need to fix that thing on the ship. That inventory?"

"Right. We do. Great seeing you, Clair. Say hello to

Tanya for me."

"I will. Don't forget about that job."

Jake and Nadine headed back to where the ship was berthed.

Nadine opened a hatch and motioned Jake forward. "Why did that lady want you to take that stupid job? I don't know exactly what your boss wants you to do, but I know you make more than that."

Jake stepped through the hatch. "Not relevant here. They don't really understand how things work elsewhere."

Nadine ran back through the conversations in her head. "Jake, they didn't ask you a single question about work. In fact, they didn't ask you a single question about anything."

"They don't do that here."

"Why not?"

"They just don't. Nobody cares about your life or work elsewhere. If it didn't happen on the Rim, it didn't happen."

"Don't they care that you're successful?"

"You told me I'm useless."

Nadine smiled. "As a spy, you are useless. Still, even I will admit that if you need a records search done, or, I don't know, something hammered or wrenched or screw-drivered, you're the guy."

"I don't think 'screw-drivered' is a word," Jake said.

"It is now. It's your new job description. J. Stewart. Screws turned, policies read."

"Thanks for that ringing endorsement, Nadine."

"Happy to help. What do we do now, Jakey?"

"Wait for Ari to call us, tomorrow afternoon. Once he needs the money."

"Can't we just organize this ourselves?" Nadine asked. "We could just meet out behind a rock somewhere."

"That would be suspicious," Jake said They might tell somebody. The people looking for you. The Militia. Whoever."

"And they won't see us at this docking place?"

"They might, but they won't tell anybody outside of here."

"Why not?" Nadine asked.

"Then they're turning one of their own in," Jake said. "They'd have to deal with their friends, and they wouldn't like that."

Chapter 23

"Does this guy ever clean this place?" Nadine said. "We could catch something just standing here."

She and Jake had just latched the *Castle Arcturus* onto Ari's friend's docking station. As predicted, Ari had held out for less than twenty-four hours before caving and giving an introduction. For a small fee, of course.

Ari's friend, Rafuse, had been completely incurious. "I'm thinking of going prospecting for a spell. How long do you want to use it for?" he'd asked.

"About a week, starting tonight," Jake had said. They'd haggled over the price, and finally Rafuse had collected his money and the twenty kilograms of pancake mix Jake had offered to seal the bribe, boarded his small Launch, and headed out. The docking station had no gravity, nor power—just four manual docking ports that opened on a central area. It took ship power to heat and had no life support or other services.

"It's just a giant, dirty hole in space," Nadine said.

"Yep, but for a week it's our dirty hole in space. Have you talked to the Committee?"

"That's a stupid name for a couple of Francais hicks from the Verge."

"How can you tell they are from the Verge?" Jake asked.

"Same way I knew you were form the Belt when we met—their accent. They have that soft country accent." Nadine kicked the floor again. "I don't see why we didn't just meet these girls out in the dark somewhere."

"They said they needed a transfer station, and they insisted on one with atmo, so here we are," Jake said.

"Well, I sent them the message they wanted. They should be here in the next two shifts or so. They must be hovering somewhere nearby."

"I didn't ask about payment. How are you handling that?" Jake asked.

"I've got an encryption key for them. They've already been given a chip, but the money's encrypted. With the key, they can decrypt and spend the cash."

"You set that up."

"An associate of mine set it up."

"Your boss."

"Fine." Nadine glared at Jake. "My boss set it up. I'm just going to pick up the container of the goods, load the ship, and then we can get out of here."

"I'm sure I can find somebody who wants a whole bunch of guns," Jake said.

"Jakey, those are my guns, not yours."

"Yet they will be on my ship."

Nadine touched a pocket on her suit, where, Jake assumed, she had one of her many weapons. "Don't get any ideas, Jake."

"Once you get them, what are you supposed to do with them? You said your boss was missing. How are you going to find out where your boss wants them?"

Nadine opened her mouth, but stopped. "I didn't think of that. Usually I just transport stuff to where he wants, but he just said to get the guns and bring them to my contact. I don't have any idea who my contact is or how to get them there."

"So you're buying a bunch of guns you don't know how to get rid of?"

Nadine looked at Jake for a moment. "What's your deal here?"

"We can put them on my ship for now, but you're going to owe me a lot on this one...."

Their comms bonged. "What?" Nadine said on the radio.

"We're on approach to your closet," the radio said.

"Closet?"

"It's not really a station. Which lock are you opening

for us?"

"None of them," Nadine said. "They're all manual. Pick one you like and hit it."

"We shall. Do you have the money?"

Nadine toggled the comm off and rolled her eyes. "It's like they're in a bad vid soundtrack." She toggled her comm back on. "Do you have the goods?"

"Of course."

"Then of course I have the money."

"Stand by."

There was a slight push against the station and a bunch of banging. The lock door screeched open, and the aroma of the Committee ship wafted in.

"What's that stench?" Nadine asked.

"Garlic, or onion," Jake said. "There's a food tray that has it. I've never tasted it, but I recognize the smell. It's cold-hardy, so they plant it on the marginal land."

"Jakey, you just can't help providing useless information, can you?"

Yvette floated through the lock, carrying a box of ten food trays. "Hello, Jake."

Another girl rolled through the lock behind her with a strange gun strapped across her chest.

"Hello, Yvette. That's a nice gauss boarding shotgun you have there," Jake said.

"Who's your friend?" Nadine asked, her hand hovering near a suit pocket. There was no gun visible, but with Nadine, you never knew.

"She is from our organization, sent to monitor this transaction."

"Hello, Marianne," Jake said.

The second girl, Marianne, jerked the gun around to point at Jake. "How do you know my name?"

"I sold you that gun. I mean, I didn't sell it to you, but I brought it out to you, and you took a bunch of crates of them away after I blew out an airlock.

"Oh," Marianne said, raising the gauss gun. "You are

that Jake Stewart. I think I know your friend, too."

"We've met in passing," Nadine said, hand in pocket. "Never done business with you before."

The silence stretched until Jake coughed. "Perhaps you can show me the container the guns are in, and Nadine and I can pull a few of them and check things out. If they are up to spec, then we'll arrange payment."

"There is no container," Marianne said.

"What?" Nadine said. A gauss pistol had appeared in her hand. She pointed it at Marianne. "What do you mean, 'no guns'?"

"I didn't say 'no guns.'" Marianne pointed her gauss shotgun at Nadine. "I said 'no container.' We are not a cargo ship."

Jake pushed himself over to a viewport and looked out.

"Imperial anus," Jake said. "You're in a Launch. Where is the cargo container?"

"It is here," Marianne said, gesturing to Yvette. Yvette pried the top off the box and pushed it over to Jake. Instead of food trays, revolvers were piled inside, surrounded by boxes of ammunition.

"Did you just dump everything in here like screws in a drawer?" Jake asked.

"We had some transport issues at one location. We couldn't smuggle an entire container, but we could move a few boxes of food every day. Took us a month, but we got them off-station."

Jake looked in the box. "We have to count them and test a sample. This is going to take forever."

"Why don't you just trust us?" Marianne said.

Everyone laughed.

The logistics were complicated. Jake had to move the *Castle Arcturus* around so that the engineering lock was latched. The girls hauled thirty boxes into the central area. Nadine pulled a gun and bullets from each, and went into the airlock and test-fired them five at a time.

As she approved each, Jake hauled them into the Castle Arcturus's engineering spaces. There was only one nozzle, so there was space to pile the boxes. Jake had learned how to strip a gun from his video studies, so he commenced stripping and oiling each gun as Nadine passed them over.

"Is that really necessary?" Nadine asked as she came in.

"It's good practice for me. After I've done a couple hundred of these, I'll be a pro."

One of the test bullets misfired.

"You have tested one-third of the shipment with no problems. That is not a bad ratio," Marianne said.

"We paid for everything to work," Nadine said.

"Well, in the real world, everything doesn't always go smoothly. What do you want us to do? Take them back to the factory and demand a replacement?"

Nadine shook her head. "I guess not."

"You can deduct the cost of one gun from your payment. Speaking of payment, we agreed that you would inspect only one-third of the goods."

"Let's get this settled now." Nadine produced a chip. "Decryption key is on this."

Yvette produced a pad and put the chip in it. "We have the payment here. We just need to decrypt it. If this is the proper decryption key, then we will be able to get our money."

Nadine touched her gauss pistol, and Marianne held her gauss shotgun. Yvette peered at the pad. Jake stretched, spinning a pair of pliers in his hand.

Everyone relaxed as the pad bonged—a successful decryption. Nadine pocketed her gun, and Marianne stuck hers to a holster on her chest.

"There you go, Nadine said. "Worked. Let's get the rest of these out of here."

Yvette examined her screen. She showed it to Marianne with no expression. Marianne nodded once, then ripped the gauss shotgun from her chest and pointed it at Nadine. "There is a problem."

Yvette produced a revolver from a holster on her back.

Nadine raised her hands. "What problem? I just heard it work. Is this a double-cross?"

"We are not double-crossing you. You are double-crossing us," Marianne said.

"How?" Jake said. "We just heard you get paid."

Yvette reversed the pad and held it out to Jake, but she kept the revolver in her other hand. Jake looked down. "Oh. Never seen one of those. Nadine, do you have another decryption key?"

"No. Why?"

"It's definitely a payment voucher, but it's double-encrypted."

The bickering went on for several minutes. Everyone but Jake had a gun out, though pointed at the ceiling.

"If we were going to steal them from you," Nadine said, "we'd have just shot you when you first got here."

"We can just shoot you and take our guns back," Marianne said.

"You could," Nadine agreed, "but you have a certain reputation to uphold. Shooting us would be problematic. People would talk."

"I want my money," Marianne said.

"Besides, those crates are heavy, and you'd have to carry them twice as far. Anyway, what would you do with them then?"

"That is not your concern," Marianne said.

"I'll bet it's somebody's, though," Jake said. "Some of your people wanted us to have those guns for a reason, or they wouldn't have sold them to us."

"Well, we'll have to work something out."

BANG.

The station shook.

"What was that?" Nadine said.

Jake looked out a viewport. "Somebody just docked."

"Why didn't our proximity sensors notify us?" Nadine

asked.

Yvette, Marianne, and Jake looked at her.

"Because we don't have any," Jake said. "We're just a cargo ship, remember?"

"Shouldn't the radar have seen them, at least?"

"We have the bargain-basement radar. It only looks in one direction. Right now it's pointed at an asteroid about twenty kilometers away."

"Right," Nadine said. She looked at Yvette and Marianne. "Why didn't your sensors show anything?"

"We're in a Launch," Marianne said. "We don't have any sensors."

"Right," Nadine said again.

Everybody looked at each other. The other lock door spun.

Marianne aimed her gauss shotgun at it, then back to Nadine, and shook her head. "Imperial testicles." She pointed her gauss shotgun at the ceiling and gestured to Yvette, who shifted her own gun to face the ground. Neither put her weapon down.

The lock door spun open, and a man stepped through. His uniform read, "Passion Transport."

For a moment his eyes tracked the guns. Then he turned to the group. "Package for a Jake Stewart and a Marianne. Need two signatures."

Nobody moved. Then Jake said, "I'm Jake Stewart. How big a package?"

"Complete container." The man walked over and extended his pad. "Thumb here, and here, and here. There you go. Which one of you is 'no-last-name' Marianne?"

"I am," Marianne said. "You have a package for me as well?"

"Just one package for the two of you. Can only release it to both of you at once, though. Thumb here." He extended the pad. "Here too. Okay."

His screen flashed green. "Come with me."

Jake and Marianne looked at each other. Jake shrugged

and followed the deliveryman. Everyone else followed. They stopped at the lock. Two women armed with shotguns stood there, blocking access.

"Just the two of you," deliveryman said.

Jake looked at Nadine, who frowned but stopped. Yvette and Marianne had a whispered conversation, and then Yvette stepped back.

"How did you find us?" Jake asked as he and Marianne followed the deliveryman down into the ship.

"Had directions. Changed a couple times. Seemed like a tracker."

"On us?"

"On something. Don't know, don't care." He led them into the lock of the Passion Transport ship, down the access corridor between the containers, and into a lock. "Got a powered container here. The package is inside. You two go in, check it out, then tell me where you want it. We'll latch it for you, but we won't take it any farther." He spun the wheel of the lock, walked to the container, and flipped the door open.

Jake followed. The container had a complete life support system built in, and heavy-duty power couplings. Inside was a clean, modern room, including an acceleration couch. Jake had seen the type before—a special medical couch. Monitors were affixed to the walls of the container and connected to the patient reclining in the bed.

His eyes opened as they walked in.

"Hello, Mr. Stewart. Hello, Ms. Marianne," Dashi said. "It is my great pleasure to see you. We have a lot of work to undertake, so we'd best get started."

Chapter 24

"Mr. Dashi! You're alive," Jake said. He surprised himself by stepping forward and hugging Dashi. After a moment, Jake stepped back and got control of himself. "I was told you were dead, sir."

Dashi smiled at Jake and patted him on the head. "The report of my death was an exaggeration, Mr. Stewart," Dashi said. "I've always wanted to say that line. I read it somewhere. I have a great deal of important work to finish yet."

"What about the explosion, sir?"

"I was in a suit and in a protected first-class cabin. Jose had apparently put three different operatives, including a combat medic, in the room next to me, and they all had armored skin suits on. The pilots were somehow in my employ as well. Jose's explanation was somewhat nebulous. After the explosion, I was swaddled into a life pod, knocked out with drugs, bundled onto a shadowing tug, and sent away for medical care."

"That's wonderful news, sir."

"I will be in bed for some time. After they fixed the nitrogen embolisms and my general shock, they discovered that I have broken both legs, which will take some time to heal."

"That's bad news, sir."

"As an additional complication, as a result of my emergency surgery, I no longer possess a gallbladder. That is neither here nor there, though. Ms. Marianne—a pleasure to finally meet you."

"I don't think I know you, sir," Marianne said.

"We have never met, but we have spoken, in a style. But I must identify myself. I believe I am supposed to say, 'Have you ever been to the church of St. Surplice?'"

"Then my answer would be 'That is an Imperial

pleasure I have never had.'"

"A pity. There are many things to be learned from the old fraternities." Dashi smiled. "Codes are so tiresome. Is that sufficient?"

"You are not what I expected," she said.

"Then I have achieved one of my goals. Were you in the process of shooting Mr. Stewart for the second key code?"

"We were going to start by shooting Nadine."

"I do not believe that will help you, as she does not possess them. However, if you feel it is an important step, please continue. Will this shooting take long?"

"Probably not. We could skip it," Marianne said.

"I'd rather you did," Jake said.

"Did what, Mr. Stewart?" Dashi asked.

"Skip shooting her. Did that. I mean, didn't. Not shoot her."

Dashi regarded Jake for a moment. "You would prefer her alive, Mr. Stewart?"

"Yes, sir."

"Why are you of that opinion, Mr. Stewart? If we shoot her, Ms. Marianne will get paid, we will have the guns, and I have arranged for the assistance of some of the more excitable Free Traders. They will help us reclaim our stations from the Militia. We have no further need of Ms. Nadine's services."

"Well, I...uh...." Jake took a breath. "Sir, I don't believe you need to have her shot."

Dashi smiled. "Do you think I'm that capricious, Mr. Stewart?"

"Yes, sir," Jake said. Then he frowned. He didn't know what "capricious" meant. "No, sir?"

"Which is it, Mr. Stewart? Ah, never mind. If Ms. Marianne brings her comm here, I will arrange payment. I presume you acquired a ship of sufficient magnitude to handle a small cargo of weapons."

"We have room, sir, but I do need to repack them for

transport. Make sure they are greased up and such."

"Please make the arrangements, Mr. Stewart. Ms. Nadine can help if you wish, or not. Have you made any progress on my assignment for you?"

"My assignment?"

"Surely you haven't forgot that you were tasked to investigate a particular course chip? I'm disappointed in you, Mr. Stewart. You were so punctilious with your responsibilities before."

"The course chip, sir? Yes—yes, I've been looking into that."

"Have you any results?"

"Yes, sir. I've decoded part of it. We will pass near the orbit generally. We're not far from it right now, but I have no idea where on the orbit the item is located."

"What do you need?"

"I need to decode the second half of the orbital equations, sir."

"That can be dealt with. I believe I can locate somebody who can acquire that information for you, if they don't already have it. Anyhow, I see my doctors are hovering behind you. I promised them only a short visit, and then I will have to rest for some time. Mr. Stewart, I'm afraid you will have to arrange the transfer of this medical container to the next ship that arrives here."

"Next ship, sir? There will be another ship arriving?" Jake asked, then paused. "Of course there will be. Yes, sir. When will this ship be arriving?"

"Soon. If you two could deal with your tasks, I will sort things out. I have to brief some others on their role, and I have a call to make."

"What about the guns, sir? What happens with them?"

"Well, since I'm paying for them, they will be my guns. I'll have a delivery address for you. You can show it to Miss Nadine. I think she will approve when she sees the person who encrypted the message."

A few minutes later, Dashi adjusted himself on his bed and pressed a button on his comm to make a call. The doctors were not happy, but they had been overruled. He didn't really need three of them, but Jose was prone to overkill in many matters, and it was easiest just to go along with it.

The call took a long time to connect, and when it did, he didn't speak at all, just waited for the person on the other end to react to the video. A man with gray hair and a lined face answered. The background behind him was steel, with some sort of piping and conduit. A station. The man didn't speak for several seconds, then began a monologue.

"Hello, Dashi. Been a long time. Thought you weren't going to talk to me ever again. Almost fifteen years. I'm glad you responded to my message. I haven't got much time left. It's nice to talk to an old friend before I run out of time. Not that I call you 'friend' anymore, but you know what I mean. A voice from the past."

He continued, "Still got what you want—well, still know where it is—and I'm still not going to give it to you. It's not for you. I don't care if you made sure I got those contracts all those years ago. Needed the money, and a man has to live." The man tilted his head. "How are you getting this call through? You must have a hidden relay station somewhere. Good thinking, but you were always the planner." He paused and looked at the screen. "Over."

"Hello, Mr. Fletcher," Dashi said. "It has been a long time. Yes, I put the relay station in a long time ago—so I could keep track of you. You are welcome to the money. It's my gift to you. I haven't bothered you all these years because I know you. You weren't going to give me anything. I still believe it wasn't my fault, but that doesn't matter. I'm sending somebody to see you. You decide what you tell him. It will be, as it always was, your decision. I just wanted you to know he was coming out that far. Over."

There was a long pause before the man finally answered. "Waste of time sending him to me. I saw a vid. It looks like you started a war. I hope you know what you are doing, but you always did seem to. Why would I give this man anything? Over."

Dashi waited a long time before answering. Finally, he said, "You make your own decision, but he's the image of his father at that age, and I remember what you told John Andrew Keith."

Dashi cut the connection without waiting for a reply.

Jake and Marianne had met Nadine and Yvette at the lock.

"Well?" Nadine said. Her hand hovered near her gun pocket.

"My boss is here. He wants me to load up the guns and secure them for transport. Another ship is coming here, and he wants me to transfer him and some equipment to it. Then we're going looking for a ship or something that he's had me tracking. After that, I've got coordinates to meet some Free Traders who will take the guns off our hands. You can come along if you like. "

"If I like? No thanks, Jakey. No likey. You're just going to do this for him?"

"Yes. He's my boss."

"Jake, you may have noticed, but things have been changing the last few days. You don't have to follow everything your old boss says."

"I'm afraid of him," Jake said.

"What about my guns?"

"He says they're his guns. He also gave me a message for you to decrypt."

"Who is it from?"

"I have no idea, but I'm willing to bet it's from your boss and says something like 'Give the guns to whoever Dashi says.'"

"I'll believe that when I see it," Nadine said. "Gimme."

Jake handed her the chip. She inserted it in her pad, put in a code, and took her time reading it.

"What does it say?" Jake asked.

"It says sell the guns to the highest bidder, keep the money, don't trust that loser Jake Stewart, and if you meet some Francais girl called Marianne, shoot her in the leg. Twice."

"It does?"

"Of course not, Jakey. It says he's busy and that a certain 'Mr. Dashi' will 'provide you with additional delivery requirements that you are to respond to.' That's quite a word salad."

"It does sound like Dashi," Jake said. "He has that effect on people around him. Marianne?"

Marianne had been chattering with Yvette in Francais. "Jake Stewart, we will help move all the boxes of weapons to your ship. That will allow us to leave faster."

"Don't you want to wait to get paid?" Nadine asked.

"Mr. Dashi has said we will get paid. Therefore, we will get paid. Best to do what he says quickly."

Nadine shook her head. "I don't believe this. Who is this guy? He says, 'Drop,' and you all say, 'What orbit'?"

"It is best to do what Dashi says."

"Why?" Nadine asked.

Marianne looked at Jake for a moment, then shrugged. "He is always ahead of everybody. Things work out for him. If you go along with him, you win. You get something, and he gets something. If you try to oppose him, you lose. Always. Even if you think you are winning, you will find out later that you lost."

Nadine looked at her, then back at Jake. "What if I don't give you the guns?"

Marianne hefted her rifle.

"I mean, things seem to have changed here," Nadine said. "I may have lost my old job, and a girl has to look out for herself."

Jake shrugged. "What's your plan here, Nadine? You

can't point your pistol at all of us."

"True. I'd have to shoot two or three of you."

"I've seen you shoot people, so I'd probably do what you say. But it's just you. You have to sleep eventually."

Nadine turned to Marianne. "Interesting how you described things with Dashi. I've noticed that when I interact with Jake Stewart, I often think I'm winning when I'm not."

Marianne looked at him. "How so?"

"Sometimes I think I've beat him, when he's actually pulled one over on me."

"How does he do that?" Yvette asked.

"I'm not sure, but I'm going to find out. Jakey, let's go find this ship."

Chapter 25

"For a hole in the middle of space, this is a pretty busy place," Nadine said. She stood by the dock to the Castle Arcturus, watching all the activity.

There were now four ships connected to the lock. Jake and Nadine's ship, the Castle Arcturus, was loading guns. Across from them, the Committee/Francais Launch with Marianne, Yvette, and Odette had just finished unloading guns. The crew of the Passion Transport ship was outside swapping Dashi's container with an unnamed Free Trader on another lock. After the courier had Jake sign, none of the Passion Transport's crew had left the ship, and the unnamed Free Trader had never even opened the lock to the station. Jake could see them outside through a viewport manually chaining and unchaining the containers.

Jake had started repackaging all the guns. He'd unboxed them, stripped them, and cleaned them before putting them back together in a more logical packaging, and had started to put them back into one of the containers.

"Is he really doing all one thousand guns?" Yvette asked, standing next to the lock leading to their Launch.

"Meaningless, repetitive tasks that make no sense? It's a Jake type of thing to do." Nadine looked at her. "Why are you still here?"

"You do not want us staying here?"

"No, I don't." Nadine gave Yvette her sunniest smile. "I don't trust you."

Yvette beamed back at her. "I don't trust you either."

"I'll shoot you if I get a chance."

"You will not get it. We will shoot first."

Jake chose that moment to arrive. "What are you two

girls talking about?"

"How we'll shoot each other," Nadine said.

"Then why are you smiling?"

"Because it will be fun," Nadine said, and Yvette nodded.

Jake shook his head. "I don't understand women."

"That is evident," Marianne said, stepping off the committee Launch. "Are we ready to leave?" she asked Yvette.

There was a brief discussion in Francais.

"Well, that's not much variety of food, but it will do," Marianne said in Standard. She turned to Jake and Nadine. "We are leaving. Goodbye."

"I'd say it was good to see you again, but I'd be lying," Nadine said.

"Free trades," Yvette said. "We can all agree on that, yes."

Everybody nodded, then the girls pulled their lock shut.

Jake spoke to Nadine. "Dashi says the Free Traders will be out of here in less than an hour. He's been transferred to the other ship. We'll be the last to leave because we're the power source for everything. He's also given me a place to go to find the code to decrypt that course chip. If you have any messages, go send them to him now. He's got a link to some sort of relay that can forward them."

"Where do we go now?"

"So you've decided to go with me, then?"

"Shut up, Jakey. I have a boss too."

"Rim-37, then off to the dark. We're going even farther out. Have to fuel up first."

"You have fuel on the brain," Nadine said.

"Better than freezing in the dark," Jake said. "The course is on the board, if you want to look at it."

The station cleared rapidly, and less than an hour later, Jake clanged the lock shut behind him and pulled away. He and Nadine settled into the short journey back to Rim-37. Jake got on the radio and arranged to have a delivery of food and some spares on the dock waiting for them.

"I'll take the fueling crew. I know how they operate. I used to work there. You go on the dock and deal with the shipment. If there is anything else you think we need, get it there. There's a chandler, money changer, commo shop—everything—right there. Expensive, but this is our last stop for a week. Let's not screw this up."

Nadine smiled and ran her hand down Jake's arm. "Don't worry, Jakey. I'm good at not screwing things up."

They arrived at Rim-37. Jake suited up, climbed outside, and began arguing with the fuel crew. He made a special effort to make sure the fuel was topped off, even going back in to check the tanks from the inside with a manual gauge. Nadine loaded three small packages of spares and five large boxes of food, which she left in the lock and piled in the corridors, before climbing outside.

"How much longer, Jake?" she asked over the channel.

"Two hours, if these guys move any faster than space snails," Jake said.

Another voice came over the channel. "It would be faster if we didn't have to fill two reserve tanks and then top off and manually measure both."

"I'm paying for it, so you have to do it, and I don't trust your numbers on that pump," Jake said.

Plenty of time to make some calls while they bicker Jake Stewart style, Nadine thought. She made a visit to the commo shack, sent some messages, and was back in the pilot's seat before Jake unlocked them and joined her in the control room.

Nadine tapped her screen to spin them out. "So, who is this guy we're going to see?"

"His name is Fletcher," Jake said, playing with the comm screen on his console. "Dashi says we have to meet up with him, and he will decrypt the rest of this course chip. Once we've got the course, we can see what there is on it."

"How do we find this Fletcher guy?"

"Dashi gave me a comm address and directions to a relay satellite. I'm having problems locking on."

"What, with all this excellent gear Mr. Vince provided?"

"You can ask him for a refund if you want."

"I could get a refund from Vinnie. I can be very convincing when I want," Nadine said.

"I can't seem to lock onto this satellite."

"Just send the message in that general direction."

"Blind?" Jake asked.

"Is it encrypted?"

"Yes."

"So send it."

"That's not how it works, Nadine. We need to lock on."

"Jakey, I've sent blind messages before. If the other side is waiting, they'll get it."

"How will we get a handshake?"

"Just send it," Nadine said. "If you don't, I will."

"Fine," Jake said. "I'll just send a blind message. We'll just send it out into the ether and see what happens. After I send it, we'll just wait two minutes, 'cause there's nothing farther away than ten million kilometers that should answer, so if we don't get a message in that time, there's nothing there." Jake hammered on his comm and glared at Nadine.

"Good idea, Jakey. Thanks," Nadine said.

They waited.

BONG.

"Was that an incoming message, Jake?" Nadine asked.

"Could be," Jake said.

"Sure sounded like it. Is it possible the great Jake Stewart is wrong?"

"It's a text. An orbit. An asteroid, it looks like."

"Stop babbling and give me the course," Nadine said.

It was some distance, but not exactly an outer orbit. It

took long enough to get there that Nadine was glad Jake had loaded the extra fuel, but she certainly wasn't going to tell him that. There were so many asteroids in the Belt, it would be hard to find their destination if you weren't looking for it exactly.

"No beacon," Nadine said. "Nothing to lock onto."

"He doesn't like visitors."

"What about supplies and such?"

"If he's got an asteroid with water, and a fusion plant, he doesn't really need much. He can crack water for oxygen and hydrogen, recycle a lot. He'll need food, but that's not that heavy."

"Who is this guy again?"

"I have no idea. His name is Fletcher, and Dashi says he can decrypt this course chip for me."

"What about the guns?"

"Dashi said to see about this first, then to deliver the guns to some Free Traders down-orbit. This Fletcher meeting is time-limited."

"Does he have a busy schedule of asteroid meetings?"

"We'll know in a shift or so, I guess."

A few hours later they were close to the orbit they had been sent. There was a large family of icy asteroids spinning along.

"Big chunks," Nadine said.

"Lots of them. Smart place to hide."

"How so?"

"You don't prospect ice clusters at this orbit."

"I've been to stations that are based around ice processing."

"Different rings. If you're in a rocky ring, you go prospecting all over the place. Any one of those rocks could be your lucky strike, but you still need ice from time to time, so the few ice rocks are valuable there because they are in that ring."

"I always thought ice itself was valuable."

"In a regional sense. Rim-37 makes good money out of

fuel because it's close to the ice rings, but still inside a rocky ring, so prospectors can headquarter there but still get supplies, and passing ships can load up on hydrogen and oxygen from the local neighborhood."

"Thanks for the economics lesson, Jakey, but what do we do now? We're here, and this guy isn't."

"Let me think. Let's do a scan."

"We don't have scanners, remember?"

"I meant let me look this cluster over with the telescope."

Jake put them co-orbital with the cluster and worked his screens. "I've created a grid pattern, and I'm taking pictures with the telescope. Once I've done that, I'll examine all the pictures to see if I can see any abnormalities, then focus in and see if I can get a better idea of what we're looking at."

"Empress's anus," Nadine said. "That will take forever." She flipped through screens on her control console, found what she wanted, and pressed the comm button. "We're here. Talk to us." She smiled at Jake. "Broad-beam blind broadcast."

"I don't think that will work."

BONG.

"Is that the sound of an incoming comm request?" Nadine asked.

Jake grimaced.

"Point Nadine," Nadine said. She pushed a button, and a man's face appeared on her screen.

"I don't know you," he said. "Go away."

"Wait," Nadine said. "I'm not alone. Jake, over here."

Jake moved until he was in the camera pickup.

The man looked at him for a long time. "Well, if you are a counterfeit, you are a good one. Let me give you directions."

A half-hour later, Nadine and Jake were sweating in transit.

"Don't go so fast, Nadine," Jake said. "Do you see that one over there?"

"Shut up, Jake. I see it. I'm busy." Nadine angled the ship around a cluster of ice. "There are hundreds of these little ones. If we hit one of these small chunks, will they damage us?"

"No."

"Good."

"Just bang us around till we hit a bigger chunk of ice, and that will crush the air out of us."

"Thanks for your support, Stewart," Nadine said. "Who puts a station in the middle of a minefield of rocks?"

"I thought you said you were best pilot ever, and this minefield of ice rocks would be no problem."

"I did. It isn't. It's all part of my plan."

The ship *tinged* as a fist-sized hunk of ice smushed against the viewport.

"You planned to hit that one?"

"Shut up. I'm piloting. Go read some cargo logs or something."

"Please don't kill us," Jake said.

"Maybe you should put your suit and helmet on."

"I'm already sealed, except for the helmet," Jake said.

Nadine glanced sideways. Jake had boots and gloves on, and his suit sealed up to his collar. His helmet was attached.

"It's not that bad," Nadine said. "I got this."

THUNK. The ship banged sideways.

"All evidence to the contrary," Jake said.

"He said there was a clear spot in the middle."

"Well, this definitely isn't the middle, then. Head for that big one over there."

"And what? Crash into it?"

"No. Just put the nose on it and push gently."

Nadine did as Jake specified, pivoting the ship. Ignoring the *splat* of ice balls smashing against it, she directed the nose of the hull up to a ten-meter-wide ice rock and, with great care, accelerated with the navigation thrusters.

"Use it as a plow—push all this slush ahead of us," Jake said.

Nadine raised the thrust a bit, and the ice rock shoved ahead of them, pushing everything else out of its path. "That's not bad, as long as it stays in one piece."

Jake looked out the viewport. "Well, there are some cracks there, and as long as they don't split, we're...."

"We're what?"

"Imperial testicles," Jake said.

The ice rock began to fracture down the middle and broke into two pieces.

"Hang on," Nadine said.

Jake gripped the console in front of him. The ice rocks slid off the bow of the ship.

"We'll be fine if they don't catch on anything," Nadine said, "and if there aren't any actual metal rocks inside that ice."

The ship suddenly swung to one side.

"They caught on something," Jake said as an alarm began to flash, "and there was a big rock inside. Decompression. Put your helmet on while I fix this."

Nadine had already yanked her helmet closed and slapped on her gloves.

"What about boots?" Jake said.

"I've got a skin suit on. I'll be fine at the controls."

Jake slid out of the seat and began to pull himself hand over hand down the ship. He could have pushed off and floated, but he didn't want to be in mid-float when Nadine's inevitable collision knocked the ship a meter to the right and into his head.

He pulled the airlock behind the control room shut, went through the first hab module, and pulled the lower hatch shut as well. The damage was in the container walkways, from the looks of it. He arrived at the head end of the containers and pulled a smoke can from his tool belt. A quick spray, and he was able to follow the smoke right to the hole. It was more of a dent, really—a seam had given away. Jake took a look at it. *Not even worth a patch.*

"Nadine," Jake said over the radio, "I need to fix the leak. Can you not hit anything for a while?"

"Hitting things is fun, Jake."

"I'm serious. I'll be using a torch."

"Fine, fine. You sure won't let a girl have fun. I'm just going to sit here for now. You need to come up here and see this when you're done."

He took a hammer with a large, flat head from his belt, magnetized his boots to the wall, and walloped the dent. Once. Again. Once more.

Now the dent was more or less flattened, but the edges were ragged. He pushed the hammer back into his belt, selected a small torch, checked that it was charged with oxygen and hydrogen, and pulled the trigger. The spark ignited the gas mixture, and Jake moved the flame over the metal.

It took only a few minutes for the metal to start melting, but the remaining air pressure complicated things by blowing the melted metal out of the ship. He stopped, took a magnetic clamp, and stuck the torch to the wall. Checking that the hatch to the rest of the ship was closed, he reached up and shut the valve that connected that end of the ship to the air supply.

Then he went to the hatch on the wall of the container head end. It was a hatch, not an airlock, so after he pulled all four levers, including the one that was two feet away, it popped open. The air ran out of compartment in a whoosh of crystallizing water, and all the lights and shadows sharpened.

"Jake, a hatch just opened," Nadine said.

"That was me. No problems. Just stand by."

He returned to his dent. With no air leak, the metals didn't flow out, but rather floated around the weld. Jake used the back end of the torch to smooth out the liquid metal, ignoring the small amount that stuck to the bottom of the torch. Soon the weld was solid. After waiting a minute for it to cool, he pulled the hatch shut and opened the valve. His crystal-clear view of the interior began to muddy as the rising air pressure refracted the light.

"I see pressure," Nadine said.

"Yup. It's coming up now." Jake walked up to the hatch to the main area. Since that was an area normally inhabited, the hatch there would only open in, so any pressure differential would hold it firmly shut. Jake waited for the pressure to rise. When his vision told him it was about half, he spun the locking wheel and pushed. He had to push hard—air was heavy—but he managed, with an effort, to shove the hatch partway open.

Wind whooshed past the hatch, but the weight almost immediately lessened as the two areas equalized.

"Jake, pressure just dropped 20 percent in the hab module."

"Me again. I'm on my way back. It'll catch up."

Jake pulled his way through the hab module and into the control room. "What's up?"

"Look at this," Nadine said, pointing out a viewscreen.

Ahead of them was a large, pockmarked asteroid, spinning almost in slow motion. Anchored to it by a cable was a derelict spaceship, slowly venting atmosphere out the back.

"That doesn't look promising," Nadine said. "That outgassing would kill everybody."

"We just talked to the guy," Jake said.

"Could have talked to his space ghost."

"I don't believe in space ghosts."

"I do," Nadine said, "but I'm not scared of them."

Jake got busy with the radio.

Eventually the voice came back. "See you made it."

"We banged into quite a few of those rocks on the

way."

"Need a better pilot," the voice said.

Nadine bristled. "I'm a fine pilot. What I have is a ship five times bigger than that wreck you have there."

"Shouldn't have brought such a big ship here," he said.

"You didn't give us much choice," Jake said.

"Plenty of choice. All yours. Chose to come here. Didn't make you."

"Dashi said we should talk to you."

"Do you always do what Dashi says?"

"You're the second person to ask me that. I do. He arranges things so that they always work out the way he wants."

"He does."

Jake looked at the spinning ship. "Why you are talking to me, Mr. Fletcher?"

Fletcher laughed on the screen. "Because Dashi asked me to."

"Do you always do what Dashi asks you to?" Jake asked.

Fletcher laughed, then coughed. "Not at the start. Eventually, yes. Easier this way."

Nadine stuck her head behind Jake. "Why are the two of you so scared of this Dashi guy? What is he, a mini emperor or something?"

"Kind of," Jake said. "He scares me."

"Scares me too," Fletcher admitted.

"Okay, you two be scared. How are we going to rendezvous with your wreck there, Fletch, buddy? It's spinning pretty fast, and there isn't a lot of room in this little ice clearing you have."

"Just bring your ship down and spike yourself to the asteroid. It's not spinning fast. Then go outside, hook onto my cable, and climb up it. That will take care of the spin issue."

"Huh," Nadine said. She and Jake looked at each other. "That's actually pretty smart."

"I'm old," Fletcher said, "not stupid."

Jake and Nadine did as instructed. Nadine had no problem maneuvering close to the largest asteroid. The other asteroids in the family were snowballs—loose conglomerations of water-ice and frozen methane—but this one had a rocky core. It did have a spin, but it wasn't much, so Jake could hop out of the lock and spike the ship down.

"Four points down, Nadine, "Jake said. "We're hooked."

"Let's go see your friend."

"He's not my friend—but Dashi said I should talk to him, so here we are."

The two traipsed across the surface to where a large cable was anchored to an eye bolt on the surface.

"Somebody drilled this in," Jake said.

"I don't see a mining drill around here."

"Maybe there's one up top." Jake clipped a line to the cable and began to pull himself up.

Nadine followed. "Jake, why go to all this trouble? The cable and all."

"Gravity."

"Gravity?"

"Centrifugal force. It's an old prospector trick. Rather than wasting fuel spinning your ship, attach a cable to a big, spinning asteroid. If the cable is long enough and the spin is strong enough, the asteroid will fling you around, and the centrifugal force substitutes for gravity. You save the fuel."

"Seems like a lot of work to set up."

"Not as much as you would think. We use the towing hook at the front of the ship as an anchor point, and any decent mining drill will tap the bolt in to hold you. Takes a couple of hours and a strong cable to set up, but a few minutes of maneuvering with the thrusters, and you've got all the gravity you need for as long as you need."

"What's the catch?"

"Gotta be a big asteroid, and you have to be able to anchor firmly to it. Can't do it if it's a rubble pile."

"Huh." Nadine pointed up to the ship. "Speaking of rubble piles, that's the biggest pile of junk I've ever seen."

"Looks like it used to be a tug, but somebody's attached three or four containers to it. I don't think it will fly—I can see the engine nozzles, but all the thrusters have been removed."

They reached the top of the cable, attached to the towing hook, as Jake had suspected. They eased around the side of the tug.

"How do we get inside?" Nadine asked. "I don't see an airlock.

"Tugs don't usually have one. What's that over there?"

"Looks like a hatch of sorts, welded onto a container."

"Let's try it."

The hatch proved easy to open, and once inside the container, they spotted another hatch welded to the far side. The container functioned as a simple airlock. Nadine pulled the far hatch closed. Once she gave a thumbs-up, Jake yanked the docking wheel on the other hatch. It popped open, almost knocking him over. There was pressure inside, and, strangely, the interior hatch opened outward.

"Not very safe," Jake said over the radio.

"Don't be a wimp, Jake." Nadine climbed over the hatch coaming.

"It's dangerous. People could get hurt."

"I couldn't agree more, but I think we have bigger problems than leaky hatches."

"How so?" Jake turned around. Fletcher was pointing a shotgun at them. "Oh."

Chapter 26

It took a minute, but after a few radio commands and some rude hand gestures, the three took their helmets off. Fletcher peered at them, but didn't put down the shotgun.

"Mr. Fletcher, my name is Jake Stewart," Jake said. He coughed, then gagged. It smelled like a thousand farts, and some chemical had leaked into the air. "This is my partner, Nadine."

Fletcher kept his eyes glued on Jake. "John Andrew Keith, good to see you."

"Sir? I'm Jake. Not John."

"John Andrew Keith it is, and will be, as far as I'm concerned."

"Uh...yes, sir."

Fletcher kept the shotgun pointed at Jake and leaned forward. He sniffed. "You smell weird." He turned to Nadine and sniffed. "Smell good. Flowers."

"You smell like you crapped your pants," Nadine said.

Fletcher shrugged. "Happened more than once. Dashi told you how to find me, did he?"

"He told us how to contact you, but I don't think he knew how to find you."

"Think Dashi didn't know where I was? He's always known. He pretends he doesn't, but he knows things."

Jake looked at Nadine. Nadine shrugged. "'Things,' sir?"

"Contracts. Shipments. Dashi's kept an eye on me for years. He wants what I have in my head."

"Yes, sir," Jake said. "Could you put down the shotgun while we talk?"

Fletcher looked down at his hands for a moment, then brought it up to where he could view it. "This is a shotgun," he said.

Jake looked at Nadine again, then back at Fletcher.

"Yes, sir, it is."

Fletcher flipped the shotgun over in his hands, studying it. He turned it back and forward, then brought it close to his eyes and peered at it like it had tiny, secret writing embossed on it. "A shotgun. A boarding shotgun."

"Yes, sir," Jake said.

"Well, imagine that," Fletcher said, then spun the shotgun around and pointed it at Nadine's nose. "Hands up."

Nadine quickly raised her hands. Jake noted that they had been near the special pocket on her skin suit where she kept her gauss pistol.

"Easy, easy. We're just here to talk," Jake said.

"'Talk'? Boarding my ship uninvited?"

"You invited us, you Imperial turd," Nadine said.

"This is a boarding, and I oppose it. Suppose that Emperor's scrotum Dashi told you to kill me."

Jake shook his head. "No."

"He didn't?" Fletcher asked.

"No," Jake said.

"Too bad." Fletcher lowered the shotgun. "Was hoping he did. Are you sure you didn't misunderstand?"

"Sir?" Jake said.

"Are you sure he didn't tell you to kill me? Maybe infer it, and you missed it?" He raised the shotgun again.

"No, sir, he didn't."

"That's disappointing." Fletcher pointed the shotgun at the ground.

Nadine lowered her hands. "I can kill you if you'd like."

Fletcher swung the gun back toward her. "Hands."

Nadine put her arms back up. "I'm just saying. If you want to be killed, I can help."

"I want him to do it." Fletcher looked at Jake. "Ever killed a man, John Andrew Keith?"

"I'm not sure," Jake said.

"Not sure? It's a simple question. Yes, or no?"

"I've shot people, or tried. I'm a poor shot. I'm not

sure anybody died."

"It's a relatively simple thing to determine if a man is dead. Are you telling me you can't tell the difference between a dead man and a live one?"

"Yes, sir, I can, but—"

"No 'buts' about it." Fletcher turned back to Nadine. "He's not the brightest, is he?"

"In some ways, not really," Nadine said. "He's good at fixing things and paperwork—stuff like that—but he's pretty helpless with a lot of practical things."

"That would be his mother. Nice lady. Friendly. Cheerful. Happy, but a twit."

"You know my mother?" Jake asked.

"Oh, I knew her. Definitely knew her. Before your dad did. Knew her several times a week before he met her."

"What?"

Fletcher took a deep breath, then another. His face began to pale. "Oops. This might get nasty."

"What do you mean?" Jake asked.

Fletcher bent over at the waist, pulled a bag out of a suit pocket, and flipped it open. The stench of vomit filled the room.

"Hold this," Fletcher said, extending the shotgun to Jake.

Jake took the proffered gun.

Fletcher heaved into the bag. He collapsed to his knees, then lifted his head and breathed hard. "Huuuuhhh....Hang on, there's more." He vomited again, and again.

Nadine looked at the shotgun Jake was holding. "I'll take that." She grabbed it, and cracked it open, and removed the shells.

"Now you can keep it," she said, handing back the unloaded gun.

"Whoops. Sorry," Fletcher said. "Gets worse and worse every time. Can you help me take my pills? They're in the wall bag in the fresher. Green bottle, and a gray one with red stripes."

Jake looked around and spotted a door to a fresher. He stepped inside and returned a moment later with the two bottles.

"Here you go. Do you have water?"

"Basic," Fletcher said, pointing down a corridor. Jake walked down, found a glass and a basic tap, and filled the glass.

"Here," Jake said, thrusting the glass at Fletcher, who had fumbled some pills into his hand.

"I thought you were going to help me with the pills," Fletcher said as Jake stepped back. "What's this?"

"It's basic, to help you get the pills down."

"How will it do that?"

"Throw the pills in your mouth, then drink," Jake said.

"That won't work, kid."

"Why not?" Jake asked.

"These aren't pills. They're suppositories."

Ten minutes later, Jake and Nadine were sitting at a table in the ramshackle hab module Fletcher had put up. Nadine refused to touch anything, and Jake didn't blame her.

Nadine looked over at the wall. "Jake, what's that?"

"Control console. Looks like he salvaged it from a ship."

"What's it doing here?"

"Life support and sensors, it looks like. He's set this up like a tiny station."

Fletcher stumbled back into the room, sweating and breathing heavily. "It gets worse all the time."

"You need to see a med unit, or a doctor," Nadine said.

"I don't. I know what's wrong with me."

"Something a doctor can't fix?" Jake asked.

"They can't fix hard radiation damage. Breaks down the cells. Causes cancer."

"You have cancer?" Jake said. "They can cure a lot of that. Why type of cancer?"

"I have cancer of everything. Seven different types, last time I had a checkup. Blood cancer was the worst."

"Where did you get hard radiation from?" Nadine asked. "What happened, jam yourself inside a microwave and fire it up?"

"You're a feisty one, aren't you?" Fletcher said.

"I just know a BS story when I hear one. How did you get hard radiation burns?"

"From a fusion reactor."

"Fusion reactors don't cause hard radiation burns. They don't produce that type of radiation."

"They do when you're outside fixing them and you clear the magnetosphere."

"Delta's magnetosphere is so low that everybody clears it all the time. It's probably only a thousand kilometers, and it's so weak that it doesn't protect anybody from anything. Try again."

"Who said I was talking about Delta's magnetosphere?" Fletcher said.

"You mean that you were outside the Dragon's magnetosphere?" Nadine said. "Really? Another BS story. Were you prospecting in the Belt too while you were doing this? Found an asteroid of 56 percent pure platinum? Celebrating your luck in the bar, but haven't been paid yet, so maybe a pretty girl like me could stand you a drink or too? Then you're going to tell me I have beautiful eyes, that you've never seen the like, and that I'm your soul mate, and wouldn't it be great if we bought a bottle of something and went up to my room to celebrate? You leave before I get up in the morning, and stick me with the bill for our drinks, and for the drinks with all the other girls." Nadine glared at Fletcher, her face flushed and her eyes narrowed.

Jake and Fletcher looked at each other. Fletcher raised his eyebrows.

Nadine coughed. "Just saying, that's all." She pursed her lips. "Bad memory. Is that what you're saying, though?"

"Uh, not exactly," Fletcher said, "but that is a pretty specific complaint."

"Well, yes, it is," Nadine agreed.

All of them were silent again.

"56 percent pure platinum is a pretty exact number," Fletcher said.

"100 percent wouldn't be believable," Nadine said. "Nobody believes that. It has to be more than half, though, or it doesn't sound like a big strike."

"I see," Fletcher said. "Heard that in a bar, did you? Believed it?"

"I hear lots of things in bars. I don't believe much anymore." She looked at Jake. He was moving his lips and appeared to be counting.

"Don't," Nadine said.

"Don't what?" Jake asked.

"It won't work. Not on me."

"Okay. It did, though. Once."

"Once. A long time ago. When I was younger."

"Okay." Jake nodded, then nodded again. "How much younger?"

Nadine sighed. "Fine. I thought I was smarter than he was. I wasn't. Moving on." She turned to Fletcher. "So, are you telling me you were on some sort of high-orbit course around the Dragon?"

"Nope, not the Dragon," Fletcher said.

"You can't get radiation sickness if you're still in orbit around Delta. We're shielded."

"The primary."

"What?"

"We were in an orbit, but not around the Dragon. Not around Sigma Draconis IV. We were in orbit around Sigma Draconis."

"An orbit around the primary?" Jake said. "How did you get into that orbit?"

"It's the one we were in when we arrived."

"When you arrived?"

"Yes. Arrived in the jump ship."

"Of course you did," Jake said, "and you knew my father, too, in this jump ship."

"Well, I met him earlier, in the Navy."

"The Delta Militia?"

"No, the Navy."

"Which navy?"

"The Imperial Navy. Years ago. Before we jumped here."

Chapter 27

"You were in the Imperial Navy with my father?" Jake asked. "Before the Abandonment?"

"A long time ago," Fletcher said, "and no—after the Abandonment.

"My dad was born here, on Rim-37."

"Really? Ever see a birth record? Ever meet your grandparents?"

Jake shook his head. "No. Dad's parents died before I was born."

"Maybe they did. Maybe they didn't. Not sure, really. He didn't talk much about that."

"How did you get here, then? Why did you get here?" Nadine asked.

"This was about thirty years ago. I was with a group, a group of—ah, Imperial anus, I'm dying. Doesn't matter," Fletcher said. "Can you hand me that glass of Basic? Thanks."

Drinking deep, he coughed, gasped a breath, coughed again, and wiped his mouth. "Thieves. We were thieves. The civil war was in full swing, but it hadn't affected us directly yet. Just ruined the economy."

"What civil war?" Jake said.

"The civil war. The secession, a new Emperor, all of that. The major fleet elements were recalled years before. There was all sorts of different news. A few sector governors revolted. Some sectors went out on their own. Some planets, too. The planets began to look out for themselves. We'd enlisted, figuring we'd be in the real Navy. After three years, we were in a modified cargo ship stopping other ships, 'inspecting their cargo'—which means confiscating the good stuff—as part of a local Auxiliary force."

"What happened to the Empire? The Emperor? Why

the Abandonment?"

"Didn't know, didn't care. If I had to guess, just a general slowdown in trade after the civil war started. Only one trade route goes through Delta. This place was a shortcut between two sectors, but only if you had a long-range ship. It wasn't on the main shipping lanes."

He stopped to take another drink of basic. "After the war started, all the long-range ships were impounded by the different navies. They used them as couriers or long-range strikes or something, so no more long-range cargo ships available. Delta is three times standard jump distance. Only military and scout ships would come here, and they were all busy."

"Why did you come here?" Jake asked.

"Didn't want to. That was the problem."

"I don't understand," Jake said. "You and my dad stole a ship."

"No, he just came along for the ride. Me and the others, we just arranged to get control of this Auxiliary Military ship. Just a big cargo ship with a couple of lasers. A sandcaster. And some missiles."

"Gained control," Nadine said. "You hijacked it, didn't you?"

Fletcher nodded. "Feisty and smart. I like your girlfriend, John Andrew Keith Edward."

"Why do you call me that?" Jake asked. "That's not my name."

"It was your dad's name, and you are named after him. J-A-K-E."

Jake straightened. "My dad's name was Danny Stewart."

"Nope. That was a records clerk back on...Betelgeuse, I think? Your dad knew him, so he used the name. My name isn't Fletcher, either, but it doesn't matter. Been Fletcher forever, it seems." He coughed again. "Knew your dad back when he was himself." He wheezed. It took a while to get his breath back.

"About the hijacking...." Nadine said.

"Right." Fletcher wobbled toward the console on the wall and tapped a few screens. "Let me turn up the air and heat in here. I don't often have visitors." He panned through a few screens, then faced Jake and Nadine. "There were six of us out of a crew of twenty-five. We wanted out of this civil war thing. We figured we'd take a ship and get away from things, go out to the outer sectors. Be our own men. Patrol a system somewhere."

"Pirates," Nadine said. "You were going to become pirates."

Fletcher shrugged. "We thought maybe we'd find a planet that would set us up as Militia, or something like that. We'd defend them against the neighbors."

"Prey on the neighbors, more likely," Nadine said.

"Maybe. Who knows, and does it matter now?"

"What happened?" Jake asked. "How did you take the ship?"

Fletcher drank from the basic and stared at the wall.

"What went wrong?" Nadine asked.

"Everything," Fletcher said. "We tried to take the ship during third watch. Figured that we'd be able to overwhelm the watch crew, and that some of them were with us. We figured wrong. There was shooting. We managed to lock the off-watch crew in the quarters, but the bridge and engineering shift fought. They locked themselves in." He stared at the wall again.

"And?" Nadine said. "Then what?"

Fletcher didn't say anything.

"You killed them, didn't you?" Nadine said.

"Yup. Depressurized the hull. Oh, I didn't do it myself, but I didn't argue too much against it."

"My dad was a murderer?" Jake asked.

Fletcher laughed. "No. Your dad was locked in his cabin the whole time. Slept through most of it. He was always a heavy sleeper, and we'd managed to disable the alarms. When he woke up the next day, a third of the crew was dead, a third were rebels, and we were threatening to dump the other third out the airlock unless they cooperated."

"So he helped you escape?" Nadine asked.

"He did. The Empire didn't command much loyalty back then. The war had been going on for a while. Quality of the troops was bad. Discipline was poor. Pay wasn't exactly regular, either. We said we'd pay him and feed him, and was that really much different than what he'd signed up for?"

"I'm confused. Was he or was he not a pirate?" Nadine asked.

"Might have become one, but he didn't have a chance. First we had to get the ship working. We'd had to kill most of the officers. The only one we had left was a junior steward. We didn't have any navigators. Needed a navigator."

"A pilot too," Nadine said.

"Maybe, but we hadn't thought things too far through. Plan was to take the ship, load up on supplies, and head out to the boondocks, but we had bad luck from the start. Maybe we were cursed because we'd killed the whole crew. We were trying to figure out the systems and set things up on automatic while we ran out-system. While we were doing this, another ship jumped into the system. Another Auxiliary cruiser, loyal to the Empire."

"You got in a battle with an Imperial ship?" Nadine said.

Fletcher laughed, but it turned into another cough. "Of course we didn't. We ran. We had a ship but no pilots. We had guns but no gunners. We had no navigator, so no way to calculate a jump."

"Computers calculate jumps," Jake said.

"Not true," Fletcher said. "Well, kind of. Commercial navigation computers route you to jump lanes, and use precalculated jump paths to take you to the next station. They don't have the processing power to totally calculate a complete jump path from scratch. Military ships do, but their computers are a thousand times more powerful and have the proper software, and they take an Imperial buttock-load of power. We didn't have that."

"I didn't know that," Jake said.

"We didn't either," Fletcher said, "till we did what we thought was a jump calculation, and pressed the button."

"Wait," Nadine said. "You just jumped?"

"We did a commercial jump like we were in a traffic lane. We weren't."

"Well, it worked," Nadine said. "You got here."

"True, except we weren't actually trying to get here. We mis-jumped. Didn't know what system this was when we crashed out. Could be there were Imperial troops here."

Fletcher finished the basic and held out his empty cup to Jake, who took it to the tap and filled it again. Fletcher thanked Jake and took another swig. A light on the console flashed. He turned back to his screens and tabbed through them, stopping to look at one in particular. "Also, we didn't know how to fix our fusion plant, which had failed when we jumped. So we were in this ballistic orbit, with no power, in a strange system. By the way, is your ship secure? Spiked down?"

Nadine and Jake looked at each other.

"Yes," Jake said. "Four points. So what happened?"

"Two suicides. A fight—a big one. Some deaths. And your dad, Jake. He happened. Your dad saved us. Showed us how we could alter the orbit to something reasonable if we could get the fusion plant up. Figured out it was just a fuel problem. We just needed to fix some fuel lines and some control runs, and we had to realign the grids and the nozzles.

"That's what got me. Some of the others, too. Went out on the hull to fix the nozzles. Didn't realize all the hard radiation we were getting. The sensors were down." Fletcher stopped and looked at Nadine. "It's really hard to crew a ship without decent sensors."

"Tell me about it," Nadine said. "I keep complaining to Jake about that, but he keeps buying cheap stuff."

"You were there for the purchase. You could have complained then, if you weren't so busy flirting with Mr. Pletcher," Jake said.

"Flirting with Vince?" Nadine said. "I was not, and even if I were, you are in charge of buying stuff. It's your job to get good sensors. Not the crap we have."

"It's been fine up till now," Jake said. "When we're back at Rim-37, I'll await a credit transfer for our new purchases." He glared at Nadine.

Nadine glared back. Fletcher coughed.

"Sorry," Nadine said. "Let me get this straight....You and a group of six of your friends stole an Imperial Auxiliary cruiser, killed two-thirds of the crew, jumped it to this system, and fried the power systems, but somehow escaped to become unsuccessful Belt miners? And nobody ever heard of this. Ever."

"We didn't kill two-thirds of the crew. There was some fighting when we took over, but...."

"But they're all dead now. Except you," Nadine said. "Why didn't you let people know about the ship? You could have just said everybody died in the fighting and that accident, and asked for help fixing it."

"They couldn't," Jake said. "They had to hide it. They weren't sure if there were Imperial units here, or if somebody was following them, or if they had already been reported. For all they knew, Nadine, there was a fleet base here, and the local Navy garrison was waiting for them and would arrest them."

"Still, they could have made up a story," Nadine said.

Jake snapped his fingers. "Militia codes. That was it, wasn't it?"

He looked at Fletcher, who nodded.

"What codes?" Nadine said.

Jake looked at Fletcher. "You could hear the comm traffic, and Militia codes are based on Imperial codes. Not as strong, but they would look similar on a comm unit. You thought there was an Imperial garrison here and they were chasing you. You didn't know anything about the Abandonment."

Fletcher nodded. "Thought we were in big trouble. That's why we were all out on the hull fixing things. Your dad figured out the problem with the fuel routing and the nozzles, so we were out there trying to get them sorted as fast as possible. We weren't tied into any of the navigation channels, or anything like that. We didn't have any time. We were all out there, and a big flare came by. By the time our instruments went off, it was too late. We all fried on the hull."

"All of you?" Jake asked.

"Your dad was in engineering. That was shielded, so he was in the best shape. I got a dose and was sick for a few weeks, but I recovered. Flemming was shielded as well, but she was sick when we got here. She lasted till we got the Launch off. The rest died within a week. There was just the three of us. Your dad put the ship in a parking orbit, and we piled in that old Launch with what we had. Flemming died on the way, but your dad and I made it to the Rim."

Fletcher turned back to his console. "Warm enough now. I have power, but not a lot to spare." He flipped to another screen. A light flashed red. He glanced at it, tapped it once, then ignored it.

"How'd you survive? How'd you get to Rim-37?" Jake asked.

"We had a Launch. We did courier runs, delivered supplies. We stayed in the Outer Rim till we figured out what was going on. It was a year before we were sure the Empire wasn't here. By then, the Launch was on its last legs. I was sick. Not really sick, but sick enough. Your dad met your mom, and they had become an item. He wanted to put this all behind him. I wanted to stay. I was prospecting and doing okay. I met a guy called Dashi."

Jake and Nadine nodded.

"He knows about this?" Jake asked. "This supposed ship?"

Fletcher shrugged. "He suspects. Strongly suspects. He's smart. Talked a lot with us when we were first here. Asked a lot of questions. He figured out that we didn't know things about the local system that we should have. Even back then, he was a man to be watched, but he helped us out a bit. Got a few contracts for your dad. Got me some prospecting licenses."

"In return, you were going to give Dashi this ship? This supposed jump ship?"

"He didn't know for sure that there was a jump ship, and we didn't enlighten him. I mean, we didn't tell him. Now I'm talking like him."

"He has that effect," Jake said. "He believed you?"

"I don't think Dashi believes anything," Fletcher said. "He assigns a probability as to whether something is true, and allocates his resources accordingly. He thought we might be telling some truth, so it was a bit of an investment on his part. If there was a ship, we'd owe him. If there was no ship, then no harm done."

"Who else have you told this wild story to?" Nadine said.

"Nobody except you and Jake here. Dashi suspects. There was a Militia guy who had a lot of questions. He might have told somebody. He was sharp. He became an admiral a few years back, according to the vids."

"Why didn't you just go and take this ship and fly it out of here?" Jake asked.

"To where, and with who? We had a crew of thirty, and only two of us survived. We couldn't have flown it anywhere with just the two of us. We needed a real pilot—an interstellar pilot, a navigator, an engineer, and a bunch of other crew. Plus supplies." A red light flashed on the console. Fletcher looked at it, then tabbed it off. "Besides, life here wasn't too bad. Nobody was chasing us. Life goes on."

"That's a great story," Nadine said. "I'd like to believe you, but it's pretty fantastical."

"It is indeed," Fletcher agreed. "Of course, Dashi sent you here for a reason, and even though he didn't say it, I know the reason was to give you this ship. I haven't got any family, I'm sicker than I've ever been, and I'm not going to get better. I guess it should go to Jake now."

"You're going to give an Imperial ship to Jake?" Nadine said. "What, you have it parked behind a rock around here?"

"Would it freak you out if I did?" Fletcher asked.

Nadine looked uncertain.

Fletcher laughed. "Jake, I'll bet you have a partial-orbit path somewhere. Missing a few parameters. Some entry codes, too, and a lot of encrypted stuff."

"I do," Jake said.

"Let me see it," Fletcher said.

Jake looked at Nadine, who smiled as if to say *why not?* He pulled out his comm unit, put a chip in it, typed a few things, and then gave the chip to Fletcher.

Fletcher put the chip in his console and typed on it. "Yup. Almost what you need. Let's see." Fletcher skipped screens and began to type a long access code in. "It was the best code we could determine. It will take a minute....There."

The console flashed.

Fletcher looked at it and nodded. "There you go, young John Andrew Keith Edward. Full orbital particulars. Access codes. Some schematics and such, but most of that is in the onboard computer. You picked a good time to come by. Given the orbital path, you might be able to rendezvous with this ship in a day or two. Great timing. That's probably Dashi's work." A light flashed red on his console, and he tabbed it off.

"Jake?" Nadine said.

"It's an orbital path. He's right—if this is for a ship, it

will pass not too far away from here pretty soon. I'm not sure we can rendezvous, though. I'll have to work on it."

"Well, work on it quickly," Fletcher said. The light on his console flashed red again. "You should go meet it before the warship arrives."

"Warship?" Nadine said. "What warship?"

"The one that keeps setting off my radar alert warnings here," Fletcher said. "The one that keeps coming closer. The one that's coming for us."

Chapter 28

"What do you mean, a warship is coming to get us?" Nadine asked.

"That's what the beeping means. Sensors say a warship is coming," Fletcher said.

"See, Jake? Everybody has sensors. Except us." Nadine hit him on the arm.

"Ow. How do you know it's a warship, and what do you mean by 'warship'? There aren't any naval ships in the system. Just Militia cutters," Jake said. "Besides, why would a warship be coming here, and how do you know it's not coming for you?"

"Maybe they are 'is this a warship' sensors," Nadine said.

"Could be," Fletcher said, "but I've been kind of ignored here for a long time, so it's kind of suspicious that they ignored me for years, and then when you two show up, a few hours later the Militia arrives too."

"I guess," Jake said. "How does this detector work?"

"It's basic. I have antennas rigged up on a couple of the icebergs. They're tuned to certain frequencies—Militia frequencies—and when they receive something, they radio it back here."

"So all you're saying is that there is a ship getting closer," Jake said. "That's probably not a big deal."

"A ship with Militia band radar."

"They could just be passing by," Jake said.

"Never seen the signal this strong, which means I've never seen anybody get this close before. If they are passing by, then they are passing close—closer than I've ever seen."

"Maybe they are coming to talk to you, not us," Jake said.

"Could be," Fletcher said. "Bet they'll want to search

your ship. You two have anything you don't want them to find?"

Nadine and Jake looked at each other.

"Kinda," Nadine said.

Five minutes later they were climbing into the airlock. "You sure you don't want to come with us?" Jake said.

"Nope. I'm too sick. These pills perk me up for a while, but the crash is terrible. I don't have much longer, I don't think. Anyway, I'm happy out here. Happy enough."

"If you are this sick, what happens when you...I mean, if things get too bad?"

"Don't you worry, youngster. I've got a packet of stuff that will take care of me if the pain gets too bad. It's even soluble in basic. I've got a container of frozen orange juice saved too. Special treat. I'll take care of things."

"What are you going to do if the Militia comes in?" Nadine asked.

"I've got my shotgun and lots of shells. I'll be fine."

"Are you sure?" Jake asked.

"Young John Andrew Keith Edward, one way or another, I won't live out the month. Whether it's drugs, the Militia, or killer space bats doesn't matter much to me. Free trades." Fletcher began to swing the lock shut.

"Free trades," Jake said, stepping back as the door clanged shut.

A quick exit and down the cable, and Nadine dove into their airlock. Jake began to lever the spikes out of the ice.

"I'm bringing everything online right now, Jake," Nadine said. "By the way, it smells great in here. In comparison."

"I just need a minute with the spikes."

"Jake, leave the spikes."

"Just a minute. Spikes are expensive." Jake levered the first one out and began work on the second.

"We don't have time, Jake. We need to leave now."

"Leave and do what?" he asked, levering the second

out.

"What?"

"What's your plan? How are we getting away from the Militia?" Jake pulled another lever. "Third one's out."

"We run away."

"Where? How? They can see us, they are probably faster, and they have sensors, as you have so helpfully pointed out. Fourth one is out."

"Fine. What's your plan?" Nadine said.

"In difficult ground, press on. In encircled ground, devise stratagems. In death ground, fight."

"Stewart, where do you get all this nonsense you spout?" Nadine said.

An hour later Nadine was sitting in the pilot's chair reading a stress gauge. She had sent Jake outside to winch in the towing cable. She had maneuvered up to a giant piece of ice, and he had clamped it to the front of the ship.

"Seriously? You've never even heard of Sun Tzu?" he said over the radio.

"Is he related to Cecil Tzu?" Nadine asked.

"Cecil Tzu?"

"Cecil runs a breakfast place on Transit-11. He has this rice and sausages thing he does, with soy sauce. It's great. Any relation?"

"I don't think so. This is an ancient Earth philosopher."

"Stewart, what do you think the chances of me knowing the name of somebody from some old vid you watched?"

"Well, I thought....Ah, never mind what I thought."

"Are you sure this is going to work?" Nadine checked her board. Everything was green.

"It should. What other options do we have?"

"We could fight."

"You always want to fight."

"It simplifies things," Nadine said.

"There is more than just fighting, Nadine. There is planning, cooperation, organization."

"That sounds boring. This is more fun."

"So what are you going to do? Stand on the hull and shoot at them with your gauss pistol? That's the only weapon we have."

"We have crates and crates of revolvers. I could use those. We have lots of ammunition."

"How close will they have to get to us for that to work?"

"Close is fine," Nadine said. "Is that container chained up?"

"Chained and locked," Jake said.

"Right." Nadine keyed her radio for a different channel. "We're set here, old timer. Thanks again for that container."

Fletcher's voice came over the radio. "Wasn't using it, haven't used it in years, and I've still got another spare if I need it. That ship is getting close. You'd better move."

"Where did you get all that stuff from?" Nadine asked.

"Dashi. He arranged to sell it to me years ago at a premium," Fletcher said, "but he said I had to be willing to sell it back if he asked. I figure you guys are asking."

"Too true," Nadine said. "Lucky strikes. Jake, you need to get back inside. I'm pushing shortly."

"Just battening down the last of the hatches out here," Jake said.

"Jake, please use regular-person words. 'Battening'? Isn't that making a cake?"

"Never mind. Just let me lock the tow cable, and I'm in."

Nadine began to cycle through all the different screens and settled on the hatch status. She waited while a light cycled from green to red, orange, then back to green. She began to fire the maneuvering thrusters, one at a time.

Jake arrived on the bridge. "Not doing your usual blast out of here, with all engines firing."

"The mass is unbalanced, and I don't want to crack into more things than necessary."

The *Castle Arcturus* moved away from the Fletcher's mini-habitat, and Nadine began to push the ship toward the swarm of ice rocks around them.

"Have you picked a direction yet?" Jake asked.

"Yep. I'm assuming they are chasing us spinward, so I'm going to go anti-spinward."

"Right at them?"

"Down their neck."

"Brave."

"That's the point, right? First we need to get out of this mess, though," Nadine said. "Watch out your viewport and let me know what you see."

"I see ice."

"I know, Jake, but how close is it, and how rapidly are we closing in on it?"

"I'll watch," Jake said.

Nadine pivoted the ship with the thrusters and checked her course.

"Okay, I'm going to engage the main engines," Nadine said. The *Castle Arcturus* began to accelerate. "What's in front of us?"

"We're clear for about ten meters, then there's a small iceberg to your starboard."

"Avoid it?"

"Nope, just push it. I'll let you know when we touch," Jake said.

Nadine carefully pushed the throttle. She looked over at Jake. He had climbed up and was standing on his chair, peering out the upper side of the viewport.

"Five meters. Four, three, two, one. Contact."

Nadine pulsed the thrusters to pivot the ship, then began to push away from the ice.

"We're moving. Okay, we're clear of that one," Jake said. "Another one coming up. We should avoid that. Swing up."

Nadine pitched the ship up and pulsed the main engines.

"Small one coming in fast. Stand by," Jake said. The ship bounced and slowed noticeably. "Contact."

"We're still heading out," Nadine said.

"Looking clearer up front," Jake said. "Some more small ones. They'll just crash."

The ship rocked gently as the smaller ice chunks hit it.

"Are we clear yet?" Nadine asked.

"One more big one. Dead ahead," Jake said.

"Can we go around it?" Nadine asked.

"It's wide," Jake said.

"I'm going to scrape over it." Nadine pushed the throttles to zero, and they floated.

"Coming up," Jake said. "Brace for impact." The *Castle Arcturus* rocked as something hit it, then began to shake.

"Scraping along," Jake said. "The spin is crunching into us."

"Got it. I'll scrape up over." Nadine fired the thrusters to change the aspect of the ship, and pulsed the main engines. "Going below."

"We're good as long as we don't catch," Jake said, but then the ship began to twist. "We've caught. Level up!"

Nadine fired the thrusters full-power. The twisting slowed, then abruptly stopped, and reversed.

"We're clear of it, Jake said.

"Good. I'll pivot us around on course again."

"Great," Jake said. "Emperor's anus—hang on."

CLANG. The ship jerked backwards. A screeching sound opened up. White lights flitted along all the viewports.

"What was that?"

"Hit a medium-sized one head-on. Crunched it into pieces. Blew them all over the place."

"Okay, but what was that noise?"

"Not sure. I need to go outside."

"I'll put us back on course."

"The radar's offline."

"Of course it is," Nadine said.

Jake unbuckled and clambered down to the lock.

Nadine kept the course steady and punched the comm. "Well?"

"I'm climbing out of the lock. Give me a minute," Jake said.

"Stewart, I'm flying blind here."

"And I'm climbing out into the blind, so we're even."

Nadine sat and fumed. She keyed the radio. "Stewart, you can be a condescending, supercilious, pompous twit, you know that?"

"I think of those as my most endearing qualities. By the way, where did you learn that word? 'Supercilious'?"

Nadine shut the radio off. "I'm starting to sound like him. I hope I'm not starting to think like him. Maybe less time together?" She stared at the console. "Never talked to myself before—that's for sure."

"Radar's back online," Jake said over the comm.

Nadine tapped the screen and turned her comm back on. "Good. Let me see what's out there....It's clear."

"Yeah. About that...."

"Totally clear. No ships. Hmm," Nadine tapped the screen. "Also, no asteroids. No beacons or stations, either. Want to explain that?"

"The support beam was bent back 70 degrees. It's pointing straight up now. So the radar is showing things above us, not in front of us."

"Thanks for that, Jake. I'll just pivot us to see what's in front of us."

"Good. Saves me from having to hammer this vertical. That would be a lot of work," Jake said.

"Up your Imperial anus too," Nadine said. "Let me spin. Hang on." She tapped her screen.

"You could have asked if I was locked down, or tethered," Jake said.

"When are you not tethered? I see them. Okay, let me

get a vector...and we're ready. You coming in?"

"Two minutes."

Nadine manipulated her screen again, then watched. A light flicked from green to red, then orange. "Firing engines," she said.

Chapter 29

"Then, after the colonel's speech, I thought, who could not agree that we would be better off under direct military rule? Don't you think so, Corporal?" Commander Vercher asked.

He was seated in the back of the Militia cutter. Corporal Dalon and a half-squad of six troopers sat in the hab module.

"Indeed, Commander. Good for you, sir," Corporal Dalon said.

"We'll do so much better than these corporate chumps, Corporal."

"Of course, Commander, and congratulations on your promotion, sir."

"Why, thank you, Corporal."

"Well deserved, sir. I mean, who gets a double promotion these days?"

"Indeed, Corporal. A reward for all my hard work."

"And your support of the junta, sir."

"Junta?"

"The Officers' Council, sir. A council of officers. It's called a junta."

"I did not know that, but that word sounds...distasteful."

"One of the other officers used it, sir, I'm sure. It may have been the admiral."

"Oh, well, in that case, I'm sure it will be fine."

"Hey, ground people, come up here," a voice came from the control room at the front on the ship.

"'Ground people'?" Commander Vercher said. "That's not polite."

"They're Orbital Force. Not known for their politeness," Corporal Dalon said. "Evans, you're in charge. Don't screw up." He hauled himself to his feet and climbed up to the control room with Commander Vercher.

"Status report," Corporal Dalon said.

"Yes, give us the latest updates on our glorious return of this backwater to Imperial control," Commander Vercher said.

The pilot looked blank.

Corporal Dalon rolled his eyes and pointed at Commander Vercher. "What he said."

The copilot spoke up. "A large, icy asteroid has detached from that cluster and is decelerating toward us."

"You called us here to talk about icebergs? Really? Why do you waste our time so? When will we arrive at this rogue station you've located?" Commander Vercher said.

Everybody was silent for a moment. The pilot and copilot looked at each other, then turned to Corporal Dalon.

Corporal Dalon closed his eyes for a moment. "Icebergs can't move, sir. There must be a ship involved. Attached to it or pushing it, or something. Which is it?"

"Can't tell," the pilot said. "It's a big one, and there are some others in close proximity, but it's definitely pushing back at us."

"Well, let's blast them out of space, then," Commander Vercher said. "Tell them, 'surrender or death.'"

Corporal Dalon closed his eyes again, sighed, and opened them. "Well?" he asked the pilot.

"Too big," the pilot said. "Can't blast it."

"You have a mass driver and a laser. Why can't you hit it and melt it?" Corporal Dalon asked.

"Oh, we can hit it, and the laser will cook it down. In time. Given the amount of power the laser puts out, a couple of megajoules, it should take....Daav, what's the specific heat of water?" the pilot said.

"4.2 joules per gram, assuming it's just water."

"So, one megajoule will melt...what?"

"Depends on the temperature. Let's say it's -50 Celsius, so we have to raise it 50 degrees. That's 210 joules, divided into a million. Call it...5,000 grams?"

"Sure, so five kilograms."

"There you go," the pilot said, looking at Corporal Dalon.

"Go where? What are you talking about?" Commander Vercher said.

"Are you Imperial scrotums telling me we can only melt five kilograms a shot?" Corporal Dalon said.

"Pretty much. We can pulse it to burst a bit, but it's supposed to fuse electronics and cause blast damage, not act as an electric blanket."

"But we're in space," Corporal Dalon said. "The melting point of water is lower in a near-vacuum."

"Good point. We don't need to raise it 50 degrees. Let's see....If we can recalculate using kelvin...."

"Emperor's anus. What about the mass driver?"

"Might break it up. Once again, it's for burst damage."

"Imperial testicles," Corporal Dalon said. "What can we do?"

"We shall board them and show them the error of their ways. Victory or death," Commander Vercher said.

"Of course, sir. As you said—but one question, sir."

"Yes, Corporal?"

"They are heading right at us. What if they choose death?"

"Choose death?"

"Ram us, sir. What if they want to kill us instead?"

The pilots looked at each other.

"Imperial anus." The pilot punched his console. "Stand by for rapid maneuvering."

"So we hit them and die in the crash, or avoid them and get shot to death?" Jake asked. He had just climbed back inside from his stint on the hull, and was sitting next to Nadine in the control room.

"I don't like either of those options," Nadine said. "So we'll go with your backup plan."

"What makes you think I have a backup plan?"

"Jake, you always have a backup plan," Nadine said. "Something stupidly administrative, like how they have to turn back because they are overdue for their quarterly laundry inspection, or their batteries are all going to die because they haven't paid the license on their solar charger interface, or some such thing."

"Solar charger interface? They have a fusion drive."

"It's just an example. I know you got that container from Fletcher for a reason. What's your plan for all that stuff?"

"That's easy. First, we make sure that they have sensors. Second, we throw a bunch of things away, and third, we blow ourselves up."

"We blow ourselves up?"

"Just a little bit," Jake said. He began to explain.

About twenty minutes later, Jake had filled the airlock with piles of junk. Empty food trays, pieces of metal, broken parts, door handles, crowbars, and tools, as well as a select pile of things from Fletcher's container. Nadine had cut their deceleration relative to the Militia ship, and had pivoted the ship up so she could follow its approach on radar.

"I really don't want to dump these tools," Jake said. "We might need them sometime."

"You said we had spares of everything," Nadine said.

"We do, but what if we lose the primary one and need the spare?"

"Jake, this is why you'll never be a corporate leader. You have to learn to take a few risks sometimes."

"I'm on the hull of a spaceship that we more or less stole, loaded with black-market revolvers, speeding toward a Militia ship that is probably here to shoot us out of space, and you say I should take more risks?"

"I'll bet you have double tethers on," Nadine said.

"You sure it's still accelerating to meet us?" Jake asked.

"Eat my Imperial anus. I don't tell you how to do your paperwork stuff."

"Fine. How much time do I have?"

"Half hour, maybe," Nadine said.

"Okay, let me get the first group off, and I'll try for a second group. Put us in a slow yaw," Jake said.

Nadine complied, and Jake began to heave the full airlock empty. He threw food trays straight out of the ship at a 90-degree angle. He didn't throw them hard. He mostly just gave them a slight underhand lob, and they floated away from the ship. The gentle yaw dispersed them, so soon the *Castle Arcturus* was in the middle of an expanding disc of trash.

Jake would occasionally take a round object out of a box in the corner and twist a ring at the top. He paid close attention to the settings on the first three he threw out, but after that, he just spun the dials at random.

There were three boxes in the corner, and he was almost done with the third when Nadine called, "Fifteen minutes. We have to get the rest of the ice off."

"Right," Jake said. He pulled the last few objects out, spun their rings, and dumped them out. "I'll need one more box."

Jake closed the outer door of the airlock, popped the inner one, and ran back in. He pulled himself down to the container head ends, and grabbed two more boxes, and pushed himself back toward the airlock. He clambered in, closed the door, cycled the outer door, and pushed the two boxes outside to hang about six feet clear of the ship.

Then Jake clambered up onto the top of the control tower. "Nadine, you ready?"

"You unclipping the ice?"

"Yes. Stand by." Jake went over to one of the main cargo winches and began to reel out the attached line. Since they were just floating along, the line pooled around the ship. Jake skated to the other side and unclipped a line there. "Alright, a little decel now, but be careful."

"Do we have to talk about your Imperial anus again?"

"Nope, but I'm on the top of this ship, so pivot us up so nothing will crush me. Wait—I have to grab something." Jake clipped one tether to the other and began to scan around. He locked onto the two boxes he'd pushed out earlier, and jumped toward them.

He hit the first one, grabbed it in his arms, and bounced out to the end of his tether. The tether was almost elastic, and he began to coil back to the ship. He snagged the second box by its recessed handles as he went by. Spinning around and hitting the ship feet-first, he engaged his magnets and held tight to the two boxes.

"Okay, go," he said.

The ship pivoted under him. He made sure that his boots were locked, and both of his tethers. The large chunks of ice attached to the front of the *Castle Arcturus* strained against the cables. They could now rock and strain against the slack. They slowly rolled around until they were below the ship, then caught in the mesh of cables. Nadine swung the ship around until the main engines were facing their intended direction of travel, then began to pulse them.

Some of the cables went slack, and others tightened. One came completely loose, so Jake tromped over to the winch. "Hold the accel while I fix a cable."

The ship stopped, and he released the boxes so they floated right above the ship. He reeled the line in until the entire cable was back on the drum. Then he repeated the operation on the second winch, but the second line was stuck.

"First winch secured," Jake said. "Second one is still out there. It's caught."

"Stand by for more yaw," Nadine said.

"Nadine, I don't think—"

"Shut up, Jake," she said.

The ship pivoted in a slow circle. Jake rushed to clutch at the two floating boxes. The cable loosened, then tightened again.

"It's caught, Nadine. We have to go to plan B. Hold us steady."

"Let me try reversing it," she said.

"We don't have time."

"Reversing."

Jake turned off his radio and began to curse. He had a lot of different curses, involving stubborn blond girls, crazy men who inhabited out-of-the-way stations, Rim-37 denizens, and general spacer hardship. He kept the radio off until the yaw stopped.

"Well?" Nadine said.

"Still tied to us," Jake said. "I'll go out and fix this."

"We only have a few minutes."

"I'll make it work."

There was a sudden flash of light parallel to them, off to one side.

"What was that?" Nadine said.

"Start of our counterstrike," Jake said. "Right on time."

"You can't have explosions going on while you are out there doing this," Nadine said.

"Some hotshot pilot told me I'd have plenty of time to get back in after she knocked the ice off the front of the ship," Jake said.

"Bite me," Nadine replied.

Jake tied his second tether to the two boxes and used it to tow them behind him. He pulled himself down to the bottom of the ship and examined the situation.

The large iceberg they had tethered to had broken into a number of smaller pieces that were even now floating off away from the ship, but the largest hunk of ice had become stuck in a loop of cable. The cable held tight, having coiled around the chunk several times. It would take a lot of time and maneuvering to twist free. Time they did not have.

"Right. I'm going to blow it off," Jake said.

"Jake, they're getting close. You only have a few

minutes."

"Only way for this to work," Jake said. A light flashed nearby as another bomb went off, and a small flash of metal, blown off something, streaked across the corner of his vision.

"I've got to get this done fast so we can maneuver. Just stand by." Jake looked at his tether, the iceberg, then back at the boxes he was towing, and judged the distance. He cursed, over the radio this time.

"Unclipping," he said.

"Jake, don't do that."

"Weren't you just telling me I should take more risks?"

"Yeah, but I meant dating unsuitable girls or trying strange brands of whiskey, not jumping off a ship into the void."

"It's okay. I'll have my tools with me," Jake said. He paused. "What kind of unsuitable girls? Do you know any?"

Another bomb went off. It illuminated the box Jake was towing—and the legend *Mining charges, 10 kg, qty 50.*

Chapter 30

"What was that flash?" Commander Vercher asked.

"Don't know," the pilot said. He and the copilot looked at each other for a second, then began to toggle screens in front of them and check readouts.

"Lots of metal spreading out around that ship," the pilot said.

"No radiation. Thermal says heat. Lots of heat. There's another one." The copilot pointed at a red bloom on his screen.

The pilot looked over and began scanning.

"It's just a bunch of metal junk, though. Small metal junk," the copilot said.

"What's happening? Are they shooting at us?" Corporal Dalon said.

"They don't have any guns. No mass driver, no laser. Nothing,"

"Are you sure?" Commander Vercher said. "Our enemies are devious."

"It's a cargo ship, by the Imperial beard, not a Militia cutter," the pilot said.

"So what are those explosions, the rare but seldom-seen exploding ice of the Outer Belt?" the copilot asked.

Everybody was quiet.

"How do you know it's an unarmed cargo ship?" Corporal Dalon said.

"It's the right size and shape for a cargo ship, one that can't take a mass driver. We have its registration, which said it's unarmed, and we put a telescope on it earlier and didn't see any weapons," the pilot said. "Any visible weapons," he corrected.

"Where did it come from?"

"Some podunk station out here."

"It originated from there? What were we chasing from

in-belt, then?" Corporal Dalon asked.

"Well, no, it didn't originate from out here. It came from a somewhere in-system."

"We tracked it from a broker," Commander Vercher said.

"A broker in-system?" the pilot said.

"Yes. At a repair yard."

Everyone turned to stare at Commander Vercher.

"What? Why are you all looking at me?"

"You didn't think it was important to tell us that this just came out of a repair yard?" the pilot asked.

"Why does that matter?" Commander Vercher asked.

"They could have put anything on it."

"What could they have put on it?" Corporal Dalon asked. "You're telling me it won't take a mass driver, and you don't see a laser, so what are those explosions, then?"

Everybody was quiet. Another explosion flashed in the distance.

The copilot sat up straight. "Mines. It could be mines. All that they'd have to do is fix a rack in one of the containers. That cloud of debris....It's hiding them. We're driving full-speed into a spread of mines."

Corporal Dalon punched a button on the intercom. "Everybody strap in for violent maneuvering." He grabbed Commander Vercher and propelled him into the passenger compartment. "Shoot something at them to break their concentration, and get us out of their way. Now."

Jake swung around at the end of his tether as Nadine yelled over the radio. "Why can't we have more than this stupid single-directional radar? Why can't we have a decent set of sensors? Jake, I'm not sure how far away they are."

"I've got to get this ice off," Jake said.

"You know we were heading right at them last time we checked."

"They can maneuver around us. We'll be fine," Jake said. He impacted on the iceberg and grabbed onto a protruding hunk of ice. Extracting an odd-looking tool from his belt, like a combination of an ice pick and a hammer, he swung it, ramming it into the ice. It held. "Okay, Nadine, I just have to set these bombs, and we can blow this thing in half."

Jake saw a flash out of the corner of his eye. He turned to look but it was gone. "Nadine, was that...?"

"Yes, that was a laser. Emperor's balls. We have to get out of here. Hang on."

The world shifted underneath Jake. "Nadine, I'm not totally clipped!" he said. The whole iceberg pivoted under him. Jake instinctively engaged his magnetic boots.

Nadine ignored his yell. "Maneuvering."

Ice is not, of course, magnetic.

Jake was flung from the surface of the iceberg. One arm clutched a jagged protrusion of ice, while the other grabbed the embedded ice axe. His legs spun up behind him, and his lifeline coiled out as the boxes of bombs stretched behind him. They hit the end of the line with a jerk.

The ice handhold cracked off, and he was yanked free of the axe. Only the wrist strap of the ice axe saved him. He hung dangling at the end of the strap, with a line and two boxes of bombs behind him.

"Okay, we've got that ice in front of us again, but they might be able to get the ventral side," Nadine said over the comm. After a beat, she said, "Jake? What are you doing?"

"Just admiring the view, really," Jake said.

"Well, stop hanging around. We need to get this worked out. How can you turn lazy at a time like this?" she said.

"I'll need a few seconds," Jake said. He climbed forward around the front of the ice and examined the coil holding the ice to the ship. It was deeply embedded. There was no way mere maneuvering would release this.

"Nadine, hold us steady for a minute while I set these charges here," Jake said. He again drove his ice axe into the iceberg, and used the tether to pull the box of bombs toward the iceberg. He pulled two out, spun their timers, and jammed them in the crack where the line was. He armed a third one and stuffed it in the box. Then he unclipped, turned, and jumped back toward the ship.

He began to climb up to the control room.

"Jake, they're shooting at us, and they are maneuvering, I think. They're targeting the ice, but they hit us too."

"Just wait, Nadine. Just wait. Any second, the charges will fire, and—"

With a flash of light, the first charge fired.

"The charges will fire, and what?" Nadine asked.

Jake looked at the lines holding the ice. Still taut. Nothing. "That should have shattered the ice and set us free."

"Well, it didn't," Nadine said. "There's the laser again. They keep firing at the ice. Say, Jake, what will happen if they hit one of those bombs?"

Jake started to reply, but there was another, brighter flash.

The entire iceberg burst into hundreds of pieces. A number of them bounced back toward Jake, and he pivoted, ducked, and weaved. They flew harmlessly past.

Except one. It struck him in the chest. He doubled over and saw a puff of water vapor as he began to lose air. He was forced upright and flung back as Nadine pivoted the ship and fired the main engines to slow them down and move them sideways. The forces made his head snap back and his arms wave out, and he stared off into space, getting a perfect view of the nearby Militia cutter as it spun around, fired its engines, and began to race away from them and their cloud of metallic, exploding trash.

"Jake, they're running away. We're good. We'll be past them."

"Good. Great. Good," Jake said. His chest hurt, and he was having problems walking back to the airlock.

"You coming back in?" Nadine asked.

"Yes," Jake gasped, "but some of the ice hit me. My suit is punctured. I need a minute."

"Jake, are you okay? Do you need help?"

Jake didn't reply. He had passed out.

"Stewart, answer your comm. Stewart?" Nadine craned her head and tried to look out the viewports. Pieces of ice and sprays of vapor clouded her view. "Jake, are you coming back in? What's happening?"

There was another flash out the viewport.

"Those mining charges are firing now. You need to get inside, Jake," she said.

He didn't reply. Nadine cursed and flipped through her board. No external links to infrared sensors. No remote linkages to suit computers. No short-range radar to see who was out there. No environmental links outside.

"Aha," Nadine said.

Cameras. They did a have a bunch of short-range cameras. She rapidly paged through the external views. They were poor resolution, but she could make out shapes. One of them was man shaped. It hung, unmoving, at the end of a tether.

"Empress Patma's vagina," Nadine said. "Can't that boy do anything without getting hurt?" She unstrapped herself from her console and began to swim back toward the airlock.

On the way she pulled her helmet on, checked that her magnetized boots were clipped firmly in place, and pulled her gloves from her belt. She flipped into the airlock, pulled her gloves on, and punched the airlock controls. After the exit lights flashed, she pulled the lock door inward and stepped outside.

She ducked immediately as a chunk of ice whizzed by her head. She was surrounded by a cloud of roiling chunks. Jake was floating a few meters away from the station, hanging at the end of his tether.

He wasn't moving.

A light flashed in the distance, and then a pain flashed through her arm.

"Hairy Imperial armpits, that hurt," Nadine said, looking down. There was a dent in her suit where something had impacted. Another flash in the distance, and this time a rain of small particles flashed by in front of her.

"Stewart, you idiot," Nadine said over the comm, "stop messing around and get in here. You've created a shrapnel machine out here."

Jake just hung at the end of his tether, so Nadine cursed again and flipped her way toward him.

She did a gentle roll and felt her tether spool out behind her. It continued spooling out until she was halfway to Jake, then jerked her to a stop.

"That boy would have a special double-length tether, wouldn't he?" Nadine grumbled. She reached back and pulled herself back in hand over hand until she was sailing toward the ship. Impacting with a clunk, her boots engaged.

She stomped over to release her tether, then stomped her way across the hull toward Jake's tether. Partway there, a large chunk of ice passed silently through her vision and shattered on the hull. Nadine jerked back, but then began to clomp through the shattered remnants. *It's just ice. How can it hurt me?*

BANG. Something hit her in the head. Hard.

She staggered, her vision swimming. *Like that, stupid.*

Reaching Jake's tether, Nadine carefully reeled Jake in, resisting the temptation to pull him faster and faster. He might not have weight, but he had mass, and the faster he was going when he got to the hull, the harder he would hit.

With a final heave, she braced herself to catch his limp body. He was alive, but unconscious, according to the lights on his suit. Vapor crystallized from a tear near his stomach, a tear covered in part by an emergency patch. She tapped the controls to turn his airflow to max, but the motor was already running near full speed.

His eyes fluttered open, and a weak voice came over the comm. "Nadine? What happened?"

"You got nailed by a piece of ice and cut your suit," she said, "and, as is usual in these circumstances, I have to save you from yourself."

She reached down into the outer pocket of her skin suit and groped for an emergency patch. She blinked as another bright light flashed above her.

"Now, Stewart, I have an awesome plan. You hang tight while I put this patch on."

A chunk of ice smashed into the hull in front of her. It broke into pieces, all of them bigger than her head, and she yanked Jake sideways with her as the ice bounced by.

"You hang tight while I run us to the airlock, lock us in, and then put the patch on." She began to clunk toward the lock. "That's what I meant to say." She looked up and spun all around to see what was coming at her.

Ice. Lots of ice.

"We'll be fine in a minute or so, Stewart. How's your air?"

Jake didn't reply, so Nadine looked at his suit. A red light was flashing.

"Oh, you're out of air. Thanks for telling me, Jake," Nadine said. "I'll fix that when we're inside, too."

Now she had only a minute or two. She looked up and twisted around again. The ice wasn't going as fast as she'd first thought. A few quick hops in one direction or another enabled her to avoid it. She was nearly at the airlock.

Another look up. A big, sharp-edged hunk of ice was twirling toward her in slow motion. It was going to impact right at the lock, but after that, the area seemed clear, so she stopped.

"Just waiting for that ice to hit, Stewart. We'll be inside in a jiffy." Hearing was the last thing to go, as far as she knew, so he'd still be able to hear her.

She watched as a hunk of frozen water—at least a ton

or two—hit the deck in front of her. This one didn't shatter, but cracked into two pieces that bounced lazily off to either side of the ship.

"That was a big one, Jake, but don't worry. No more for a few minutes, and here's the lock." Nadine stopped in front of the lock and looked down. "And the panel. And the spot where the handle used to be, which is gone now."

Chapter 31

"This pressure sucks," Corporal Dalon said. He was being pushed back into his couch behind the bridge.

"Why are we not shooting?" Commander Vercher asked. He had strapped himself into one of the empty consoles on the bridge of the Militia cutter—or, rather, Corporal Dalon had strapped him in.

"Because we are facing away from them, so we can use the main engines to decelerate relative to them."

"We must destroy them," Commander Vercher said. "We must not let them get away."

"On the subject of 'not,'" the pilot said, "we must not impact several hundred tons of frozen water traveling at high velocity relative to us. We must not have a proximity mine hit us and explode. Those are big 'nots.' Not letting them escape is much farther down the 'not' list."

"How long are we going to be jammed in like this?" Corporal Dalon asked. "I feel like my stomach is trying to crawl out my back."

"Better than its contents trying to crawl out of your ass," the pilot said. "We'll keep it up till that cloud of debris passes by us, then we'll go back for them. Jammy, you have a new vector yet?"

"Pivot thirty starboard. That will do it."

The pilot tapped his console. "Hold on, everybody."

The acceleration stopped, and everybody floated in their seats.

"Whoa," Corporal Dalon said. The ship pivoted and spun, and his inner ear got confused. He swallowed hard as his stomach flipped, but managed to regain control, though he heard retching sounds behind him in the troop compartment. "Do we have to keep doing this? My guys aren't used to it, and they won't be good for much if this keeps happening."

"We need to slow down relative to that pile of crap heading toward us, and we want to get out of the worst of it. We didn't have good numbers on where it was going, though, so now we're slowing down and cutting to the side."

The smell of vomit drifted up from the back of the ship. Corporal Dalon's mouth filled with a gush of saliva. He swallowed, hard.

The pilot looked over at him. "You okay, Corporal?"

"I'll be fine."

"You don't look fine," the copilot said. "Hang on. Look at your screen."

"Why?"

"Well, I'll explain what's going on so you can tell your guys. Besides, people who stare at an artificial horizon or are engaged in mentally demanding tasks are less likely to be spacesick."

"Really?" Corporal Dalon asked.

"Yes. Look here."

Corporal Dalon's screen lit up.

"That cone is the debris field coming at us," the copilot said. "The debris field might be a mine field. We need to be out of that field. We could just turn 90 degrees to our base course aspect, fire the main engines, and we'd move out of its range eventually." A yellow course line showed on the field.

"So why don't we?" Corporal Dalon asked.

"Because that ship is hiding behind that cloud. We can't track it super well with all that metal and ice in there. When we clear that cloud, we don't want to be going at full speed in some other direction. You need us to be alongside to board."

"My guys can board from anywhere. Just get us close, and we can jump across and take that ship."

"Ever done a boarding before?"

"Lots."

"So you know all the things that can go wrong,

especially with untrained troops. Do you want us to spend the next day chasing down the flyers who missed that ship?"

"No."

"Okay, then we need to slow down relative to the other ship—because you can be sure they are slowing down relative to us—and then we can turn around and catch them."

"So you're going to blast through that cloud," Corporal Dalon asked. "Emperor's blessing...that smell." More vomit smell wafted through the cabin. He gagged.

The copilot shook his head. "Too dangerous. There might be actual mines there. So we move out to the fringe of it, where the density's lower, and we also cut closing speed so that if we do hit something, we won't get damaged." The copilot looked at his screen for a moment and tapped something. "Won't get damaged as bad," he amended.

"Our armor will save us, though, won't it?" Commander Vercher asked.

"We're a Militia cutter, not a battleship. We don't have any armor," the copilot said. "We can't afford to be hit by anything. One good ice strike, and all our sensor suites are gone."

"No armor?"

"You've been watching too many vids. Militia cutters came from the Customs service, not the Imperial Navy. We're designed to chase down slow, unarmed freights— not fight it out with tons of ice bearing down on us. We'll spin around just before contact to get a look at what's there and avoid it."

"Then can we fire?" Commander Vercher asked. He was clear-eyed and didn't look the least bit sick. "That smell is quite strong, isn't it?"

Corporal Dalon pulled a bag from his belt and noisily got sick into it. Commander Vercher watched him with no change of expression. The copilot looked at Corporal

Dalon, then Commander Vercher.

"You've been in space before, Commander?"

"Only to the orbital stations. I've never been on a small ship, nor in a chase. I must say, it is quite an exciting life you lead."

"How come you're not sick like your men?"

"My family has a yacht we keep down the coast from Landing. I've been on the equatorial sea many times, in bad weather. I suppose it prepares you for this."

"A yacht. Huh," the copilot said. "What was it called?"

"*Return to Glory of the Empire*," Commander Vercher said.

Everyone looked at him. Corporal Dalon blinked once, then loudly puked into his bag again.

Nadine cursed as she scrabbled at the panel. With no handle, she couldn't get any purchase at all, never mind the leverage needed to disengage the locking pins. There were other airlocks, but Jake looked like he didn't have much time.

"Hang on, Jake. You, of all people, being killed by defective machinery would be just too ironic for words," Nadine said.

Jake's eyes were glazed, his breathing labored. He shook his head.

"I know, Jake. I know. Let me tow you to the other lock."

A small piece of ice crashed into the ship. Nadine paused. Jake slapped feebly at his leg.

"You are complaining about your leg hurting at a time like this? Man up, Jake." Nadine looked around. More and larger pieces of ice were heading for a collision. She didn't think she could get to the other lock without being crushed.

Jake slapped his leg again, and Nadine looked down. "Joke's on you, Stewart. You are always saying how much better these Belter suits are, with their titanium panels, reinforced construction, built-in tool belts."

Jake feebly slapped his hand against his leg. Nadine looked into his eyes for a moment. His eyes were glazed, but he gave her a weak nod.

"Reinforced construction, and built-in tool belt," Nadine said again. She looked down at Jake's leg, at the tool snaps. A large wrench, specially built for use in vacuum gloves, was there.

Nadine snatched it off and slid it over the flange that remained of the locking wheel. A pull of a lever tightened it, and she began to twist. After a long, agonizing moment, the pins broke contact. The wrench began to spin. Two more rotations, and the hatch opened.

Nadine hustled Jake in ahead of her and pulled the hatch behind, spun the intact inner wheel, and punched the emergency atmo button. She reached over, yanked Jake's helmet off, and let him sit on the floor. By the time she had gotten her helmet off and shaken her hair free, he was lying on his side, gasping in air.

"Jake, are you okay?"

"No, but I can breathe, and the rest isn't urgent. You need to get us out of here. I set about thirty of those charges to blow, and we need to get away from them."

"I'll run up and slow us down," Nadine said.

"No time," Jake said. "I have another plan. One that you'll love."

Jake explained.

Nadine nodded once, pulled a strap over Jake, then raced up to the control room. Strapping herself in and pulling the computer up, she fired the thrusters until she was pointing straight ahead on their original course.

"Here goes...." She pushed the throttles to maximum.

Chapter 32

"That is a jump ship," Jake said.

"How do you know?" Nadine said.

"Look at the extra engine fittings there, and those bulky wires around the rear of the hull." He stretched around to point and yelped in pain.

"Stop being a baby. It's just a cracked rib, the computer says."

"It hurts. I always get hurt when I'm with you."

"Totally your fault," Nadine said.

"Getting hit by the ice and almost asphyxiating is my fault?"

"Should've set those charges different," Nadine said. "I don't see any wires. The resolution isn't good enough."

"They're coiled on the back," Jake said. "You didn't complain about the charges before."

"You made it back to the airlock. I helped you from there. Electric wires?"

"No, they're used for the jump drive. They generate particles that compress space in front of the ship and drag it along."

"Drag it along?"

"It uses negative-mass matter. I've read about it, but I don't really understand it."

"Whatever. So that's a jump ship, huh?"

"It looks like it," Jake said. He looked at Nadine. "Thank you."

"For what?"

"Coming out to get me. Fixing me up. Driving though that debris cloud. Evading that Militia ship."

"It was nothing."

"I looked at the logs, you were on the helm for almost thirty hours while I was out."

"I like to pilot. You know that."

"Still, that was a lot for you to do. You even did some

navigation."

"That's 'cause I'm awesome." Nadine paused. "Actually, the computer did most of the navigation. You had most of it loaded already, and I knew you'd fix the rest when you woke up. Besides, we're partners now."

"We are?"

"My old boss is in jail, I can't seem to contact anyone from his old organization, and everybody I run into seems to think you can sort things out. Besides...."

"'Besides' what?"

"You always win. I don't know how you do it, but you always come out on top." Nadine shook her head. "How do you do that, Jake?"

"Planning. Don't get too close to that jump ship, Nadine. " Jake played with his screens. "That's a strange course. Up over the ecliptic. That's unusual."

"Well, we're close here, so, Mr. Navigation, think we can rendezvous?"

"What? You're not going to just jet off toward it without setting a course, calculating fuel requirements, or even having the computer determine if it's possible?"

"I'm not sure that's important, but I'm getting cautious in my old age," Nadine said. "Besides, I have you along to do the calculations."

"You can't do them yourself?"

Nadine just glared at him.

Jake turned to the console. After a minute, he spoke. "I think so. It's not tumbling or anything. Just a slow roll."

"What's that bump on the side?" Nadine asked.

"Can't see from this angle." Jake played with the telescope settings on the console. Their radar could feed information to the telescope, but only as long as they stayed on a steady course.

"It's blurry. I need to cut thrust to get a better picture."

"What crappy sensors," Nadine said.

"We're not a Militia ship. We're a freighter—and a cheaply equipped one, at that."

"We should have gotten better sensors."

"Should we have stayed behind at the station to get them fixed up while those Militia with guns were hunting for you?" Jake asked.

"Just take your picture," Nadine said.

Jake let them drift, and focused the telescope on the freighter. It had rolled so that the top of the ship was visible. Jake had to play around to get a clear view. "There's something attached to the airlock behind the control room. It looks like a ship of some sort."

Nadine zoomed in on the picture on her screen. "That is a ship. I think it's a Launch."

"It can't be a Launch. Launches are pretty long. If that's a Launch, then that ship is big. Wow." Jake put a picture of a Launch up on his screen, and he and Nadine compared the two.

"It's a Launch," Nadine insisted.

"Not a Launch. It has to be smaller."

"Looks like it to me."

"If that's a Launch, then that ship is more than twice as long as a standard Free Trader, and the container rings are bigger too."

"So?"

"So it's huge—and look there." Jake pointed. "Those must be habitat modules. I wonder how big a crew it's set up for."

"One way to find out, Jakey. Set a course for SS Jump Ship."

Jake figured out a course, and Nadine maneuvered them onto it, even though the computer could have done the whole thing, just not as fast or with their efficiency.

They continued chasing the supposed jump ship for almost a full shift, closing on it over time. At last they had managed to get below it and were catching up.

"Look at the size of that engineering section. Those coils of wires definitely look like the pictures I've seen of a jump drive."

"That's definitely a Launch, Jake. The viewports match the Launches I've seen."

"It can't be. If that's a Launch, to scale, that ship would mass almost a thousand tons."

"Is that unusual for a jump ship?"

"How should I know?"

"Haven't you read it some book, like *500 Meaningless Imperial Statistics You Can Memorize to Impress Your Friends and Amaze Your Family?*"

"I don't think there is such a book," Jake said.

"Why? Have you searched for it before?"

"What are we going to do, Nadine?"

"Rendezvous with this ship."

"And then what?"

"What do you mean?" Nadine asked.

"So we get to the ship. We board it. We figure out it's a jump ship. The jump drive won't be working, or even if it is, I don't know how to work a jump drive. Do you?"

"I can fly anything."

"Do you know how to turn it on, though?"

"That's your department."

"And then there's the radiation problem."

Nadine looked at Jake at that. "What radiation problem?"

"Fletcher's radiation problem. It's in a weird orbit. I think we might be moving out of the Dragon's magnetic field. Without the protection of the field, our radiation exposure will be ten times worse."

"Tens of thousands of people live and work in space around Delta. How can that possibly be a problem?"

"Near space. Shielded by the Dragon's fields. We haven't gone outside of the magnetic fields since the Abandonment."

"Well, that's going to change now," Nadine said.

"What about the Launch?" Jake asked.

"What about it?"

"Is somebody here already? Are they salvaging it?

What's it doing here?"

"We'll find out, won't we?" she said.

"I'm serious, Nadine. We're in the middle of a corporate war, or a civil war, or whatever. The Militia tried to kill my boss and yours, and almost succeeded. He's fighting back. We have this container of guns we're supposed to deliver to some Free Traders or GG or whoever—I'm not quite clear. But Dashi is arranging things, and he always wins. He'll tell us who to give these to. We need to get back in-system and help out. We don't necessarily have time to check out this ship."

"Jake Stewart not wanting to check out a new spaceship? Wonders never cease."

"Seriously, Nadine. We can get close enough to this ship to determine what it is, then spin around and head back and deliver those guns. That will help Dashi win the war, and after things settle down, we'll come back out here and see what this ship is about."

"Why not go out and see it now?"

"Well, for one thing, we're the only ones who know how to find it. I'm the only one that has the original course chip and the decoder, and who knows the general area of space it's in. What if something happens to us? What do we do then?"

"Nothing is going to happen to us."

"This is a big deal. The Militia or GG or any of the other corps would shoot for this advantage. Think how things would go for them if they could tell everybody they had a real live jump ship, and that we could reconnect with the rest of the Imperium."

"We'll be fine, Jake. I guarantee it. I like my fine ass exactly where it is, thank you very much."

"I'll bet they would torture us for the location."

"They would. Which is why we are not going to get captured by them till we've got more detailed info."

"What about that Militia ship that was chasing us before?"

"They're gone—or did you tell me wrong?"

"You're right. I'm just worried. This is a big deal."

"Well, let's dock with this big deal."

The docking was unusual. "What is that?" Nadine asked, looking at the tube sticking out of the airlock.

"A nexus lock. It attaches around the airlock and gives you five more locks to attach ships to. See there, are five hatches on the end. The Launch is on one of them."

"We can fit on the end," Nadine said. "Let's do it."

The docking was straightforward. Nadine maneuvered next to the lock, fired the grapples, and pulled the ship in. The outer collar sealed, and an air burst read green.

"Hard seal," Jake said. "Let's go look."

For once, Nadine fully suited up. Boots, gloves, helmet, and a tool belt. Jake was in his full semi-hard suit, with two oxygen bottles and extra tools, and he pulled an extra tool chest behind him.

"You going to take it apart?" Nadine asked.

"Maybe," Jake said. "I want to be prepared."

They stepped into their airlock, spun the door open, and spun the external door open as well.

"Air checks out," Jake said as they walked into the docking collar.

"Want to look at the Launch?" Nadine asked.

"Not really. I've seen Launches before."

They walked to the end of the docking collar and swung the airlock doors open until they could step into the ship.

"Standard airlock," Jake said.

"The controls, too," Nadine said. "Ready to see a jump ship?" She didn't wait for an answer, but spun the wheel and pulled herself through the door. They stepped over the coaming and into a darkened passageway.

"Looks exactly like every cargo ship I've ever been in," she said. "Standard lights. Standard fixtures, and the air is—" She pulled a tool off her belt. "The air is standard."

She reached up and pulled her helmet off. She looked around, then looked at Jake.

"Jake?"

"What?" he said.

"Not going to take off your helmet?"

Jake sighed, then pulled his helmet off. He sniffed.

"It smells odd," Jake said

Nadine sniffed as well. "I don't smell anything."

"Exactly," Jake said. "It's bland. No smell at all."

Nadine sniffed again, then nodded. "Yes. It's different. Well, let's go exploring.

They began to climb through the ship. It wasn't really spinning or yawing, just a gentle roll, so they drifted slowly from side to side as they approached the bow area. They climbed through what looked like two totally standard habitation modules, a standard atmospheric cargo bay, another habitation module, and then into a tiny room with two couches and two control consoles, but no viewports.

"This is different," Jake said. "Pretty small space to put two couches in. Why are they so close together?"

"Is this the control room?" Nadine asked.

Jake looked up the ladder. "That looks like a control room up there."

They climbed up the ladder and into a standard four-seat control room, with viewports in all directions. A quick tap on the screens showed that the consoles would power up.

"These are standard controls," Nadine said. "They look just like any sort of control software I've ever seen."

"It's all standard. Why would it be different here?"

"Jump ship?"

"No jump controls here. Oh, wait. That other room. That's the jump computer," Jake said. "That's why it's so crowded."

"They need that much space?" Nadine asked.

"Apparently," Jake said. "Let's go check their screen."

They returned and began to play with the control screens.

"Well, here's one labeled 'Jump Menu.' That's pretty suspicious," Nadine said.

"Here's another menu labeled 'Jump Drive Maintenance,'" Jake said. "In fact, all the menus are either for the jump drive, or jump calculations, or labeled 'Jump' something. It's a completely separate system."

"Well, congratulations, Jake," Nadine said. "You own a jump ship."

"I guess," Jake said. "Huh. You think that's true, what Fletcher said? That my dad came here in this ship?"

"We'll find out, I guess. Do we have any food or provisions here?"

"I think so. There was a standard provisioning menu in the control room that showed food. Let's check."

They went into the upper habitation module and rooted around in the lounge. There were lockers full of standard-sized food trays.

"These are standard-sized food trays, but they don't look like Delta trays," Jake said. "Definitely from somewhere else."

"Looks like a lot of food," Nadine said.

"Enough for a big crew—crew of twenty-four, Fletcher said—and plenty of basic, too. Looks like they didn't eat much."

"Good deal. We can stay here a while, if need be. Let's do a quick walk around. I want to look at that Launch, and you should go check out engineering."

"Why don't you go to engineering?" Jake said.

"Jakey, do you truly think I'd see anything wrong in engineering? Unless it was on fire, I couldn't tell the difference."

"Good point," Jake said. "I'll climb down and see if anything looks off, then meet you back here to figure out what to do."

"I'm going to try to make sense of these controls," Nadine said. "Have fun, Jakey."

☐

As soon as Jake left, Nadine abandoned the bridge and slid back to the Castle Arcturus. Jake would be busy in engineering a long time. Forever, if Nadine was any judge.

She wasn't particularly good at navigation, so she spent a good ten minutes charting her orbit. Since she was docked with the jump ship, it was also the jump ship's orbit.

Jake was right. When it was extended, it stretched way outside of the Dragon's magnetosphere. So far, in fact, that a special warning screen popped up. Nadine spent ten minutes figuring out what is said. She'd never seen a "EVA danger" warning before. All her previous traveling had been safely inside the Dragon's giant magnetic field.

She read through the things that could happen if she was outside of a shielded place when a solar flare hit. Cancer. Sickness. Death.

"Want to avoid that death thing," she said, manipulating the course screen in front of her. "Just have to deliver these guns. Jake will be fine." She began to punch up a course.

The screen flashed. *Destination?* it read.

Nadine began to type. She frowned and zeroed out the screen, then thought for a moment. Where was the best place to sell a load of guns? The middle of a war, of course.

All the major stations were on a pick list. She chose the one in the middle and let the computer do the work. If she had to, it was going to be a long flight. Very long. Well, she had time to check some messages.

Several of the guarded queries that she had surreptitiously sent from Rim-37 had received answers. Most expressed great interest, but wanted more details.

She composed a series of long messages that involved price, timing, and place. The price was high, the timing was tight, and the place was well known.

Let's see who signs on for that.

She began to play around with the controls on her

board. Jake could have locked them down, but she had been watching him closely. He'd been so excited about boarding a jump ship that he hadn't done his usual lockdown.

Nadine paged through a few screens, unlocked the magnets, and floated free. Jake hadn't done his usual chain-up, either, so she was home free. She carefully pulsed the ship away from the jump ship, spun on an axis, and pushed in the auto-pilot button.

The computer began to slowly accelerate toward the inner system. Good thing the computer knew how to do that, because she surely didn't.

She had been underway for a good hour when the comm bonged.

"Hi, Jakey," Nadine said.

"Nadine, are you stealing my ship?"

"It's not really your ship. It's our ship," she said.

"I paid for it. You didn't."

"But I helped pick it out."

"No, you didn't."

Nadine thought about that for a second. "Yeah, that's right. I didn't. Sorry. Look, I just need it for a while. Just long enough to deliver these guns."

"You've stolen Dashi's guns?"

"They're my guns."

"They're your boss's guns, and he told you to follow Dashi's instructions on them."

"Well, okay. They're my guns now. Dashi doesn't need them."

"Dashi told me to deliver them to the Free Traders."

"They have the opportunity to pay for them, just like everybody else."

"Nadine, what are you doing?"

"Look, Jake, a girl has to look out for herself. My boss, as you call him, might be dead, so I'm on my own. There are a number of people who might want to kill me. Those Francais girls. The Militia, for banging up their ship."

"Don't forget those GG guys from before, when you blew up their ship."

Nadine had forgotten about that. A previous job with Jake Stewart had resulted in the destruction of a GG heavy hauler and the death of the entire crew. "That wasn't me. That was you."

"You were driving. You were the pilot. Yours is the name they remember."

"I'm not....Damn you, Jake Stewart. Never mind. I'm going to sell these guns and get a million credits. You can't stop me."

"Wouldn't dream of it. Keep the ship and the guns. I don't mind."

"Exactly, so don't try to do anything. Wait, what do you mean? Keep the ship?"

"And the guns."

"Why are you giving me the ship and the guns?"

"Well, Mr. Vince will eventually repossess that ship, especially after his second lockdown kicks in."

"His second lockdown?"

"Sure. You don't think he had just a single thing on there, right? He's a smart dude. He'll have a second and a third one. I just didn't get around to figuring it out. You'll have to pay him at some point, and if you can't, the ship will stop working."

"Imperial ass. Fine. I'll sell the guns and pay Vince."

"Good idea. Have you got a buyer yet?"

"Not yet, but I will," Nadine said.

The computer bonged.

"Hang on." She began to peruse the message that came in. "Joke's on you, Jakey. I've got a buyer. The message just came in."

The computer bonged again.

"Was that the same buyer asking for more details?" Jake asked.

Nadine looked at the second message. "Hah. A second buyer."

"You can't sell the same thing to two people, Nadine, and given the current circumstances, the second buyer will be pretty unhappy they if they can't buy what you are selling."

"You are wrong there, Jakey. It just makes things more fun," Nadine said.

The screen bonged again. Nadine looked at it. A third buyer had responded.

"Did things just get even more fun, Nadine?" Jake asked."

Chapter 33

"Hiya, Vinnie. How's it hanging?" Nadine asked. She was finally close enough to the inner stations to have some sort of a real-time conversation with somebody.

"Ms. Nadine, a pleasure to hear your voice. Are you coming here to have dinner with me?" Vince asked.

"I don't think I'll have time for dinner. I've got lots of important things to do."

"Like avoiding that warship and that freighter behind you?"

"You noticed that, huh?"

"Hard to miss, and we have excellent sensors."

"Not like the crappy ones I have."

"You have the absolute bare minimum of electronics. I would be happy to sell you an upgrade, but Jake wanted it that way."

"I didn't."

"I thought you said that you left those details to him."

"I should have intervened, but that's fuel out the thrusters, as they say. I don't want to get my ship shot up."

"It's not actually your ship until you pay for it, you understand."

"Details, Vinnie, details. Boring details, in fact. No chance of dinner with you if you keep bringing up those boring details."

"I certainly wouldn't want to miss that opportunity," Vince said. "Well then, how about this: one way to stop those details is to make them go away. Perhaps you have something that you could trade me for the ownership of that ship?"

"Whatever would you want to buy from me, Vinnie?"

"How about all those weapons and ammunition?"

The negotiations and the discussion took some time, and Nadine didn't enjoy it as much as she thought she would. For one, the actual mechanics of it were hard—the back and forth, the pricing. For two, she thought she got rolled.

"This isn't a great deal for me, Vince," Nadine said.

"What do you mean? You come into orbit briefly, close by the station. There will be a Launch waiting. You transfer the cargo from your ship to the Launch, and then fly away. You'll own the ship free and clear."

"I feel like I should get some extra money."

"I could make you a co-loaner on a second mortgage."

"Is that good?"

"What do you think?"

"I think that I don't understand that stuff, and that Jake took care of those things. I want cash."

"We don't carry much cash here. Let me check," Vince said. She heard a rustling sound, like he was patting his pockets. "I have exactly 452 credits in credit chips here."

"That's not a lot, Vince."

"Most of my money is in ships or mortgages. I think there might be a five-credit piece in one of my space boots back at my cube. Do you want to come back to my cube and help me look for it?"

Nadine laughed. "As interesting as that sounds, I don't think I have time."

"Besides, I'll need most of that to buy you dinner."

"We already said I don't have time for dinner, Vince."

"So you can't have the money now, then. I'll need to keep it till you are around next time. Glad that's settled. We'll expect you in a few hours, and proceed unloading the ship."

"It's not....Oh, Emperor's hairy balls—fine. See you then," Nadine said. She shut off the comm and began to play with her board.

"You're in over your head, Nadine. You need to talk to an expert," she said aloud. She sighed, punched up a different code, and began composing a message to Jake.

Jake was far away, the spatial geometry wasn't the greatest for high-speed messages, and he took his time responding, so Nadine didn't get the answers she needed fast enough.

"Hi, Nadine," Jake's message said. "I'm fine. Thanks for asking. There's like ten years' worth of food here in storage, the fusion plant is working so I won't freeze, and, as you can see, communications seem in great shape, so I'll be okay. This orbit is a bit problematic, but I think I can get the main engines online to change it to something more useful. The jump drive is fascinating, and I'm spending a lot of time reading the manuals, when I'm not fixing other things. Truthfully, it's okay that you left me here. This stuff is amazing."

Nadine smiled. Jake was never happier than when reading rulebooks.

His voice continued. "As far as Vince goes, he kind of has you over a barrel. You don't have any leverage. Negotiations only work if you are willing to walk away, and he knows you can't walk away. You can fly away, but there won't be anybody else to sell those guns to, and you have to get rid of them quick before either the Militia or GG chases you down and just takes them. Really, he's the only game in town. Getting the ship free and clear is a great deal, and once this current unpleasantness is over, we'll have our trading ship free and clear. Partner."

Nadine smiled again. Only Jake would call a system-wide corporate war "this current unpleasantness."

Jake's voice went serious. "Regardless, you'll have to arrange a safe handover, and since you'll have to let them board the ship, because everything is hanging around in boxes in the engine room, you'll have to come up with something creative. You are good at things that are direct, with the potential for quick action with an overtone of violence. I would suggest things related to that."

Nadine listened to the rest of the message, then

nodded. Direct. Action. Violence. That was her. She pondered for a moment, then pressed the comm button.

"Vinnie, I changed my mind about that dinner."

The beat-up Trader flipped over, fired its main engines, and nosed to a stop relative to the Castle Arcturus about a hundred meters off the bridge. Nadine regarded it through the viewports from the control room. She keyed the comm.

"Vince, that is the sorriest-looking ship I have ever seen."

"It does the job," Vince said over the comm.

"Where's the habitat module?"

"It doesn't have one. We only use it for short hops."

"Are all five of you crammed in the bridge, then?"

"Nope. We're in the Launch you haven't seen."

Nadine cursed. With a gentle bump, something touched the ship. She unbuckled and dove down the corridor, past the habitat module and behind the bridge, snatching a grab bar and swinging to a halt next to the main airlock. She had just enough time to pull her gauss pistol out before the airlock cycled open. She held it across her chest—visible, but not pointing at anything. A smiling Vince stepped through the airlock and removed his helmet. He had sleek skin suit on. It looked tailored, but somehow practical.

"Nadine, good to see you. Where should I set up?" Vince asked.

"Just follow me to the common area," Nadine said. She pivoted and pulled back into the hab module, but spinning in such a way that she didn't lose track of Vince for even a second.

She arrived next to the galley and pulled herself down to a seat, sliding her legs into the straps. Her gun slid into the special pocket on the front of her suit, but she kept her hand close to it.

Vince pulled in behind her and sat down across the

table. His men were right behind him. The lead one produced glasses—made of real glass, not metal—and wine in a glass bottle.

Nadine was impressed. "That's expensive, isn't it?"

"Yes," Vince said. "Best I had. I'm sorry I couldn't rustle up top-notch food in the time I had, but I brought my best trays, and I figured the wine would make up for it."

"Impressive," Nadine said, and she meant it. "I see you've dressed for the occasion as well. Those are pretty expensive duds you're wearing."

"I only take them out on special occasions," Vince said.

"Like when you're planning on stealing a ship from somebody?" Nadine asked.

"No. I wear my regular clothes when I do that," Vince said. "In my business, lots of mortgages have to be foreclosed on, and I can't dress up for all of them. Can Lok pour? He and the boys need to get started so that we make our launch window."

"Of course," Nadine said.

Vince's henchman poured a careful half-glass. The engines were firing so that there was light gravity, and the wine stayed in the glasses. As soon as he'd poured, Lok and the three other henchmen drifted to the rear of the ship. There were some banging noises, and then the first reappeared with a box of guns.

"Quite clever, putting them in boxes in the engine room. So much is done by containers that the cargo inspectors rarely check the engine room."

"It was Jake's idea," Nadine said.

"I'll bet it was his idea to keep the engines running, too, so that we couldn't sabotage anything without you knowing," Vince said.

"That too. This buffalo is pretty good. It's spiced or something," Nadine said.

"It's not a regular tray. It's called 'hot buffalo,'" Vince said. "So what was your contribution to this handover, then?"

Nadine pulled her gauss gun out and spun it around her fingers a few times. "This."

It took almost an hour for the four men to move the guns around. They weren't particularly gentle, more shoveling them into the airlock than placing them. Once the airlock was almost full, they pushed one of their number outside, and he loaded everything into cargo nets, which were then towed to the decrepit freighter.

"This is the best wine I've ever had," Nadine said as they were enjoying the last of it after dinner. "I've never tasted anything like it."

"It's pre-Abandonment. I've been saving it up for a while."

"Wow, that's probably worth more than that snazzy suit you're wearing, Vinnie."

"It's probably worth more that ship we're loading out there," Vince said, "but who would I sell it to?"

"That's the most beat-up freighter I've ever seen," Nadine said.

"It's the most beat-up one I had. I'm selling it with the guns," Vince said.

"You never said who you were selling them to."

"Nope. I didn't," Vince said. One of his compatriots came up and whispered in his ear.

Nadine tensed, keeping her hand near her gun.

Vince nodded and looked up at Nadine. "That's as many as we can take. There's still a couple dozen back there and a bunch of loose rounds, but we don't have time. Those belong to you now. The boys are heading back to the Launch. I have to go." He produced his comm and began making some notes. "There you go. Full ownership transferred to the company that Jake set up to buy the ship."

"Not to me?" Nadine asked.

"I could move the remaining 20 percent to you, but that would still leave the 80 percent that Jake set up with

298

the corporation tied up there. I can't touch that. Besides, you are listed as a director and shareholder of the other corporation, so you can work that out with him."

"So who actually owns this ship?" Nadine asked.

"No idea. I don't own any of it anymore, though. You want to check your board? We have a launch window to make."

"I'll do that," Nadine said, floating up from her seat.

Vince floated back to the airlock, Nadine keeping her distance behind him. He floated into the airlock, and Nadine pushed the door shut, but locked the outer hatch. Pulling herself back to the bridge, she ran a series of quick tests and punched the comm button.

"Pleasure doing business with you, Vince," she said, releasing the airlock.

"The pleasure was all mine. After your current job is over, perhaps we can get together again," he said.

"I'd like that. Free trades, Vince."

"Free trades."

Nadine sat in the control room and watched the Launch and the pile of junk masquerading as a freighter head off in different directions. She ran a few more tests, then opened up the navigation computer and stared at it for a long time.

Finally, she sighed. "Sorry about all this, Jake. Good luck."

She punched in a course.

Chapter 34

"If I try to land, I'll explode," the pilot said.

"Don't be overdramatic," Vince said. "It will be rough for sure, but we've calculated the stresses and the fuel. You'll be fine.

"No, I mean the heat of re-entry will cause the air in the habitat to expand, and it will explode out the viewports and doors."

"They are strong enough to handle that," Vince said.

"Are you sure? I've been told it gets real hot when you try to re-enter, and things expand when they are hot."

"That's not totally true. Wait a minute—you've 'been told' this?"

"Yes."

"Who told you?"

"Pilots."

"Pilots who did deorbits?"

"Well, no. Only the Militia pilots do that, but I looked it up on the net."

Vince stared at the pilot for a moment. "Have you ever done a deorbit before?"

"No."

"Have any of these other pilots ever done a deorbit before?"

"No."

"Are you actually a space pilot?"

"Not exactly."

"'Not exactly' as in, 'you did most of your training but didn't quite finish,' or 'not exactly' as in, 'you've never been in a ship before'?"

"Imperial Anus. Stop busting on me. I drive river barges. I'm used to moving and driving stuff."

"River barges." Vince closed his eyes and shook his head. "How did you get this job?"

"Don Junior is my cousin."

"He has a lot of cousins."

"'Bout a hundred, if you count both sides of the family. Catholics, you know."

"No. What's a Catholic?"

"You've never met a Catholic?"

"I think I've heard of it. It's a religion. Like Hindus, right?"

"It's nothing like Hindus."

"You pray to gods to help you out, right?"

"Yes, but it's totally different," the pilot said.

"You don't have gods?" Vince said.

"We do, but different gods."

"You don't pray."

"No, we pray," the pilot said.

"Okay." Vince said looked at him, but the pilot said nothing more. "That's not really important right now. The ship is set to do an auto-deorbit. You're only here to take over in an emergency—if one of the thrusters fires off prematurely or something like that."

"Got it," the pilot said. "I do have one question, though."

"What?"

"What's a thruster?"

"I'm satisfied, Mr. Pletcher. It's as we agreed," DJ said over his radio link.

"Fine. Your man is on the bridge of the ship, and he's taken control."

"As agreed."

"So I can expect full payment?" Vince asked.

"I'm sending it as we speak," DJ said, gesturing to one of the vice presidents sitting across the table, who began typing on a tablet.

"Pleasure doing business with you. Till next time. Free trades."

"Free trades, " DJ said. He cut the connection and

looked at the vice president who was executing the payment. "Well?"

"He's paid, and what limited orbital resources we have left show the ship starting what looks like a deorbit."

"Good. When will they be down?"

"About two hours."

DJ nodded. The vice president tilted his head.

"What?" DJ asked.

"Your cousin Francisco....His pilot training is limited, and he is somewhat...."

"Francisco is a moron—barely able to steer a barge down a river that will take him where he's supposed to go—but he's loyal. With him there, I know those guns and ammunition have gone into that ship, and that ship is coming down here."

"But what if he has to take over the landing?" the vice president asked.

"If he has to take over the landing, that ship will be nothing more than a big hole in the ground at the end."

"Well, yes."

"But we know just where that hole in the ground will be," DJ said, "and we know how the guns are secured. They'll survive the crash. At least, enough of them will."

"What about your cousin?" the vice president asked.

"I've got lots of cousins," DJ said. "I can spare a few."

"Can we shoot it down?" the Militia major asked. He was in the shuttle launch control room, looming over the controller's desk.

"Sure. We'll just use our super anti-space laser and blast it," the controller said.

"Do it," the major said.

"Okay, but it only takes coins. Have you got any small-credit change?"

"What?"

"We don't have a super anti-space laser or any sort of orbital defenses," the controller said. "We were an agricultural resupply colony, remember? No need to protect fields of potatoes. We have no large-scale weapons."

"Well, send one of the orbital ships after it, then," the major said.

"Why?"

"To shoot it down."

The controller looked at the major. "It's in deorbit."

"So they can shoot it down."

"Deorbit. Deeee-orbit. What do you think that means?"

"It means....Oh. They are coming down," the major said.

"Yes. They are landing. We can even tell where they are landing."

"Where are they coming in?"

"About two hundred kilometers east of Landing, in a big valley near the ocean. At least, the largest pieces are."

"Largest pieces?" the major asked.

"At that speed, he's going to break up," the controller said. "I'm sure of it."

"So we can just forget about him. All the cargo will be vaporized."

"Not unless we use our super vapor-destroying meson gun."

"Meson gun? I thought you said we don't have weapons," the major said.

The controller just stared at him.

"You're an Imperial turd, you know that, buddy?" the major said.

"I don't work for you or the Militia."

"Not yet, anyway."

"What's that supposed to mean?" the controller asked.

"When the time comes, I'm going to come looking for you. You realize that, right?" the major asked.

"Looking for me?"

"Me and a few friends. Talk to you about your loyalty

to the Empire."

The controller shrugged. "The Militia doesn't run this moon."

"Not the whole moon, no, but there are a lot of us around right here, which is where you are. If you plan on staying in this job, you'd best remember that."

The controller stared at him for a moment. "Fine. He'll impact in this circle here." He pointed to a display screen. "Somewhere in there. He'll break up, but he won't turn into dust or anything."

"What about his cargo?" the major asked.

"If it's not delicate, it will probably be okay. Those containers are pretty strong. They might break open. Are they heat-sensitive?"

"Not totally. I'm not sure. Are you saying they could recover all this cargo?"

"What's the cargo?"

"Space-vaporizing meson guns," the major said.

"*Touché*. I guess. I wouldn't want to do it." The controller pointed at the screen. "Look here—those are mountains. I've got some cousins out east, so I've been on that train before, and that's not an easy walk. The monorail is on the right side of them, so they could walk down, I suppose, but there are no trails or anything, so it will be a long walk, especially carrying things."

"So even if the cargo is intact, they can't get it back to the monorail."

"It would be really hard, and even if they get it to the monorail, they have to bring it into town. You'll see that."

"We will," the major said. "We will."

The group traipsing across the hill was quite large. There were at least twelve people. A Militia squad of eight—and three men and one woman in blue uniforms, stumbling as they walked. The Militia all carried weapons and large packs. The blue-uniformed people carried extensive tool belts and backpacks with more tools attached. Everybody was cursing.

"Will you all shut up?" the corporal in charge said. "We need to be quiet."

"We don't need to be quiet, Militia man," the woman in the blue uniform said. "Nobody lives here. Nobody comes here except us."

"What if they hear us on the train?" the corporal asked, pointing at the horizon.

"That's kilometers away, the trains have their windows closed, and the air is noisy. Nobody will hear us. See us, maybe, and your magic eye in the sky tells us when the trains go by so we can hide."

"Maybe so, but it's best to be prudent."

"'Prudent' this," the woman said, grabbing her groin and making a rude gesture at the corporal.

The corporal returned the gesture and muttered, "Stupid ill-bred, lower-class princess."

His´ squad shared a smile. One turned back and whispered, "Ten credits they end up in the sack tonight."

"You think he likes her?" one of the men asked, skeptical.

"You're on," a female Militia trooper said. "He'll never go for it before the operation. After, though? Fireworks."

"Really?" the man asked.

"Likes the attitude," the woman said. "He dated a friend of mine. She had a mouth on her, and she said it drove him crazy."

"Huh," the man said. He turned to the gambler. "Twenty credits for me."

The next afternoon, the crew stood on a hill watching the monorail whizz by.

"Right. Eye in the sky says that it's outbound for the eastern terminus. We go now," the corporal said.

The whole crew headed toward a spot where the track crossed a deep gorge over a river. Upon arrival, the four in blue uniforms swarmed up the bridge. The three men

305

produced long-handled wrenches and began to unbolt parts of the structure. The woman produced an insulated rubber suit, heavy rubber gloves, and strange-looking boots.

After donning them, she slowly climbed up the structure. She stopped next to a large cable and pulled out a long, strong pair of cable cutters. The cutters' teeth were sharpened steel of some sort, but the handles were a dull red substance. It didn't look like metal.

The woman began to position herself. Running an odd-colored strap around her waist, she tied herself to a steel beam. Then she braced her boots against the truss and leaned back until only her feet were in contact. She hung away from the cable, levered the cutters into place, then took a large cable and clipped one end to the truss and the other to a metal bolt just above the cutters.

"Ready," she said.

"Stand by. These are pretty sticky," one of the crew said, tugging hard on the wrench handle. The nut screeched around. As he pulled again, the nut screeched some more, then came free and began to spin without resistance. He spun more and more until the nut bounced off and clattered into the gorge below. Then he reversed his wrench and used it as a hammer, clanging repeatedly against the bolt until it fell through.

The screeches, bangs, and clatters continued, and the men yelled at each other, coordinating their activities.

There was a momentary pause, and the foreman climbed up higher and looked down at the crew members below. "You two ready?"

"Yup," the first said.

"Yes, boss," the second said.

"Go," the foreman said.

The two men below began to bang away at a bolt, one on each side of a long beam. The beam began to shift. With another screech, it slid down the nearly disconnected bolts, then dropped and clanged its way down the truss.

"Done," the boss said.

"All you apes get off now," the woman yelled. The three men who had accompanied her dropped their wrenches to hang from their belt lanyards and scrambled down the structure. When they reached the ground, they scampered twenty meters away and gathered in a group with the Militia.

"What happens next?" the corporal asked.

"We've dropped that beam, so the bridge structure is weakened. They won't want to drive a train over that, even on local power, so the train is trapped on the far side of the gorge until they repair the bridge."

"Is that hard?"

"That beam weights about two tons, so you have to get it here, in the middle of nowhere."

"I've seen vids where they fly stuff like that. Construction planes. With big fans on top," the Militia corporal said.

"Helicopters. They use them in the capital—and on Old Earth and the bigger Imperial planets—but we're just a moon. Our atmosphere isn't that dense. Helicopters can barely get off the ground, and they sure aren't going anywhere with a two-ton load."

"How did they build this stuff to start with?"

"They used a monorail car with a construction crane. Built the monorail out to the end of the line, brought the train along from behind, and used the monorail itself to move the beams out."

"How do we stop that?"

"Look," the electrician said. He pointed at the woman. "She's going to cut the superconductor cables—no power for the monorail out east."

"Won't the power fry her?"

"She's totally insulated from the structure. The boots have ceramic soles, and the handles of the clippers are ceramic, but the cutters are tungsten. Very sharp. When she slices the superconductor, the power will run down the cable into the truss and won't hurt her."

"Really?" asked the corporal.

"That's the theory," the tech said. "She's the best live electrician we have. She has more balls than the rest of us put together."

"Brass ones?"

"Well, probably ceramic, in her case, 'cause she would want something non-conducting, but you get the idea," the tech said.

"What happens if she messes up?" the corporal asked.

"Krispy Kate," the tech said.

The woman turned back and glanced around. "I'm cutting in five. Last chance for anybody to get away." She held up a gloved hand. Her fingers counted down from five to one, then gripped the cutter handles and pushed them together.

The results were spectacular. It started with a flash of lightning from the cutters to the beams. Then the lightning began to snap and crackle from the cutters. With a loud sizzle and pop, the ends of the cable parted, and a stream of sparks sprayed out both ends like pressurized water.

A bolt of lightning flashed around the woman. She screamed. With a massive crackling sound, she was propelled away from the bridge, sparks streaming behind her.

The corporal dove to the left and the electrician to the right as the woman's smoking figure impacted the ground right in front of them. She was still holding the cutters, but the metal part was totally gone, and even the ceramic handles had melted together.

Then everything was quiet except for a quiet popping from the flapping cable, which soon quieted down to nothing.

The corporal approached the smoldering body. The boots' soles were melted and smoking, and the cutter's handles were still a bit liquid.

He jumped back as the woman sat up. She ripped her

facemask off and looked around with a grin. "That was awesome. Let's do it again."

Chapter 35

"So we just sit here while they capture the station?" Singh asked.

"Yes, that's the plan," Jose said, concentrating on a screen before him.

"What are you looking at?"

"Procedures for changing the head of the emergency council, doing business as the Delta Corporation."

"Is that a good way to spend your time right now? Shouldn't we be fighting the enemy?"

Jose flipped his screen down and looked at Singh. "The enemy is mostly conscript Militia soldiers, possibly former allied corp staff, who don't give an Imperial testicle for the Officers' Council. They just want to go home. We just need to delay them until they decide to leave."

"They'll be down here in a few hours at the most, and TGI will be out of business. Why would they leave?"

"They are fighting with GG in Landing. Once GG gets their act together, there'll be even more fighting in town. The Militia will need to withdraw all their troops from here for the fight with GG in Landing."

"You have no troops defending the corridors," Singh said. "They'll be here shortly."

"No, they won't," Jose said. "They have to burn through all those barriers. There is no path to the reactors or to the control room or to life support that doesn't go through at least seven or eight barriers."

"How long does it take to burn through the barriers?"

"Let's see." Jose flipped his screen up and began to do a search. "We did a number of tests and did some comparisons. With a trained welder and a laser cutter, between twelve and fourteen minutes each."

"So they could be here in an hour," Singh said.

"In theory, with a trained welder and proper

equipment, between eighty-four minutes and one hundred twelve minutes."

"You are a coward, you know," Singh said.

"Really?" Jose looked surprised. "How so?"

"The Council left you in charge of this station. They expected you to fight for it."

"I think they expected me to defend it. Fighting isn't exactly required."

"How can you defend it if you aren't ready to fight for it?"

Jose stopped typing and looked up. "You tell me."

Singh shook his head. "I'm going back to my office. I have a small security detachment with me. They're ready to fight. Every one of them is a better man than you."

Jose looked at him. "What's better, fighting or winning?"

Singh blinked. "They're the same."

Jose shook his head. "No, they're not. Look, I'm busy. Can you come back in three or four hours?"

"I just told you we don't have three or four hours. The Militia has already landed. By your numbers, they'll be here in, at most, two."

"That's not what I said."

Singh stood up. "You are an Imperial turd. I'm going to stand with my troops."

Jose glanced at his screen. "You do that. I have time after lunch at about 15:00. Come see me then. We'll talk."

"You are completely out of touch with reality," Singh said.

Jose looked up at him. "One of us is, for sure."

"In the name of the Emperor, what is taking so long?" Commander Roi surveyed the group in front of him— Sergeant Russell, some troopers, and a number of station officials.

"Have to cut through all those barriers, sir," Sergeant Russell said. "Need to get to the control room and the fusion reactor—and life support, of course."

"Why is it taking so long?"

"We only have two lasers, and they are carbines, pulse shots. They're not designed as cutters."

"Why does it take hours?" Commander Roi asked. "What is the problem?"

"Turns out that they are some sort of special alloy. Resistant to heat. The lasers don't work well on them."

"If the lasers don't work, then blow them up," the commander said. "Bring some grenades."

One of the station officials looked up. "Uh, excuse me, Your Supreme Executiveness," he said. "There is a bit of a problem."

"It's 'Commander,'" Commander Roi said.

"Sorry, Commander Supreme Executiveness, but that explosive thing...not so good."

"Why is that?"

"Well, the thing is....Those extra bottles—the ones with nitrogen? They're no problem."

"Yes, and?"

"Well, it's the oxygen ones...."

"Yes?"

"They could sort of cause a giant explosion, and we don't know where they are. That first one—the one that blew up right away—was only about one-tenth full, and it still hurt two people and depressurized the corridor. There's also this whole 'Empire Reborn or death' thing...."

"This current regime is corrupt and decrepit. We shall replace them with a proper Imperial government, one that is faithful to the tenets of Imperial rule."

"Oh, I'm fond of tenants myself," the official said. "I rent out a place in Landing. Nice place. Has a hot tub. Do you like hot tubs, Commander?"

"Do I what?" Commander Roi asked.

"Like hot tubs. You know....Girls in bikinis, big breasts, floating in the water. That sort of thing."

"I like bikinis," Sergeant Russell said, "and girls with

big breasts. Especially in hot tubs. How much is your place?"

"Oh, reasonable, I assure you," the official said. "In fact, for you, Sergeant, we'd have a special deal. How many of you?"

"Well, there's my wife, and then my girlfriend, and then her girlfriend....How many people does it sleep?"

"Well, six, normally, but that's with three rooms. Will it be two per bed, or three, or four?"

"Well, it depends," Sergeant Russell said. "Could be three. Could be four. Is there enough room?"

"Always," the official said, "but if you are...enthusiastic visitors, as they say, I'll have to charge you a cleaning fee. I can't waive that—it goes to an external contractor. Will you need food and booze delivery? I know a place. They'll stock it up for you."

"Silence," Commander Roi said. "What does this have to do with burning through these barriers?"

The official and Sergeant Russell looked at each other, apparently working their way through their thoughts.

"Right." The official snapped his fingers. "Oxygen bottles. A full bottle will make your bomb ten times more powerful. Blow the corridor out. Snap the spokes. Destabilize the station. Kill lots of people." He turned to Sergeant Russell. "See, nobody is really worried about this 'Empire or death' thing. I mean, why not the Empire, right? That's where we all came from. But this 'death or death' thing might not attract as many people, so we'll have to take our time with those barriers—disconnect those bottles, and then burn the struts."

"How long will that take?" Sergeant Russell asked.

"We'll have plenty of time to plan your vacation, Sergeant," the official said. "So, fall or winter? Which do you prefer?"

Jose's door bonged. "Enter," he said.

Singh came in with two heavily armed troopers behind

him.

"You said they would be here by now," Singh said.

"I did not," Jose said.

"You said they could burn through those barriers in eighty-four minutes."

"I said that a trained laser cutter technician with proper equipment could do it in eighty-four minutes."

Singh stood silent, looking around Jose's office. It was packed with equipment.

"What's all this stuff?" Singh asked.

"Laser cutters."

"Oh," Singh said. "How many?"

"All of them," Jose said.

"All of them?"

"Every single laser cutter on the station," Jose said. "I paid good money for all of them."

Singh thought about this. "How about the trained staff?"

Jose waved a hand. "Down the corridor, drinking basic. Standing by."

"For what?"

"They will be able to cut all these barriers out of the way in eighty-four minutes once I give them the word. Starting from the inside, of course."

"Why would they do that?"

"Because the Militia troops will have left."

"Why will the Militia troops leave?"

"Because they are needed to defend against the forthcoming GG offensive in town."

"Why is GG staging an offensive in town?"

"Because the best Militia troops are occupied up here."

"How does GG know that?"

"Because I told them," Jose said.

"I see," Singh said. He turned to walk away, then stopped. "Wait. GG knows that the Militia's best troops are up here because you told them, so they are staging an offensive to take over Landing while they are occupied.

You said the Militia is defending against this offensive, though. How do they know it's coming?"

"Oh, that's easy. I told the Militia that I told GG," Jose said.

"I thought that GG was short of weapons. How did they get enough weapons to launch an attack?"

"I arranged it so they may soon be acquiring some though extralegal means."

"Enough to win the war?"

"No." Jose frowned at something on his screen and tapped a few buttons. "Enough to think they might win a battle, though."

Singh waited in the doorway, processing this.

One of the troopers cleared his throat. "Excuse me, sir, but are you running all the sides of this war?"

Jose looked up and at each of the troopers. He nodded. "Of course. It's much more efficient to have one person in charge of the whole war."

Chapter 36

DJ surveyed the wreckage on the screen. He turned to the vice president. "That's a big pile of junk."

"Yep. Engines are toast for sure, and that big hole in the ground over there—you see that?" the vice president asked.

"Yes."

"That's the control room, where the pilots sat."

"Can't be much left there, can there?" DJ asked.

"Nope, but it looks like the cargo made it."

"Are you sure?" DJ leaned closer to peer at the screen.

"Pretty sure. The containers are there—and there. They look intact."

"Well, crack 'em open," DJ said. "Take all the guns you can find, and put 'em to work."

"Yes, sir. About that....That's a good day's walk from the monorail, even assuming that we get it working...."

"Right. Status on that?"

"The train is stuck in East-32. It coasted into there under local power. It's not going anywhere till we get those cables reconnected."

"How long will that take?" DJ asked.

"There's a problem."

"What's the problem?"

"Superconducting cables. We have to unbolt some from the end of the line, one of the bridges."

"So?" DJ frowned.

"We'll end up cutting off about eighty kilometers at the end—that's the last bridge. We have some settlements out that way that depend on the monorail for supplies."

"All of our settlements depend on the monorail for supplies. We need this backup."

"They could just do it again."

"They won't," DJ said. "That was the closest bridge to

Landing, the only one they could reach."

"They could cut the power from the reactor, or remove one of the superconductors somewhere."

"Cutting a cable is one thing. Removing a superconductor magnet is another. Now that we know what they're capable of, we know we have to respond. Send armed groups along the length of the monorail. We'll be able to find them before they do this."

"What if they shoot down the satellite?"

"If any of the sides here start destroying pre-Abandonment assets, things will escalate quickly," DJ said. "Our satellites are vulnerable, but so are theirs. I don't think it will come to that. Even so, put a ship with a rail gun up into high orbit. I want a high guard."

"A high guard?"

"I want something far up in the gravity well. If they start doing anything funny, we'll drop rocks on them."

"So it begins," the vice president said.

"We won't start it, but I'm sure to end it. Let's get this started. I've got to get into Landing."

"You are going to Landing, sir?" the vice president asked.

"Yes," DJ said. "My father has sent me in to take charge of things. I will be in contact with you from the city. We may have to walk a bit."

"Either way, we have to do something about getting those guns."

"Let me see that screen again, but give me a wide-angle view. Zoom out."

The group of GG workers stood on the bluff overlooking the sands. There were about fifty workers, half with a crate of some sort, and half carrying packs that appeared to contain food and water. A small group of GG internal security stood nearby, shotguns prominently displayed.

The head of the security detail walked over to the well-dressed man who stood alone at the top of the bluff. Don Alexi was another of DJ's many cousins, and by his conduct so far, he appeared to be one of the more competent and ruthless among them. "Don Alexi, we are ready."

"We have to wait."

"Yes, sir. What are we waiting for?"

"High tide."

"How will we know when it is high tide?"

"The water will be splashing against the cliffs. Here," Don Alexi said, pointing down.

The security head looked down at the bone-dry beach. "I see. I've never seen sand this red before."

Don Alexi looked at him. "You know a lot about sand?"

The security man shook his head. "No. Just what I've seen in vids. It's usually white."

"Delta sand is red. Lots of iron."

There was a roaring sound in the distance, and they both looked seaward. A line of white showed on the horizon.

"What's that?" the security head asked.

"Tidal bore. Watch," Don Alexi said.

The line of white soon resolved into a wave, rushing forward.

"How fast is that going, do you think?" the guard asked.

"Faster than you walk. Not as fast as you can run."

"So you can outrun it."

"Yes."

"Good. I'll tell the boys," the guard said.

Don Alexi watched the wave roll in. When the first part of it began to lap against the bluff, he pulled a pair of binoculars out and began to scan the horizon. After several scans, he narrowed in on a particular spot and adjusted his focus.

A ship appeared in the distance. It had sails like a

sailboat, but also a large selection of solar panels. He turned to the waiting group and pointed.

They shaded their eyes and looked that way. Most couldn't see it, but a few with better vision could just make it out. They pointed, gestured, and called to their friends. Don Alexi walked down from the head of the bluff to meet the group.

"You leave as the tide begins to fall. It will go out as fast as it came in. One hundred credits each for carrying a crate to the ship. It's two kilometers. Remember to run both ways."

Don Alexi watched the water carefully. In forty minutes, he was sure the waves were receding and the depth was going down. He released the crew and yelled at them to wade into the water and begin running. They did initially, but once out of range of his voice, they fell back into an easy walk. The guard captain watched him.

"Will they make it okay?"

"I think so."

"What about coming back?"

"That's up to them."

The ship's crew was composed of three brothers. The youngest brother, Melchior, had the best head for navigation, so he was in charge.

"Get ready to drop anchor," Melchior said.

"Already, Mel?" Estephan said.

"I said get ready, and I meant get ready."

"The water's still deep, though. How will they load us?"

"We need to be in deep water so we can float off when the tide goes out again."

Estephan looked at the third brother, Balthazar, who shrugged.

"Okay. You're the boss," Estephan said.

"Yes, I am. Get the side tracks ready as well."

The three brothers bustled around. The boat had a rounded bottom and a heavy, full keel that ran from the front all the way to the back. Two different anchors hung off its rear corners. The chains rattled as they went out, and Estephan and Balthazar snubbed them both at the same time, pulling the boat to a halt. It bobbed slowly in the waves as the tide finished rising.

"Heave out a bow anchor too," Melchior said. "We can wait here."

The other two brothers heaved a third anchor off the bow and reeled the stern anchors into the water together so that the boat bobbed in the middle of a triangle of anchors.

"How long do we have till the satellite goes overhead?" Estephan asked.

"There's one overhead right now, but that's GG," Melchior said. "For the Militia one, we've got a couple of hours. We just have to be floating out there fishing when it comes over."

"What do we do now?"

"Now we wait." Melchior ducked inside the main cabin and glanced at the helm station. "High tide will be soon."

The boat bobbed as the water flowed forward and ran into the bluffs in the distance.

After about forty-five minutes, a strip of sand appeared in the distance and began to creep toward them. The creep turned into a walk, then a hustle. The tide was definitely running out. The boat strained at its anchors, then began to bump softly as the water shoaled.

"Settling," Balthazar reported. The three brothers rushed to the corners of the boat and stood by the anchors.

"How does it look, Bal?" Melchior said.

"Okay up here."

"Esty?"

The boat thudded into the ground as the waves raced by.

"We're hitting hard," Estephan said.

"Stand by," Melchior said.

The boat continued to bump, harder and heavier, but then the vertical motion decreased as the water rushed out underneath them.

The boat heaved up on a large wave, then slammed down again. Balthazar lost his footing and fell to the deck. Melchior and Estephan grabbed a railing and held on. The boat stayed down this time.

"We're down," Melchior said. "Get the ramp ready."

The two other brothers bustled around to the left side of the boat and opened a gate in the railing, then ran around to the front and manhandled a large gangplank along the side. They hauled it up vertically with a line attached to a boom off the mast, then clipped it into metal fittings with large bolts.

All this work took only ten minutes, but in that time, the water had fallen considerably. The water was now less than a meter deep and racing at high speed.

"Drop it?"

"No. The current will bend it out of shape. Wait till you see sand."

All three of them stood watching the water race out. Within ten minutes, patches of sand and small rocks appeared in the racing water. They lowered the gangplank down, and it splashed into a puddle about six inches deep. Esteban and Balthazar raced down and pounded spikes in to hold it steady.

"Looks good down here, Mel," Balthazar said. "Where's our cargo?"

Having stepped up to the front of the boat, Melchior pointed to a group of men sauntering down the sand in the distance. Most of the men carried a single crate on a large harness on each of their backs. Some walked in teams, holding two crates slung between them on ropes. None seemed in a hurry.

Balthazar and Estephan returned to their brother on the bow.

"They're not moving super fast," Estephan said.

"Don't they know about the tide?" Melchior asked.

"Not our concern," Balthazar said. "If they ask to stay onboard, they can't. Put your revolvers on. Bring me my gun."

The other brothers looked at Balthazar, then climbed below. Mel was in charge of the sailing and navigation, but Balthazar was the roughest of the three. If there was any possibility of violence, he stepped up.

Melchior and Estephan reappeared with revolvers in holsters and handed a third holster to Balthazar, along with a shotgun. Nobody spoke.

Almost an hour later, the first group of men arrived. Balthazar stood at the bottom of the gangplank. His pistol was loose in its holster, and his arms were crossed over the shotgun. Mel stood on the deck with a hand on his holster. Balthazar covered the gangplank, and Mel kept an eye in all directions.

Joining Balthazar, Estephan spun a crowbar in his hand as the first team of two men approached with a crate.

"Hello. Drop it here," Estephan said, pointing at his feet.

The two men dropped the crate and stepped back as Estephan pried the top off and looked inside. Satisfied, he levered the top off the second crate. He nodded, put the first crate on his shoulder, and staggered up the gangplank. Once onboard, Estephan plopped the crate down on the deck and slid it into an open hold. There was a lot of banging before he reappeared.

The two men had watched the whole incident with interest. When Estephan reappeared at the top of the gangplank, one of them spoke. "*Señor*, we have carried the crates for two kilometers. We can carry it a little farther."

"We're fine." Balthazar reached into a pocket and produced two small metal disks with a stylized GG logo on them.

"This is your receipt. You give that to your boss, and you should get paid, okay?"

The men watched Estephan drag the crate up onto the ship. "You sure you don't want us to help you load?"

"We're sure. We'll take it from here."

"Okay." They stepped a few paces away and started chatting in Spanish.

The main group began to arrive and stood in line chatting in a good-natured way. Estephan pried open each crate, glanced inside, and dragged it up onto the boat. The work was hard, and soon he was sweating. Balthazar gave out receipt disks as necessary, but kept most of his attention on the workers in front of him. After about twenty crates had been loaded, Estephan stayed on the boat and spoke to Melchior. Leaving Estephan on the bow, Melchior scurried down the gangplank.

"This is taking too long," Melchior said to Balthazar. "The tide is coming in. We need to go faster, but Estephan needs a break."

"Is everything here?" Balthazar asked.

"Not really. We don't have a great count, but some are missing...maybe 5 percent."

"Five crates?"

"No, just maybe one or two from each crate."

"Where?"

"I think these guys took them," Melchior said. "They stole them. Figured we wouldn't notice.

The porters stood in the distance. A few of the ones who had dropped their crates had taken their metal receipts and begun the trek back to shore, but the bulk of the men stood around chatting with friends or acquaintances. The rest were still lined up to receive their disks. The sun was bright, the sand was firm, and they looked relaxed.

"Don't they know about the tide?" Melchior said.

"Not enough," Balthazar said. He raised his voice. "You men—attention."

All eyes turned to him.

"Thank you for bringing us these. Our spot checks show everything is in order. By my count, there are nineteen more crates left to load." He paused.

Many of the men obviously didn't speak Standard, and their friends were translating for them.

Balthazar continued, "The tide is coming, and I don't want to make you wait. This man here...." He pointed at the porter closest to him, who looked at his friends and shuffled his feet. "Yes, you. Here are receipts for the nineteen remaining crates. Count them out for him," he told Melchior, handing him a bag of the metal disks.

Melchior stepped up to the man and counted out, in Spanish, nineteen disks. The three brothers spoke Standard, Francais, and Spanish.

"You should go now. High tide is in less than ninety minutes. You will have to move quickly."

"*Señor*, we can help you load the ship," one of the men said.

"Thank you, but no. We will take care of things," Balthazar said. "Mel, get them on board. Don't bother checking the contents."

Melchior began to load the ship. He didn't bother to load them into the hold anymore, just dumped them on the deck as soon as he boarded and ran back for another. Estephan joined him in running up and down the gangplank.

Most of the porters had started walking back toward the distant bluffs. The first group that had left were quite far away, but the porters were scattered in groups of two or three heading off to the horizon. Almost all of the men were gone, but a core group of six still stood there.

"*Señor*, we were wondering if you need more help," one began, turning toward the ship.

"Hey, Rube, " Balthazar said—a merchants' code call that meant there was trouble brewing with outsiders and the caller needed help.

The other brothers stopped what they were doing. Their hands drifted to their holsters.

"We just want to help, *señor*," the man said.

Balthazar fired his shotgun into the air.

At the sound, everybody turned to Balthazar. Estephan and Melchior had known what was coming. Their revolvers cleared their holsters, and they pointed them at the closest men.

"Time to go," Balthazar said. "The tide is coming in. If you run now, you can beat it. We want you far away."

The remaining group of porters had drawn back, but their hands hovered around pockets and behind their backs.

"That is not very hospitable, *señor*," their spokesman said.

"The tide is coming," Balthazar repeated. "You need to go. Now."

The six porters grumbled among themselves. One cocked his head and shouted at the rest. In the quiet, a background hum could be heard.

The three brothers were still standing with their weapons out, facing the group. "That's the tidal bore," Balthazar said. "If you leave now and walk quickly, you can beat it. Otherwise, the water will get you."

"It's just water, *señor*. We can walk away from it."

"It's travelling at four kilometers an hour. You'll have to run to get away from it."

The spokesman produced a revolver. "Maybe we will stay here and take this fine ship for our own. Watch the tide from the deck."

All three brothers pointed their guns at him and cocked them.

"Perhaps the others might, but you...." Balthazar said. "You we will shoot first, and you will have to kill all of us before you take our boat."

Another low-voiced discussion began in Spanish. The hum of the approaching water was clear now, and four of the men broke off and began to stride away. The remaining two—the spokesman and a friend—scowled and stood their ground, hands on weapons.

"Mel, load up," Balthazar said. "Estephan, down here with me." Estephan ran down and stood next to his brother.

Estephan and Balthazar stood tall, their guns never leaving the porters. Melchior ran down, grabbed a crate, and ran it up on the deck, then another, and another. The standoff continued.

After the fourth crate, Melchior ran down and began to lever up the spikes that held the gangplank down.

"Empress's vagina. What are you doing, little brother?" Balthazar said, not taking his eyes off the two men with revolvers.

"Ship first, crew second, cargo third. The tide's almost here, and I don't want to lose the gangplank. You two will need it to get onboard." Melchior levered the last spike out, then ran up the gangplank to get back onboard. Grabbing a winch, he spun it until the gangplank was a foot clear of the mud. Then he ran down, hoisted another crate on his shoulder, and clambered back onboard.

"You should run now. The tide will be here any minute," Balthazar said.

"We're not afraid of any Imperial-dammed water," the spokesman said, pointing his gun at Balthazar.

"Estephan, back onboard. Keep your gun on them," Balthazar said.

Estephan backed toward the gangway. Melchior stepped behind him and helped him step up, guiding him back onto the boat. Once Estephan was settled, Melchior resumed pointing his revolver at the group. Estephan took a spot forward of the gangplank and grasped a metal shroud line with one hand. His other kept his revolver aimed at the porters.

Balthazar shouldered his shotgun, grabbed a crate and threw it on the end of the gangplank, then went back twice more. After the third, he threw himself on the gangplank and walked them onto the deck. The crates were strewn all over the boat now.

"Bal, that's all we're getting," Melchior said. "Tide's here. Hang on till we float."

"Cover those guys," Balthazar said. "When they see the water, they'll do something stupid."

Balthazar dropped down behind a crate on deck and aimed his revolver at the two men. Estephan did the same. Melchior retreated to the wheelhouse and checked the engines.

The tide rolled in with a muted roar. A rustling wave of water, perhaps a foot tall, rode in over the sand. It was only a small wave, but it moved fast. The two porters glanced down as the water flowed over their feet, perplexed. The water continued to deepen.

The approaching water raised to a rattling howl, and the short wall of water slopped over them. The other man, realizing his peril, pointed his gun down and began to tramp toward shore. Soon he was straining, then running.

The spokesman kept his gun pointed at the ship, but frowned down at the water.

The inrushing water had already covered the end of the gangplank and the crates there. Melchior put his gun down and began to winch the gangplank higher and higher. Soon it was six feet out of the water, and the boat began to groan and work a bit. The water was now almost two feet deep.

The spokesman began to wade toward the ship, but Estephan shot the water in front of him. "Stay put. Nobody but family aboard."

"For the love of the Imperial family, I can't swim," the spokesman said.

"Doesn't matter. The tide will take you in," Balthazar said.

"To the Imperial hells with you," the man said and fired his gun.

The brothers fired back. Mayhem broke loose.

The incoming tide tossed him toward shore. The brothers shot from behind their crates. They weren't particularly good marksmen, but there was three of them.

The spokesman was left floating facedown in the water, red pooling out around him.

"Bal, get the crates. Esty, winch that gangplank up, then stand by the rear anchors," Melchior said. "I'm letting the front ones loose so we can get out of here." With the threat of violence neutralized, Mel was in charge again.

The brothers rushed to obey, and soon Melchior was gunning the engines against the tide, backing the boat out to its anchors while Balthazar stowed the crates in the hold.

Melchior glanced ahead. He could just make out the other man, splashing forward in the rising tide, trying to stay ahead of it.

After a minute, the splashing stopped, and the tide streamed in, unmolested.

Chapter 37

"How many revolvers?" Molina asked. They were all standing on a ramshackle dock on the edge of Landing. Molina had been there when the brothers had arrived, and he'd had all the correct countersigns. He didn't identify his faction, but his GG coveralls gave his allegiances away. He had brought only a small crew of workers, who loitered onshore at the end of the dock.

"642," Melchior said.

"There were supposed to be a thousand."

"That's what we were given. You can count them yourself, if you want."

"I'll take your word on it. What about ammunition?"

"Enough for about half of that. We think."

"What? I thought there was supposed to be more."

"You can count that yourself as well, if you want. Actually, I'd like you to do that."

"Do what?"

"Count it. We just weighed it. We have two tons of boxes of stuff—revolvers and ammo together."

"Emperor's anus," Molina said. "There were supposed to be more. I think you stole them."

Melchior pushed his lips into a sour line. "First, we've done smuggling runs for your people for years. Second, it was your carrying crews that stole them. The boxes were opened when we got 'em, and we gave receipts for what we got."

"We will be inspecting these receipts after this fight," Molina said.

"Only if your guys are really, really good swimmers," Balthazar said. He laughed. "I doubt one in ten of those guys beat the tide back."

Molina put a finger on his belt. The brothers did likewise. "Suspicious that those men didn't come back."

"No, it's not," Balthazar said. "We told them how fast the tide would come in. We told your guys the same ahead of time, and anybody who wanted to listen. Look, you know about this. We've done midnight pickups before for people, and other things, with your guy Ascanio. He has a crew. They've done this before. They know how to unload a boat. Why not use them?"

Molina shook his head. "He was killed in the fighting, along with some of his crew. We didn't have time to get the rest together."

"Too bad. I liked Ascanio. Well, here're your guns."

"Yes. I need you to bring them into the city."

"Nope," Melchior said.

"What?"

"FAS."

"What does that mean?" Molina said.

"'Free alongside ship.' That was the deal. We'll unload and pile them here if you want, but if I were you, I'd bring a few more guys." Melchior gestured at the man and women standing at the end of the dock, out of earshot. They wore GG colors and were watching closely.

"What good are they to me here? They have to get into the city to be of use."

"We know that," Melchior said. "That's why we suggest you get some more guys."

"Fine. We'll carry them ourselves."

"2,000 kilograms? You're stronger than you look."

"I will go round up some more people, and we will take care of it. Start unloading. I'll be back in four hours," Molina said.

"One hour. It will take us less than an hour to dump all this stuff on the dock, and then we sail."

"I will remember this, later," Molina said. "You'd better have powerful friends."

"Well-armed ones, anyway."

"I will be back in two hours. If you leave before then, there will be much trouble for you."

"Fine. Two hours," Melchior said.

"Very well. It will take that long to carry them into the town," Molina said.

"Don't carry them," Balthazar said. "Give them away."

"What?" Molina said.

"Look, you guys and the Militia are fighting it out for something, right? So don't bother hauling the weapons up there. Get your guys down here and give them a revolver and, say, three handfuls of bullets. Then send them back into town. They can cause trouble individually."

Molina looked at him. "That is a good idea, but it will be hard to find enough of our regular staff."

Balthazar shrugged. "So recruit some new ones."

"Recruit some new ones?"

"Yeah. Sign up some new GG people, give them a gun, and send 'em into town to play."

"I see," Molina said. "Unload now. We will be back in two hours."

He strode down the dock and walked up to the group at the end of the quay. Balthazar watched as they conferred, then all began to talk into their comms.

"Mel, where did you hide the crates of ammo we stole?" Balthazar asked.

"Spare anchor chain down-channel, in the cove around the corner. Dropped them and the buoy when we were in deep water."

"Tide won't uncover them?"

"Nope. Not till the next spring tide. We can get them before then."

"Alright. Let's unload this stuff and get out of here."

"Call everybody back from orbit," the lieutenant ordered. He was in the main control room of the shuttle launch building.

"Everybody?" the comm tech said.

"Yes. All the ships. Bring them all back."

The comm tech shrugged and began to type on his

screen. "It's your war. I'm just working in it."

A door banged open behind them, and a uniformed figure barged into the control room. "Report," the captain said.

The lieutenant saluted. "There is a coordinated attack going on," he said. "The Growers have pushed out from the train station on one street and overwhelmed the units we had guarding there. We did a lot of damage, but they broke through. Our units are retreating toward the shuttle dock here, but there is pretty confused street fighting."

"What're all these fires going on down here?"

"A unit of Growers is coming up the river. There's been fighting with one of our pickets, and they're reporting heavy casualties as well. They're retreating toward us."

"How did they get that many people down there?" the captain asked.

"We don't know. The situation is confusing. There are reports of fighting between different groups, and a lot of them seem to have fake guns."

"Fake guns?"

"Guns that don't work, anyway," the lieutenant said. "I've called everybody back in—everybody in the city and everybody in orbit."

"Leave a squad on TGI Main. How many ships are up there with actual troops in them?" the captain asked.

"Maybe a dozen?"

"Have half of them land down here, and suggest the other half storm GG Main."

"'Storm,' sir?" the lieutenant said. "We were trying to avoid any orbital damage. Everything up there is vulnerable. One mistake, and who knows what could happen."

"I don't care," the captain said. "It's time these people remembered they are part of the Empire."

"But, Colonel, can I not go with you? Bringing this

fight to our enemies will be glorious," Commander Roi said.

"I wish I could let you, young man," Colonel Savard said. "We will bring Imperial chastisement to our enemies at Galactic Growing. I am here only to collect as many troopers as you can spare before we attack the traitors' home station. But somebody must stay here and command in my absence. You are my trusted aide. Your place is here."

"My place is at your side, Colonel, as we face death or glory together!"

"I wish it were so, but I must have somebody reliable here," Colonel Savard said. He motioned the commander closer and lowered his voice. "In truth, I do not trust that lieutenant back at our orbital station. I want a more loyal officer within reach of our high shuttle port. I am leaving you a small shuttle, suitable for station-to-station travel, and a squad."

The colonel turned back to the sergeant. "Sergeant Russell, have you chosen who will stay behind to guard our interests here?"

Sergeant Russell braced to attention and saluted. "Sir. Myself and eight troopers will be staying with the commander."

"You're not coming with us, Sergeant?" Colonel Savard asked.

"Sir, with all this chastising gloriousness going on, we felt the only fair way to...ah...apportion the righteousness of Imperial enterprisingness was a lottery."

"A lottery?"

"We rolled dice for who would accompany you to the Growers' station, sir."

"And you lost? How sad."

"Lost?" Sergeant Russell blinked. "Oh, sure. Yes, sir. Lost, as you say. Lost, or something like that, sir. I'll stay here."

"Well, fear not, Sergeant, there will be glory enough for

all. They also serve who stand and wait."

"And live longer too," Sergeant Russell said under his breath.

"What was that, Sergeant?" Colonel Savard said.

"Long live the Emperor, sir," Sergeant Russell said. His squad shouted in agreement.

"I salute you both," Colonel Savard said.

The troops returned the salute as the colonel marched into the waiting airlock.

Commander Roi watched the door close with a glum expression, then turned to Sergeant Russell. "Well, we must do our part."

"Indeed, sir. I understand that you took computer science at the university?"

"I did, Sergeant, but I was horrible at it. I failed it twice before squeaking by. Why do you ask?"

"I'm sorry to hear that, sir. Regulations require that upon regaining control of an Imperial asset, it's necessary to audit the main computer and inventory all Imperial items."

"Audit? Inventory?" Commander Roi asked. "Surely not now, in the middle of a battle."

"Well, there's no battle actually going on right here, right now, and Imperial regulations are quite specific."

"Well, deal with it, Sergeant."

"Sorry, sir—has to be an officer. Regulations."

"An officer?" Commander Roi said.

"Yes, sir," Sergeant Russell said, "in case there are any classified things I'm not supposed to know about."

"I see."

"I've loaded up your task list on your tablet, sir. It's quite extensive. I'm not allowed to help out directly, of course, but I thought I'd take over berthing, payroll, provisioning and supplies, mounting a sensor watch—all the boring administrative stuff—while you handle the more important things."

The commander smiled and clapped Sergeant Roi on

the shoulders. "Truly, you are a loyal servant of the Empire. Well, to each the Empire has set his apportioned tasks. Obedient to the will of the Emperor, I will retire to my office. You will contact me if you need anything?"

"Immediately, sir."

"Very well." The commander turned and walked down the hall.

Sergeant Russell watched until he turned the corner, then turned to the troopers. "Right. Shamus, draw a couple hundred credits from the chips that the commander left us. You are in charge of administration and payroll."

"Yes, Sergeant."

"Chaudhari."

"Yes, Sergeant?"

"Find us a bar that sells beer and food and has a working screen display. You are in charge of provisioning and supplies."

"Yes, Sergeant. What for?" Chaudhari asked.

"Sensor watch," Sergeant Russell said. "We'll watch the war from there. Move out."

The streets around the shuttle control building were absolute mayhem. There was smoke everywhere, and DJ and his men had engaged three different groups with gunfire on the way over.

Another group had attacked them with bats before being driven off. It had taken almost an hour to fight to the cross streets.

"Emperor's testicles, these are supposed to be our troops," DJ said. "Where is Alfonzo?"

"Should be around the corner here somewhere, DJ," said one of his men.

"Any answers on the comms?"

"No, sir, but with Diego dead, we won't get much," the man said.

"Never mind. I'll go look." DJ ran to the exposed

corner to look down the side streets.

"Say what you like about Don Junior, but he's brave," one of the men said, swinging a shotgun to cover them.

"Maybe he just doesn't have a good understanding of consequences," said the other. "Don't confuse bravery with a lack of imagination."

DJ turned and waved his men over, then slipped around the corner. The twenty or so men with him rushed the corner. They ran as a disorganized mob. They were heavily armed, but not soldiers. DJ was around the corner, conferring with the leader of a small group of men.

"Alfonzo," DJ said.

"Don Pedro," Alfonzo said.

"That is my father," DJ said. "You know that."

Alfonzo looked at his men, then back to DJ. "You have not heard?"

"We haven't heard anything for four hours."

"Your father....He, well...." Alfonzo squared his shoulders. "He was an old man. He passed peacefully. You are the new Don."

DJ blinked. "He's dead."

"Yes."

"Now, of all times."

"We do not choose our times."

DJ stared up at the sky for a moment. "We do not choose our times, but perhaps others do. This is the work of our enemies. I will remember this." He shrugged. "Well, in his memory, let us bring his grand adventure to a victory. How many men did you bring with you?"

"These. Seventeen."

"Seventeen? You were given weapons for a thousand."

"Don Pedro, I was given weapons for six hundred. I was given working weapons for two hundred, and ammunition for perhaps one hundred."

"What?"

"Not all were delivered, and of those delivered, perhaps one in three actually fires. They were sabotaged."

"How?"

"The firing pins were removed from most of them. They are so much scrap metal without them."

"What's happening now, then?"

"We gave out guns to our loyalists and spread the rest out with local recruits."

"Local recruits?"

"Gangs. We armed the gangs and told them to cause mayhem. This is the result."

"We must find out what is going on. Our communications specialist was killed, and the Militia is jamming our comms. We need better communications. Where can we find them?"

The two men looked at each other, and then turned to look at the shuttle control office, in the distance.

"Hands up! On the floor," a GG trooper said as he and his companions stormed the shuttle office.

"Sure," said the tech at the board. "Which first?"

"What?"

"I can't get on the floor if I keep my hands up. I'm belted in, and the chair is bolted to the ground. I could try to kind of slide down." The tech demonstrated, slouching. "Won't work, exactly. Want me to get down first, and then put my arms up? Isn't that some sort of yoga pose? 'Seated orbital warrior' or something?"

"Don't do anything stupid, or I'll shoot you," the trooper said.

"In a room full of pre-Abandonment equipment? Special computers we can't make here, ever? No, you won't. Your bosses will flay your skin off if you do that."

"You're right." The trooper lowered his weapon and turned to one of his men. "Fuego, go find a wrench or something and break this guy's knees. Make sure you don't hit the equipment when you do it." He turned back to the tech. "That safe enough for you?"

"Just joking with you," the tech said, but he did raise

his hands again.

DJ and Alfonzo strode in. "What is going on?"

"Not certain, sir," the trooper said. "We just secured the control room."

The tech cleared his throat.

"Where are the Militia guards?" DJ asked.

"Don't know, sir," the trooper admitted.

The tech cleared his throat again.

DJ turned to him. "What?"

"The Militia troops ran off about ten minutes before you got here. Most of the staff left right after to go home. I'm it for the building."

"Why didn't you go?"

"It's dangerous out there. Lots of crazy people with guns. We had a vote—whoever came back first, we'd help."

"You will help us?"

"Bud, I just want this revolt or riot or whatever to be over."

"You would work for the Galactic Growing Corporation?"

"I worked for a corp before this thing started. I figure I'll be working for one when it's finished, so yeah, why not yours?"

"You have reliable communication equipment? Equipment that will reach the orbitals?"

The tech pointed. "Right over there."

The newly minted Don Pedro and Don Alfonzo moved to the board and began typing. The tech turned back to his board.

The guardsman stepped up and pointed his gun at him. "Don't do anything."

"Didn't we talk about this shooting thing?"

"Right. Still plenty of time to go looking for a wrench, though."

"Okay, I'll keep my hands where you can see them. Not much for me to do. Say, how long have you worked for GG?"

The guardsman looked at him and tilted his head. "Ever since I was eighteen. My dad worked there. He got me the job. "

"They good to work for? Take good care of their people?"

The guard shrugged. "Good enough. Why do you ask?"

"Well, they'll probably be my new employers. Them or the Militia."

"We will win."

"Sure. Whatever. But GG....They take good care of you, right? Food, some rooms? Some stuff?"

"Sure."

"Okay, well, I'm on team GG, then," the tech said.

The guard looked at him. "That's it? That's all it takes to change allegiance?"

"I'm like you. My dad got me my job. It's not like it was a choice or anything."

The guard watched him for a moment, then shook his head. "When did we become feudal?"

"About ten minutes after the Abandonment," the tech said.

There was a commotion from across the room.

"Technician, do you have a shuttle?" DJ asked.

"Got two."

"Prep one. We have to go. GG's main station is under attack."

Chapter 38

The door of the cell clanged open. A squad of heavily armed Militia troopers stormed in and pointed guns at the prisoner.

The man on the bed stood up. A helmeted female figure limped in behind them and leaned on a cane. "You're the one they call the admiral?" the woman asked.

"Yes."

"They say you are a traitor to the Militia."

"I've served the Militia my entire professional life, and I've always been loyal."

"You are a traitor to the Empire," she said.

"Is that a question or a statement?" Admiral Edmunds asked.

"What?"

"Are you asking, or telling?"

"I don't understand," the woman said.

"The Empire hasn't been here for years. How would you know what is and isn't loyalty?" Admiral Edmunds asked.

The squad remained silent.

"So, why are you here? I have some reading to catch up on. I don't really need an interruption," Admiral Edmunds said.

The lieutenant pulled her helmet off. "Do you remember me, Admiral?"

The admiral stared at her, then nodded. "Lieutenant Shutt. I do. That accident. What are you doing here?"

"I'm interested in your loyalty."

"I'm a traitor to the Militia, or so I've been told. Why would I care what you believe?"

There was a large amount of shouting, a banging noise, and then the room shook.

Admiral Edmunds looked up. "I hear you started a war. How's it going?"

Lieutenant Shutt leaned on her cane. "We're losing."

Admiral Edmunds, Lieutenant Shutt, and her squad walked down the stairs in the foyer of the city hall. Large groups of men and women in Militia uniforms sat or stood along the walls.

"GG came boiling out of the train station this morning. At the same time, a group came up from the docks down south," Lieutenant Shutt said. She was struggling with the stairs, so the admiral slowed down to match her pace. "We were prepared at the station, but didn't expect the docks part, and it overwhelmed our resources. We gave as good as we got—better than we got—but we took heavy casualties and were forced back."

"What about the farmers?"

"They got hit hard as well. Much harder than us. They sent a well-armed group out of the train station in a compact mass and headed into the city. They overwhelmed the groups we had stationed there. We couldn't hold them."

"Who's left at the monorail station, then?" Admiral Edmunds asked.

"Whoever's left has retreated into buildings. We've got scouts who can see them, but we haven't done anything about it," Lieutenant Shutt said.

"Uh-huh, and what about down south?"

"That's a different story. They came up from somewhere near the docks, shooting up anything that moved, or trying to. It seems that about two-thirds of their guns have been sabotaged."

"Sabotaged so they look fine, but won't shoot when you actually put ammunition in them?"

The lieutenant stopped and leaned on her cane. "Yes. What do you know about that?"

The admiral stared off into the distance. "How to make

them pass a cursory inspection." He snapped his fingers. "Firing pins. They're missing the firing pins, right?"

Lieutenant Shutt nodded. "That's right. Did you have anything to do with that?"

"Nothing, but I know who did. What's the situation down south?"

"Confused. Some of these groups are shooting at each other. Some have set fires or are looting buildings."

"GG security is doing that?"

"Gangs, we think. Not sure. I told everybody to pull back."

"Good idea. What about comms?" Admiral Edmunds asked.

"We don't really have any," Lieutenant Shutt said.

"Right. What's that room over there?"

"Cafeteria."

Admiral Edmunds stretched his arms up over his head and cracked his knuckles. Dozens of the men and women in uniform were watching him and muttering to each other. He gazed at each group, making eye contact with each person before moving on. Most eyes dropped when he held them, but one senior sergeant held his gaze, then smiled.

The admiral smiled back. "Sergeant Sumita, do you have a moment?"

The sergeant strode over and saluted. "For you, sir, always."

Admiral Edmunds clasped Sergeant Sumita in a stiff-armed shoulder hug. "It's good to see you again, Hugo."

"You too, sir. Are you back to fix things up?"

"I'm retired."

"Just a little bit of work, sir. Won't take long. You can do it before dinner and then be back to enjoying your retirement."

"That simple, is it, Sergeant?" Admiral Edmunds asked.

"Absolutely, sir," Sergeant Sumita said. "Just kick a few Imperial buttocks, and we'll be fine."

"If it's just a few, why didn't you do it yourself?"

"Don't know which ones to kick, sir. That's an officer's job."

"Indeed. Indeed. Hugo, if you're not too busy, could you send out runners to all detachments within a mile? Officers and senior NCOs are to be here within thirty minutes for a short meeting. Get the names of who is coming. Nothing on the radio."

"I will pick the runners myself, sir," Sergeant Sumita said.

"Good," Admiral Edmunds said. "Returning runners report to you and the lieutenant here. Have a second group of runners ready to go if there are any waverers that the lieutenant wants here."

"Me, sir?" the lieutenant asked.

"You." The admiral nodded. "I want everybody here. If somebody looks like they're not showing up, I want to know if you care—if they have to be here. Think about who you can trust."

"Yes, sir," Sergeant Sumita said.

"Go, Sergeant."

Sergeant Sumita took off. Admiral Edmunds nodded in approval.

Lieutenant Shutt looked at the admiral. "What made you think I was going to let you take charge and issue orders?"

"The only other reason to take me out of jail was to shoot me," the admiral said, "and you wouldn't shoot me in the lobby."

"Oh." She watched the sergeant's squad start jogging away. "How did you know he would help you?"

"I saved his life on the south continent once."

"The militia doesn't operate on the south continent."

"No, they don't, do they?" Admiral Edmunds smiled at the lieutenant. "Anyway, now for the most important part of the day."

"Getting out of jail wasn't the most important?"

"Nope."

"The conference, then?" Lieutenant Shutt asked.

"Not that, either," the admiral said.

"What is, then?"

"Breakfast, Lieutenant. Breakfast is the most important part of the day."

"Another conference," Amelio Vargas said. "It's a waste of our time. I don't know why I let you talk me into this. We should have stayed with the troops. You are an idiot." He stepped up the front steps of the civic building.

"That's Captain Idiot to you," Amelia Vargas said, returning a salute. "The troops will be fine. We told them not to do anything stupid."

"You are only an officer because Father liked his daughters better," Amelio told his twin.

"You are only not an officer because you are a stiff-necked, pig-headed Imperial prick who always irritated Father," she retorted.

They glared at each other.

"There's some truth to both statements," Amelio said. "Let us see what was is going on, and what the admiral has to say. What is that smell?"

"Smells like heaven," his sister said.

"Or breakfast."

"I just said that."

They walked through a door and into the cafeteria. An orderly handed them two steaming hot trays of food as they came in and pointed to the cafeteria tables facing the front. There were about forty people in uniform sitting there, wolfing down food.

They sat and surveyed the room.

"Lots of lower ranks here," Amelia said. "Sergeants. Technicians."

"Yes," her brother said. "Not many of the political types, either." They exchanged a significant look.

"Pierre," Amelia said, turning toward a man at the next

table. "How are you?"

"Good, *ma petit*, good. You are looking ravishing, as always," Pierre said. He wore a Militia captain's uniform, but his was tailored. And ironed. And clean.

"Nice uniform. I see you haven't been out in the streets much," Amelio said. "Where is your sergeant?"

Pierre's face darkened. "Killed by the Growers. A lucky shot. This is my formal uniform. My other was damaged."

"Damaged how?" Amelia asked.

"Ashok bled out before I could get him to the hospital. I ran the whole way carrying him. I was not fast enough." He looked down at his clothes. "I do not wish to wear that uniform again. This one will suffice."

Everyone was quiet for a moment. Amelia ate her food and looked around. "The senior officers....There are hardly any here."

Pierre shrugged. "They have mostly gone to orbit with the Officers' Council. They are trying to storm the orbital stations."

"Storm an orbital station? How do you do that?" Amelio asked.

Pierre shrugged again. "I do not know. I have my own problems."

"Who's that over there?" Amelia pointed.

"It's the admiral."

The room quieted as Admiral Edmunds stepped up onto a chair, then climbed up to a tabletop. He surveyed the crowd. "Good morning. I hope you are enjoying your breakfast."

The room burst out in laughter and applause.

The admiral did a mock blow. "I thought so. I have been unavoidably detained for the last few days, but I am back now. Our situation is as follows: There is widespread insurrection in Landing, spread by the GG household security forces. They have attacked government buildings and killed Militia troopers, citizens, and security forces.

The monorail has been sabotaged, fires are reported in the factory district, and several food production and manufacturing facilities have severe damage. There are reports of fighting near the shuttle dock and, more importantly, damage to the main fusion plant."

Admiral Edmunds paused and took a breath. He gestured, and one of the officers at his table gave him a glass of water, which he took a long drink from before turning back to the crowd. "We are in an extremely bad place. We are outnumbered, outgunned, short on ammunition, our enemies are numerous, and they have backed us into a corner."

He paused again and drank the rest of the water down. "There is only one thing to do. We will attack."

Cheers broke out in the room. He waited for them to subside.

"Our priorities are as follows. First, we will withdraw all our troops from around the monorail station. The Growers can have it. We will move in force to the main fusion plant, secure it, then power down the shuttle docks and the monorail as well. After that, we will push the Growers into the dock area and pin them there. I expect we will receive some reinforcements, or at least weapons, from TGI security forces at that time, and we will clear the warehouse area and disperse the rioting elements in the streets. All the while, we will collect the 'malfunctioning' weapons for later use. "

A man at the back stood up.

"Yes, Captain Lapoint?" the admiral said.

"Sir, where will these reinforcements come from?"

"I will be speaking with some people at TGI shortly. They will be providing us with a small number of troops, but also additions to our weapons and ammunition."

"TGI, sir? The Officers' Council tells us that they are our enemy. An enemy of the Empire."

"Have you fought any TGI forces today, Captain?"

"I have not, sir."

"Have any of you fought any TGI forces?" Admiral Edmunds asked, looking around the room.

The room stirred as everyone looked around.

"I believe, Captain," the admiral said, "that our enemies are those actually shooting at us and actively destroying property. Not those targeted as the result of some theoretical corporate dispute. Do you agree?"

Captain Lapoint smiled. "I do, sir." He saluted and sat down.

"What about the Officers' Council?" a voice from the back yelled.

"The Officers' Council has left to orbit. I do not know why. Perhaps they find it safer there," the admiral said.

The crowd laughed.

"I thought you were in jail," somebody else yelled.

"I was. I am not anymore. I'm here, fighting with you. Unlike the Officers' Council."

The crowd laughed again, and Captain Lapoint back stood up. "Who will be in charge, sir?"

"On behalf of the Empire, I am taking personal command till this crisis is over," Admiral Edmunds said. "Now, finish your breakfast, and let's get to work."

Cheers erupted as he climbed down.

"Well done, sir," Lieutenant Shutt said.

"Well enough. Let them finish, then get them moving as we talked about, Lieutenant."

"Of course, sir. Victory or death, as those Empire Rising dorks would say."

"Indeed, Lieutenant, indeed—but what if it's both?" the admiral said.

Chapter 39

"How are you feeling, sir?" Jose asked Dashi.

Jose was sitting at his desk having a comm call with Dashi. Dashi hadn't volunteered where he was, and Jose hadn't asked.

"Much better, thank you, Jose. The second surgery seems to have done the trick. The doctors tell me the internal bleeding has finally stopped."

"I didn't realize how much danger you were in. They wouldn't tell me anything."

"I told them not to. You had enough on your hands as it was. Is that welding equipment I see in the background?"

"You could have died, sir."

"I could have, but that can happen at any time, and it is best you be prepared for the inevitable. In any event, should you have the time, I would appreciate a briefing on our status right now. Do you have time?"

"Of course, sir," Jose said. "It is much as you planned, sir. The Militia mutiny by the Empire Rising cabal is falling apart. Most of the troops in Landing are back under the control of their regular officers. There have been substantial casualties in the rebel officer ranks."

"The admiral is back in control, then?"

"He has captured the power plant and begun to shut off power to different areas of the city. The remaining GG troops at the monorail station have surrendered. He has disarmed them, given them seven days of rations, and told them to walk home."

"Walk home?"

"At least to the next GG station. Down the monorail line. Regardless, a great number, several hundred, have taken up his offer. He is fighting in the southern part of the city now. Things are going slowly, but he sounds confident."

"Good, good, and DJ?"

"DJ is now Don Pedro."

"What?"

"His father died yesterday."

"Jose, did you...?"

"No, sir. It was just one of those things. Heart attack, my information says."

"Does DJ believe that?"

"I don't think so. I haven't spoken to him directly—his comms are a mess—but there has been renewed fighting around the shuttle port. First the rebel officers were in control, then they took a shuttle, then a mob of GG security forces captured the shuttle port, and then they took a shuttle up from there."

"Are they chasing each other?"

"No, sir. They appear to have started an orbital battle."

Alarms were going off all over the place. There were so many that it was hard to tell them apart. Colonel Savard crouched behind three overturned tables in the cafeteria. Shotgun-armed troops fired around the corners. One of the troopers leaned out and fired a blast, but jerked back and fell down. The colonel dragged him back around the corner and began applying first aid to the wound in his chest.

The colonel turned to the lieutenant with a comm next to him. "Report," the colonel said.

The lieutenant looked up from his comm. "Colonel Savard, there is much confusion. The operations center was under our control, but comms are down—the Growers many have recaptured it. We can see fighting in the power plant area on the screens. There is a hull breach on Ring D and one on Ring E. There are fire alarms going off everywhere, and most of the automatic systems that still have power have closed, isolating much of the station."

A white strobe light began to flash brightly in the cafeteria.

"What is that?"

"Sir, that is the depressurizing alarm."

"From Ring D?"

"Sir, that's the local alarm. We are losing pressure in this room. Right now."

Colonel Savard looked around. They had been ambushed as they crossed the cafeteria area. Their retreat was far behind them, across an open foyer. They had not expected the Growers to fight this hard.

"What is beyond those doors over there?"

"Ring stairs, sir."

"Can we get to the power plant from there?"

"Down the stairs, one quarter anti-spinward, and up again, and we'll be at the core."

"Very well." The colonel was having trouble breathing. Even the light was changing as the air thinned. He stood up as much as he could while still crouching behind the overturned table. "Cease fire and listen."

He waited as his words were passed down the row of men. All stopped and crouched behind their hiding places. A single revolver was firing from the corridor in front of them. He timed his words between shots.

BANG.

"We are losing air here. If we do not leave this compartment and get to safety, all unsuited personnel will die."

BANG.

"Our comrades are fighting in the power plant. They need our help. If we take that, we have the station."

BANG.

"If we can reach that corridor, the way is clear to the fusion plant."

BANG.

"There cannot be many of them. Perhaps only one or two. We outnumber them. We can rush them."

BANG.

"Most importantly, that is a six-shot revolver."

BANG.

The colonel stood up to his full height as the sounds of the last round echoed.

"I am attacking. Follow me." He ran toward the corridor, firing as he went.

The lieutenant followed him. "The Empire will return!"

"The Empire," chorused the troops as they pursued them.

"Exterior lights are out, Don Pedro," the pilot said.

"Keep going. We must reinforce our troops there," DJ said.

"Yes, sir. We can't dock this orbit, I don't think."

"We must dock."

"Not up to me, sir. Mr. Newton is firmly in control. We've been firing thrusters as much as we can, but all this extra mass has messed us up."

"You told me you've docked a thousand times."

"I have, sir, but I normally have time to calculate our exact mass before we lift, and delay launch to catch a launch window, and wait an extra orbit if we need to."

"We don't have time for this," DJ said.

"Doesn't matter if we do or not. We're stuck with gravity. Too bad we weren't going to TGI Main rather than GG Main. We have an excellent solution on that one, after only three orbits."

"We need to get to GG Main before those Empire Rising freaks take it over."

"No can do, sir. Check out the computer." The pilot showed him his screen.

DJ barely glanced at it. "I can't read nav computers. I don't know how to navigate."

"This is a special military one," the pilot said. "Look here. There are really only three variables—your current orbit (which it gets from the computer at Militia headquarters), the orbit you want to intersect, and your points of closest approach and closest velocity on your current orbit."

"Why do I care about this?"

"Look here," the pilot said. "This number here. That's our velocity relative to GG Main at closest approach. If I change this to zero, it will show the course changes. Here, you see—there are three, and then we'll be down to latch."

"I cannot wait three orbits. We must get there now."

"Sir—Don Pedro," a voice called from the back.

"I'm busy," DJ said.

"Sir, there are reports from the station. There is some sort of panic going on over there."

"What's happening?" DJ asked.

The pilot fiddled with his screen. "I've got them on the telescope. Let me enlarge the image." They looked at the display. "It's drifting out of orbit slightly. Those plumes are atmosphere escaping. They're pushing her around."

The radio man pulled his way forward. "Sir, there are reports of fighting near the fusion reactors. There has been damage. One of our squads is asking for assistance defending it. They say a small group of Militia is inside."

"We can't help them from here." DJ banged his fist on the console. "Pilot, get us there."

"I can't just push a button. We have to worry about orbits and fuel, and we—oh crap."

Everybody turned back to the screen. The center of the ring had exploded with a bright flash. The screen blanked in the glare, and as the display came back, they could see pieces of the station spinning off in all directions.

"Emperor's balls," the pilot said. They all just stared at the screen.

"Thousands of people lived on that station," the tech said.

"Many of my family. I don't know how many where there, living or visiting. Dozens," DJ said.

The pilot leaned over and began to type into the

console.

"What are you doing?" DJ asked.

"We can't go there. There's too much debris. We'll impact something."

"What about survivors?" the tech asked.

The pilot just shook his head. "Anybody not in a suit is dead already, and anybody in a suit is going to orbit right into the ground.

DJ spoke up. "This is the Militia's doing—and their allies, TGI. They have done this. They killed my father. They killed my people." He turned to the pilot. "Take us to TGI Main."

"As good as anywhere else, I guess," the pilot said. He typed on the screen some more. "We have some luck, for a change. We're on a good course for them. Just have to slow down a bit."

"What do you mean?" DJ asked.

"See? Look at the screen. We'll be almost on top of them, just going too fast relative to them. Give me one shorter orbit, and we'll be right on top of them, zero-zero. First one, we'll go screaming by."

DJ began to question him about the numbers on the screen, tapping one or two and having the pilot explain them. Finally, DJ nodded and yelled back to the hab module. "Good. Technician, come up here."

The comm technician appeared. "Don Pedro?"

As easily as if he were drinking a glass of water, DJ pulled the revolver from his holster and shot the pilot in the head. Blood spattered all over the screen. The comm technician gasped.

DJ held up his hand and smiled. "Relax. Relax. It's okay. I have discovered that he is a traitor, in the pay of our enemies. He has been communicating with them all this time. Take this body and throw it out the airlock."

"But...Don, he was our pilot," the comm technician said. "How will we get back?"

"It is alright. I had him set our course before I killed

his cursed soul. We are on target to dock at TGI Main. I have much to discuss with them. We'll be there soon."

"Yes, Don."

"Good. Dump him outside, and when you are done, come back here and give me a tutorial on the comm gear. I will need to record some private messages."

Chapter 40

"Orange juice, please," Nadine said.

After selling the guns to Vince, she'd dropped far and fast. A Militia ship and the unnamed freighter had initially followed her, but then the Militia ship had made a radical change of course and headed toward some inner station. The other ship, which looked suspiciously similar to a Francois ship she had tangled with some time ago, had also followed her, then gone dark and disappeared. She'd managed a rendezvous with a Free Trader station that was in the lowest part of its orbit.

"Do we look like the type of place that has orange juice?" the bartender said.

"I'm sure you have some for special customers." Nadine gave him her best number-three smile.

The bartender looked at her for a moment, then walked over to the end of the bar, thumbed open the fridge there, and produced an opaque bottle. "Have you got the money for this? It's expensive."

"How much?"

The bartender named a figure. Nadine raised her eyebrows. That was high. She upgraded her smile to number two and said, "How much after the pretty girl discount?"

The bartender shook his head. "Not on the orange juice...but do you like mimosas?"

"What's a mimosa?" Nadine said.

Two hours later Nadine had decided that she did like mimosas—very much. This wine with bubbles in it was great. She'd have to get more of that.

She climbed onto her ship and stumbled up to the control room, remembering to shut and lock the airlock. Wouldn't want somebody coming by and stealing the ship she had stolen. She sat down and looked around. Having her own ship was nice, but...well, a bit quiet. On an impulse, she hunted up a comm code and began to record a message.

"Hi, Jakey. Thanks for the ship. It's great. I've finally got my own thing now, and I don't owe anybody. All thanks to you. I know I kind of, well, 'acquired' it from you, but you've got that whole other ship to play with. I'm sure you be fine. It's quiet around here without you, though. I hope you're okay and up to things. I see that war thing isn't going well for your side. Lots of fighting and stuff. I'm going to stay far away from that. I'll be sure to be anti-profligate with my fuel. Maybe we can meet up for a drink when this is all over. Write back soon."

Nadine burped and decided that was a good time to end the message, so she saved it and pressed send. She wondered how long it would take for Jake to respond.

The message came back in a surprisingly short time— only minutes. The message light flashed, and the screen read, *Message from J. Stewart.*

Then a gong sounded, and a different message flashed. *Control board locked*, it said. Her control board went dark.

"You are a giant Imperial turd, Jake," Nadine said, and waited. They had a voice relay setup, and the delay was noticeable, but not too uncomfortable.

"You stole my ship," Jake said.

"It was our ship, and I didn't sign on for a war."

"You were trying to escape being arrested, and I stopped to help you."

"Great help, Jakey. I'm stuck in the dock of a Free Traders' station, running up docking fees as we speak."

"You were spending our cargo credit on booze and orange juice."

"Truth," agreed Nadine. "I think you'd forgive me if you tasted those drinks, though. That champagne stuff is pretty awesome. Wait, how did you know that?"

"I have a tracer on your bank account."

"On my bank account? You hacked into my bank account?"

"No, I helped you set it up, remember? I just put my name in the 'email a copy of receipts' column. It's a standard setting."

"It's on my account, though."

"No, it was the ship account, and you stole it, remember? Besides, we need to keep receipts."

"I saved your life when that ice hit you."

"You also left me to die out here."

"You said you had plenty of food."

"Did you know that before you left?"

There was silence for a long time.

"What happens now?" Nadine asked.

"We need your help. I've been talking to Jose. There is a big war going on. GG Main exploded. There is fighting in the city. The Militia can probably take the city, but they need more weapons—the weapons from the ship."

"I, uh...." Nadine blushed a tiny bit. "I don't have the revolvers anymore."

"You sold them to GG. I know. That was the plan. Only about one in three of those revolvers work. By the way, they want to kill you. They've put a contract out on you. 10,000 credits, dead or alive."

"All the more reason for me to get out of here."

"I need you to help the Militia equip themselves with more revolvers. This way they can recapture Landing and put down GG's rebellion."

"Jake, I already told you I don't have any more revolvers. I sold them all to GG."

"Yes. I know. That was the plan."

"The plan was for me to sell those weapons to GG?"

"Either to GG or the Militia, or both."

"Either. Both. But you knew they didn't work."

"Yes."

"Your plan was for me to sell malfunctioning weapons

to one side of a civil war," Nadine said.

"Yes, or both sides," Jakes said. "It really didn't matter."

"And because they don't work, you knew they would want to kill me."

"Exactly."

Nadine started to yell at Jake, but stopped. There was always something, with Jake's schemes. "Jake."

"Yes?"

"Those revolvers don't work."

"Correct."

"Why don't they work?"

"They don't have any firing pins," Jake said.

Nadine banged her head against the console, then tried again. "Fine. They don't have any firing pins. Why not?"

"I took them all out—well, as many as I could—while I was cleaning them. That's why the cleaning took so long."

Nadine nodded once, then again. "Of course...and where are the firing pins, then?"

"In the engine room, in a secret compartment. Could you get them and deliver them to the Militia, please? We don't have a lot of time."

It took a bit longer than Nadine would have guessed to get the firing pins. They were in a sealed metal box that was actually inside the fuel tank. When they'd modified the ship, Jake had had the spare H tank converted into a smuggling hideaway. She had to unbolt a flange, and turn some valves, and use a pump, but eventually she popped a panel and pulled out an ice-cold box.

Jake had warned her, so she was wearing her suit gauntlets, and she was able to pry it open and check inside, then returned to the bridge. The message light was flashing at her.

She opened a new channel. "Okay, Jake. They're all here. I'm sure you have somebody here to bring these down to the surface, so send them over, and I'll give 'em the box. Just unlock the board, and I'll be on my way."

The board flashed green before she finished speaking, and Jake's voice broke in. "New plan, Nadine. I need you to hurry over to TGI Main and defend them. Don Pedro has gone nuts. He's heading over there on an intercept course, and he says he's going to crash his ship into it and destroy it."

"Surrender or die," Commander Roi said. He was in his office staring at his screen. Sergeant Russell was ranged behind him, along with four of his troopers.

"That's seems to be a somewhat extreme statement, given that 80 percent of your combat force is standing behind you," Jose said. He could see the entirety of the office. The commander had not shrunk the view field of the camera.

"We have substantial reserves available. Tell him about the reserves, Sergeant," Commander Roi said.

"Our reserves are substantial, Mr. Jose," Sergeant Russell said.

"No, they are not," Jose said. "There are only eight of you total on the station, and the six of you in that room are all your effectives. Chaudhari broke his wrist trying to bend one of the straps he was cutting, and Kim is sick with alcohol poisoning. You are it."

The commander looked back at the sergeant. "Alcohol poisoning? How much beer did he drink?"

"He drank only a single beer, sir. Affected him badly. Some sort of allergy."

"I see."

"He wasn't so allergic to the six shots I bought him before that," one of the other men muttered. Sergeant Russell glared at him.

"Nevertheless, we demand your surrender," Commander Roi said.

Jose began to speak, but then looked off-screen. He watched something for a second, then typed on his console. "You need to see this, Commander."

The face of Don Pedro appeared on the screen. He was in the middle of a transmission. "....punish them both equally—those in the Militia who have destroyed my family's station, and their allies in TGI who had my father assassinated and assisted them in hunting down my people. I have nothing left to live for. I name my cousin Rico my successor. As the head of the family, I will give my life destroying our enemies. Revenge will be mine."

The message clicked off.

"What is that? Who is that?" Commander Roi asked.

"That's Don Junior. He took off after his father died. He's in a shuttle, and he's on a collision course for this station," Jose said.

"That is of no consequence to us. We are here to discuss your surrender."

"We don't have time for that. We need to get some of my people out there. We can re-point some of the spin engines and use them to shift the station's orbit a bit. We'll start cutting right away so we can get out there."

"If your men come out here, they will be fired on—unless they surrender and agree to be interned," the commander said.

"'Interned'? Commander Roi, you're in the Delta Militia, not the Imperial Marines, and this is somebody ramming a derelict ship into a space station, not the Battle of Rigel Seven."

"The Battle of Rigel Seven was a glorious victory for the Empire. I feel I am I fine company if we—"

"Sorry to interrupt, sir," Sergeant Russell said. He didn't sound sorry. "Mr. Jose, can you put that collision course thing on the screen so we can see exactly what's happening?"

"Sergeant," Commander Roi hissed, "do not interrupt my negotiations. This is obviously a ploy."

"Oh, no doubt, sir," Sergeant Russell said, "but I wanted him to think we were taking him seriously so you could have more maneuvering room—you know, if you wanted to pretend and let his people come out here so we could capture them and whatnot."

The commander blinked. "Outstanding, Sergeant. You have hidden depths. A true servant of the Empire."

"They also serve who stand and wait, sir," the sergeant said. He was copying numbers from the screen and typing them into his console.

Commander Roi had again forgotten to hit the mute button, and Jose had heard the whole conversation, but he kept his face blank.

"I do not believe you, Mr. Jose," the commander said. "If you want out of the cage you rats have locked yourself into, you will have to submit to our authority. I have prepared a document outlining the surrender procedure. Firstly, there is the matter of a formal declaration...."

Jose tuned out the commander's speech and watched the motion behind him. Sergeant Russell had finished checking things on his comm and turned to his men, whispering orders. One of the men bent down and began to remove his boots, then his socks. He handed the socks to Sergeant Russell.

"Article Two. After the formal renunciation, those who are willing to return to the bosom of the Empire—God save His Imperial Mightiness—will need to provide written documentation...." Commander Roi continued.

Sergeant Russell had ordered another man to take off his socks, and now he had four socks that he was pushing together, combining them into some sort of sack. One of his troopers had stepped out into the hall and returned with a can of something, which he offered the sergeant. The sergeant shook his head and berated the man, but not loud enough to be heard. Sergeant Russell pointed out the door, and the whole squad disappeared, including the two barefoot men.

"Article Five, Responsibilities of the Senior Officer in the Prison Compound," the commander said. "The most senior officer, as recognized by the competent Imperial authority—that would be you, Mr. Jose, unless you think somebody else should do it. Mr. Jose? Mr. Jose, are you listening to me?"

"Of course I am. I am clearly the competent authority for TGI here. Please continue."

"Right. As I said, Article Five...." The commander continued on.

One of the men had returned behind Sergeant Russell, shaking his head, then another, but the third man came in with a smile on his face. He handed Sergeant Russell a small sack. Jose recognized the logo. It was frozen turnips that were sold in bulk for add-ons to food trays.

"...so those are the preliminary articles," Commander Roi said. "Do you accept these, Mr. Jose?"

"Pardon?" Jose said.

Sergeant Russell was stuffing the socks full of frozen turnips and swinging it experimentally.

"Don't play coy with me. This is our best offer. If don't accept it, I can't be responsible for what might happen," the commander said.

Sergeant Russell was swinging the loaded sock around his head now, taking aim at the commander's head.

"Oh, I'll take my chances, then," Jose said.

THUNK. The loaded sock impacted just above the commander's ear. His eyes rolled, and he slumped back. Three of the men wrestled his floppy form out of the chair. Sergeant Russell sat down and faced the camera.

"Sorry for the delay, Mr. Jose. I didn't want to kill him, and he has a sidearm, so this was the best way to avoid any unpleasantness."

"Why not kill him?" Jose asked.

"He's not a bad guy, really. He's just....Well, he's just an idiot. How do we keep this crazy guy from crashing into this station and killing all of us?"

"My men are already cutting their way up through Ring D, Spoke 2. There's an engine maintenance team there with them. Meet them in the hallway and take them where they need to go."

Sergeant Russell knew an officer speaking when he heard one. "Sir," he said, and saluted the camera.

"I said, Jake, that I'm not going to kill myself for your stupid war."

"Nadine, we need you to go to TGI Main and see this guy off."

"How will I do that, huh? Shower him with good intentions? Speak harshly to him on the comm? As you are fond of reminding me, this isn't a warship."

"I really don't know. Can't you do something?"

"Perhaps I'll just crash into him and kill us both?"

"Well...."

"Jake, I'm sure that you are all noble and dedicated, but that's not me. Now, I gave that box of firing pins to your Free Trader friend on the station here, and she said she'd get them to the Militia on planet. I've done my bit. Now I want to get away from all this. Unlock my board and give me a course that takes me away."

"Away to where?"

"A station, a safe orbit, your old Rim station—I don't care. Just get me away from here."

"Nadine, if that crazy guy hits TGI Main, with the loss of GG Main and the damage to the Militia stations, plus the collateral damage from the debris already, we're going to be down perhaps one-third of our orbital capacity, and with the shortages, things will be bad."

"Blah, blah, blah. More Jake Stewart stuff. I just want to get away on my ship. This isn't my fight, Jake."

"It kind of is. It's all our fights. All our fight? I don't know the right grammar."

"Well, look it up and let me know sometime. In the meanwhile, I got your package to who you wanted. Now unlock my board and give me a course out of here."

"Fine." Jake began typing.

Nadine watched her board. Eventually it unlocked, and a new course popped up. "Jake, this is taking me by TGI Main."

"Yes. That's the only course I'm giving you."

"I'm not going to impact this guy somewhere, am I?"

"No. Your radar would pick it up before then, and besides, you could swing away easily enough. Doesn't take much to avoid somebody who's on a fixed course."

"I'm going to take the console apart and remove the locking circuit."

"You can do that or, better yet, fix the radar so you can see where you are going. You'll want to do that to avoid them."

"Glad you know that. Especially when I see them on radar. Well, it's been fun, Jake. Look me up after the war."

Nadine reached forward and cut the link. She stared down at the course for a long time before finally reaching down and pushing "Execute." The ship pivoted and fired its thrusters for about forty seconds, falling into another orbit. But the ship didn't rotate, indicating that it had more engine operations to do. Nadine stared out the control station screens, watching the station fade slowly away.

She tabbed through screens until she got to the radar screen, which showed up clear even though the station was visible out the window. She nodded once, then again. Nadine pulled herself out of her seat and back to the hab module, threw open the lockers and selected some tools, then began to suit up to go outside.

Chapter 41

TGI Main was a beehive of activity. Jose's crews had cut a path through his booby traps and met up with Sergeant Russell's crews. Four crews, including one from the Militia, were out in the rings, unbolting and re-bolting the motors that gave spin to the station and changing their aspect so they could push the station sideways.

"Is this going to work?" Sergeant Russell asked.

"After a fashion. 'Will it work enough?' is the real question," Jose said.

"So, you just point them at 90 degrees to our course and fire?"

"Not really. The mountings aren't built for that. Full power would snap girders, break the rings, and do Don Pedro's work for him. We'll do a slow, steady push that will force him to correct, then a bigger push at the last moment, hoping he'll miss us."

"Have you got any warships in place to intercept?"

"No warships, no. We have one cargo ship that's coming by, but there isn't much it can do."

"Could it push him out of the way or something?"

"'Or something'?"

"Well, you know—crash into it or something?"

"You want to ask her to do that?"

"Sure. It's an option."

"It is. I would do it, but I can't."

"Why not?"

"She's not answering her comm."

"'That's the only course I'm giving you, Nadine,' he said. That stupid brat," Nadine was out on the surface of the Castle Arcturus, carrying a hammer.

Taking great care, she climbed toward the truss. It was bent back out of shape, attached by only two of the four legs.

"Thinks he's smarter than me." *BANG*. The hammer hit a metal bar. "He never trusts me." *BANG*. "I won't miss him for a second." *BANG*. "Stupid ship. Doesn't have decent radar." *BANG*. The truss bent a bit. "Lousy food. Was there a sale on rancid super-potatoes?" *BANG*. The truss bent some more.

"'I'll just lock the board, Nadine,' he said." She hammered on the one truss arm until it was almost beaten through. "and WHY can't we have real sensors?!" Nadine hammered the truss again.

"Don Pedro, please let us in," the tech's voice said through the intercom while hammering at the bridge hatch. "We don't want to die."

"Cowards," DJ said. "We must avenge my father. Are you not loyal to your house?"

"Don, killing us all will not bring your father back."

"I agree, but it will punish those Imperial testicle-lickers at TGI. 'Trans-Galactic Insurance.' Should be 'Totally Godless...Something.'"

"There is another ship approaching. It is moving fast."

"Yes, I see it." DJ examined his screen and looked forward. He was close enough to TGI Main that he could see it visually, if he looked in the right direction. "We're moving too fast. They cannot reach us."

"The computer says it can," the tech said.

"The computer is wrong. I will have my revenge."

"If they impact us, we will be destroyed."

"They will too," DJ said. "The ship and the station. Even destroying us will not be enough. The pieces will shred those imbeciles."

"Don—"

DJ reached forward and flicked the intercom off, then leaned back and watched TGI Main grow in his viewscreen.

Jose and Sergeant Russell were sitting in Jose's office. Sergeant Russell had a large green bottle of beer. Jose sipped at a clear liquid. Jake Stewart was on the screen.

"We're ready with the engines," Jose said. "We'll give a big boost just as he comes into range. That might be enough to have him miss."

"Not if he can look forward," Jake said.

"This is good beer," Sergeant Russell said. "What's it called?"

"La Verge," Jose told him. "It's from the surface. It's a pale ale."

"Crisp. I like it."

"Good."

"What are you drinking, Mr. Jose?" Sergeant Russell asked.

"A vodka. Triple-distilled. Pure, but strong."

"Excuse me," Jake asked, "but why are you talking about alcohol when a spaceship is going to crash into the station in a few minutes?"

Sergeant Russell answered. "The sergeant I had when I went to boot camp told me, 'If you look relaxed, the troops will be relaxed.' Tense troops make mistakes, so it's more important to look relaxed than to be relaxed."

"Mr. Dashi told me something similar once," Jose said. "Make your plans, follow them, and wait for the outcome. Often, once you start something in motion, there isn't much you can do till it's over but wait."

"How much longer do we wait?" Sergeant Russell asked.

Jose hit a button on his comm. "Are you ready down there?"

"Yes," a voice said. "We'll start firing when he's about fifteen seconds out. Long enough to get out of the way, but short enough that he may not be able to correct."

"Not short enough, though."

"No, he'll still have a chance."

"How long?"

"About three minutes till impact."

"Well, let us know." Jose sat back. He and the sergeant gazed out the window in silence.

"Two minutes," the voice said.

Jose took another sip of his drink. He offered it to Sergeant Russell, who accepted, and they swapped drinks, taking a sip. Sergeant Russell coughed, and Jose grimaced.

"Too hoppy," Jose said, handing it back.

"Too biting," Sergeant Russell said, swapping with Jose.

"One minute," the voice said. "Emperor's balls."

"What?" Jose said.

"There's another ship out there. It's coming in hot. Very hot. On a collision course."

"Ha! Ha!" Nadine slid out from under the control board and brandished a screwdriver. "Take that, Jakey. Locking me out of my own board....Not happening."

She sat down at the pilot's seat and belted herself in. Then she carefully sealed her boots and made sure her gauntlets and helmet were attached to her suit. She tapped a few buttons.

Helm control restored flashed on her screen.

"Gotcha," she said. She tapped a few more screens. "Now to make him cool his jets." She punched a few more screens and waited for a call to connect. The other side answered almost as soon as the call went through.

"Hi, Jakey," Nadine said. "You must be close—not much of a delay."

"Nadine, can you stop that ship? The one heading for TGI Main?"

"You mean by crashing into him? I'm an awesome pilot. Of course I can."

"Will you?"

"Of course not, Jake. I'm not going to kill myself for some stupid corporation."

"It's not just about a corporation. It's all of Delta.

Without that station, we're going to be in serious trouble. GG Main is gone, there's damage all over the place, and we might not be able to go on."

"Boring, Jakey. Boring," Nadine said. She pivoted the ship around and did a roll. "Looks like I have altitude control now. I'm just going to move a smidge off this course, Jake. Miss that shuttle about to crash into TGI Main. Computer says I only have forty seconds."

"Nadine, please. I need you stop them."

"Oh, you need me, do you? What's in it for me?"

"What do you mean?"

"Well, this ship, for starters. I want this ship."

"But if you stop them, you'll be dead. You won't survive that."

"And lunch. A really expensive lunch. With orange juice and that olive oil stuff. Two lunches—and a dinner."

"Whatever you want, Nadine. I'll miss you."

"I think you would. I do think you would. Well, I have a course correction to make. Don't want to hit shuttles." She began to type a course correction into her console. "Goodbye, Jake. I'll talk to you after all this."

"Goodbye, Nadine. I love you."

"Known that for a while, Jake. Right back at you. We can talk about that later—and for once, I'm glad you bought that cheap radar."

"What?"

"I hate wasting good sensors," Nadine said. She looked at the visual display and poised her hand above the "Execute" button.

After a long moment, she tapped it.

The display port in Jose's office flashed, and for a second there was a bright light.

Then nothing.

"They hit. Glancing blow. Something clipped the shuttle. It's broken into two pieces. Both missed," the voice reported.

There was a pattering sound, like lots of small shoes falling on the floor, then a large cracking sound.

Jose and Sergeant Russell looked at the display.

"Play that back in slow motion," Jose said.

"What in the name of the Emperor's anus is that?" Sergeant Russell asked, pointing at a device spinning off to the side.

"Looks like part of a cheap radar system," Jose said.

Chapter 42

"Do you have enough supplies to last for the next few weeks, Mr. Stewart?" Dashi asked. He was back seated at his desk on TGI Main, taking the conference call.

"I do, sir. There is plenty of food, I've restarted the reactor, and environmental is up."

"Good, good. You are happy with your orbit?"

"It will take some work, sir, but we will be able to rendezvous with TGI Main."

"Excellent." Mr. Dashi beamed. "Have you had time to familiarize yourself with the jump controls?"

"I'm working on it, sir. There is a great deal to read."

"You are a great reader, though, so I'm sure you will work it out."

"Yes, sir," Jake said, then frowned. "Sir, this ship has excellent sensors, and I've taken the time to scan Landing...."

Dashi grimaced. "Yes. Things are bad there. Jose?"

"There is widespread insurrection on the surface," Jose said. "The admiral and the Militia have been concentrating on the Growers and any organized groups. They have been successful breaking up large concentrations, but there are still small, random groups causing mayhem. The issue is not in doubt, but the details are troubling."

"Will we be able to feed ourselves after this, sir?" Jake asked Dashi.

"An excellent question, Mr. Stewart. Under the current situation....No, we will not."

"Then we're all going to starve?"

"We were all going to starve eventually—all the projections agreed—but now we have a jump ship, which we will send back to the Empire to request relief. Maybe even evacuation."

"All this maneuvering was just for this jump ship?"

"Mostly, yes."

"The fighting, the destruction, the stations destroyed?" Jake asked.

"They were inevitable. I—or, rather, Jose and I, since he is now in charge of most of this, have simply arranged for it not to be us who would be destroyed. We still have a large amount of space-based infrastructure, we have food for many months, and once the surface quiets down, we can restart limited production. With us and the Militia in control, we will be able to save the maximum number of people for the minimum length of time."

"At the cost of the entire Galactic Growing organization and most of the Militia."

"They were not sufficiently advanced long-term thinkers," Dashi said.

"That seems quite cold-blooded," Jake said. "Ruthless."

"Thank you, Mr. Stewart. That was the nicest compliment that you have ever given me." Dashi smiled.

The room was silent for a moment.

"Although you are an excellent navigator and becoming a skilled engineer, Mr. Stewart," Dashi said, "you are well known as a nervous pilot. We will be sending you a pilot to help you dock and get acquainted with the new drive system."

"Of course, sir," Jake said. He sounded disappointed.

"Excellent. Until then." Dashi signed off.

It took a while, but eventually Jake was close enough to TGI Main to rendezvous with a shuttle. It would be many orbits before he could dock with the station, but Jose had insisted on getting a pilot out early so they could practice on the new systems. Jose seemed to be running everything on Dashi's behalf, and Dashi seemed to be closeted with leaders of different factions. There were rumors of him becoming the new planetary executive.

The shuttle matched orbits, or close enough, and a

single, suited figure fired her jets and jumped across the intervening distance, not even bothering to use a tether.

Risky. Jake opened the outer airlock and waited till the person clanged inside, then walked down to greet them. The inner hatch swung open, and a skin-suited figure stepped inside. She was female, by her shape—a fit, attractive female.

She took off her helmet and shook a head full of blond hair out.

"Hi, Jakey. Miss me?" Nadine asked.

Jake's mouth dropped open. "You're dead."

Nadine extended her arms out and twirled. "Do I look dead? I think I'm too sexy to be dead."

"Your ship exploded."

"Nah. The GG shuttle exploded, not me."

"Your ship hit the GG shuttle and exploded. I saw the explosion."

"You saw *an* explosion, not *my* explosion."

"How is this possible?"

"Turns out that a hotshot pilot like me can just clip a passing ship if she's got a long enough hook. That radar was the charm. I bent it out and into a giant spaceship-catcher and weakened all the supports. Hit it like a giant needle into the drive unit, and the rest is history." Nadine smiled, then shuddered. "Put horrible roll on the ship, though. I was puking nonstop by the time the thrusters righted us. Let me tell you, that was expensive to get cleaned up. Now that I have my own ship, I've begun to realize why you were so focused on the cost of things. There are so many bills."

Jake just shook his head. "I can't believe you're alive."

"Believe it, Jakey. Say, do you remember what you said when you thought I was going to die?"

Jake nodded.

"Are you going to take it back, or say it again?" she asked.

Jake cleared his throat and turned red. Then he looked

right at Nadine. "I love you. I have for a long time."

"Do you remember what I promised?" Nadine said.

"That we'd talk about it?"

"Yep." Nadine began to peel off her skin suit. She didn't have anything on underneath. "We've got about two weeks of orbit time to talk. Let's get started right now."

a Free Ebook

Thanks for reading. I hope you enjoyed it. Word-of-mouth reviews are critical to independent authors. Please consider leaving a review on Amazon or Goodreads or wherever you purchased this book.

If you'd like to be notified of future releases, please join my mailing list.

https://dl.bookfunnel.com/utkw99vv1s

I send a few updates a year, and if you subscribe you get a free ebook copy of Sigma Draconis IV, a short novella in the Jake Stewart universe. For updates on new releases, you can also follow me on Amazon, Bookbub and Goodreads.

Andrew Moriarty

ABOUT THE AUTHOR

Andrew Moriarty has been reading science fiction his whole life, and he always wondered about the stories he read. How did they ever pay the mortgage for that spaceship? Why doesn't it ever need to be refueled? What would happen if it broke, but the parts were backordered for weeks? And why doesn't anybody ever have to charge sales tax? Despairing on finding the answers to these questions, he decided to write a book about how spaceships would function in the real world. Ships need fuel, fuel costs money, and the accountants run everything.

He was born in Canada, and has lived in Toronto, Vancouver, Los Angeles, Germany, Park City, and Maastricht. Previously he worked as a telephone newspaper subscriptions salesman, a pizza delivery driver, a wedding disc jockey, and a technology trainer. Unfortunately, he also spent a great deal of time in the IT industry, designing networks and configuring routers and switches. Along the way, he picked up an ex-spy with a predilection for French Champagne, and a whippet with a murderous possessiveness for tennis balls. They live together in Brooklyn.

Please buy his books. Tennis balls are expensive.

BOOKS BY ANDREW MORIARTY

The Further Adventures of Jake Stewart

Available soon on Amazon

The electric ground car skimmed to a stop in front of the Imperial Department of Planetary Agriculture building. Armed Militia surrounded it, facing outward, looking for threats.

An officer stepped up and opened the door. "Let's move along now. There are too many unaccounted-for guns out there."

Jose stepped out and looked around. "It's too far for anybody to hit us with a revolver. We'll be fine."

The guard shrugged. "Your call." He handed Jose a credit chip. "My bet is Vasilly."

Jose nodded, then reached inside to help Dashi out of the car.

Dashi's cane clicked as he snapped it onto the stone walkway in front of him, then clicked again as he stepped forward. He stumbled, and only the quick reaction of the younger man saved him from falling. The smoke still swirling around made him cough.

"No need to rush, sir," Jose said. "Nothing will start without you. I've already been in contact with everyone and stressed your physical condition."

Dashi gestured to the uniformed group standing at the head of the stairs. "Those people are waiting. For us, Jose. Punctuality is the courtesy of kings."

"Would you like to be a king, sir?"

Dashi turned to Jose and smiled. "Do you think you could arrange that?"

"Yes, sir. I think I could, if you thought it wise."

"The student has become the master, but I will not be a king." With great care, Dashi levered himself over a single step in the walkway.

"What will you be then, sir?"

"What I have always been—a loyal servant of the Empire."

"Until it returns, sir?"

"It has never left. It's just been quiet for a time." Dashi paused at the base of a new set of steps. "Ladies and gentlemen, good morning. Admiral, you smell awful."

"A good Imperial welcome to you too, Dashi," Admiral Edmunds said. "The remaining Growers set fires as we stormed the warehouses. I was on fire for a while."

"Were you able to secure the food stores?"

The admiral turned to a soot-covered woman with a commander's insignia who was standing behind him. She also leaned on a cane. The insignia was bright and shiny, as if brand new.

"Not enough," she said. "Not enough."

"The power plant?" Dashi asked.

"It won't explode, but it won't send any power either," she said.

"Are you in control of the city?"

"There is no more organized resistance, but lots of unorganized groups roaming around."

"I see. Any good news?" Dashi asked.

"Reports have arrived that you have somehow acquired

a functioning jump ship," the admiral said.

"Mr. Jose has been handling that for me." Dashi turned to Jose.

"We have one," Jose said, "and it appears to be working. The crew are on their way here."

"You can't choose a crew without consulting us," Admiral Edmunds said.

"Why did you choose the Imperial Department of Agriculture for this meeting without consulting us?"

"Because it was the only Imperial building not actually on fire, and it has computer access and a room big enough to be a council chamber."

The two groups looked at each other for a moment, then the admiral shook his head. "Neither of us have any choice. We need to work together, or we're all going to starve. Let's get to our council chamber and formalize this. Jose, here is one hundred credits, and my bet is Clarence."

Jose nodded and made a notation on his comm. Dashi looked at Jose with his "query" smile, but, out of his usual character, Jose ignored it.

Then the admiral stepped up beside Dashi, and they began to walk down the hallway, speaking in hushed tones.

Jose and a group of officers followed. Jose seemed to know them all by name and shook each of them by the hand. Each of them chatted with Jose for a moment, then offered him a credit chip and a name. Their guesses included Benjamin, Alesky, Aristride, Zebediah, and many others.

The group approached a set of double doors. A stylized depiction of a group of stars, including Polaris, hovered over the door.

Armed guards stood in front of the doors, but they were not in Militia uniforms. Rather, they had shoulder badges from the Free Traders' Council.

A woman approached them. "Admiral. Mr. Dashi."

"Ms. Marianne," Dashi said. "Thank you for coming. We welcome your participation in this new endeavor."

"Participate or starve?" she asked.

"Just so you know, I voted 'starve' for you," Admiral Edmunds said. "Self-serving treacherous opportunists, the lot of you."

"A hearty good morning to you too, Admiral," Marianne said. "The less powerful have to take the hand they are dealt—in particular, if they are caught between two more powerful allies. The question is, can we work together?"

"I've promised to work with you. I keep my promises," the admiral said.

"We can all agree on that, but I rather wish you hadn't promised to destroy the Growers headquarters."

"I lost a lot of good men keeping that promise. I'm not going to betray their trust now," the admiral said. He turned to the officers with him and introduced them.

"You know Mr. Jose, of course," Dashi said when Jose's turn came.

"Good to see you again, Ms. Marianne," Jose said.

"You as well, Mr. Jose. My guess is Pradeep," she said, handing him a credit chip.

Mr. Dashi gave Jose another questioning smile, and Jose again ignored it. Dashi frowned. Jose never ignored his questioning smiles.

There was a bit of a commotion behind them, and then they all heard a new voice. "I said we have an invitation to the ceremony, and we're going to go, you Imperial turd, so get out of my way, or I'm going to shoot the lot of you."

"Ms. Nadine is here, sir," Jose said to Dashi.

"So I hear," Dashi said.

The admiral's expression blanked for a moment as he turned toward the noise. Then he started forward, running toward Nadine. He shoved the arguing guards to one side and grabbed her in a giant bear hug. Her twirled her around, tears running down his cheeks before he finally stopped and put her down.

"Well," he said, pushing away his tears. "Well," he said

again. He coughed. "You look okay. Are you okay?"

"I'm fine," Nadine said.

"I heard you rammed that Grower ship."

"I hit it with Jake Stewart's patented starship grabber and food storage hook. Worked great. You should install one on all the Militia ships," Nadine said.

"Maybe I will." The admiral turned to Jake. "You're Dashi's troubleshooter—Stewart?"

"I'm Jake Stewart, yes," Jake said. "I wouldn't call myself his troubleshooter, though. More like his auditor."

"Yet every time there is some sort of trouble involving Dashi, you seem to be around."

"I g-guess so." Jake seemed intimidated. For some reason, he also had his hand on his holstered revolver.

The admiral stared at Jake for a long time. "I thought you'd be taller," he said.

Evidently not knowing what to say to that, Jake just blinked.

"Treat her well, or I'll have you killed," the admiral said.

"Pardon?" Jake said.

"Just kidding," the admiral said.

Jake let out a breath. "Oh. Funny joke."

"Just kidding. I won't have you killed. This is personal. I'll do it myself."

"Good to see you, Mr. Stewart," Dashi said, "and you, Ms. Nadine. Have you learned a lot in the last two weeks together on that jump ship?"

"Sir?" Jake blushed. He and Nadine had been left alone on the jump ship for the last two weeks and had done quite a bit of exploring, albeit not always the technical type.

"Jump systems. Propulsion. Interstellar navigation," Dashi said.

"Oh, that. Yes, sir. We've learned a lot and done a lot of system tests."

"What did you think I was referring to, Mr. Stewart?"

Dashi asked.

"Uh...." Jake said.

"I protest again," Ms. Marianne said, "that they will be the main part of the crew. We should be providing a Free Trader pilot. They are much more experienced than these two."

"You will get your representative," Jose said, "as agreed. We also agreed that the most experienced crew should be given priority. Since there have been no functional jump ships in this system for more than eighty years, Mr. Stewart is actually the most experienced jump system operator and engineer, so he will be going. Ms. Nadine is an experienced pilot, and they are used to working together, so she will be going as well."

"You manipulated us into this decision," Marianne said.

"Of course," Jose said. "That's my job." He smiled, looking much like a younger Dashi. "Right now it's time for the ceremony. Jake, you and Nadine are upstairs."

"Thanks, Jose," Nadine said. "Oh, and I've got Peter."

"And I'm taking nothing," Jake said.

"Nothing?" Jose asked.

"He doesn't have one. It doesn't exist," Jake replied.

All three of them looked at Dashi.

"I have no idea what you are all talking about," Dashi said. "What is this?"

"See you later, sir," Jake said. "Let's go, Nadine." With that, the two hustled off.

"Jose, I insist you tell me what's going on with these names," Dashi whispered.

Jose smiled and pointed forward. "Showtime, sir. Smile for the cameras."

They both turned toward the door and began to march into the temporary chamber.

Jake and Nadine had reserved seats on a set of

bleachers that overlooked the council tables.

"Nothing?" Nadine asked.

"Yes. I don't think he has another name at all."

"He can't be just 'Dashi.' He has to have some other names. A family name. A house name. A corporate extension, if nothing else."

"I have a suspicion. I think he's just 'Dashi.'"

"Why do you think that?" Nadine asked.

"Something I read a few years back. We'll find out shortly."

Even as they spoke, the ceremony was going on below them. A master of ceremonies was speaking. "...meeting as the new emergency council of Delta. Until the Empire returns."

"Until the Empire returns," the crowd said back in chorus.

"I'm still not happy leaving that ship up there," Nadine said.

"We need a better name than 'that ship.'"

"Something could happen to it."

"You just want to be up there playing with the controls."

"There are plenty of things I want to play with. That's just one of them," Nadine said.

Jake blushed again. "We need to test the jump power system shunts."

"I'm willing, as long as we can do it naked," Nadine said.

Jake blushed even harder. His comm gave a soft beep, alerting him, and he began to page down.

"State your full legal name and all Imperial titles, for the record," the master of ceremonies said below.

Jake and Nadine listened. The chancellor was just the chancellor, and the corporate and Free Traders had no Imperial titles. The admiral, for some reason, had missed his queue and was paging through his own comm. Then the admiral turned and looked at Jose, who was steps behind Dashi.

Jose was watching his comm as well, but caught the admiral's glance and jerked his head toward the spectators' gallery, at Jake.

Jake leaned over and grabbed Nadine's arm. "Nadine, we have to get back to the ship. Now."

"Easy, tiger," she said. "There's plenty more where that came from. We ought to pace ourselves."

"Not that," Jake said. "Sensors on the ship have detected another ship."

"There are plenty of ships in this system, Jake."

"Another jump ship. Another jump ship just arrived. I copied all the alerts to me, Jose, and Dashi, and Dashi copied them to the admiral. We have to get up there and get more info. Now."

Nadine nodded. They stood up and began to shove their way to the door.

The admiral finally stood up and did his part. "Bryan Edmunds, Admiral of the Delta Militia, Lieutenant in the Imperial Customs Reserve," he said.

Nadine slowed a bit. "Imperial Customs Reserve?"

"It was the only Imperial department actually present here after the Abandonment," Jake said. "At least, the only one that the computers agree there is continuity for. Wait—here's Dashi. We need to see this."

Dashi had climbed up using his cane and now faced the imperial seal at the front of the room. "Dashi, president of this council," he said, then sat down.

There was silence for a moment, then the master of ceremonies said, "Sir, the computer requires your full legal designation for registration, as well as all Imperial titles."

Dashi sighed and looked down at Jose. Jose just gave him a bland smile.

"Fine. I am the Count Von Dashi, Warden of the Marches, Count of the Greater Cluster, knight of the realm, and seventh of the house of succession to Pradeep IV. Heir of the Empire."

There was a collective gasp, then a murmuring all across the council.

"Emperor's testicles," Jake said, "do you know what this means?"

"He's claiming to be one of the heirs to the Empire?" Nadine said. "Can that be true?"

"Computer would have rejected it by now if he wasn't. But what's more important than that?"

"What?"

"I just won the bet. He only has one name.".

Made in United States
Orlando, FL
29 May 2024

47302682R00232